HRT
Husband
Replacement Therapy

HRT

Husband
Replacement Therapy

KATHY
LETTE

HEAD
& ZEUS

An Aria Book

First published in the UK in 2020 by Vintage, part of Penguin Random House

This edition first published in the UK in 2024 by Head of Zeus,
part of Bloomsbury Publishing Plc

9 7 5 3 1 2 4 6 8

A catalogue record for this book is available from the British Library.

ISBN (PB): 9781035906338
ISBN (E): 9781035901586

Cover design: Simon Michele | Head of Zeus

Typeset by Siliconchips Services Ltd UK

Printed and bound in Great Britain by
CPI Group (UK) Ltd, Croydon CR0 4YY

Head of Zeus Ltd
First Floor East
5–8 Hardwick Street
London EC1R 4RG

WWW.HEADOFZEUS.COM

This book is dedicated to my witty, warm and wonderful sisters, Jenny, Liz and Cara, whose unbridled love, loyalty and joie de vivre light up my life. And to the lovely man who finds us funny, Michael Brian O'Doherty.

All names in this story have been changed to protect the desperate, the hilarious, the deranged, the fabulous and the not-so-innocent.

I

Once upon a time there was a woman who discovered she had turned into the wrong person . . . That's me, by the way. I'm going to tell you a story about three months that upended my life. And you are not going to like me. You may even hate me – honestly, I hated myself at times. You're going to think I'm a conniving, duplicitous, selfish monster. You're going to think I'm the worst sister, mother, daughter, wife and friend in the whole wide world. But, believe me, there were pretty extenuating circumstances. Once I've explained it all to you – and no doubt been hospitalised for chronic gravel rash on the knees from grovelling – well, I'm hoping I can change your mind.

It started on my fiftieth birthday. I was standing on a beachside balcony peering back through the glass doors at my birthday shindig. I've watched the video of what came next a gazillion times through mortified fingers, so I can give you a blow-by-blow account of the day my life went tits-up.

Hello, everyone! Thank you for coming to celebrate my Fuck it, I'm Fifty *birthday bash!*

The words were forming in my head but not quite reaching my mouth. This could have been something to do with the fact that I was completely intoxicated. In the lead-up to the event my friends had told me that it would be downright rude not to get drunk on my fiftieth. As instructed, I'd downed one bottle of vintage vino at home and then, upon arrival at my party half an hour later, more or less dunked my whole head in the punch bowl.

The function room of the Sea View Hotel was filled with a rolling boil of noise. The excited hum of voices was broken only by the cheery clatter of silverware and china from the buffet. Looking in at the party, I could see my mother's mass of dyed blonde hair, swept back from her forehead and coiffed into a great, towering croquembouche atop her haughty head. Her slim, aquiline nose gave her a hawklike, predatory air. I knew that nose well, as I'd spent most of my adult life being looked at down it. Our family matriarch was seated at the top table, bookended by my two sisters, who were studiously avoiding each other while simultaneously competing for her attention. In sync, both stressed siblings made a grab for one of the exotic cocktails wobbling by on a tray held aloft by a weary waiter wearing a spray-on smile.

Also grabbing a passing cocktail was my husband, Harry. I'd always thought you had to go to Iraq or Afghanistan to get post-traumatic stress disorder, but it turns out you can also get it in a quiet cul-de-sac in suburbia, a lesson I'd learnt that very morning. The dark ocean behind me hissed as waves broke onto the rocks below. Thinking about Harry's betrayal made me contemplate just diving off the balcony into the cool, inky water right there and then. But, resisting the urge to flee, I shoved open the balcony doors with a *whoosh*. A cold blast pushed against me, as if to force me back outside. The conversational murmur swelled for a moment before my ears became accustomed to the babble. I saw my guests through a haze. As if seeing a play unfolding before me, I watched people move around, altering their inflections as they found new friends or were reacquainted with old ones.

I seized another drink I didn't need and downed it in one long gulp. On the stage, to my left, the microphone was set up, ready for the rock band and the toasts my kids had undoubtedly been press-ganged into delivering after dessert. But if anyone was going to deliver a speech at my fiftieth birthday party, by god, it was going to be me. Normally the thought of public speaking left me more terrified than a mouse in a python cage, but, emboldened by the booze I'd consumed, I suddenly found myself lurching up the stairs towards the mic to utter my rehearsed line of welcome, this time out loud.

'Hello, everyone! Thanks for coming to my *Fuck it, I'm Fifty* birthday bash!'

I clocked my mother, whose high-rise hair teetered precariously as she shook her head in warning at me, her youngest daughter.

'Oops. Sorry, Mum . . . We're not allowed to use the F-word in our family. We have to say "fudge" instead, or it's six cuts of the feather duster. But not tonight, Mother dear. Tonight I am fucking doing it my fucking way, thank you very fucking much.'

This outburst was so out of character that the undertone of conversation abated as surprised guests swivelled their heads in my slightly dishevelled direction.

'And thank you for all the prezzies, too. Kind friends have been asking what I most wanted for a gift, you know, besides a one-way ticket to a tropical island in the arms of a poetry-quoting gymnast with a ten-inch tongue . . . And I joked that the only thing I *didn't* want was a worm farm. Well, guess what my husband gave me? A *worm farm*. I hate worms. Although it appears that I've m . . . m . . . married one!' I slurred tipsily.

A ripple of polite but puzzled laughter ran around the room. I felt myself sliding sideways, like a ship off the slips, and held on to the mic stand for anchorage. 'Oops. God, I nearly went arse over tit there. That would have been attractive, flashing a fiftyyear-old fallopian at you!'

This inspired a rowdy cheer from a few of the beer-sodden blokes at the back of the function room. I felt as if I were a cruise ship entertainment officer trying out edgy new material to keep the crowd in their seats, or an action hero who has just discovered her superpower and realised that she's not merely a suburban housewife after all.

Through the fog of inebriation, I became dimly aware of a hand on the small of my back and registered, faintly, that it was my husband.

'I think you've had a bit too much lady petrol, there, love,' Harry joked into the mic.

'And I think you've had a bit too much sex on the side in our marriage,' I retorted.

Well, that's one way to silence a crowd, I thought, as the entire room reeled and stared.

I looked up at my spouse. Harry had slicked his hair back for the occasion – a shellacked wave of sun-kissed locks. He's always had great hair. It's one of the reasons I first fell for the bronzed surfer boy, because he boasted the longest hair in high school. But it was about to stand on end now.

'Father Gallagher married us,' I clarified for the crowd. 'We said our vows – for better or worse . . . Sadly, he didn't ask you to clarify exactly how much worse, Harry. I mean, flossing your teeth in bed is bad enough, but having an affair?' I swerved my head back towards the audience so fast I felt my blotto-ed brain crashing into the sides of my cranium. 'For any guests who don't live in this comfortably padded lunatic asylum known, euphemistically, as the "Insular Peninsular", my Harry runs a service called "Hire a Hubby". He does odd jobs for women all over the area . . . I just didn't realise he was s . . . s . . . servicing them, literally. You've been wielding your toolbox here, there and everywhere, haven't you, my'—I paused to punctuate my accusation with a small burp—'*love?* You're always telling me how the ladies love the tradies.'

There was a quick and nervous burst of laugher from somewhere, but most of the room remained awkwardly spellbound.

'Don't be ridiculous, love. Pay no attention to the silly, sozzled sausage!' Harry instructed the gathering, with mock bonhomie. 'Turning fifty has been a bit traumatic for the poor possum. She's not exactly in her right mind . . .'

'G . . . g . . . gosh, have I lost my mind?' I stammered. 'I guess it's around here somewhere. I'll find it when I tidy up, which I do *every day*, despite holding down a full-time job – as, clearly, you're too busy fixing your girlfriend's most intimate plumbing.'

'That's enough!' Fury was radiating off Harry now like cheap aftershave. 'Let's go outside and get some fresh air. Still,' Harry made one more stab at jocularity before bundling me offstage, 'it wouldn't be a fiftieth birthday if the party girl didn't get bladdered and talk complete bollocks, right?'

'Complete bollocks, is it?' In quick succession, I kneed my husband in said area, then whisked a mobile phone from the pocket of my sequined cocktail frock. 'I took a screenshot of a text message you received while you were in the shower this morning, right after our traditional birthday bonk. Shall I sh . . . sh . . . share it with our best friends and family?' I swooned a little, then squeezed my eyes half-closed so as to focus on the screen. 'From you: *Hello, sexy. I'm so sorry, but I'm not going to be able to make our anniversary. Work has reared its ugly head. And, unfortunately, I can't send your gift, as it's attached to me.*'

Although bent double in agony, Harry made a grab for the phone, but I rebuffed him, continuing, 'And then, her reply to you: *My heart is breaking! I was especially looking forward to unwrapping your gorgeous gift . . . What is the job that is keeping you from me? I have a job in mind too, with the word "blow" in front of it. P.S. Don't forget to delete this in case Ruby starts prying.*'

Silence was now bouncing off the walls. Even the waiters had stopped circulating and had turned to gawp at the slow-motion marital car crash unfolding on stage.

The shock on Harry's face was intense. He appeared to be midway through an experiment to see how long a person could stay in a wind tunnel. 'It's just harmless banter . . .' he spluttered.

I could see my sisters working their elbows like oars to get through the sea of people to the stage, signalling to their respective husbands to *Do something!*

'I wasn't going to s . . . s . . . say anything till after the party – well, obviously that worked well, didn't it? So, who is it? She's listed in your phone under "Stiff Nipples – Air Conditioning". You talk of an "anniversary". So how long's this s . . . s . . . sordid little liaison been going on? And how does this two-faced bitch even know my name? . . . Oh, god.' Once more I realised I'd been caught with my synapses down. 'It's one of my friends, isn't it?' I turned back to face the audience and started jabbing my finger accusingly around the room. 'Which one of you so-called pals has wrecked my marriage? I just wanna know so I can'—I racked my befuddled brain for an appropriately awful revenge—'pack your tampon tubes with live funnel-web spiders. Is it one of the Yummy Mummies?' I demanded of my dumbstruck husband. 'I bet it bloody is! You're all so sanctimonious, aren't you? Swigging your kale juice at the school sports day, constantly going on body-cleansing retreats . . . yet unable to survive without collagen injections and wine o'clock. But if it's a s . . . s . . . s . . . school mum,' I beseeched my husband, 'how the hell do you tell them apart, with their identical floaty Camilla dresses, bolt-on boobs and botox?'

I had a vague awareness that I might be drunker than I had realised, and that it would probably be prudent to shut up, but then I thought, *Hey, it's my fucking fiftieth. Why interrupt my journey into self-annihilation?* I bent down from the stage to snatch a glass from a surprised guest and drained it in one go. The booze re-ignited my recklessness.

'Well, if it's one of the school mums, Harry, I'm disappointed in you. I really am. How could you be attracted to any woman who'd name her kids "Sage", "Moon", "Melody" or "Apple" because they think they're so "unique" and "gifted"? Guess what, ladies? Your kids are *not* going to be special. They're going to be average – just like all of you.' Certain guests were now shrinking from my words as if they were body blows. 'All those lectures about what your lactose-intolerant brats could and couldn't eat on a sleepover . . . Only spoilt middle-class kids are lactose intolerant. Nobody working class has ever bloody well heard of it!'

I could not believe what was coming out of my mouth. I was the nice sister – the one who remembered the birthdays of extended family members and sent gifts proxy-signed from the three of us. The one who volunteers to pick up pals from the airport, mind their disgusting pets or watch their untalented offspring's pathetic attempts at creative dance or comedy improv. I give money to buskers even when they're singing that awful 'Blurred Lines' song. I apologise when someone's supermarket trolley bumps into mine. This drunken diatribe was as out of character as the US Republican Party signing up to a climate change agreement.

My sisters had reached the steps leading up to the stage and were waving at their husbands to hurry up. Harry tried once more to forcibly steer me away from the mic. In the tussle, my dress shed a shower of sequins, which made me even madder. I'm only five foot three but, fuelled by fury, I shoved my husband so violently he crashed backwards into the drum kit and fell to the floor in a cacophonous rattle. 'Now you really can call yourself a sex cymbal,' I scoffed. This bonsai ball of Aussie sass who was impersonating me then lifted the mic off the stand so she could prowl around the stage in order to scrutinise the startled female guests more closely.

'So, who is it, Harry? Oh, god, it's one of the women from

book club, isn't it? Though *they're* not so s . . . s . . . s . . . special either. They watch movie adaptations of the assigned novels. D'you know that? Most of their reading material's limited to Instagram captions – oh, and your phone sexts, clearly.'

Who *was* I? I felt estranged from myself, but the imposter pressed on, rashly.

'But, wait . . . It's much more likely to be one of the smug yoga crowd. Those girls are so *bendy*. Shit. It's Jaynie, isn't it? My so-called "best friend". Oh, god, Harry. Do you have any idea how many years you need to practise the downward dog to be able to kiss your own arse like that?'

A crisp, steely voice cut across the room. 'Ruby, *sit down*! You're making a spectacle of yourself.'

The voice went through me like a chainsaw. My attention was immediately drawn back to the top table. 'Oh, hello, Mother. I didn't recognise you without your cross. Mum's always criticising her three daughters for juggling our kids and careers so badly . . . even though you haven't got out of bed for a full day's work since about, what, 1974, have you, Mother? She blames us for protecting our darling dad, you see, and hiding his affairs. Well, you can gloat now, Mum, because clearly I've married a man just like him.'

My mother retreated into stony indignation, wreathed in an air of outraged integrity.

'Where are my darling kids? Zoe? Jake?' Shielding my eyes against the lights, I located my gobsmacked offspring by the side of the stage. They were peering up at their normally sunny, funny mother with open-mouthed incredulity. 'Thank god I've never given you what my mother gave me – the gift of self-loathing, insecurity and anxiety.'

The predatory look my mother sent my way could have secured her the title role in a Dracula movie. But I pushed on regardless, as another realisation hit me with the impact of an Exocet missile from Life's Blindingly Obvious launch pad.

'Jesus.' I swivelled to stare at Harry, who was still noisily untangling himself from the snare drum. 'This morning, you were thinking of *her* the whole time, weren't you? That's why you had your eyes closed! Oh, well, whoever you are, I'm sorry you've had to experience that. Harry's never been that good in bed. I did once scream "Oh god! Oh god!" but that was only because I'd just seen a huge huntsman spider on the bedroom ceiling over his shoulder.'

With the help of my brothers-in-law, Harry had now scrambled back to his feet. 'Start the bloody music!' he called out in desperation.

'My advice to your girlfriend?' I tottered to the front of the stage and scrutinised the women below. 'Don't make the mistake of turning f . . . f . . . fifty. Stay young . . . Although, ironically, I should probably offer to pay you child support. I mean, you've just taken a fifty-one-year-old teenager off my hands. Our priest is here somewhere. Hello, Father Gallagher? Can you show yourself?'

'Music! Goddamn it!' Harry demanded, as the band fumbled into position.

'Well, Father, wherever you are . . . My query is, can we get an annulment after twenty-eight years of marriage? My other question is, can a fifty-year-old woman with a varicose vein wear heels and date again? . . . Oh, fudge.'

My eyes landed upon my boss, a statuesque, thirty-something brunette with alabaster skin, who'd been mysteriously parachuted into the role of editor at the local paper despite a total lack of qualifications. I groped down the cerebral equivalent of the back of the sofa and remembered something else.

'Bloody hell, Harry, you're rooting Angela, aren't you? You told me once you fancied her . . . Even though she has about as much personality as she has hair. She's nearly bald, you know. It's all extensions.' What I lacked in clarity I now made up for by hiccupping heavily. When I recovered, I added, 'I know you think you're god's gift, Ange, but truth is, you've passed your bore-by date. You light up a room by leaving it. Last week you held a meeting to discuss our overuse of paper clips. We have a desalination plant going rusty, holes in the s . . . s . . . shark net and a crack in the nuclear reactor, and our "editor" gets us to write about a kitten that looks like Hitler, a mum finding a gecko in her fridge and grass growing quickly after rain. These are the things that keep me awake at night, I can tell you.'

The alcohol in my system made the guests a little blurry; rather than a group of well-dressed suburbanites, they now appeared to be one giant, indistinct, gasping amoeba. A voice from far back in my cerebrum told me to maybe call it quits. I suspected I was about one drink away from waking up in an unfamiliar nation with nipple jewellery, but it was too late, because my mouth had already set off on another sortie down self-destruction street, despite it being clearly signposted *TURN BACK, YOU ARE GOING THE WRONG WAY.*

'And we all know about the kickbacks, Ange. Why else would you ask us to go easy on certain developers and local big shots? Plus, you shred paperwork faster than Trump's accountant. The whole office knows you only got the job because of your big-boobed, playboy-pet look . . . So, did you crawl through Angela's cat flap, Harry?'

'For the love of god, Ruby, put down the bloody mic!' Harry begged, as band members frantically plugged in their instruments.

'D'you know what? It's my birthday and I'll implode if I want to. Actually, it feels pretty damn good. One of my greatest regrets, apart from not being Nora Ephron, is that I've never s . . . s . . . said what I really think. Nope. Not to anybody, really.'

'Why not buy a vineyard, Ruby, and cut out the middleman?' a high-pitched voice heckled from the crowd.

My eyes snagged onto the culprit. It was Karina, one of the school mums whose company I'd endured since our now-eighteen-year-old daughters had met on the kindergarten mat. Karina rolled her eyes condescendingly in my direction and puckered her collagen-filled lips in disapproval.

'Oh, Karina, by the way, your husband sent the babysitter a dick pick. She showed her mum, Shaz, who showed all the other mums. Oh, and Shaz, your perfect hubby groped me at your anniversary party. Isn't that right, Robbo?'

There were some hoots of drunken male laughter scattered around the room like tiny explosives, which my confused, befuggered brain took as a sign of encouragement.

'Oh, and Robbo, so cocksure, aren't you, entering every room scrotum-first. Well, guess what? And this goes for all you steroid-addled ex–footy players. Your trophy wives tell you they're at Pilates in the mall, but they're really meeting their toy boys. A much more effective way to strengthen the pelvic floor, apparently.'

Every head in the room was now tilted towards me in a hyper-alert way. The audience blinked and blinked at me, like a giant, multi-eyed insect. But I just couldn't read the signs; and to be honest, not even an intensive course in advanced semaphore could have helped me now.

'To my own kids – I would take a bullet for you both, you know that, but being your mother is like being an unpaid PA to two pushy A-listers. It's my own fault. I've s . . . s . . . spoiled you rotten.'

The mic gave a croaking gasp, like the cough of a dying man, as Harry unplugged it. But the room was so quiet my voice still carried, clear as a bell.

'Zoe, I love you to pieces, pumpkin, but just to be clear, you are *not* a multi-millionairess top model accidentally trapped inside the body of a girl in the burbs. You're bright but lazy. If you use your gap year merely to Instagram photos of yourself pouting, then forget uni; you're clearly headed for a career gyrating in your pants in a lap-dancing club.'

There was an indignant gasp from the head of the P & C, Debbie Darlington, another of my 'besties'.

'Oh, shut up, Debbie. You let your fifteen-year-old get botox! When she next asks for botoxed lips you should give her a good smack about the chops . . . But then again, would she be able to feel it?'

I cackled at my own quip, not noticing that nobody else was laughing. The alcohol had made me totally oblivious to the fact that I was no longer a shoo-in to win 'Ms Popular of the Peninsular' this particular year. But once I'd started mouthing off, I just couldn't stop. All my pent-up frustrations were exploding out of me like uncorked champagne. Two or three bottles of truth serum will do that to you; after all, drunken words are only sober thoughts.

'And Jake? I love you, kiddo. But you're smoking too much weed. Unless you're s . . . s . . . secretly staring in a reality TV show called *Hash in the Attic*. So, here's the sermon. Verily I say unto you, either knuckle down at your apprenticeship or leave home. I mean, do you have any idea how much you cost? You wolf down food as though you're a slave in Egyptian times, bolstering yourself for a day of heavy pyramid building. Out the door by twenty-four. That's the motto. The Bank of Mum and Dad is shutting up s . . . s . . . shop.'

I felt my elbows gripped in a vice-like hold and slowly realised that I was now flanked by my brothers-in-law.

'Ah, Scott and Alessandro! Do you know what we call you behind your back, Scott? "*I've Got* Scott". As soon as you meet someone, you're like, "I've got a boat . . . I've got a new SUV . . . I've got a waterfront home . . . I've got a dirt bike . . . I've got a jet ski . . ." You're one of the richest blokes on the peninsula – and we know that because you keep telling us so. Scott's a human rights lawyer,' I told the crowd. 'You've probably heard him jauntily talking to his junior all night, saying things like, "So, exactly what kind of electrodes did they use to torture his testicles?" Or "How many dead bodies were exhumed from the mass grave?" And yet, you abuse my s . . . s . . . sister's human rights all the time, bragging about never having changed a nappy or cooked a meal, you hypocritical dipshit.'

The heady taste of honesty flooded my mouth. How long had it been since I'd let myself say something I really meant?

'Oh, and meet Alessandro, my other brother-in-law. He's

the Dent Boss. He takes dents out of chassis – we call him "the car whisperer". But it's all cash in hand. Everyone knows you do your mates' drug laundering through your business, Sandro – that's why we secretly call your garage "the laundromat". D'you know that?'

My brothers-in-law then attempted to lift me up off my feet and simply carry me off stage. My legs pedalled in the air for a moment, like a cartoon character, before I delivered two quick kicks to their shins.

'You boys have really got to work on your people skills. It's my fucking birthday!'

'*That's enough!*' My mother had now pushed her way to the front of the crowd. She thrust a forefinger up at me as if she might impale me upon it. Her glare was icy enough to turn volcanic ash into snowflakes.

'Oh, s . . . s . . . sorry, Mum. I stole your limelight. Mrs Ruth Ryan is only happy if people float out of her presence backwards, like flunkies at Buck House.'

I demonstrated the walk, teetering in reverse in my heels. This drew a splutter of laughter from my flummoxed guests, especially when I fell over and lost a chicken fillet from my push-up bra. It lay quivering at my feet like a stranded jellyfish. Perhaps the guests would mistake it for a stress-relieving executive squeezy toy, I thought, vaguely, kicking it into the crowd.

'Ruth's only mothering advice? To never go out without lippy. You should never have had children, Mum – that's like feeding live chickens to an alligator. You think I'm joking?' I asked nobody in particular as I hauled myself back up to standing. 'She named her three daughters after precious jewels – Emerald, Amber and Ruby – but she tells us now we're little more than cut glass, our lives a cheap imitation. At least Dad was warm and fun and loved us. Sure, he didn't exactly regard matrimony as an exclusive carnal arrangement, but we loved him. Why would you punish us for that?'

My mother made a face like a snail that had just eaten a slug pellet. I had never, ever spoken back to her, but I was sure as hell making up for it now. After such a brilliant demonstration of ambassadorial diplomacy, a job as a UN hostage negotiator surely beckoned.

'My sisters aren't talking to each other, by the way, thanks to Mum poisoning them against each other. And I'm always left rushing around trying to patch things up . . . I'm the youngest, you see, so my family tend to bounce me back and forth like a shuttlecock on a badminton court.'

The band were finally tuning up. Insulted guests were making for the doors, led by Debbie and Celeste. Abandoned plates were being lofted back to the kitchen by waiters wearing rictus smiles. Some guests started booing from the back. 'Hey, Ruby, you really should get out less,' someone heckled. 'Do you intend finishing this diatribe any time in my life span?' bemoaned another.

'Okay, okay, I'll finish,' I said, trying in vain to shrug off my two burly manhandlers, who were back with a vengeance. 'But one more thing before I go . . . The principal news, aside from my birthday breakdown, is that I have metastatic pancreatic cancer. Terminal.'

The collective intake of breath sounded like an asthma attack.

'I only found out today. With so little time left, you're probably wondering what would I like most in the world?

16

To patch things up with my sisters, actually. Mum, you've successfully alienated us from each other for so long, making us compete to be top of your speed dial. Well, enough is enough. Emerald, Amber . . . I've booked the three of us onto the next cruise ship leaving Sydney. On S . . . S . . . Saturday. For three weeks – to clean the slate before I cark it. You can't say no, girls, it's my dying wish . . .'

I saw my surprised sisters turn instinctively towards our mother.

'And forget what Mum thinks. Mum always has to have the last word. But this time *I'm* having it – engraved on my epitaph.

'So, there's not much else to say, except to thank you once again for coming to celebrate this special night with me. Quite a birthday present, right? Hooray. Happy Birthday! You're fifty . . . now die!'

2

The registered letter was lying on the doormat when I woke the next morning. It was from my doctor.

Dear Ms Ruby Ryan,

Please ignore the letter you were sent in error yesterday. It was addressed to the wrong patient. You do not have cancer and are perfectly healthy, to the best of our knowledge. We are terribly sorry for the mix-up and hope that this unfortunate clerical error didn't cause you undue distress. The staff member responsible has been disciplined.

Yours sincerely,

Dr Zahra Hanbury
Golden Sands Medical Practice

I flumped onto the hall floor. Oh, fudge. Oh, fuckity, fuckity, fuckity fudge.

3

Scrunching up the letter, I realised that my world had humptydumptied, never to be put back together again. By the time I'd thrown up and taken a cold shower, my hangover had left my temples and was now throbbing behind my right eye like a displaced heart. I had absolutely no idea how to cope. I'd always been known as the soft, self-deprecating, easygoing, knockabout Ryan sister. This was like going from a beginner's slope straight to a black diamond ski run with no instruction. When I'd opened the doctor's letter saying I had terminal cancer, a steel vice had wrapped itself around my chest. But today's letter explaining the misdiagnosis had squeezed the vice so tight, it left me gasping to the point of asphyxiation.

There was no going back. I hadn't just burnt all my bridges, I'd nuked them to oblivion. Sprawled on the cold bathroom tiles with my head above the toilet bowl, waves of regret washed over me as I remembered the hurtful things I'd said to my friends and family the night before. It all came crashing back – a kaleidoscope of horror. I couldn't recall how I got home, but I could remember throwing Harry out with the words: 'Never darken my vag again.'

My kids, torn between agonising grief at the news of their mother's illness and mortification at my humiliating performance, had decamped in shock to stay with friends.

By midmorning, when I finally summoned the courage to open my laptop, it was to a barren inbox, apart from a message from my boss, Angela, offering her condolences but curtly suggesting I start my sick leave immediately. Angela normally monologued for hours, we staff writers listening patiently, hoping that by the time she stopped talking about herself she'd want to hear our story ideas, but chances were we'd all have died from old age by then. Today, however, she'd got straight to the point.

There were no messages from my normally loquacious girlfriends, either, which spoke volumes. My best friends, Jaynie and Debbie, had blocked me on Facebook and Twitter, which said it all, really, loud and clear. I'd have to get a change of address card marked 'Social Siberia'.

My mother had left a message on my landline in her most severe, church-pew voice. 'You've disgraced the whole family. Consider yourself well and truly out of my will' – a pointless gesture if I had been dying but a rather annoying development now that I wasn't. My mother had never let self-doubt cloud her judgement. She loved to hate things. She could write off whole countries without even going there, whole nationalities without meeting any members of them – and daughters with the stroke of a pen.

'You've always been a drama queen, Ruby. Chemo will sort you out,' she post-scripted in a blasé tone, as though offering me a stale scone. 'At times like this you need to crack hardy.'

Or just crack up, possibly.

Harry's voicemail message was furious and confused in equal measure. 'You disgraced and libelled me in front of all our mates. As if I could ever cheat on you. That stupid shit on my phone . . . It was just silly banter with an old client. Oh, and thanks for telling everyone I'm bad in bed. That added the fucking icing to the happy fucking birthday cake. But I'm putting your insane behaviour down to this shit-awful disease, which we can fight together. Because . . . I love you,' he added, tonelessly, ringing off.

Anger welled up in me – anger bitter enough to taste. *Love?* The bastard had given me a *worm farm* for my birthday. A bloody worm farm. I wanted to feed *him* to the worms at that moment, that's for sure. I'd trusted him completely. We were a team. We shared so many in-jokes about our kids, our friends, even our mortgage, threatening to go along to a police line-up to identify the house that was attempting to steal our wallets.

How could I not have known he was cheating on me? Clearly, I was one neuron short of a synapse. Could there be life after infidelity? Well, maybe, if he'd admit it: perhaps then, after a lot of kowtowing and pleas and abject begging, I could forgive him. It would hurt, but my heartache would eventually pass. But Harry's denial via voicemail echoed in my head like an explosion. The refutation hurt even more than the affair itself.

Both my sisters had called. Amber, a chef, had left a message of anguished love and distress and the offer of chicken soup and/ or internal organs; Emerald, a vet, left a list of medical questions and advice.

I rang back my oldest sister first.

'Emerald, I'm so, so sorry about yesterday,' I blurted at the sound of her hello.

'Due to a technical error, you seem to have missed out on having a cyclone named after you,' Emerald responded, dryly.

'Oh, god. Was I that bad? A mix of alcohol and shocking news brought out the worst in me. Am I in much trouble?'

'Trouble? Oh, no, you're not in trouble . . . Not unless you count dangling over a cliff face by a single pube "trouble".'

'Oh, Jesus. *That* horrendous, huh? I feel sick. Can I come over?'

'Ah . . . Only if you happen to have a bombproof, flame-retardant, armoured vehicle handy in your garage, because my apparently "money-laundering" husband wants to kill you. Which in itself is ironic, as you told the world that you have a death sentence already.' Her voice softened. 'Is it true, Rubes? Or were you just shit-faced? Tell me exactly what the doctor said.'

My mouth felt like the bottom of a budgie cage and my teeth were all furry, as if they were each wearing a little coat. 'I need protein. Meet me for lunch.' I tried to think of a venue appropriate for social lepers. 'Convict Cafe. One o'clock . . .'

'What? That's miles away! I'll need a list of edible berries and a compass to find the place. Plus I have a cat hernia op scheduled this arvo.'

'You still have to eat. Just for half an hour. *Pleeeaaassseee.*'

'Is Amber going?'

'I'm going to ask her, yes. It's an SOS emergency. This is not a drill. Repeat: This is not a drill.'

It was a code we sisters only used for times of dire distress – like coming home from school to find our mother totally pissed, lying in a pool of her own vomit. Or our father being shot at with an air rifle by the husband of a woman he'd been seeing on the sly.

'If Amber's coming, then no. You know I'm not talking to that cow right now.'

'Not even for my dying wish?'

There was a pause big enough to accommodate a fleet of semi-trailers. 'Fudge,' my older sister finally said.

Amber's words were tumbling out of her mouth before I even had time to say hello.

'I feel sick . . . sick with disgust at life's cruel and haphazard nature. I just can't believe that you've been crushed, so indiscriminately, under the black jackboot of fate.' Amber let out a strangled sob. 'I know we've had our differences, Ruby – well, only when you've taken Emerald's side against mine – but you also know I'd do anything for you. You do know that, right?'

'Great. What you can do for me is meet me for lunch. One pm. Convict Cafe.'

'What? Why not meet at the International Space Station? It's closer.'

'I don't want to run into anyone I know.'

'Yes, well, you have a point. Though – wait. Is Emerald coming?'

'Yes.'

'Then no. You know I'm not talking to that bitch ever again.' 'This is an SOS emergency. This is not a drill. Repeat: This is not a drill . . . Besides, it's my dying wish.'

A pause. 'Fudge, fudge and triple fudge with ice cream on fudging top.'

★

I vowed that, once I'd wrangled both sisters into the same room, I'd tell them right away that the diagnosis had been a mistake but how the shock was a wake-up call for us to bury the hatchet and be friends again, hopefully on the three-week spring cruise I'd drunkenly paid for in the belief that my life was nearly over.

I'd gone to the doctor for a simple blood test to check my hormone levels. When I'd received the consultant's letter on the afternoon of my birthday and read that I had stage four terminal cancer, straight after discovering my husband's infidelity, I'd sobbed, drunk the most expensive bottle of claret I had in the house, then searched online for the first available cruise sailing out of Sydney.

At least the sham diagnosis would get all three Ryan sisters sitting at the same table at the same time, which during our adult years had proven about as easy as brokering a peace deal in the Middle East. Driving to the cafe, I told myself I must come clean about the misdiagnosis straight away, without delay, come what may. I was dying to tell them that I wasn't dying. Hooray!

4

I'm dying!' were the first words past my lips as my estranged sisters arrived at the same time from opposite sides of the cafe. 'So you cannot stay mad at me!'

Just moments earlier, while waiting for my siblings in the snack bar at the far end of the peninsula, way out past the sand dunes and the oil refinery, I'd read the small print on the ludicrously expensive cruise tickets I'd drunkenly purchased the previous day only to discover they were totally non-refundable, which is why the truth would have to wait. My life had just collapsed like a Chilean mine. My husband had moved out, my friends had disowned me and my kids were busy with their own lives. I had no one else in the world to take with me. And aside from all that, I really did want to reunite my estranged sisters, who were both so dear to me. Nope, there was nothing else for it. I would just have to pretend I was dying for a teensy bit longer – at least until the boat set sail. I'd fess up the moment we weighed anchor and just hope my furious siblings didn't give me too severe a lashing with their cat-o'-ninetongues, or keelhaul my sorry arse then hang me from a yardarm.

'How are you holding up?' Amber gushed before emitting a high-pitched gasp, swallowing a sob and grabbing me into a bear hug. I glanced over her shoulder at Emerald in astonishment. Amber was more of a pat-on-the-back type of person. Physical contact was usually so abhorrent to her that Emerald and I couldn't imagine how she'd ever got pregnant.

'What's the exact diagnosis?' Emerald demanded, heaving herself into a chair. She wanted details, dates, doctors' names.

We continued like this for ten minutes, Emerald peppering me with practical questions while Amber just clutched me and cried.

'Stop blubbing, Amber. That's not going to help the situation,' Emerald barked.

'You have the warmth and compassion of a piece of granite, do you know that?' Amber retaliated, between sobs.

'Cease and desist, both of you. My dying wish is to have my meals brought to me by a naked Chris Hemsworth . . . But I'd settle for some sisterly love.'

I was making it up as I went along, but what the previous day had given me was a deep and overwhelming desire to carpe the hell out of the diem; I intended to carpe diem as if there were no tomorrow, even if I had to lie a little longer to do so.

'But you still haven't answered my question. Tell me exactly what the consultant said,' Emerald probed, her tone as sharp as a scalpel.

I felt as if I'd been pushed on stage in a play where I didn't know the lines. 'I'm calling him Kev. The cancer, I mean. He's squatting in my pancreas like an evil little toad. I could have surgery to try to evict him, which would mean weeks in hospital with tubes running in and out of me . . .'

'What about chemo?' Emerald persisted.

You're lying to your sisters, I thought, with a savage burst of self-loathing. Who *was* I – Richard bloody Nixon? But then I just ploughed straight ahead and lied some more.

'The point is, it's terminal. I can either have loads of expensive, invasive, hideous, shit treatments and still end up dead, or I can enjoy my last moments.' I handed the menus back to the passing waitress. 'I've ordered for you both, by the way, as I know you've gotta get back to work,' I said, buying time while working out what on earth to say next.

'I bet your doctor wasn't too happy about that frickin' decision,' Emerald said. 'Shouldn't we get a second opinion?'

Deceiving my sisters like this was making my cheeks flush so hotly I could have roasted marshmallows on my face. But I continued pushing the lies out of my mouth the way an instructor shoves first-time parachutists out of an aircraft.

'Basically, Kev has spread so far that the doc understood my decision to avoid additional torture and just let Kev have his way with me with good grace,' I ad-libbed. 'At least I won't lose my hair.'

I might be the runt of the Ryan litter, but I had been blessed with my father's wild, curly, Celtic red hair, which makes it look as though I'm having a million brainwaves all at once. Which I suppose I am, most of the time, for short stories and poems and novels I start and never finish. Yes, I'm afraid I have literary leanings, which my mother has always discouraged. 'You can barely write a cheque,' she'd chide, or something along those sarcastic lines.

'What about targeted gene therapy?' Emerald persevered.

I know that liars look shifty – their eyes dart and their heart rates accelerate, so I tried hard to breathe evenly, to keep eye contact, my hand covering the jumpy pulse in my neck. 'The doc reckons it's insufficiently tested to be of any use to me.' *Liar, liar, pants on fire!* 'I don't know how much longer I'll have, but I won't be wasting any of it poisoning myself . . . because I'll be on a cruise with my beloved sisters.'

'Seriously? Your first reaction was to book a cruise with us? That's nuts, but I do love you for that response,' Amber said, tears trickling through her rouge.

'Ditto,' grumbled no-nonsense Emerald. 'Nuts but nice.' She squeezed my hand under the table.

I gave a grateful, inward smile. We three sisters did love each other, despite our mother's spiteful manoeuvrings. Yes, we could quite happily drown each other under a wave on a regular basis, but we would also give each other a kidney if required. We were the Ryan sisters – the prettiest, wittiest girls at a school renowned for the fact that the girls were forward but the boys were backward, who nevertheless married the first guys we dated in high school just to get away from our unhappy home. As kids, we'd kicked and fought and bruised each other with Chinese burns, but had also huddled in the linen press together to avoid our mother's drunken rages, cheered each other on at sports days and ball-kneed any bloke who dared to badmouth, grope or malign a sibling. We'd taken care of each other after break-ups, too, going en masse to an ex-boyfriend's place to retrieve bikinis and David Bowie albums, and to secretly key his car. We were like Orion's Belt: always there, lined up alongside each other.

My whole life I'd felt I could never live up to my big sisters' competence and achievements. Even now, aged fifty, I was still the little sister, always running along behind, trying to keep up, calling out for their attention, attempting to make them laugh, ingratiating myself by offering to do too much.

I was also the fixer in the family, constantly trying to bridge the yawning chasm of contempt between my two warring siblings, layering on the psychological salve to soothe the emotional wounds inflicted by our manipulative mother. Ruth Ryan had wanted a son but got three daughters, which was another disappointment she hardly bothered to conceal.

'What about alternative treatments? Surely there's something you can do diet-wise?' Amber was doing her concerned head tilt and moist-eyed look, as though already preparing to dash into intensive care with kale cakes and tofu shakes.

'Oh, Christ, don't start with your frickin' fish oil tablets and fruit enemas.' Emerald rolled her eyes. 'Ruby does not want to waste any time at a vegan healing festival, urinating in her yurt because a mudslide has barred her exit flap. And, do you know what? No woman should *ever* be urinating in a yurt next to her own bed.'

Amber bristled. 'I just couldn't get the flap open in time. And, anyway, I'm only trying to help. Something you're too selfish to know about, Emerald.'

'I'm very *unselfishly* choosing to ignore that bitchy comment, because we have bigger things to worry about. The point is not to give up, Rubes,' Emerald pep-talked. 'A Kev-ectomy could be possible with surgery and chemo. Almost any abdominal operation can be performed laparoscopically—'

'Which is just Greek for "much, much slower". I don't want keyhole surgery. I just want to go on a cruise with my sisters. That's a much better cure than chemo.'

'And I just want Death to Kevin!' Emerald appealed. 'Statistically, with chemo, one in three pancreatic cancer sufferers live another six years after diagnosis . . . You just have to beat the other two losers.'

'Oh, there goes that warmth and compassion again,' Amber said, with a sucked-on-lemon expression, throwing her hands in the air.

I looked at my two sisters. They were opposite in every way. To observe the Ryan girls from a distance, you wouldn't think we were related. Whereas Emerald announces herself in a confident, full-volume boom, Amber speaks softly and breathlessly, as if always telling secrets.

While Amber is as glossy and nervy and stylish as a first-placed thoroughbred at Ascot, Emerald is more of a plodding draught horse. Her face is heavy and world-weary, without any delicacy, but her big eyes, strong mouth and defined eyebrows give her a handsome aspect, in contrast with Amber's dainty features, which are as supple as her deft and slender fingers.

Their hair is also completely different. Amber's is light as spun gold and usually piled up onto her head in a cloud, whereas Emerald's chocolate-brown locks are cut short into a sensible bob – a helmet of hair she was now shaking at every one of Amber's suggestions.

'Let me book you in to my Korean health retreat. They do the most amazing deep-tissue detox.'

While Emerald maintains that the secret to good skin care is to be, well, Mediterranean, and the secret to beauty is to have Nordic parents who are prone to height, hair and Viking ice-blue eyes, Amber went in for exotic facials with obscure ingredients. Her most recent fad was discarded foreskins collected from South Korean circumcisions.

'Maybe those bloody foreskin facials you so adore explain

why you're such a complete dickhead,' Emerald deduced, violently ripping apart a bread roll and stuffing it into her mouth.

Where Amber was immaculately made-up at all times, waxed, tanned, trimmed and eyebrow-tinted, Emerald's beauty routine took two to three seconds a day, during which time she used her car's rear-view mirror to whack on some lipstick on the way to work. On special occasions, birthdays or New Year's Eve, she would occasionally go all-out and add a dab of blusher.

Amber believed that most things in life could be cured by a mix of Pilates, chakra yoga, yogalates, acupuncture, angel channelling, astrological charting, craniosacral therapy, meditation, mindfulness, reiki, swearing off carbs and giving half your annual salary to a self-styled Intuitive Heart Healer who would awaken your inner Warrior; Emerald, on the other hand, felt most things could be cured with a Xanax tablet and a vodka bottle.

Their approach to food was also at odds. Amber had been through every food fad, feasting on bone broth, fasting, following the scripture of Paleo or Atkins or only nibbling organic, non-irradiated, biodynamic, fair-trade tofu, and was currently incredibly keen on quinoa. Emerald preferred food that was cooked in fat, drenched in salt and coated in chocolate, preferably simultaneously.

As if on cue, a huge plate of pasta arrived to interrupt my ruminations. Emerald grabbed her fork and started shovelling carbonara into her mouth with gusto. Still hungover, I'd ordered only soup, as everything else was too noisy. Kale-nosher Amber picked at her super salad while eyeing Emerald's meal as though it were some long-lost childhood sweetheart.

As she forked in another huge mouthful, curvaceous, big-boned Emerald looked at Amber's lithe limbs and dexterous movements. I could see that she was assailed by a consciousness of her own heavy clumsiness, which is why she snapped, 'Eat a goddamn carb, why don't you, Amber? It won't hurt you.'

Amber shook her expensively highlighted blonde hair and swallowed the lettuce frond she'd been chewing. 'It most definitely *could*. Have you girls had your cholesterol levels checked?'

'Cholesterol?' Emerald repeated. 'Jesus, who cares? Yes, Ruby, why don't you just get your *cancer doctor* to check your *cholesterol*. You must be very frickin' worried about that.'

Amber started to retaliate but I raised my hand, in traffic cop mode, before placing the three cruise tickets on the table. 'This is the remedy I want.'

My sisters greeted the tickets with the same enthusiasm you might welcome a syphilitic ulcer on your wedding night.

Amber was the first to speak. 'Ruby, darling, I so appreciate the gesture, but I can't leave the kids at such short notice. Bella has an exam. And Justin's soccer final is on Saturday.'

'You'll only be away for three weeks,' I persisted. 'What's the worst that could happen? Bella gets a bellybutton piercing and Justin a tattoo that says *Love the Universe* in Sanskrit?'

Amber shuddered theatrically, a strand of hair falling into her pretty face. 'That's what the tattooist says. In reality it probably reads *khichdi and curry chicken*.'

'You forget, Ruby, that everything rates high on Amber's parental anxiety meter,' Emerald added disapprovingly.

I contemplated our middle sister. 'Emerald's right, you know, Amber. Stop letting your kids walk all over you. I love you so much, but you might as well get your own tattoo, right on your forehead, reading *Doormat*.'

Amber's determination to be the perfect mother our own mother most definitely was not meant she spent her life spraying tiny pine cones silver for homemade potpourri and never *ever* letting the sun set on an empty slow cooker in her spotless kitchen. She was constantly in full nail-me-to-the-cross mother– martyr mode. Over the years she had passed on to me a barrage of 'how-to' books and advice columns listing ways to be a better parent/book-week-costume-maker/cake-baker/ gardener/ hubby-pleasing fellatrix, while also being thinner, prettier and less cellulite-riddled. I'd endured conversation after conversation about whether she should be a helicopter mum or a tiger mum or a snowplough parent, a domestic goddess or a sex goddess, or possibly all at once. Now it was *my* turn to offer Amber a 'how-to' manual, as in 'How to enjoy whatever goddamned years you have left, starting today'.

'It's pointless even trying to be a perfect mother, Amber, because you know what will happen?' I counselled. 'Your kids will grow up and then start whining "Why didn't you screw me up more when I was young? I've got nobody to blame now!"'

'Too bloody right,' Emerald decreed, mid-mouthful. 'Bottom line? If you've steered your kids safely into adulthood without them developing a drug addiction or a penchant for collecting Nazi memorabilia, you deserve a motherhood medal.'

'I'm sorry, Ruby.' Amber bridled. 'But I am not taking mothering advice from a woman whose son is doing drugs.'

'For god's sake, the kid smoked one joint. He's not exactly Pablo Escobar.'

As I watched my sisters furiously try to justify why they didn't deserve an all-expenses-paid break in the lap of luxury, I convinced myself that I might actually be able to do them a favour. Amber was running herself ragged trying to create some kind of Von Trapp happy-family mirage, and unhappy Emerald was comfort eating her way into being prematurely old; I'd recently heard her actually groan when getting up out of a bean bag. The wake-up call I'd had from my cancer scare could be the catalyst to snap us all out of our collective coma. Yes, this trip away together would be good for *all* the Ryan girls, I decided. It wasn't just a cruise, but a life-raft.

'Aren't you tired of living a life that revolves around balanced nutritional meals involving quinoa?' I insisted, putting my hand atop Amber's. 'You dash from school appointment to work meeting to kids' orthodontic check-up like your life is some kind of maternal decathlon. We all do. Yet nobody ever gives us a bronze, let alone a gold, trophy.'

'Ruby's right. You should be having a nervous breakdown . . . except you'd only have time for that in your lunch hour. Oh, wait, I forgot, you don't usually take a lunch hour, do you?' Emerald said, mopping up carbonara sauce with a chunk of bread. 'I'm amazed you don't just sleep in your office pantry overnight.'

'Put yourself first . . . Just this once,' I persisted, pressing the cruise ticket into Amber's hand. 'Why not?'

'Because the guilt would kill her,' Emerald guessed, licking the last of the cream from her lips.

'Oh, that's so sensitive, Emerald, really,' Amber snapped. 'Talking about death at a time like—'

'Look, if your offspring complain of neglect,' I pushed on, 'simply point out what you've given up for them – uninterrupted sleep, your privacy . . .'

'Our pelvic floors,' Emerald added, gloomily. 'The ability to wear a bikini – we have nipples down to our knees because of those bloody kids!'

'Speak for yourself, Emerald. I am perfectly pert, thanks very much.'

'Perfectly anorexic, you mean.' Emerald leant over and honked Amber's left breast. 'How much foam is in that frickin' thing?'

Amber slapped her hand away. 'Get off me! You only have big tits because you're overweight.'

'At least I don't starve myself to fit into size six pants, which are giving you a bad case of camel-toe, by the way.'

'These are perfectly tailored designer trousers, I'll have you know. Some of us make an effort. I mean, really, a long skirt and trainers? Is that appropriate work wear?' She pointed at Emerald's attire.

'There's a gym on board, Emmy. Or we can just get in shape by dancing the night away. The disco diet!' I enthused.

'I'm in shape . . . I do at least twenty sit-ups every morning, hitting the snooze button on the iPhone so I'm too late to go power-walking with my health-nut husband.'

'Look, if it meant protecting our kids, we mums would contract a slow, flesh-eating bacteria that resulted in all our limbs falling off. But, having coddled, caressed and kissed bumps better for decades, tethered to the stove by our apron strings, it's time we took a break from nurturing. Don't you agree?' I asked hopefully.

'Oh, Ruby – my heart goes out to you.' Amber wrung

her manicured hands. 'And I'm sending bad vibes to Kev. Down with Kev! Death to Kev! But I can't go. I'm sorry. The kids need me so much right now.'

I deflated faster than the British economy post-Brexit, then turned to my other sister.

'What about you, Emerald? Running your own veterinary clinic, at the bossy beck and call of our overbearing mother, two demanding kids – you must feel like a gymnast trying to balance on a beam. Surely *you* need a break?' I thrust the cruise ticket towards my oldest sister.

'Yeah, I do, but if I buggered off for three weeks at such short notice, Mum would kill me,' Emerald sighed resignedly, pushing the ticket back across the table.

Amber's eyes flared. 'Once again, *not* the most sensitive analogy.'

'Then just don't tell Mum,' I argued. 'Negotiating with terrorists is pointless. Everybody knows that.'

'But I can't leave her. I'm her main carer.'

'Clearly, where there's a will, you'd really like to be in it,' Amber said, coldly.

'I resent that! I take care of Mum because *somebody* has to, and you're too busy being mother of the bloody year.'

My stomach knotted. The will was a contentious point within our family as there was quite a bit of money involved. Our father was basically a tradie who made good thanks to the mining boom. He'd started out as a boilermaker but then began building those big metallic parts for diggers way out west. Although whenever he got into trouble with the cops, for speeding or drink driving, he'd give a twinkly wink and revert, saying 'But I'm just a tradie, mate!'

'Come on, girls,' I placated, 'we all do our share. But since giving up the booze, Mum's never looked better. Surely she can take care of herself for three weeks?'

I pictured our matriarch. Aged eighty, she was so much more glamorous than any of her daughters. She sported better clothes, better hair – she'd been with her hairdresser for longer than she'd been married. Ruth's social life had also always put her daughters' to shame. The woman would only babysit if you booked her a millennia in advance, and even then nearly always cancelled because something *faaabulous* had come up.

'Ignore the thought of what she will say. Our mother is good at emotional blackmail in the same way that a tornado is good at uprooting trees and hurling vehicles,' I pointed out.

'And, by the way, Emerald, you are *not* her main carer,' Amber chipped in.

'Then why am I top of her speed dial?'

'Mum told me *I'm* at the top, actually.'

'Stop it, both of you. Competing for our mother's affections is pointless. She dislikes all three of us equally. We're a huge disappointment. Look, I know Mum's not all bad . . .'

Emerald stared at me incredulously. 'That implies either short-term memory loss or a brain tumour,' she surmised.

'Once more, medical analogies? Really!' Amber chided our older sister in a brittle voice. 'But, Ruby, there's no doubt that our mother is a gargoyle.'

'It's true, Rubes. She'd look perfectly at home perched on a flying buttress guarding a Gothic monastery . . . Which is exactly why I can't spring this cruise idea on her. She'll just morph into the Goddess of Wrath.' Big, tough, capable Emerald quaked at the thought.

I knew what they meant. My heart gave a wrench of protective love. This was my chance to break my mother's vice-like grip on my sisters. If I could convince them to escape her acrylic-nailed clutches, just this once, I felt sure they could learn how to be happy again. It was time to lay it on thick. Hell, it was time to get out the industrial-sized cement trowel.

'My darling sisters. The cancer diagnosis has made me suddenly reassess everything.' I was amazed at how good I'd become at lying in such a short time. I patted myself on the back, metaphorically. Then another cold wave of self-loathing hit me. In a spasm of guilt I made a quick mental list of all the people worse than me – Mussolini, Stalin, Hitler, Pol Pot, Dick Cheney, that bastard who invented Spanx – then made another silent, sacred promise to confess the truth the minute I got my sisters aboard. But I just had to get them on that bloody boat first.

I grabbed hold of their hands. 'A now-or-never feeling has taken hold of me. I can't stop thinking about all the wonders of the world I've never glimpsed. The Great Wall of China. The Taj Mahal. Machu Picchu—'

'Chris Hemsworth naked,' Emerald reminded me, licking her lips.

'Exactly. My brain is jumping from one missed opportunity to another. I've never skydived. Not that I want to . . . But I want to have the opportunity to at least chicken out of it at the last minute! I want to ride an elephant and swim with a whale. I want to learn astronomy and read the night sky. I haven't seen the aurora borealis, let alone a solar eclipse. I've never read Proust. Or been in a threesome.'

'Darl, you've never even played doubles at tennis!' Emerald mocked.

My hangover was finally abating. I felt energised and determined. 'Exactly. I want to have adventurous sex, say, in a broom cupboard – a broom cupboard aboard a scientific research ship heading to the South Pole.'

My sisters looked at me quizzically. I couldn't blame them. I sounded weird even to my own ears, as if I were trying out someone else's personality, someone much more feisty and fabulous than me. But maybe this *was* my true self, finally shining out from beneath the family bushel?

'Look – when I was at school, I always thought I would take the world by storm. Well, weather experts have downgraded my career trajectory from "storm" to "light drizzle". Do you remember when I won a place on that creative writing course and Mum said, "You? A writer? You don't even know that a double negative is a complete no-no!" I just accepted her dismissal of the idea, like it was an edict from the Vatican. I should have taken that cadetship with the *Herald*, but Mum just gave me that smile that can burn five layers of skin off your face—'

'Oh, I know that smile.' Amber shivered.

'—then she laughed and said, "You're not exactly Ita Buttrose material, dear." I could have finished that novel that's been languishing in my drawer for decades . . . But there was always Mum's negative voice ringing in my ears. "No matter how much you push the envelope, Ruby, you'll still just be stationery." Clearly I need a twelve-step program to break my low self-esteem habit. I mean, what am I? A fifty-year-old has-been hack on the local rag. Could have, would have, should have. Well, no more! This is my season of "Yes". From now on, I'm going to eat carbs, I'm going to eat salt, I'm going to drink martinis. Today is the first day of the rest of my hedonistic life. I want people to say, "She died with her eyelashes on in her battle with Kev, that hairy aggressive pancreatic tumour dude."'

I was talking such shit I could have qualified as a lifesaver at a sewage plant. But a little lie like this wasn't a *huge* sin, was it? I wasn't coveting my neighbour or taking a life or anything. A couple of Hail Marys on the way home should do it . . . Okay, more like a couple of decades' worth of dedicated rosary-fondling. But it would be worth it if I could get my sisters aboard that cruise and patch things up between us.

'Look, I didn't just have a light-bulb moment yesterday, I had a blinding nuclear fusion flash. I don't want to be a member of the exploited, exhausted, taken-for-granted mothers club anymore. Or put up with an unfaithful spouse . . .'

'Has Harry confessed who he cheated with?' Amber asked, cautiously.

'No, the arsehole.'

'Harry's not an arsehole, he's a regular ankle – three feet lower than an arsehole,' Emerald decried in a gravelly undertone.

'It's just opened up an old wound. Remember when he cheated on me with Tracey Chapman in Year 12 and we broke up for two years? Maybe he's a sexual kleptomaniac.'

Driving to the cafe an hour earlier, I'd rung Harry to say that unless he told me the truth about his affair, I was going on the cruise. His reply? 'Make sure you have your inoculations before you go – inoculations against rednecks and bloody bogans.' I'd been planning to tell him about the misdiagnosis, but his cool, condescending response made me think *Why the hell should I?* My irritation was now scratchy as sandpaper.

'Screw Harry!' I said. 'This is about *us*. I don't want to communicate with animals, angels, fairies, archangels, ascended masters, guides, stars or those who have crossed over. Nor do I want to fry myself with chemo and get tattooed eyebrows and a muff merkin.'

I cringed inwardly. The lies were just rolling off my tongue at this point. Obviously, I had a personality guaranteed to give a shrink wet dreams.

'All I want to do is take a little bonding cruise with my dear sisters and reset our sibling compass before I cark it. Don't you want to learn what turns you on as a person, rather than as a wife or mum? I don't want to go screaming down memory lane thinking, *Gee, these are shit memories!* Do you?'

'You are *not* going to cark it,' Emerald said, emphatically. 'We are going to fight this wretched Kev.'

For a moment all animation left my face. I couldn't believe that both of my sisters, while solicitous, had refused my invitation point blank. It was insulting to think that, if I really *did* have cancer, they wouldn't put their lives on hold for three measly weeks. I could feel a peeved frown puckering my forehead.

'But you have to come with me. I've got *cancer*! How long do I have left?' I started frantically fingering those mental rosary beads. In desperation, I began to cry. Not because I had cancer, but because I didn't have it and had to keep pretending I did, and it *still* wasn't enough to win over my warring sisters. Both of them immediately wrapped their arms around me.

'Ruby, I'm so, so sorry you're sick. But I can't just bloody well drop everything. I'll be here for you in every way I can: I'll drive you to every appointment, but I have responsibilities – to Mum, to my clients. And to Alessandro. Now the kids are away at uni, he gets so lonely. If we don't have sex every night, Sandro sulks. The man's hung like a pachyderm, which means he gets MSB – maximum sperm build-up. Besides, you know that I never do anything spontaneous without a warning!' Emerald concluded, trying for a note of levity.

'And Scott would be at his wits' end without me, too. His cases are so harrowing. He just doesn't cope without my emotional support. I'll cook wholesome food to build up your immunity, Ruby. I'll massage unguents into your temples. But . . .' Amber's face flickered and tensed. All her eye make-up had washed away with her tears, leaving her looking young and vulnerable. 'I can't just abandon my family. Or Mum, for that matter. Not at such short notice.'

Defeated, I slumped back into my seat. Feeling the sludge of desolation in my heart, I signalled to the waiter and ordered a Bloody Mary. My hangover was back with a vengeance. I didn't just need hair of the dog, I needed a whole canine pelt. 'Oh, and hot chips,' I added. My head had started thumping so badly I wanted to ask the woman at the next table to mute her knitting needles.

Emerald squeezed my hand. 'Don't be angry with me, Rubes – after all, I'm the one who'll be plucking your chin hairs for you when you go into a coma.'

'Emerald! Is that comment entirely necessary?' Amber snapped, her eyebrows taut as an archer's bow.

'It's okay, Amber. I'm not upset.' *I don't even have cancer,*

I wanted to add, but said instead, sorrowfully, 'You're lucky that you're both so happily married. Just promise me that one of you will always come to the hospital with those tweezers.'

I felt exhausted. No wonder – I'd been on my metaphorical toes for so long, I could've joined the corps de ballet.

'We will,' my sisters said, in another odd display of unity.

I sat there long after Emerald and Amber had dashed back to work. The nudging and jerks and winks and whispered asides of other customers were not lost on me. Even out here, at the very tip of the Insular Peninsular, it seemed word had got out about my bravura birthday meltdown. I felt like a balloon that had lost most of its air. What the hell would I do now?

One thing was for sure – when fate closes one door, it crushes your fingers in the hinges of another.

5

Later, when it was all over and the dust and drama of that summer had finally settled, Amber told me what happened post-lunch, after we parted that day. Let me draw the picture for you . . .

Amber's life was like a giant jigsaw puzzle, with all the little pieces perfectly slotted together to match the coloured photo on the box marked 'happy family' and 'successful working mother'. But timing and organisation were everything. The woman juggled so much she could be in the Cirque du Soleil. After our anguished meal at Convict Cafe, Amber had scurried back to her office to supervise the catering for three parties. They were one chef down, so she'd had to stay late dicing and slicing.

At least she'd prepared a beef bourguignon for the family's evening meal before leaving for work that morning. At 5 pm she'd texted Scott to remind him to put the casserole dish in the oven at a low temperature so dinner would be gurgling away aromatically by the time she walked in the door at eight. Then it would just be a matter of steaming some greens, cleaning the kitchen, helping the kids with their homework, finding lost sports kits, putting the washing on, issuing some regulation nagging about flossing and digital detoxing, then falling into a bath before bed. She often wondered if Scott noticed that she had two jobs, chief bread winner *and* chief bottle washer – a role she preferred to describe as 'domestic engineer' or 'president of in-home pedagogy', but which still boiled down to being a woman who was so busy she needed to employ staff to chew her food and have friends and fun on her behalf.

When Amber pulled her car into the driveway of her lovingly restored sandstone Federation home, framed by waratahs and wattle and other native flowers, in her mind she was already in her PJs, curled up around her book. If she got to bed before Scott finished working on whatever legal opinion was currently obsessing him, she could also avoid a carnal encounter. Despite what she'd said to her sisters and the image she projected to the world, Amber often feigned sleep so that she didn't have to have sex with her priapic husband. Amber was far too polite and husband-pleasing to ever rebuff his advances. It wasn't non-consensual, but nor was it sensual.

But if she couldn't sidestep Scott's advances, her plan B was to bring up every detumescing subject she could think of, from global warming to shower grouting to Korean nuclear proliferation, in the hope of deterring his ballistic missile. Maybe she could just wear her designer trousers to bed? The snug fit could prove to be an excellent contraceptive – once she got into them, they were nearly impossible to get off again. But, in fact, her family were about to provide the straw that would break the woman with the camel-toe's back.

Amber could smell the fire the moment her key hit the

lock. Skeins of thick, pungent smoke lay in the air. Groping her way by braille to the kitchen, she found the grill shooting flames and the casserole sitting, uncooked, in the oven. Scott had clearly turned on the grill by mistake before retreating back to his man cave at the bottom of the garden.

When she stormed into the converted boat shed to confront her husband, he replied, nonchalantly, 'Sorry. Thought I'd turned the right knob. They all look so alike.'

Amber stared at her husband in astonishment. 'You mean we've been married for twenty-five years and you don't know how to switch on our oven?'

He shrugged. He *shrugged*!

'I could make my signature quiche . . .' he suggested, barely looking up from his paperwork. 'Although the recipe says to beat twelve eggs separately. That sounds too cruel, don't you think? Maybe I could just reprimand them sternly,' he joked. He *joked*!

'No.' Amber went into full persecuted, burn-me-at-the-stake Saint Amber mode – as he knew she would. 'I'll just rustle something up.' *Sitting duck, or sacrificial lamb?* she thought darkly. *Underdog in a chump sauce?* Turning to head back to the scorched earth that had become her kitchen, she paused. 'But why wasn't the smoke alarm going off? Did you change the batteries like I asked?'

'Oh, shit. Meant to, but then this case came up and it's been all-consuming . . . Refugee crisis.'

Amber was very restrained – after all, she didn't stuff Scott's briefcase up his nose. She merely retreated to the kitchen while her domestically impaired legal eagle husband was in mid-humanitarian flow.

The second blow was delivered when her seventeen-year-old

son, Justin, and fifteen-year-old daughter, Bella, trailed in from swimming training, hungry and on the sniff for supper. Amber, way behind schedule, asked them to help out by putting their dirty sports clothes in the washing machine.

'Which one is that?' Justin asked. 'The top one or the bottom one?'

Mother looked at son, aghast. 'Wait. You're seventeen years old and you don't know the difference between the washing machine and the dryer?'

'Is it the one on the wall or the one on the floor?' her son drawled.

'Bella, will you please show your big brother which machine is which.'

'Um . . . I would, but . . . I'm not sure either.'

Ruby was right; she might as well have 'doormat' stamped on her forehead.

Amber, who'd always maintained an attitude of detached and courtly irony towards her family, suddenly transmogrified into Attila the Mum. 'I am sick of being taken for granted!'

'Take a chill pill, Mum.' Her son's tone bordered on surly. 'What's wrong?'

Amber sighed with exasperation, 'Oh, you know, life.'

Justin looked perplexed. 'But I *am* your life, Mum.'

It was true that the kids were the glue that kept her marriage together, but, of late, things were coming unstuck. Perhaps it might help if she were to actually *sniff* their homework glue a bit more often. Amber loved her children with a passion, but tonight she found herself considering the guppy approach to parenting – that is, eating your young.

After the kids and her husband had disappeared to go wherever it is they vanished whenever dishes piled up in the sink, Amber thought about her life. Not only was she running a boutique hotel for all the people in her radius – people who apparently believed the dirty crockery levitated itself in and out of the sink of its own accord – she was also expected to quietly guide and advise her kids and her hubby and the pets and her employees and her clients and her demanding mother and her mother's maligned manicurist/ gardener/pool boy/etc. with the patience of a police officer talking someone down off a ledge.

After putting the laundry on, stacking the dishwasher, defrosting a big tray of lasagne for tomorrow's dinner, checking that all teenagers' electronic devices were off and putting the cat out, Amber finally crawled, exhausted, into bed. The one thing she was fantasising about was sleep – and then she felt her husband's hand groping for her across the sheets. As he tweaked her left nipple, she found herself contemplating a subtle hint to let him know she wasn't in the mood – such as smashing the ceramic bedside lamp on his head.

It wasn't that Scott was unattractive. While many of her girlfriends' husbands' six packs had become blobs of mozzarella dangling there over their dooverlackies, Scott was still fit. He didn't have time to help around the house, but he miraculously found hours to jog and cycle and play squash. Scott was the kind of man who would hire a gardener to cut the lawns so that he had time to play golf for the exercise.

As her husband's hand moved down her belly and under the elastic of her pyjama pants, she wondered how it was that a man who hadn't spoken to her all day, and had nearly burnt down her kitchen, could think she'd be in the mood for love. No. She was in the mood for garrotting him with his jockstrap. As he prodded away at her clitoris as though it were an ATM machine, all she wanted to say was 'Out of order. Not dispensing. And definitely no deposits.' There's so much emphasis on women faking orgasms, Amber thought, but what about men faking foreplay? She'd toyed with starting a His and Her orgasm chart to highlight discrepancies, but would he even care? Her husband was so self-obsessed, Amber often thought Scott should have just asked for his *own* hand in marriage. But part of Amber's 'happy marriage' mirage meant keeping her husband content, and so she rolled towards him.

She never felt that Scott made love to her. It was more of a naked mugging. No finesse, no tenderness, a hit-and-run romance. If he did talk at all, it was to feed her lines for some legal sexual fantasy that was playing out in his head: 'Say "I yield to the authority of the bench,"' he'd urge, or 'Fondle my gavel.' He clearly had no idea that a busy mum's top bedroom fantasy involves discovering that her husband has picked up his underpants off the floor.

While Scott thrust away, Amber contemplated menus for two future events she was catering. Scott had no inkling of her distraction. The night she'd conceived their son she was mentally planning a Moroccan lamb recipe with fennel and garlic. Their daughter? Mango, crème and ginger meringue.

Scott definitely had his turbo-booster rocket thruster on tonight, with no moon landing in sight. The metronomic regularity of his lovemaking was inducing sleep. 'Were you faking it last night?' she imagined him asking her over breakfast. 'No . . . I really was asleep,' she'd reply.

Bored rigid and beyond exhaustion, Amber now used her

emergency guaranteed ejaculation technique and tickled her husband's prostate with a finger. It was disgusting but effective. In her mind she pictured herself just shoving stuffing up a bird's bottom.

After scrubbing her hands in the bathroom, she returned to the bedroom to hear Scott snoring cacophonously. Great. Now she still wouldn't be able to sleep. Exasperated, and at the end of her familial tether, she stomped back into the bathroom and rang my mobile.

'I'm in, Ruby,' she said as soon as I answered.

'What?'

'I'm coming on the cruise. I mean, how bad can it be?' Amber rationalised. 'If Emerald annoys me too much I'll just make her walk the plank.'

'Oh, Amber, that's wonderful! What made you change your mind?'

'Well, don't tell Emerald, who will just gloat in a most nauseating fashion, but having sex with Scott puts me into a coma. And that whole doormat thing? It's true. I am being walked all over.'

'Don't worry, you coma-sexual! You're not alone. Perfect marriages are like orgasms – a lot of them are fake. Just look at Harry and me,' I said, sadly. 'I thought we were happy.'

'And I also really want to be there for you, Rubes. I love you.'

'I love you too. And. . . .' Now was the time to tell the truth, I thought, as I lay all alone in my empty house, cradling the phone, looking up into the darkness. How could I continue to lie to my dear sister, especially after Amber had uncharacteristically revealed a vulnerability of her own? If not now, when? Just spit it out . . .

'I'll see you aboard HMAS *Hedonism*!' I heard myself say.

You are going straight to hell, Ruby Ryan, I chastised myself. But, at least by going on a cruise with my sister first, I'd be taking the scenic route.

6

In our post-summer post-mortem, when we were scrubbing the metaphorical blood out of the shag pile, Emerald also confessed to me what really happened after our lunch at the Convict Cafe that day . . .

Sliding into bed beside her dozing husband, all Emerald craved was some carnal comfort. Alessandro's tousled mass of curly hair on the pillow was nearly as dark as when they'd first met, with just the odd fleck of grey at his temples. Daily gym workouts meant that he still sported the whole Greek god look – the man looked seriously underdressed without a plinth.

She played with him gently, rubbing her nipples up against his chest while trying to forget her shitty day. After her poor little sister's cancer confirmation, Emerald had dashed back to work to deal with a kangaroo that had been hit by a car in the national park. It had been lying on her table, concussed, when all of a sudden it leapt up off the slab and jumped around the surgery, smashing up everything in its path. Shelves of fish food and chew toys and dog toothpaste all went flying, including a glass tank that contained a cantankerous brown snake. Emerald was torn between catching the venomous viper or tackling the roo before it bounded onto the busy road.

In the midst of the chaos, Emerald's mother rang to say she needed her daughter urgently. Once the roo was corralled, Emerald had to leave her nurse to catch the snake, clean up the wreckage and cancel her cat hernia op as she sped to her mother's house – only to discover that the 'emergency' was Ruth's inability to work her Netflix account. Emerald was then dragooned into going through the mail, paying the bills online, untangling the pool sweep, weeding the flower bed, cooking her mother's dinner then watching 'a bit of telly', which turned out to be an episode of *Midsomer Murders* – that was two hours of Emerald's life she'd never get back again – only to be informed by her mother that if she dared to go on that cruise with Ruby, Ruth would change her will to leave everything to the Catholic Church.

Emerald's nipple rubbing soon had her moaning with lust. She nibbled on Alessandro's ear and stroked him faster. Sandro half woke up and moved towards her, aroused. He looked at Emerald, his eyes as bright and intent as they had been when they were first in love, back in high school. Then, as he woke more fully, a film of indifference settled over them. He kissed her on the cheek, then patted her on the shoulder – three pats, like you would give a trusty old dog. He pushed her leg off his thigh and rolled to put his back towards her. He couldn't have made his rejection more obvious if he'd built a Trump-style wall down the middle of the bed.

She thought back to when they'd first wed; when the sex was so great that it took up her whole life. When she wasn't in bed, she was planning how to get back there. Oh, how Emerald craved that deranged, rip-each-other's-clothes-off, screw-in-the-hallway-then-the-living-room-then-the-hallagain-and-then-finally-the-bed kind of sex they'd once enjoyed.

Emerald had a penchant for the wilder reaches of sexual behaviour and, over the first few years of their marriage, had introduced Sandro to a number of new concepts that aroused and terrified him in equal measure. But even before their second baby was born, she'd felt he was making love more out of a sense of duty than any actual desire.

Now here they were, two drowning empty-nesters, clinging to their sides of the bed like separate life rafts.

Determined to rekindle their passion, Emerald crept her arm around her husband's warm, naked body and stroked his belly. She nuzzled his neck and pushed her hips into his broad, strong back. She moved her hand lower down – to find him limp as a piece of wilted lettuce. Of late, she would only be able to locate her husband's cock with the Hubble telescope. She felt like a dog trying to nudge its dead owner back to life.

Alessandro brushed her hand away with more resolve this time. Once more he kissed her half-heartedly on the cheek and said 'Goodnight' with the finality of a submarine hatch closing.

Emerald lurched to her feet, feeling furious. Weren't men supposed to be the ones gagging for sex all the time? Yet here she was, with extremely erect nipples and wet as an oyster down below, and he wasn't in the least bit interested.

She trudged down the hall of their blond-brick bungalow to the kitchen. Through the sliding glass doors she could see three or four cars waiting for her husband's attention in their adjoining garage. If only the car whisperer would care for her the way he caressed those chassis – massaging the metal, teasing out bumps, coaxing out scratches, rubbing and petting and polishing the body to a satisfying sheen. Most of Alessandro's clients were female. They came in secret, not wanting their husbands to know that they'd bumped into a bollard or that the kids had dinged the car during a driving lesson.

Emerald knew that they fancied him, too. 'It's his attention to detail I love,' women marvelled, implying that if the Dent Boss took that much time and care over a car body, imagine what he could do to *her* body?

'Hey, Dent Boss, can you polish out my cellulite too?' flirted one.

'I just can't curb my enthusiasm for your gentle touch,' bantered another. 'How do you feel about my sassy chassis?'

As Emerald flicked on the kitchen light, the dog gave her a glottal bass bark of welcome. At least her kelpie was pleased to see her. She opened the freezer and was bathed in its icy blue light. Only a tub of salted caramel ice cream could hit the spot right now; sadly, not the G spot, as she'd intended. The kitchen was spotless except for a can of engine lubricant Alessandro had left on the counter. She read the label – it was cheekily branded *Start Ya Bastard*. She was momentarily tempted to rush back to the bedroom and spray it onto her husband's flaccid appendage.

Instead she ripped off the lid of the ice cream container she kept hidden under the ice packs at the bottom of the freezer. Alessandro had no idea that she secretly snacked on the side. She pretended to like the mung beans and tofu he stir-fried for them each night for supper, but she gorged on biscuits, chocolate and cakes when he wasn't around. If this rejection kept up, she'd soon be the size of an emerging nation. She was full of fast food, but starved of slow sex.

As Emerald licked the spoon, the longing to have sex with someone, *anyone*, felt like a raging thirst. She seemed to have evolved from tranquil, middle-aged mum of two to male-hunting predator. Within minutes of meeting a good-looking bloke, she found herself imagining him naked. At the beach, while pretending to be immersed in some learned tome, she was actually surreptitiously perving on the nearest chiselled pectoral, imagining herself bivouacking in the shade of his bulging bicep.

'Just because a woman can hide the primal engorgement of her libidinous organ doesn't mean she doesn't want to discover the supple hydraulics of a love god's manhood on a regular basis,' she confided to her dog. 'As a young woman I longed to meet the right man. But now, aged fifty-five, I'm wondering if I've had enough of the wrong ones.' Emerald realised, with a slight shock, that she felt no qualms about making love to a perfect stranger except that she didn't want him to be perfect – she wanted him to be really naughty and dirty and bad.

Yet the one man she really wanted did not want her. And she wasn't unattractive, was she? The fuller Kardashian figure was in vogue – a peachy derriere was now de rigueur. Why, just last week a bloke on a building site had given her a long, slow wolf-whistle when she'd dashed across the road to pick up a tray of mangoes. And what a tingle of illicit delight it had given her. She reckoned it should be illegal to wolf-whistle at any woman under fifty, but mandatory for women over it. Alessandro's rejection was so humiliating. She was too young to be tossed onto the sexual scrap heap.

Emerald had tried to talk to him about it but Sandro just shut down the conversation. She'd suggested some vitamin V, but he saw Viagra as an affront to his masculinity. She had slyly purchased a packet and left it lying by his side of the bed anyway. She bought him oysters by the bucketload. But still nothing. They were living like brother and sister.

Emerald stroked her kelpie as it nestled contentedly in her lap. 'Ah, it's so easy for you, girl, isn't it?' Animals are so much better at mating than humans, she mused. Her mind flitted to the female emperor moth, which simply discharges a perfume from her abdominal glands to be picked up by the long feathery male antennae, bringing him frantically fluttering to her side. Female red-backed salamanders choose male newts by inspecting their droppings. If she liked the bloke's diet, she moved on in and copulated between courses.

Lacking a perfumed abdominal gland and a dung-detector, maybe she needed to migrate somewhere, forcing Alex to miss her? Creeping obsolescence flickered in her peripheral vision. From adolescence to obsolescence – it had all whizzed by in a heartbeat.

She dialled my number from the landline.

'Does this cruise go to Bangko?'

'Bangko?'

'I don't say "cock" – it's not the way I was brought up,' Emerald joshed.

'No, we aren't cruising to Bang*kok*,' I said, laughing. 'But Vanuatu, New Caledonia and lots of exotic Pacific islands.'

'I'm eating double-choc mini rolls by the tub. We can only go to places where they don't discriminate against fat people.'

'Relax. Caftans are in this summer.'

'Caftan? I'll be wearing a bloody tarpaulin. Amber's not coming, is she?'

'She is, amazingly! Isn't that fantastic?'

There was a pause. 'She's my sister and I love her, but you do realise we'll have our teeth into each other's throats before you can say "anchors aweigh".'

'And that's exactly why we need to do this trip together. To get over all that crap. What changed your mind?'

'I've decided that what I need is some equine therapy.'

'Um, there are a lot of activities on offer on these big ships, Em, but I'm not sure about horses.'

'No, I mean I want a man who is hung like a horse. That's equine therapy for middle-aged women.'

'What?! What about Alessandro? I thought he was your Italian stallion?'

'I lied. Okay? Sandro hasn't touched me for years. Don't tell Amber. She'll only gloat. The reason I comfort eat is because I'm suffering from chronic hetero hunger pangs. I want to put "men" back on the menu. Our last hormonal hurrah. I think it's okay to be physically unfaithful, as long as I'm not emotionally unfaithful. What happens on board, stays on board, right? For you too. Harry's infidelity has given you a "get out of the bedroom free" card, I'd say. Especially after Kev's vile appearance.'

Now, I thought. This was the right time to tell the truth about the misdiagnosis – except that I'd tied myself up in so many knots with all my lies, I'd need to hire a top escapologist to help me get the hell out of them.

'Great. See you aboard HMAS *Hedonism*!' I heard myself say instead of the truth. 'Love you, Emmy.'

'Ditto,' she replied. Coming from rational, unsentimental

Emerald, it was the equivalent of a Shakespearean love sonnet.

As I hung up, my main worry now was that the cruise ship would sink under the weight of all my excess emotional baggage.

7

'Emotional roller-coaster' is an overused expression, but I felt it was far too tame a description for the nail-biting, knuckle-gnawing, vomit-inducing big dipper ride my life had become. In the past week I had been diagnosed with cancer then miraculously cured, discovered that my beloved husband was a cheating bastard, thrown a party with all my friends and family to celebrate my fiftieth birthday, then promptly alienated them all and been exiled as a pariah to the persona non grata parish, been excised from my mother's will and drunkenly booked a cruise for my two estranged sisters, who'd flat-out refused to come . . . but who were now, astonishingly, leaning up against the railing of an ocean liner, sipping cocktails with little umbrellas in them.

'Where are we going again?' Amber asked, slugging down her second piña colada as we slipped moorage at sunset and cruised past the pale, shimmering sails of the world's most famous opera house.

'We're sailing out of the heads and turning left, then we'll simply keep going until the ice cream melts,' I explained, gesturing vaguely towards the Pacific. I'd been too plastered at the time of booking the tickets to take note of any exact geographical details.

Emerald's work schedule and Amber's helicopter parenting

meant we were the last passengers to board and had only just made it to the departure gangway with moments to spare. Emerald had been delayed by a bereaved pet owner who'd insisted on hiring a medium to connect with her dead dog from beyond the grave, and Amber had run overtime with her tutor studying 'fronted adverbials' and 'gerunds', and how to calculate the kinetic energy of a two-tonne car travelling at thirty kilometres an hour. Apparently tutoring for kids is so common, Amber had decided that the only way to guarantee better grades for her precious progeny was to get tutored herself as well, enabling her to offer even more effective homework help.

I'd promised myself I'd level with my sisters about the cancer misdiagnosis the minute the boat set sail . . . but the moment was so perfect, with the tangerine sunset lighting up the sparkling harbour, which lapped like a contented cat on the sides of our ship, that I postponed my confession until after another round of cocktails. And then another.

I vowed to make a clean breast of things as soon as we found our cabin and were changing for dinner . . . But that didn't go to plan either. Amber and Emerald had always pooh-poohed cruising; Emerald feared a cabin so small even a sardine would feel cramped, prompting Amber to fret that she'd have to 'go outside to change her mind'. So, when my sisters saw our spacious, three-bedroom suite, complete with expansive balcony, they had to tilt their heads backwards so that their eyeballs wouldn't fall out in amazement. They leapt about as though doing a Californian aerobics class.

'You should get drunk and surf the net more often!' Emerald exclaimed, dive-bombing onto her capacious bed.

'Yes, let's just keep our little sis in an alcoholic stupor!' Amber agreed, popping open the 'welcome aboard' champagne that had been in an ice bucket, awaiting our arrival.

My sisters were agreeing. That was a first. How could I burst their bubble – their champagne bubble? My confession was on the tip of my tongue, but so was the Bollinger, which fizzed and frothed like the sea beneath our balcony.

I then pledged to come clean at dinner, but both my sisters were being so uncharacteristically attentive and kind – 'May I buy you another drink? I'm thinking champagne – vintage'; 'You take the best seat, Rubes, the view should be all yours – especially of the cute buns of the boys in the band', and so on – that I didn't want to break the fragile spell.

Sipping nightcaps on the top deck beneath a canopy of stars seemed the perfect moment to fess up, but I took another dose of pathetic pills and gave in to cowardice by convincing myself that it was best to just have *one* night of harmony before my guilty admission and the avalanche of fury that would follow.

But the next day was so blissfully happy . . . and then the next . . . By the afternoon of day three, the truth still hadn't found its way onto my lips – perhaps because my lips were far better employed working their way through the colourful cocktail list of 'Slippery Nipples', 'Orgasms', 'Corpse's Revenge', 'Sex on the Beach' and big full glasses of a lethal beverage called, appropriately, 'The Bull Shooter'.

Besides, I had other things on my mind, notably the number of handsome young men on board. Ship life was like being afloat in a huge aquarium. Every imaginable species drifted by – tall women as pencil-thin as trumpet fish; big, bloated wrasse with lugubrious lips; contented, kimono-ed whales who seemed to eat as though they had seven rectums; little darting types in coordinated sporty clothing who tended to swim in schools – all filtering luxury through their gills like oxygen. The men aboard, on the other hand, seemed to be of one breed only: muscled, chiselled and bronzed.

We Ryan girls were lying on our sun loungers, poolside, on the afternoon of our third day at sea, with me positioned between my two older siblings, the ham in the sisterly sandwich as usual. I was enjoying the view – that is, the passing pulchritudinous male parade – when a forty-ish man with cultivated perma-stubble bounded on deck and boomed a boisterous, American-accented *'Hello, Laaadeeez,'* into his microphone. *'I am Brent, and I'll be your entertainment officer for the duration of the cruise!'*

It takes a lot of personality and a lot of chutzpah to be an entertainment officer, and let's just say that this bloke was over-qualified. To disguise the fact that he was losing his hair, Brent had shaved his head, giving the overall impression of a billiard ball with a sneer. *'I need three of you bewdiful ladies to volunteer for a very special assignment . . . judging the "Neptune, Sea King of the Cruise" competition! And, of course, I need some extremely sexy male competitors. The only rule, dudes, is that contestants must check out of the judges' cabins by nine am tomorrow, okay?'*

The pool area was suddenly overpopulated with generouslybuttocked mining heiresses in spiky heels, waving money to help influence the judge-selection process. Spray-tanned, bling-embellished, floral-bikini- or leopard-print-sarong-wearing and highly G-strung middle-aged women from all over the sundeck whooped and hollered as they gravitated poolwards, giggling.

I instantly felt dowdy and underdressed in my old olive-green speedo with questionable elastic. I'd always loved how the colour set off my red hair, but I hadn't noticed until now that the cossie had lost its elasticity – much like my marriage, which I also hadn't noticed had faded and sagged. Clearly 'costume drama' isn't a description of a BBC series with bustles and bonnets, but indecision over whether I was too old to buy a fashionable bikini from the onboard boutique. No other female afloat on HMAS *Hedonism* seemed to share my insecurities. I longed to be more like them, but right now my confidence level was so low I'd need a pressurised mini-sub to locate it.

By now, twenty or so eager young male contestants had stampeded to the makeshift stage. Clad in bathers tight enough to reveal their religions, the young blokes struck Adonis-type poses to fully display their biceps, triceps and undulating six-packs. The men's abdomens were so sculpted I wondered if they'd simply swallowed loaves of bread without chewing, which were now lined up in those taut tummies. One Nordic Viking was rippling his stomach muscles with such rapidity it resembled a horde of hamsters hiding out under a flesh-tone doona.

'Has either of you noticed the inordinate number of handsome young men aboard?' Emerald inquired, peering over the top of her Ray-Bans. 'Young, single men who seem footloose and fiancée-free? There's not a beer belly or a food-stained footy shirt in sight.'

'Well, yes, now you mention it,' I agreed. 'Including the entertainment officer, who clearly believes in life, liberty and the happiness of pursuit.' I pointed at Mr Charisma, who was flashing his blinding-white teeth as he sauntered through a crowd of female passengers, casually patting posteriors and planting kisses.

'Well,' the waiter chimed in as he placed our next round of technicolour cocktails on the side table. 'It is kinda to be expected on a cougar cruise, right?'

The sight of the three Ryan sisters simultaneously spitting out their Slippery Nipples must have been accidentally captured in the background of at least ten iPhone videos, and would surely be the cause of much puzzlement when replayed by other passengers anon.

Amber was the first to regain her composure. 'I'm sorry – a *what*?' Shielding her eyes, she squinted upwards to survey the Herculean hulk clad in black shorts and a tight white tee who had made this revelation.

'A cougar cruise.' The waiter flexed his muscles, then stood in an inverted-V position, legs apart, his formidable groin at eye level.

Emerald gave a swoon worthy of an Elvis concert circa 1956. 'So, what does that mean exactly?' she asked, in her most velvety voice.

'Youse older chicks pay, and cubs sail free.' He winked. 'Didn't ya know?'

'"*Cubs*"? No, I certainly did not know. Did you?' Amber asked me, her voice prissy with disapproval.

I shook my head so vigorously that my sunhat fell off. 'Jesus, no! I was so drunk when I booked. I just paid for the first available cruise out of Sydney. Hey, at least it's not a swingers cruise, or a nudist cruise or, god help us, a Republican Mormon float-fest.'

'Bloody hell. How excellent!' Emerald exclaimed. 'And are these young "cubs" required to provide flirtation and frottage?'

she asked, tucking a ten-dollar tip down the front of the waiter's black shorts. I gazed, agog, at his, um, effrontery. His penis seemed to be in a separate time zone from his body. The male waitstaff had clearly been hired from Rent-a-Bulge. Unless they were wearing padded underpants – a kind of Wonder-pant for men.

'Well, it ain't compulsory.' The well-endowed waiter smiled. 'But you know what we blokes say – every hole is a goal!'

'How romantic.' Amber glared disgustedly at the waiter before covering her retro, designer polka-dot two-piece in a thick white towel and strangling her lovely long blonde hair up into a tight bun.

'The only thing my sister wants in bed is breakfast,' I explained to the waiter, with an apologetic smile.

'Breakfast I don't have to cook for myself for once. But what I definitely *don't* want is another man wanting something from me.' Amber shuddered.

'Speak for yourself,' Emerald purred, peering lasciviously at the poolside meat market. Even though she was strapped into the kind of sturdy orthopaedic bathing suit that wouldn't have looked out of place on someone swimming the Channel in the 1920s, she coquettishly lowered one thick strap. 'I knew cruises offered an all-you-can-eat smorgasbord, but I wasn't expecting a boy buffet.' She turned her head to watch the waiter's peachy posterior retreat.

'Emerald, you're a vet. Surely you see enough animals on a daily basis,' Amber chided. 'I mean, he's not exactly a conversationalist.'

'Yes, but he does have other charms, like a ten-inch cock. Sure, we could sit around discussing the benefits and drawbacks of the adaptive unconscious, applying economic theory to sociological problems, and the difference between instinct and measured thought . . . or we could just go get laid. Hard call,' she said facetiously.

'Did you not hear him? "*Cubs*" cruise for free. That's practically prostitution,' Amber declared from within her terry-towelling cocoon. 'Plus, it's so insulting. We're in our prime! Those boys should be paying *us*!'

'Don't kid yourself, possum. Just look at poor Ruby, traded in by Harry for a younger model. Boys will be boys . . . and so will a lot of middle-aged hubbies who should know better.'

'Emerald's right,' I concluded with dull resignation. 'Only two things improve with age: red wine and George Clooney.'

The entertainment officer's Californian drawl rang out once more over the deck. '*There are three categories, dudes. Dance moves, underwear modelling and a talent round. Let's get started, ladeeezzz!*'

'The loudest insect on the planet is a two-millimetre-long species of water boatman that uses its penis as a violin bow. Now *that's* talent,' Emerald mused. 'Not to forget the swallowtail butterfly, which has eyes on its penis to help to position itself correctly during mating. And Indian stick insects, which stick together to have nonstop sex for seventy-nine days.'

Her zoological observations were drowned out by the opening chords of 'It's Raining Men', which burst forth from the speakers. Twenty young male contestants immediately began busting out their moves, grinding and gyrating, wiggling and waggling, much to the tipsy delight of the mumsy throng.

Emerald immediately forgot all about stick insects, water boatmen and butterflies. 'Woman overboard!' she adjudicated as the song climaxed. 'And it's every woman for herself. I think I definitely need some mouth-to-mouth-resuscitation . . . although, full stomach-to-stomach-resuscitation would be even more life-saving.'

Entertainment officer Brent played the theme music from *Jaws* to allow time for the exuberant judges to put their hennaed and highlighted heads together in heated discussion.

Emerald was quick to give her own verdict. 'Did you see the size of number seven? That guy could pole vault to Vanuatu on his own appendage. I definitely want to get to know *him* better . . .'

Amber jabbed Emerald in the thigh with a stiletto nail. 'I'm sorry, but isn't that a wedding ring I see on your finger? What about Alessandro? You're always bragging about the prowess of your Italian stallion.'

Emerald's face closed like a clam. 'Sarcasm doesn't suit you, Amber.' Then she looked daggers at me. 'I told you not to tell her!'

'I *didn't*. My lips are big but sealed,' I protested.

'Tell me what?' Amber asked.

'Come on, Emmy. I think we've drunk too much from the bottle to put any genies back *in* it,' I pleaded, raising my glass in her direction.

Loosened up by two Slippery Nipples and an Orgasm, Emerald acquiesced. 'Oh, Christ. Just don't gloat, okay, Amber? I hate it when you exceed the daily recommended amount of smugness . . . My Italian stallion's gelded.'

'What?' Amber canted a pencilled brow.

'What's said on the cruise stays on the cruise, understood?'

Emerald insisted in a piercing whisper. 'I was relining a hamster cage with newspaper at work last week and glimpsed an article about marital sex. The headline read "Sex Ten Times a Year", and I thought *Gosh, that much?*! I sneaked it back to my office to read it, and it went on to say that sex ten times a year means your love life is defunct. Hopeless. Dysfunctional.'

Amber shed her improvised beach-towel burqa and pivoted to face her older sister, leaning across my prone body. Emerald mimicked the manoeuvre, swivelling sideways. I lay between my warring siblings in a kind of human no-man's-land.

'Seriously? When was the last time you had sex?' Amber probed, astounded.

'On my birthday, if you must know . . . my birthday three years ago. It was like being ravaged by a tree sloth. The only frickin' physical contact I get these days is checking my breasts for lumps. It's got so bad I look forward to my bloody mammogram. There, are you happy now?'

'Happy? I'm jealous,' Amber groaned. Her mouth was a calligrapher's thin line. 'Look, as we're being honest with each other . . . I lied about my marriage too. It's hard, hard work. Most days I feel as though I'm stirring wet cement with my eyelashes.'

'What do you mean?' Emerald slurred, reaching for my Slippery Nipple and downing the dregs.

'You didn't tell her?' Amber asked me, scrutinising my face for signs of sincerity.

'Of course not! I never tell either one of you what the other says. I keep all your secrets. It's bloody exhausting! The real secret, as far as I'm concerned, is why the secret to a happy marriage is such a well-kept bloody secret,' I quipped, but neither sister was listening to me, so intent were they on each other.

'Remember when I got mugged at the ATM by the train station?' Amber confessed. 'And the thug threatened to break my legs? My first thought was *Great! I won't be able to have sex* . . . Don't gloat, okay?'

'Gloat? I'm jealous. Mum always made us believe that the male libido was an untameable beast: that sex was all men wanted. Well, now sex is all *I* want. Why did I ever say no? I can't believe all the cock I batted away in my youth. My husband told me that he loves me, but he just doesn't find me attractive anymore. Do you know how that makes me feel?' Emerald screwed up her eyes as if in pain. 'Am I so repulsive?'

'No!' Amber and I said in unison.

'You're gorgeous, ' I added.

'Thanks, but I still want to enrol in a rejection course, except I'm scared I'll get rejected from that too. A bit of flirtation will do me good.'

The entertainment officer interrupted my sisters' disclosures to announce round two. '*And now, ladeeezzz, the category you've all been waiting for: underwear modelling! Okay, dudes – Versace are looking for their next David Gandy and Channing Tatum. Are you ready to strut your sexy stuff? Then suck it in and push it out! Let's go!*'

As the Village People's 'Macho Man' erupted from the speakers, the contestants turned the pool edge into a catwalk, sashaying, posing, dancing and prancing.

One thing was clear – Emerald didn't need to take a dip, as she was swimming through a pool of her own drool. 'It's so weird when the tables are turned and *I'm* the one begging and *he's* not interested,' she clarified, her eyes fixed on male flesh. 'My vag has become the Greta Garbo of sexual organs. No sightings. She never comes out . . . Tell me the truth, how often do you girls have sex?'

'You mean per day? On a bad day, three times. On a good day? Only once,' Amber divulged. 'Ruby?'

'Well, Harry and I make love about twice a week. But for the past six months, he's insisted on turning off the lights or closing his eyes. And I was suddenly not allowed to talk, either. Now I know why,' I said, sadly. 'I mean, obviously, in his head, he was having sex with *her*, whoever she is – and clearly she was getting many more orgasms than I was!'

A chill descended despite the warm, tropical sun beating down onto the deck. Emerald turned a greener shade than her namesake. It was the first case I'd ever seen of pre-coital depression. Amber also noticed the drop in temperature and tried to placate us.

'Okay, Alessandro may be letting you down in the sex department, but at least he's domesticated. I spend my whole life picking up Scott's underwear, which is a total turn-off.'

'Darling, my husband *irons* his underwear. It's the only stiff thing about him. I know what I'd bloody well prefer!'

'*Ooze charisma, boys!*' the entertainment officer encouraged. '*There are top designers here talent-spotting. Now give me laser-beam eyes. I'm talking Blue Steel!*'

The contestants complied. I thought their facial expressions more closely resembled patients trying to pass kidney stones than an attempt to arouse sexual desire, but Emerald was besotted. 'I feel like a woman with a fork in a world of soup. Lovely, yummy sexual soup,' she sighed.

'You're such a sensuous woman,' I comforted my oldest sister. 'Maybe there's some other reason Alessandro's not interested. Has he got brewer's droop? Maybe he's a secret alcoholic – or, as they say in Adelaide, "likes wine tastings"?'

'No. Only the odd beer. Plus, I've checked his online browsing history. No dogs or dominatrices. It's just me he doesn't want,' Emerald admitted, forlornly.

'Oh, god, count yourself lucky. Scott's got genital myopia – he has a hard time seeing past his penis,' Amber said. 'Sometimes I don't think he knows who or what is on the end of it. I could be a room-temperature apple pie, or a piece of rolled liver.'

'But Scott's hot. Why don't you fancy him?' Emerald said, almost crossly.

'Because he doesn't *talk* to me.' Amber's skin was bone white, her lips a slash of glossy crimson. 'Talking is foreplay for me. Scott's always in his office, only stopping by the house occasionally for clean underwear, when he may or may not remember my name. Lack of emotional libido leaves me drier than . . .' She trailed off.

'Prince Andrew's armpit?' I suggested.

'Exactly! It's a wonder Scott can get it in without a shoehorn,' she added, in a moment of tipsy candour.

'Ah, the dreaded menopause,' Emerald diagnosed.

'That could explain why the only thing you're getting between the sheets is an anticlimax,' I agreed.

'What are you taking for it?' Emerald asked.

Amber shrugged. 'Herbal infusions for my hot flushes.'

'Fuck that. That's like taking an aspirin for a leg amputation. You need oestrogen, progesterone and a dab of testosterone.'

'You take testosterone?' Amber queried. 'Well, that explains why you've turned into a complete hornbag, wanting to bed every man you meet.'

Emerald eyeballed Amber. 'Do you *know* me? Hello, I'm your sister. I think it's safe to say that I've been chewing holes in the furniture since puberty. And anyway, why shouldn't women enjoy sex? Females are criticised for sowing their wild oats but then we also get punished for going to seed.'

'HRT is mare's urine, you know,' Amber pointed out, cringing, an unspoken reprimand in her brusque manner.

'Really? Soon you'll be saying "yeah" or "neigh", tossing your mane and counting with one foot,' I joked, in an effort to placate Emerald.

'I suggest you donate any dosh you were going to spend on all those Scandinavian menopausal "remedies" to the charity of your choice, Amber, and make the world a better bloody place, because it will have more of an impact than swallowing a herb to counteract hormonal upheaval,' Emerald sniped.

I could feel a clash escalating and went into full appeasement mode. 'One thing's clear, girls. God is a bloke. What else would explain all the biological ordeals women endure?' I Neville Chamberlain-ed. 'Getting taken hostage by our hormones once a month, then pregnancy, where you swell to sumo-wrestler proportions, followed by childbirth, where you stretch your birth canal by the customary ten kilometres . . .'

'Yes, then mastitis, followed by the menopause.' Amber started counting off biological inconveniences on her fingertips.

'And then, just when everything goes quiet, do you know

what happens? *You grow a beard*. How can that be fair?' I kvetched. 'I could make a macramé hanging basket with my chin hairs right now.'

I pretended to plait my chin hairs, which caused Amber and Emerald to cackle like kookaburras. Making my sisters laugh has always been my favourite achievement. As they caught their breath, I felt a fierce rush of tenderness towards my siblings. I loved to hear them bantering, just like when we were girls – it was a pleasure I'd enjoyed so rarely of late.

'What about you, Rubes? Now you're fifty, are you having your own weather?' Amber inquired.

'Yeah. Are you sweating so much you feel as though you're undergoing interrogation by the Gestapo?' Emerald insisted.

'Why have a hot flush when you can have a hot tropical holiday somewhere exotic?' I replied. 'One thing I *do* know is that we've raised our kids and paid our dues. It's time to start living again. Living – you know, the bit between being born and dying?'

At the mention of the D-word, my sisters' faces froze. I'd momentarily forgotten my fake case of 'Kev', and instantly regretted my choice of phrase.

'Ruby, I just want you to know that if Kev gets bad,' Amber said, her pained smile spackled on, 'I'll take you to that clinic in Sweden.'

'It's in *Switzerland*, you idiot. At least get the country right. She doesn't want to end up at an ABBA appreciation society meeting for her final moments, for fuck's sake.'

As my sisters started to flare up again, I placed a calming hand on theirs. 'Listen. The greatest gift our mother gave me is my sensational sisters. We haven't been together, just the three of us like this, since we were teenagers. But this time, there's no parental supervision! We need to make this time count. Agreed?'

Amber lay her other hand on top of mine. 'Agreed.'

Emerald followed suit. 'Agreed. So, what are our objectives?'

'Well, Amber is going to stop thinking about her kids. How many times have you WhatsApped them so far today?' I snatched up Amber's phone from the side table and read aloud. '*Your clean socks are in the bottom drawer* – really? You're an awesome mum. You get your kids to eat salad and don't allow sugar after four pm. You make them wear sunblock. You do their art homework assignments for them. But it's time to cut that psychological umbilical cord.'

'Your other objective should be to *eat* now and then, and actually enjoy it. One carb won't kill you. I mean, I can see the three-course raisin you had for lunch!' Emerald scoffed, poking Amber's concave midriff.

The underwear modelling round must have come to an end, as the entertainment officer's voice boomed once more over the tannoy. '*And now, it's time for Neptune, Sea King of the Cruise to reveal his hidden talent. But I think we already have a winner, girls – Jack here has just told me he can play the didgeridoo. Do you know what that means, laaadeeez? A guy who can breathe through his ears!*'

As the all-female audience squealed with delight, the more agile male contestants executed backflips, handstands and cartwheels while the burlier ones concentrated on shows of strength, one even picking up a substantial-looking judge and lifting her over her head.

'Look at those sad women, flaunting themselves in front

of boys young enough to be their sons. What are they going to do – date them, or *adopt* them?' Amber mocked.

I felt a twinge of ill ease. 'Amber's got a point. Isn't it sexist, Emerald? To ogle men like this?'

'Hmm. I passed that question on to my loins, which stirred then answered loudly, *Hell no!*' Emerald said. 'Women have been mercilessly subjugated by the patriarchal theonomy for eons. Now it's our turn!'

'I suppose your only objective for this cruise is to get laid?' Amber asked Emerald, disapprovingly.

'You bloody betcha. I'm gonna have my beefcake and eat him too.' Emerald laughed. 'And also drink the boat dry, obvs! Let's do the wine tasting course that's on offer. Maybe we'll finally solve the conundrum of why men like their wine old and their women young.' Emerald picked up a wine list and studied the descriptions. '"Nuanced", "mature", "complex" – surely these sommeliers could be describing we three middle-aged sisters?'

Amber laughed, finally relaxing. 'Okay, so I'm going to stop being the perfect mum, and Emerald is getting back her sexual mojo, but what about you, Rubes? What's your objective?' Amber squeezed my hand once more and looked into my eyes with a mix of love, pathos and pity.

The truth tingled on the end of my tongue. Now was the time to spill the beans. *Now, now, now . . .*

'Well, my objective is to . . .' I began tentatively. 'To have fun with my sisters, who are going to be nice to each other and become friends again, and rebuild our sisterly bond.'

Now, do it now, you gutless wonder. Level with them, I admonished myself. My lips parted to divulge my dark secret . . .

'Otherwise, the next time you need my help to patch up your friendship after some stupid fight fuelled by our mother, you might be talking to me through a ouija board.'

Oh, that went well, I congratulated myself as my two sisters came in for a group hug. *Well done.* *Time to pop over to Parliament House to pick up that bravery medal.*

'*Ladeeezzz, thank you.*' The entertainment officer brought proceedings to a close and began tallying up the judges' scores. The male contestants, eager for the crown, stood in a long line – flexed, nostril-flaring, feisty, caressing their undulating abs with sunscreen SPF 50-lust. The appreciative female audience members were purring like canary-filled cats. Eyeing those taut, brown buns in such skimpy bathers had women preparing to leave their partners pronto and have a love child.

As the virile Viking was crowned Neptune, King of the Sea and awarded his prize by Brent, I tried to tell myself that there were worse things than lying to my sisters – like, I dunno, clubbing a baby seal to death. Purchasing weapons-grade plutonium from a Russian mercenary. Or, even more damning – voting for Bolsonaro, Boris, ScoMo or Trump. I'd made my sisters abandon their lives for three weeks under false pretences – three weeks during which they could feed me to the fishes at any time once they discovered the truth. Who wouldn't want to postpone that pain?

Yes, I felt a knot of remorse in my tummy, but it passed momentarily, like acid reflux. As I was already bound for hell, I added, 'Oh, and I don't want to be treated like a patient or have cancer define me. So, will you please stop crying, Amber? You seem to be welded to that box of Kleenex. And no more medical questions, either, Emerald. I just want to enjoy time with my sisters. Let's make a pact not to talk about it till we get home. Okay?'

That reprieve would allow me a little guilt-free time to enjoy some sisterly solidarity. I knew the amount of arse-kissing I would eventually have to do would require the purchase of lip balm in bulk. But, for now, I wouldn't think about my lie, my job, my mother, my empty nest and least of all my cheating, duplicitous drongo of a husband. That was my real objective. No, I wouldn't give Harry a second thought for the rest of the trip.

8

That cheating bastard! All I could think about was Harry. He consumed my waking hours and haunted my nights. Who had he cheated with? That was the question. No doubt some young, designer-vajazzled goddess who could easily guarantee my elimination in a wet T-shirt contest. In the witching hour I'd lie twitching, glaring wild-eyed at the ceiling or staring through the glass balcony doors at the velvety night sky dotted with diamanté stars, racking my brain for clues. It infuriated me that he wouldn't confess his carnal crime. Every instinct in my body told me it was true; when a husband starts helping around the house without being asked and begins making meals unaided, that's the signal for a wife to hire a private eye. The trouble is, I thought, tossing around in my bed until I became as twisted as a French braid in the plush linen sheets, that I had thought we were happily married, but he cheated on me, so obviously we weren't happy at all. I'd been living a lie. This fact filled me with a deep despair that clung to me like melted plastic. If he'd just confess and grovel a bit, maybe we could climb out of this marital Mariana Trench. But grovel, email, text message, WhatsApp or Messenger apology came there none.

I checked my inbox so often I developed RSI from hitting

refresh. He was no doubt using his hands for other things – clit-tweaking, or twirling his girlfriend's nipple rings, whoever the hell she was. Pacing around my deluxe cabin, I ground down my molars until there was practically nothing left but a pile of powdery enamel. Yes, Harry may have graduated top in his year at technical college; yes, he may be the famous Mr Fix-it, but, ironically, Hire a Hubby had broken my heart. It deserved to be a country-and-western song, it really did.

In a pre-dawn, sleep-deprived fury I texted him: *We are now officially separated*. Surely he'd now be so racked with remorse he'd get carpet burns on his knuckles from crawling back to me? But still nothing.

When there was no word from him when we first left port, I initially tried to convince myself that the cruise line had accidentally outsourced all communication services to one of the more slovenly former Soviet satellites, which was saying *nyet* to the net.

When there was no word on day one at sea, I had told myself that he was probably too busy buying me 'make-up' jewellery; the traditional gem of a way to show contrition.

When there was still no email on day two, I had imagined he was flying to meet me at the next port, or maybe rowing solo across the Pacific to prove his devotion.

Maybe he's been injured, I'd thought happily, on the third day of radio silence.

Maybe he's dead, I reflected on day four. Obviously, he must have fallen off the ladder as he was topiarying our front hedge to read '*I love you, forgive me*', and accidentally whacked his head on the driveway and died. Tragic but touching.

On day five I thought, *He'd better be dead, because otherwise I am going to kill him.*

Clearly, while I was out of town, my husband's cock had become a heat-seeking missile that wasn't reporting to mission control. The low-down, lying scumbag.

Yes, yes, I sobbed into one of my six goose-down pillows – pot, kettle, black. Believe me, there's truly no need to point out my hypocrisy. I'd lied so much of late it was a wonder my lips hadn't fallen off. When I thought about how and when to tell my sisters that I'd fibbed about the cancer diagnosis, I just adopted the position of a defensive echidna, rolled tightly into a ball, and willed myself to think of something else. But the lie I'd told my siblings was accidental, whereas Harry had blatantly deceived me.

Abandoning all thoughts of sleep, I leant on my balcony railing, looked down into the dark water and listened to the hiss of the sea against the side of the ship. As the warm wind whipped through my hair I crossly cross-examined myself. Had I ever lied to him? Well, yes, but just little white lies. Off-white, even. Maybe beige. But that was normal. I mean, how terrible would life be if couples told each other the complete truth all the time? There's a word for couples who tell each other the truth all the time – divorced. Complete honesty is not always the best policy in marriage. Surely it was perfectly fine for wives not to showcase their flaws and foibles. How many women does it take to change a light bulb? None: on certain things, it's best to keep men in the dark.

Shoes, for example. Has any woman ever fessed up to a partner about the true cost of shoes? One of the biggest differences between the sexes is that men only need one pair of shoes the whole year round, and maybe only four pairs for his entire life. Consequently, they just don't understand that it's genetically impossible for most women to walk past a shoe sale and not buy something irrational and strappy. Sometimes Harry would ask how much I'd spent. I usually dodged the financial truth bullet by fobbing him off with a little jest – 'Hey, my foot's so often in my mouth, it simply has to be well-shod, right?' while surreptitiously hiding the receipts. Well, don't you?

And then there were the little white lies about the car. Like all men, Harry thinks he's an excellent driver. The first time he got a note under his windscreen that read 'parking fine', he presumed it was a complimentary comment on his driving skills. I know that he also secretly believes that every woman is bad behind the wheel – which is why I've never, ever, let slip when a postbox had dented my door or another car had failed to take evasive action when approached by my bumper bar. I would just sneak over to my brother-in-law, the Dent Boss himself, for some surreptitious chassis restoration, bribing Alessandro with a slab of beer to keep schtum.

What else had I lied about in my marriage? I pondered, pouring myself a vodka from the minibar. Allergies. Yes, I'd developed some imaginary late-onset allergies to a few things, but this wasn't deceit so much as survival. One of life's great mysteries is why people are divided into those who like the outdoors and those who like the indoors, and why they invariably end up married to each other. On our honeymoon, I'd foolishly confessed how much I hated camping, only for Harry to then spend every holiday for the next five years trying to convert me. A couple of nights under canvas and I discovered that the worst aspect of tents is that it's so hard to be tense in them; it's just not so dramatic, storming out and slamming the flap. But I soon realised it was easiest to keep my loathing of camping a secret from my husband and invent some allergies – to flies, ticks, flowers, frogs, even fresh air itself. We've been holidaying in comfy coastal rental cottages ever since. But was that really such a terrible crime on the morality rap sheet?

What else had I lied about in our 28-year union? I lay on the soft cream couch in the cabin and contemplated this query. Well, as far as Harry knew, I was sponsoring a goat in an African village; I saw no need whatsoever to tell him it was actually an entire goat herd, and all of the village's goat herders and their extended families.

As the clouds parted and the moon shone silver through the balcony doors, I wondered, what were my other little white lies? I knew for sure that no wife ever admitted to her husband the true number of men she'd slept with before him. When we got engaged, I'd told Harry about some of my sexual encounters during our two-year break – the ski instructor, the guitarist from that band in Byron on the schoolies weekend – but not all of them. But that's not lying, really. It's more a case of selective honesty. I'd also always exaggerated the size of his equipment. In my view, Freud got it wrong: it's not women who suffer from 'penis envy' but blokes. 'Is mine big? Is mine the biggest?' How many times I'd been tempted to snap, 'Look, I'd love to sit here all night discussing your appendage, but I'm just not into small talk.'

Clearly, the secret to a happy marriage is to keep most things, well, secret. But not an affair. That wasn't just a lie, that was a betrayal. I would never lie about an affair. Mainly because I would never have one.

No, if Harry wasn't going to tell me who he was screwing, then I was not going to tell him I was okay. I wanted him to sweat, the worm. Of course, I didn't want my kids to suffer, so I answered Zoe and Jake's texts and emojis with the news that I'd had a second opinion and was going to be fine! It was all a false alarm. If they told their dad he'd probably just think I was being brave for their sakes – which should only make him feel worse, I thought. Surely his guilt would be so strong it'd be radiating from him in zigzags visible to the naked eye. But still, nothing.

You know you're in a bad way when you wake up with a terrible 'morning after' feeling and you didn't even do anything fun the night before. Watching the sun rise over the sapphire sea, I wrote up my to-do list.

1. Stave off breakdown.
2. Divorce husband.
3. Become lesbian.
4. Have a great time bonding with your sisters.

Yes, sisters fight. Look at Jo and Amy's rivalry in *Little Women*, the Queen and Princess Margaret's power struggles in *The Crown*, and the one-upwomanship of those literary lionesses Charlotte, Emily and Anne Bronte. But loyalty and love are encoded into our DNA. I would literally die for my sisters, which was ironic, because when they found out about my lie, they would literally kill me.

9

My mind was going around in circles so constantly, I felt as though my dress had been caught in a revolving door.

'Some therapists believe there are times when an affair can rescue a marriage, and even make it stronger,' Amber counselled as we sat down to breakfast. 'It's not about assigning blame, but finding out the root causes of the infidelity so you can improve your relationship from the ground up.'

By the time our cappuccinos arrived she was more pragmatic. 'Sometimes I wish Scott would have an affair. Then I wouldn't have to have sex with him so often!'

'Don't get sad or mad, get bad,' was Emerald's advice. 'After marriage, a cougar needs to be rehabilitated and released back into the wild. Let me lead you astray. Leave it to Diva!' She laughed.

To alleviate my Harry-induced despondency, both sisters were determined to distract me, but in very different ways. It was a tug-of-love. While Amber liked to work hard at having a good holiday (attending Cardio Combat sessions, spin classes, acro-yoga, tango lessons and 'enrichment lectures' where she sucked up information on the Pacific's cultural and historical aspects like a human hoover), the only thing Emerald wanted to work on was her tan.

'Come join me in the jacuzzi for a cocktail, Rubes,' she tempted. 'I usually need a holiday to recuperate from my holiday, but on a cruise you just go with the flow. Literally. I'm just sitting back, drinking it all in – while drinking. What's not to love about that?'

On the drive to the departure terminal at Circular Quay, Emerald had predicted that a cruise would be like a three-week wedding reception, complete with notoriously bad band. 'The promotional brochure may promise the "new Beatles", but what that means is four frickin' Ringos,' she'd moaned. But it had taken only one day for her to be converted.

'No. Ruby's coming to a photography class with me, aren't you, Rubes?' Amber had been equally critical of cruising. For the duration of the taxi ride to Circular Quay, she'd predicted the worst. 'I've heard too many horror stories – the salt, the sand, the exotic insects – and that's just in the sandwiches!'

But it had also only taken about a day for Amber to eat her words – well, she would have eaten them if she wasn't too busy devouring the gourmet tucker. 'I'm comfort eating, clearly. It's the only time I stop worrying about you, Ruby. The chefs really need to install speed bumps to slow down my progress to the buffet,' she'd said between mouthfuls of marinated crabmeat gateaux, tournedos of black Angus beef and waggles of lobster tails.

I was used to Amber spending more time chewing over the merits of each mouthful than actually masticating, a habit that made the rest of us want to impale her on our fork prongs. So it was a novelty to see her delighting in food as though it were a whole new experience. In some ways it was;

it was rare for her to have the opportunity to eat anything she hadn't had to cook.

Emerald, meanwhile, was more interested in the human menu. Her carnal appetites were just a different form of comfort eating, really. 'It's a male smorgasbord out there. Shall I go for the athletic or the aesthetic? The manly, the laddish, the beardy or the blondie, the purple-tipped dreads, the man bun or the baldy? Two glasses of white wine and I'm anybody's,' she giggled.

While drowning your sorrows in semen may not be recognised by therapists as a legitimate coping strategy, it'd been decades since I'd seen Emerald so upbeat and happy, or Amber not short-tempered due to hunger pangs and low blood sugar.

I did feel wretched about causing my sisters angst over my false diagnosis, but I convinced myself that I was also doing them some good, as both had embraced my 'carpe the hell out of the diem' approach to life with alacrity. Displaying my professional dedication to the truth, the whole truth and nothing but the varnished truth, a commitment that has clearly made me the respected and acclaimed journo I am today – ha-ha – I said to them, 'The best thing you can both do for me is to have fun.'

The first sign that Emerald was going full cougar was when she burst back into our suite fresh from the boutique, festooned with shopping bags – including one that held a new olive-green bikini for me.

Amber and I were in the middle of changing out of our wet cossies to get ready for lunch in the Tuscan Grille when she summoned us to survey her purchases.

'Jesus,' I laughed, riffling through the bags. 'David

Attenborough could make a documentary on your wardrobe. I mean, there's more leopard print in here than on the Serengeti.'

With pincered talons, Amber picked up a jungle-print halter-neck dress. 'Gosh, Emerald, you'll have to start taking malaria tablets.'

'Perfect for prowling!' Emerald chortled, stripping off to her bra and pants before pouring herself into a figure-hugging leopard-print minidress that offered maximum décolletage.

'Your neckline's got lower as your hemline's got higher,' Amber said disapprovingly. 'You're the inverse of an iceberg – ninety per cent of you is visible.'

'It's just camouflage for when I go hunting in the disco. You've got to come with me, Ruby.'

'Two old chooks on the dance floor? It'll be poultry in motion,' I punned, but, as usual, my sisters were too focused on their bickering to pay me any attention.

'Ruby's far too busy for such inanities,' Amber said, squeezing my arm proprietorially. 'I've signed us up for the rock climbing wall, yogalates, macramé . . .'

'What about man-cramé? I'd rather tie up a *man* in knots,' Emerald chuckled, appraising herself in the mirror and giving a twirl.

Amber continued obstinately circling activity start times on the information sheet. 'Ruby, there's a general knowledge quiz every night after supper, oh, and charades. You love charades!'

'Bondage charades would be more fun – one bloke on each team is tied up and the rest of us make him guess what we'll do to him,' Emerald tittered as she changed outfits.

'A lot of blokes are better imagined in your bed than found there in the morning,' Amber warned.

'I'm sorry, Amber, but *how would you know?*' Emerald struck a pose in her next outfit. 'So, what do you think of this?'

Amber and I surveyed our sister's mammaries, which were now encased in a bustier big enough to house Meatloaf and his twin brother.

'Well, you've certainly perfected your drag queen look,' Amber adjudicated.

'Hey, there's a lot of female competition on board, so I thought I'd better go for the full MILF.'

'MILF,' Amber decoded, sternly, 'is a guerrilla movement in the Philippines.'

'Farc!' Emerald replied, with mock shock.

'Emerald, darling, you're regressing.' Amber tut-tutted. 'Plus, you're too old to be a "mother I'd like to fuck". Picture it. Once you take off all the scaffolding, he'll go to grab a boob and find it halfway down your thigh!'

'Emerald, you are not setting booby traps,' I consoled, patting our big sister's arm. 'Goddesses never age.'

'Don't humour her, Ruby. She's so old she'll have to say to her toy boy, "Shout dirty to me!"'

'I know it's ridiculous,' Emerald admitted. 'But we've accidentally set sail on a cougar cruise, and I, for one, am not going to waste the frickin' opportunity. Nor should you, Rubes. You'll never get this chance again. If you and Harry do split up, you'll have to start dating again.' Emerald's face clouded as she remembered my 'condition'.

'Speed dating, clearly,' I interjected, so she wouldn't feel bad. I knew it was wrong, I knew it was bad. I hated myself for perpetuating the lie, but I just wasn't ready yet to put my head between my legs and assume the brace position for the truth to come out.

'Sorry.' Emerald faltered. 'Anyway, I've been talking to other women on board and let me tell you, back in the real world, men our age expect to date women half our age, and women our age are forced to date men twenty years older; blokes who are always calling on their mobiles from hospital fore-courts saying "It's okay. It's not malignant." You spend nearly every first date in casualty because another part of him has fallen off.'

'I think you'd have to call that "going out on a limb",' I joked, seemingly for my own amusement, as my sisters were wholly focused on each other again.

'Ruby is not going to divorce Harry. There's no need to split up her family. All marriages can suffer from a little fidelity fatigue. You'll get past it. And, anyway, younger men aren't so great,' Amber countered. 'You'd have to spend all your time reversing out of rooms so he can't see the backs of your thighs and compare them to the last teenager he dated.'

'Speaking of teenagers, I quite fancy our cabin steward,' Emerald said, practically drooling. 'He's Russian. I can think of nothing better than doing the horizontal hopak with a couple of carnally inclined Cossacks, can you? It's practically a poem. Is there anything more masculine than a husky Ruskie?'

'Well, if you insist on having a fling with a toy boy, make sure you use the dimmer switch,' Amber teased, watching as a now-topless Emerald examined her breast buoyancy in the mirror. 'On second thoughts, forget the dimmer switch. Just turn the lights off. In fact, *unscrew* the light bulbs.'

'Use it or lose it, kiddo. That's my motto. My basement has atrophied from lack of use. And I don't feel guilty about Alessandro, either. He should feel guilty for leaving me high and dry for years.' Emerald's face lost its vibrancy and a shadow came over her. 'I'm just tired of feeling invisible,' she said, sadly, then rallied. 'Just because a woman's getting closer to her pension, why should "a bit of rough" refer to a leaf of bloody lettuce and not a tattooed toy boy? In the real world you'd have to endure caustic cracks about childproofing your love life and needing to buy a booster seat for your car. But not on a cougar cruise! We're on the Love Boat, baby, headed for Fantasy Island.' Emerald, having settled on the jungle-print halter dress, slipped on a pair of brand-new Roman-inspired gold sandals and announced, 'Right. I'm ready. Let's go get 'em!'

Locking our suite and striding to catch up with my sisters, I realised that of all the onboard activities offered, the fine art of table-turning was the favourite. Women who'd been judged, ranked, rated on their looks from car windows and building sites their whole lives were now judging, ranking and rating men, with a casual sweep of a hungry eye.

All except Amber, of course, whose preferred leisure pursuit was turning out to be 'raining on parades'.

Emerald hated gyms, especially the illogical instruction to wear loose-fitting clothing. 'If I had any loose-fitting clothing, I wouldn't have to come to the gym, now, would I?' she always said. But strolling past the fitness area on the way to lunch, Emerald paused to watch a tanned he-man with pneumatic buttocks performing chin-ups with one hand. 'Now *that* could tempt me to the gym. What machine should I use to impress that hunk of spunk?'

'Um . . . the ATM?' Amber suggested.

As we passed the rock-climbing wall after lunch, Emerald paused to watch a taut-torsoed Apollo hauling himself upwards with gravity-defying ease.

'Oh my god. Check out the guy with the pecs. I'd like to ride that bucking bronco all over the rodeo!'

'Okay, this is getting pervy, now,' Amber rebuked. 'The guy's so young his pyjamas probably have little feet.'

At dinner, the spectacle of middle-aged women flirting with cubs had Amber rolling her eyes so often I worried people would think she was having a seizure.

'Emerald, as a vet, aren't you finding these human mating rituals a tad dull? I mean, at least in the animal kingdom you're occasionally treated to a flash of bright feathers or a cascade of lovely song. Braindead boys strutting and flexing and setting fire to their farts doesn't quite compare,' she said.

'Just because they're young doesn't mean they don't have things to offer,' Emerald countered. 'Or that they're not smart. Millennial males get a bad rap. To be fair, quite a few defy their stereotype . . .'

On comedic cue, the boys at the next table, most of whom seemed to have only recently been introduced to cutlery, started throwing food at each other and attempting to catch it in their mouths like Sea World seals, which set Amber off on another bout of frenetic eye-rolling.

'You keep doing that and you're going to shake something loose in there,' Emerald said, laughingly.

Our big sister kept right on cooing over the selection of men on offer as though she were trying to find the Caramel Indulgence in a box of Milk Tray. The more she looked, the more determined she became to sample every flavour, even if it meant taking a nibble of one then popping him back in the box.

The first toy boy Emerald brought back to her cabin didn't pass the taste-test. Emerald described him as the hard toffee that's always left over in the chocolate box.

'He expected me to deep-throat his chrome dome!' she reported after kicking him out and joining Amber and me in our shared living area for a hot chocolate. '"Blow me, babe!" he said. I told him not to be ridiculous, and that the last time I was on my knees was two years ago when I was looking for a contact lens.'

Her second cub, however, was more appetising. 'Apparently he loves skydiving,' she told us, after finally emerging from her bedroom, spent and dishevelled and ravenous for breakfast. 'You name a sky and he's dived from it . . . I hate being in the air, but I thought it best not to mention that until after the wedding.'

'I'm sure your husband will be pleased to hear that,' Amber said through a clenched picket line of perfect white teeth. 'And please tell me that's mayonnaise on your dressing gown.'

That night Amber wore earplugs so as not to hear the laughter and shrieks coming from our older sister's cabin, but I listened on, enviously, and yes, salivating slightly.

At breakfast the next morning, just as I was polishing off a tower of cinnamon pancakes, while Amber played with some exotic concoction involving coconut and quinoa, Emerald staggered into the dining room, late.

'You're starting to look as though you've just crawled out from under a Stone . . . most probably Keith,' I ribbed her.

'Hey, it's not my first rodeo, kid. That's why I'm having a mimosa for breakfast.' She winked.

'So, who was your poor victim last night?' Amber asked, censoriously.

'An engineering student.'

'How was it?'

'Put it this way – he turned on his bow thrusters and counter-propellers and shoved his rudder hard to starboard. But I'm afraid I had to scuttle him this morning. He talked all this new-age "woke" crap.'

'Oh.' I grimaced, laughing. 'All that PC "woke" stuff puts me to sleep.'

'Me too. In the end, I was like, hey, buddy, I don't want to "tap into cuddle power" or "ditch the ideal and love what's real" or be a "dream-maker not a dream-breaker". I just want you to ride me, cowboy, and pillage like a pirate!'

I stifled a covetous sigh. While Emerald was having flirtation, fun and frottage, I was flat-out having 'fun' with Amber – activities that would make Albanian daytime television look riveting. When we weren't at a flash mob dance rehearsal, discovering the art of glass blowing, or playing bridge, blackjack, shuffleboard, backgammon, indoor golf or mini tennis, we were catching waves on the flow-rider; that is, until my new bikini bottoms managed to catch a different wave from me all together.

'Oh, god, what torture have you got planned for me tomorrow?' I asked, grimacing, after dinner on day seven. 'Abseiling off the bow? Walking on hot coals? Knitting my own straitjacket?'

'Scuba diving lessons in the pool,' Amber enthused.

'Let me see – dressing up in a rubber Batsuit, dragging ten

kilos of equipment around on my back before plummeting into deep water, only to have to drag it all back up onto dry land again an hour later . . . It's just way, way too much like marriage for my liking.'

'Speaking of which – any word from that mongrel you wed?' Emerald asked, curiously.

I shook my head and continued laying out my pyjamas on the bed. There were daily loving messages from my kids: *So glad you're going to be okay, Mum. Have fun!* and so on, and a few from friends I hadn't slagged off at my infamous birthday bash, but total radio silence from Harry. The truth began to cling to me like a chill – he no longer loved me.

Emerald was fuming on my behalf. 'What a pain in the arse he is.'

'If I could isolate the pain just to my arse, that would be a relief.'

'Well, bugger that bastard! Come with me to the disco and nab yourself a joy boy. Let's give ourselves something to talk about when we're in the old people's home.'

'How could *I* ever get a joy boy? Not even my husband wants me.' I checked my email inbox for a message from Harry for, oh, only the hundredth time that day. Nothing, as usual.

'You're the one who talked about seizing the day and carpedieming like there's no tomorrow,' Emerald reminded me.

I automatically checked my WhatsApp, in case I'd missed something. Nada.

'Don't you want to get into a man's pants and not have to launder them later?'

'Yes, but . . .' I checked Messenger for Harry's name. Zip. Zero. Zilch.

'Good god,' Emerald gasped, as she struggled with the zipper of one of her new dresses. 'I'm piling on the pounds. It's that bloody dessert trolley. Thank god I'm going to shag it off later.' Tonight she'd settled on the whole Belle Époque courtesan look, complete with pearls draped on her near-naked breasts.

'I'm sure the extra seven pounds is just your eyelash extensions,' I joshed.

'It's probably not the cake, but the cocktails,' Amber rebuked, as Emerald poured herself another glass of champagne.

'Hey, I drink responsibly . . . I haven't spilt one drop while climbing up to sit on the face of an R-rated Romeo.'

I was only half listening as I scrolled through friends' Facebook updates. And, suddenly, there was Harry at the beach with his board, smiling, surrounded by laughing young women from the surf club. Surfing! Laughing! Smiling! Surrounded by adoring young women! It was a punch to my solar plexus. His wife was dying and there he was, having fun in the sun. Well, okay, his wife wasn't exactly dying, but what if I *were*?

'Maybe I will come tonight,' I heard myself say, tossing my phone onto the couch. 'Why not? My husband's clearly deserted me, meaning I'm footloose and Spanx–free!' I paraphrased Emerald.

'Good on ya, Rubes. It's time to be daring and bold and walk on the wild side.'

I slipped off my wedding ring. 'I am single and ready to mingle,' I said.

'Forget *Eat, Pray, Love*. What about Drink, Dance, Shag? That's what women want. Sex is a life force. It's so intoxicating it takes over your whole imagination. I'd jump off tall buildings or stop speeding trains to get that passion fix. You've just got to send out the right sexy signals.' Emerald yanked my T-shirt over my head. 'What are you going to wear? Let's start by tightening your bra.' She shoved her hand into my left bra cup and hoisted my breast towards the ceiling. 'Get those tits right up.'

'Hey, what little I have is already up and out, okay?' I said, affectionately slapping her hand away.

'Stop being such a goddamn wuss and make it work!' Emerald commanded, hitching up my skirt by folding the waistband over itself. 'And here, wear these knickers. I bought them today but they're too small.'

Amber intercepted the lacy black pants Emerald had thrown my way and read the label. '"Lover's Spark" Brazilian briefs?' She shook her head at us in despair. 'I'm starting to rethink Darwin, I really am. You girls are evolving backwards into teenagers.'

'I'm not sure I want to wear an outfit that reveals parts of me only an obstetrician should see!' I chuckled, tugging my hem back down.

Amber's scowl grew deeper. 'What do they call this disco? Grab a Granny?'

'The disco's called The Erogenous Zone, and Ruby will soon see why. Here.' Emerald thrust her glass of bubbly at me. 'Have a quick personality drink before you go out.'

'But we'd planned to win the trivia quiz tonight,' Amber protested with pinched lemon lips and a pitying tone. 'I can't win without you. The literature category's your forte. And it's been so much fun. We learnt a great Japanese word last night – "Yugen", a description of the awe that overcomes you when you regard Mother Nature's mysterious beauty.'

'Yes, it was fun, Amber, but honestly, when am I ever going to use a word like that in my drab little life?' I said, forlornly. 'No more brain aerobics. I wanna hear my body talk,' I sang, launching into an Olivia Newton-John impression, which Emerald joined.

After we'd collapsed, panting with laughter, onto the couch, Emerald said to Amber, 'Why don't you dismount your high horse and come with us?' She stood and unzipped a bag of recently purchased make-up products, and turned my face to the light to apply eyeshadow.

'You're wearing make-up now?' Amber asked, astounded. 'Honestly, at this moment, it would be easier for me to grasp quark nuclear physics than to understand what the hell is going on with my sisters. I'm going to lose the quiz and then get an early night,' she said, pitifully.

'Sure ... you *can* go to sleep early, but that will only tempt us to shave off one of your eyebrows when we get in!' Emerald laughed as she layered eyeliner on my eyelids. Amber was right – we were totally regressing. Next it'd be pillow fights and short-sheeting each other's beds.

I laughed then, too, jerking my head backwards, which caused Emerald's charcoal eye pencil to etch a bold stroke from my right nostril to my left earlobe, which only made us laugh more. While Emerald fetched a make-up wipe, I slugged down another huge slurp of personality.

'I'm just window-shopping, Amber, I promise. I'm not going to do anything. So don't get your horny hopes up about me, okay, Emerald?' I called out after her. 'Besides, as if any man would ever fancy me.'

'You're still hot . . . it just comes in flushes now,' Emerald said convivially, returning from her room.

I suspected the only heat I'd feel in the disco would be from blushes of embarrassment. *Gosh, what's that noise?* I thought, as my big sister squirted me with perfume. *Oh, just the sound of millions of men laughing themselves to death at the thought of Ruby Ryan pulling a toy boy.*

In truth, I didn't think it would be possible to take the amount of drugs required to hallucinate that I was attractive. My sex appeal was so miniscule, it'd take a microscope to find it. When it came to sending out sexy signals, I might as well be relaying transmissions from Alpha Centauri.

'Don't worry, Amber, my eyes are bigger than my vag, so to speak.'

And with that, before I could chicken out, Emerald ushered me out the door to go double-park in The Erogenous Zone.

10

'Yugen! Yugen! Yugen!' was the only word I could summon from my vast vocabulary as an athletic man half my age extracted his tongue from my mouth. I ran my hands over the satiny skin of his muscular forearms and gazed into his dazzling azure eyes.

I rocked back on my heels to examine the hair-gelled Adonis who was pressing his groin up against me – his *enthusiastic* groin. As a recently rejected wife of twenty-eight years I lapped up the attention as if I were a rescue dog from the pound. He was nearly six feet tall, with a mop of sun-kissed, chestnut-brown hair. His face was a complex geometrical configuration of bronzed bone structure. Basically, the boy had hit the DNA jackpot. Sadly, when he spoke, I realised he was big for his brain, like a dinosaur.

'Yeet. What a rig,' he said in a rush.

'What?'

'You're a tight little number,' he added, squeezing both my butt cheeks.

'Pardon?'

'How's our vibe! Let's go back to your cabin,' he said hotly into my ear. 'My room's so small, you gotta be a ventriloquist to get in there.'

'I think you mean contortionist,' I corrected him.

'I'm, like, totally woke, by the way,' he added.

'Must have been that espresso martini,' I joked.

'Huh?' he replied.

When I'd walked into the whoosh of body heat that was The Erogenous Zone an hour earlier, I'd immediately executed a 180-degree swivel on my high heel to get the hell out of Cougar Country. But Emerald had seized my elbow and frogmarched me to the bar.

'There's so much cock in here. Act half normal and you're going to get laid,' my normally straight sister shouted in my ear. 'Any woman could pull on this boat. Jabba the Slut could pull. Indeed, I think I snogged her myself on the dance floor last night!' she laughed. 'But first you need some cougar juice,' she explained, ordering cocktails.

All around us, waterfalls of neon light cascaded down the walls as inebriated young men careered like toddlers, pinballing around the dance floor, shouting over each other in rapid-fire lingo. Older women wobbled on too-high heels in overawed orbit around the cubs, their smiles welded on with a mix of desperation and desire.

How pathetic, I'd thought – only to find myself, three martinis later, bumping and grinding along with them to Hot Chocolate's 'You Sexy Thing', feeling happier and hornier and freer and more fabulous than I had for decades.

Now, I am to dancing what an African dictator is to world peace – I definitely move to a different drummer. But, unfortunately, the cocktails had affected my critical abilities to the point where I thought I could dance, which is why, moments later, mid ABBA medley, I'd found myself hitting my head on a disco ball as only a girl from the Insular Peninsular can, before toppling backwards into the arms of the young bloke with whom I was now entwined. And, good lord, could the guy move. He danced as though his feet had taken steroids.

As Cyndi Lauper's 'Girls Just Wanna Have Fun' morphed into 'Sexual Healing', a slow beat reverberated through the floor. Marvin Gaye's crooning had couples moving sluggishly through the warm air, and my dance partner and I swayed sensuously with them.

'What's your name?' I shouted, tipsily.

The young man gave me a scorchingly hot look. How hot? Put it this way – if I were an egg, I'd have hard-boiled. 'Wave,' he replied ardently into my ear. 'Spelt W-A-Y-V-E.'

Wayve? That sobered me up. How young was this guy? Was it even legal to be rubbing nether regions with him? Was I about to be carted off in handcuffs by the water police? I suddenly imagined myself cutting up his food, tying his shoelaces and carrying him on my shoulders to see The Wiggles in concert. I had a precipitous dread of the fluorescent lights coming on, enabling him to discover my real age, then watching him fleeing from the dance floor wearing an expression reminiscent of Munch's *The Scream*.

I immediately broke free and fought my way back to Emerald's side. My big sister was holding court with some young men on a leather banquette, her mouth lipsticked bright red with bravado – the very shade favoured by our mother.

'How much have I d … d … drunk?' I slurred. 'If I gave a urine sample right now, would it have an olive in it?'

'Hope so. Speaking of which . . .' Emerald turned to address the nearest cubs in her coterie. One was a dome-headed hunk who looked as though he lubed up monster trucks for a living. The other was extravagantly tattooed in ill-conceived reptilian motifs. 'Boys, you need to do something to improve your personalities – go get me a cocktail, will you?'

When the bite of her remark passed them by, she simply handed over her lanyard for payment. 'Buy yourselves a beer too. And some more lady petrol for my sister here.' Once more the boys stared at her blankly. 'A martini on the rocks,' she decoded, and when they departed in the direction of the bar she turned to me. 'So, did you nab a dance partner?'

'Well, yes, actually. English doesn't seem to be his native tongue, but I think he's just invited himself back to my cabin.'

'Who?'

I hitched a brow in Wayve's desirable direction.

Emerald's eyeballs jumped out of their sockets, rushed across the dance floor, gave the young bloke in question a full-body once over, then snapped back into place. 'Well pulled,' was her verdict. 'What's stopping you, then?'

'His name's Wayve – W-A-Y-V-E – but I don't think he's quite breaking on the rocks.'

'So? Low IQ's not sexually transmittable.'

'Okay, but . . . but . . . then there's the fact that I can't get naked in front of a stranger! I haven't even gone sleeveless in five years! And what about the stretch marks on my belly?'

'Those are your tiger stripes, Ruby. You've earned them. Be proud of them. Alessandro always makes me feel so fat – like one of those giant jellyfish in a Jacques Cousteau doco, floating in the sea like a flesh balloon. But the boys on board think I'm Kardashian-esque. It's all free sex to them. Besides, if *you* don't nab the guy, someone else will.' Emerald pointed back to the dance floor, where a woman with a particularly steatopygous derriere was waddling on fragile heels towards Wayve, beaming at him like an overeager game show host.

'Do you fancy him?' Emerald asked, with an appraising eye.

I looked at the strapping young man and felt my salivary glands shift into third gear. 'Yes, but I don't speak his language. He keeps going on about things being "lush" and "frothy" and "totes awkie" and "triggered", and how he's looking for inner peace. I don't know how to break it to him that there's no such thing – only anxiety, insecurity and alcohol.'

'Who cares? As long as he's fluent in body language.'

'No, no, I can't. It's been so long since I've been with any other bloke besides Harry. Decades!'

'Well, all you need to know is that young men have foreskins. Uncut guys are great, by the way. The head of the cock is like a big, giant man clit. And there will be dick picks. Sending genitalia selfies is to courtship rituals what compiling mixtapes was in our day.'

'But what if I'm no good?' Since Harry's betrayal, I'd been gorging compulsively on self-loathing. 'No. I can't go through with it. It's too embarrassing.'

'You won't be doing anything that your lying, cheating husband isn't doing right now with the girl of his wet dreams.'

The thought of what Harry might be doing with whom prompted me to fumble for my phone. It was about the millionth time I'd checked for a message that day. Silence, I realised then, is not golden. It's pitch black, cold and cruel. Jealousy and rejection churned sourly in my stomach. I had loved my husband with every fibre of my being, and what had it got me? Heartache, loneliness and self-esteem so low not even a limbo dancer could retrieve it. Love should be classified as a Class A addiction, I pondered. Well, from now on, I was in romance rehab – starting with taking the phallic cure and being as shagadelic as womanly possible.

But then I faltered. No, I just couldn't break my marriage vows.

This decision prompted an urgent message from my clitoris, along the lines of *'Hey, haven't you ever entertained the idea of wild, inventive, spontaneous sex?'*

'Yes, of course,' I replied, mentally.

'No, I mean, with a partner,' clarified my clit.

'Ha-ha. Clit, calm down. I just cannot betray my husband . . . Can I?'

'Why not?!' my clitoris urged. *'Live dangerously!'*

'I live dangerously,' I countered. 'Just last week, I let a parking meter run over by five minutes!'

'Live large!' urged my clit. *'Sure, there are worse things than celibacy – like leprosy, and death.'*

Emerald, who was obviously in cahoots with my clitoris, pressed some condoms into my palm. 'Now, go kick him to the kerb, sis.'

The disco floor was kaleidoscopic, with dancers weaving, coagulating, dispersing and swirling all around me. As I took Wayve in my arms, Emerald called out after me –

'Coo-coo-ca-choo, Mrs Robinson!' My big sister winked at me lopsidedly before starting a conga line and dancing back to the bar.

'Ding-dong! Time for him to ring your devil's doorbell,' urged my clit. *'Hello, I'm coming!'*

A muscly-thighed Chris Hemsworth impersonator with

the IQ of a houseplant was tempting me to break my most sacred marriage vow – and I was discussing the pros and cons with my clitoris.

Clit: '*I'm so happy I could jump for joy.*'

Me: 'Yeah . . . right off the nearest cliff.'

II

No, I am not going to sleep with him, I told myself as he pushed me up against the wall of the elevator and kissed me ravenously. The man was a force of nature – a lightning bolt.

No, no, I am not going to sleep with him, I told myself as I grabbed the fragrant, muscly-thighed one and drew him closer.

'You're so hard,' I murmured into his ear. But making conversation was also hard. When the lift door opened and other couples poured in, we drew apart and made another attempt at dialogue. It's safe to say that Wayve was not about to make Cicero quake in his oratorical boots. He talked in brief spurts, every comment directed several inches below my head, directly at my cantilevered breasts. Each utterance drove home what a mistake this was, when in quick succession Wayve said, 'What happens to the ice sculpture, after it melts?' – 'Is Mystery Island completely surrounded by water?' – 'Are there any undiscovered caves there? I bloody love caving.' – And 'Have you seen the flamingo dancers in the ship show? That's some awesome shit, right there.'

'Flamingo dancers, eh?' I looked at him quizzically, trying to picture the dance troupe standing about on one leg. But when we were out of the lift and alone in the corridor, Wayve said things like 'I can't wait to lick your pussy,' 'I'm going to spread your legs and fuck you,' and other sexy sentiments whispered hotly in my ear all the way to my cabin. Okay, it wasn't exactly Shakespeare, but it was certainly hitting the spot.

All I could think of were things *not* to say, like 'Do you still choose your cereal for the toy?', 'Does your Mum know you're here?' and 'I'm old enough to be your mother.'

Once inside the cabin, I seemed to step outside of myself and watch proceedings. I paused by the bed, arrested by the vision of the young man lifting his shirt over his head, revealing a broad back, the skin varnished to a violin shade after days of fun in the sun and then, oh, the peachiness of his perfect posterior as he lay stark naked across my bed.

No, no, I am not going to sleep with him, I told myself as I slipped out of my dress and kicked off my heels.

On my bed the towels had been shaped into an elephant, a swan and a dog that clutched the TV remote control in its sculpted paws. *No, no, I am not going to sleep with him*, I repeated, sweeping this terry-towelling menagerie to the floor.

No, no, I am not going to sleep with him, I told myself as I unhooked my bra and dive-bombed onto the bed and under the sheet at record speed so he wouldn't have time to see my stretch marks, whacking my shin on the end of the bed and somehow grazing my nose on the sheets in the frantic process.

No, no, I am not going to sleep with him, I told myself as I saw his cock thickening, the glans enormous. Unlike me, he was so at ease in his skin – including his foreskin. As he applied the condom I noted how different he looked from Harry. The fleshy turtleneck, of course – thank you for the tip about his tip, Emerald – and then that dark mat of pubic hair at the base of his shaft. His excited cock was waving back and forth like a windscreen wiper.

No, no, no, I am not going to sleep with him, I thought . . . but as the young man ran his firm brown fingers down my spine, my tongue was hanging so far out of my head that the cabin carpet got a free shampoo. He bunched my hair in his hands, pulled my head back and kissed me ravenously. I dwelt, once more, on my husband's infidelity and lack of contrition, then grabbed the stupendous joystick before me. It was the size of rocket ship ready for blast-off. T-minus ten seconds, nine, eight, seven, six . . .

Just as I was giving in to the moment, Wayve suddenly spoke. 'Dominate me.'

'Sorry, what?' I sought clarification. 'What did you say?'

'Dominate me.'

'Oh, oh, right . . .' What the hell did he mean? I had no idea, but, trying to look worldly and suave, I straddled Wayve and pinned his arms down on the bed as forcefully as I could. But then what? I wasn't sure what my next manoeuvre should be. It struck me that boys his age have watched so much porn that they must expect a pretty sophisticated repertoire. Especially from an older woman. I immediately experienced a performance anxiety I hadn't felt since those hedonistic hours of enforced folk-dancing in primary school. It was obvious he wanted me to play a role – but of what? Teacher? Prison matron? Mother? Good god, not mother! *Paging Doctor Freud to reception* . . .

I racked my brain, not sure of the script he craved. I am

firmly of the opinion that handcuffs are only acceptable if you're an undercover police officer. The only thing I'd ever whipped was cream for Amber's famous pavlova. Ironically, I would have quite liked to be dominated myself: since he'd roughly grabbed my hair to kiss me, the whole *Poldark* fantasy of the strong young stud unable to control his passion was playing on repeat in my head. The only area in which I was clearly dominant was intellectually. Maybe I should ask him sternly to name the square root of the hypotenuse, or to triple an entendre, or maybe to do a little light quipping in Latin? Discombobulated, I dismounted and rolled to the side.

'So, what *are* you into?' Wayve asked, rubbing my nipple between his fingers. 'Rope play? Rough verbal? Anal? BDSM?'

'Um . . .' was the only reply that leapt immediately to mind. It seemed that *I* was now the one failing the audition for the Algonquin Round Table.

He kissed his way down my body and my pulse quickened. I felt his tongue flick under the lacy edge of my lingerie and brush back and forth across my vulva for a blissful few seconds. Just as I was surrendering to the joyous idea of finding myself in one of those subtitled European movies, Wayve said something I couldn't quite catch.

'What?'

'Hair?!' he said, perplexed, before drawing back.

'Um . . . yes, well, we are mammals,' I pointed out, reassuringly.

Wayve tugged Emerald's 'Lover's Spark' Brazilian briefs down to my thighs and gazed, amazed, at my nether regions. I kissed the top of his head, stroking his shoulders encouragingly . . . but, glancing down at his naked body, I realised that my toy boy's impressive appendage had deflated faster than a beachside li-lo at the end of summer.

Beer dick, I surmised. Well, it was getting late and he'd no doubt been drinking all day. Or, wait, could it be . . . the bush? Maybe he'd never seen a woman with bush? No way . . . he'd told me in the lift that he'd grown up on a sheep station, so surely the bloke was used to a little light bushwalking? I had been hoping that he might actually be partial to a bit of bush tucker.

But Wayve was making a repulsed face, like a kid who'd been offered a plate of spinach. The condom hung limply from his cock the way washing hangs lifeless from the Hills hoist on a breeze-less day. For him, this was clearly a Bush Tucker Trial. Suddenly, instead of starring in a black-and-white French film, I'd been unceremoniously recast in an episode of *I'm a Nonentity . . . Get Me Out of Here!*

'Do you prefer your women waxed?' I inquired. 'A waxed pudenda may sound erotic, but when it's growing back it looks like a shag pile that's been terrorised – a super-itchy shag pile.'

Judging by the intense look of revulsion on his face, Wayve was thinking that waxing wouldn't be enough to achieve deforestation on the scale this situation required. No, my mons was obviously going to require several months of strategic bombing with napalm.

I pulled him back up into an embrace, snuggled into his arms and inhaled his delicious scent – musky, tantalising, what was the word I was looking for? Oh, yes – *young*. Determined not to be rejected, I slid down his body this time, flicked the condom floorwards, as though I did this every day (dear god, I hadn't even seen a weenie beanie since teenhood) and aroused him with my mouth. He got hard straight away but then I felt his body convulsing and pulled back in annoyance. I wasn't going through all this just to give a toy boy a blow job, I thought, angrily. Men are just like holidays – they never last long enough. If I'm going to cheat on my husband, I want to do it properly. Or *improperly*, actually.

'Getting off at Redfern? I don't think so. I like to do the whole City Circle,' I said, trying to employ some blokey, euphemistic vernacular. I rolled on another condom and then sat astride Wayve, tossing my hair theatrically as if I were in a shampoo commercial. (Isn't that what women did?) But his flaccid penis just flopped around inside me, like a dead salmon in a tumble dryer.

'Reckon I'm just feelin' a bit guilty about me girlfriend,' he explained.

'Oh? Right,' I said, dismounting once more.

It may not have been true, but we both clung to the excuse like two drowning people to a tiny piece of verbal flotsam.

'Yeah . . . I'm s'posed to be on a fishin' trip with me mates, not on a cougar cruise with MILFs.'

'A mother you'd like to fuck – is that what I am?' I asked, huskily, in full Mrs Robinson mode, caressing him once more with confident strokes.

'Well . . .' he said thoughtfully. 'You're more of an MP.'

'An MP?'

'Mature pussy.'

Now it was my turn to feel all desire deflate. I fell back onto the pillow. It seemed that when he'd pulled my hair back tightly it wasn't part of a take-me-roughly *Poldark* fantasy at all. He was obviously just trying to iron out my wrinkles to make me look younger – a 'Fairfield face lift', we used to call it. 'If you're in love with your girlfriend then why did you come on a cruise like this?' I asked, curtly.

'Well, all me mates were comin' for the free holiday and, well . . .' He shrugged. 'I'm a country boy. If it's got a hole and a heartbeat, we fuck it then count the legs afterwards.'

Unless it has pubic hair, apparently. 'How poetic,' I muttered. 'The post of poet laureate clearly beckons.'

'I see no problem divin' and munchin' when needed, either. It's just the "Me-Tarzan-You-Jane" jungle look kinda threw me, ya know?'

'You're plagiarising Shakespeare again, aren't you,' I said, facetiously.

'Who?'

'Oh, lord. William Shakes . . . never mind.'

I felt the chasm of the generation gap yawning between us across the sheets. 'Body hair is sensual and essential. It captures your pheromones, which are nature's invisible perfume . . . All those girls waxing to make themselves more attractive to men, they're basically losing their secret weapon. Bring back bush, I say. A woman should only wax lyrical . . . Hasn't your mother explained these things to you? I'm sure your Mum doesn't wax. And she's probably about the same age as . . .'

I tried to claw back the words as they left my mouth, but it was too late. A look of repugnance crossed the boy's smooth countenance. This whole encounter was turning out to be a disaster on par with the Hindenburg. What had I been thinking? The short answer was I hadn't been thinking, I'd been drinking. And it was all Emerald's fault, the fact that I was now lying here with a tumesced toy boy, totally unbegotten.

This was not what I'd envisaged. Just for one night I no longer wanted to be Julie Andrews and Mary Poppins and Pollyanna all rolled into one big, self-sacrificing ball of niceness. I'd wanted to be Bette Davis in *All About Eve*, claws out and sequins flying. I'd wanted to be Glenn Close in *Dangerous Liaisons*, eating men for breakfast. I'd wanted to be Rosamund Pike in *Gone Girl* – dark, duplicitous, wicked. I'd wanted to be Scarlett O'Hara, giving zero mint juleps about getting what I wanted, when I wanted it. Spurred on by this impromptu mental pep talk, I tried to arouse him again with my hand. There was a brief spasm of life and he turned towards me eagerly, but then he suddenly pulled another disgusted spinach face and pointed at my stomach. 'What's *that*?'

I followed his gaze to below my navel.

'Oh, you mean my baby marks? They're just slight stretch marks from growing two humans in my abdomen.'

Once more the turbo-thrusting twenty-something's manhood dwindled to a limp shrimp lying on his leg. I was so embarrassed, all I could think about was which South American country I could flee to without a visa at short notice. Even the terry-towelling animals seemed to be looking up at me from the floor with pity. *Come on*, I rallied myself, *you've been humiliated by people a lot higher up the food chain than this bit of beefcake*. To disguise my mortification I quickly adopted the unfazed facade of a Henry Higgins type, or Henrietta Higgins in this case, briskly explaining about the Bard and island geography and *flamenco* dancing and how no one could know if a cave was undiscovered, because it was, well, undiscovered . . .

Wayve turned to me with an expression so intense I thought I may have missed my vocation as a high school teacher. I leant in, all the better to hear his appreciative, awed compliments on my intellect and erudition. 'Yes?'

'Think I'm gonna puke,' he said.

I went straight into mum mode – fetching the ice bucket and a towel and placing them by the bed, dissolving aspirin in a glass, applying a cold flannel to his burning forehead. Then I sat by his side, stroking his arm soothingly and chatting away to him like . . . well, like mother and son, really.

I'd soon forgotten about being begotten. Fucklessness is often confused with celibacy, the difference being, of course, that the state of celibacy is voluntary. Yes, I may be a shagless tragic, but being shagless is better than being badly shagged. Isn't it?

Yep, I thought, *tonight I really turned my life around – I used to be insecure and frazzled, and now I'm frazzled and insecure.*

As I nursed the boy off to sleep, I thought the night could only be made worse by one thing – my sisters finding out that my daring walk on the wild side had led me straight off a cliff. There's nothing bad about sisters that sharing personal and intimate details won't aggravate.

No, I swore to keep the whole catastrophic encounter to myself. I'd never give my siblings the comedic satisfaction – never, ever, ever. I'd rather chew off my own tongue.

12

Total catastrophe! I WhatsApped both sisters, pre-dawn, my head hanging over the toilet bowl. I couldn't chew off my own tongue now as promised, as it was stuck to the roof of my mouth, coated in fur. *From mojito to finito in, like, less than one hour.*

One thing I'd learnt is that a separated, middle-aged woman who gets drunk enough to sleep with a boy toy will be rewarded with the sight of herself vomiting up five martinis in the middle of the night.

I'd woken an hour earlier with a vague recollection in my fuddled, muddled brain, that I'd brought home a souvenir from the disco; a two-legged souvenir. I cautiously began to roll in his direction, wondering what kind of small talk could save me from the crippling humiliation of our unconsummated evening. What did boys his age like to talk about? Football? Surfing? Instagram influencers – whatever the hell they were?

When I discovered the other side of the bed to be empty, the wave of relief that washed over me felt tsunami-like in scale. But it was quickly followed by a wave of nausea so strong it propelled me to the bathroom – where I'd been lying ever since, my hot cheek pressed up against the cold tiles.

When I finally felt confident I could stand without listing starboard, I eased my way into the shower to wash off all remnants of the night before. I showered with my eyes closed to avoid the too-bright light. It hurt to walk. As I was dressing, I also noticed a raised welt the size of a crockpot on my shin, a bruise rapidly turning the colour of an aubergine on my ankle from where I'd whacked it during my diva dive onto the bed the night before, and a stiffness in my hips which could only have been from some overexcited disco moves, rather than the horizontal tango, as I'd hoped.

Worse, catching sight of myself in the mirror, I noted that my labia had swollen. No wonder it hurt to walk. Honestly, it looked as though someone had taken to my nether regions with a bicycle pump. No, that didn't quite explain it. It looked as though pirates had moored a rubber dinghy between my thighs. *At least if there's an accident at sea, I can ride my own inflated labia to shore*, I thought, amazed. I also had a sheet burn on my nose – not the best look on a middle-aged mum of two.

Eventually, with minty breath and hair turbaned in a towel, I limped like a saddle-sore gunslinger into the living room I shared with my sisters. Emerald had one foot up on the coffee table and was uncharacteristically painting her toenails a blood-red shade, while Amber was curled up on the other end of the couch in her cupcake-patterned Peter Alexander PJs, peering at the computer open on her lap, no doubt emailing instructions to her over-protected progeny about what to do in case of a cyclone, tsunami, bushfire, flood, nuclear attack or Martian invasion.

'Well, well, well, here's a cowgirl who's been ridin' the risqué range!' Emerald greeted me, approvingly.

'So, what was such a catastrophe, and why are you hobbling?' Amber asked, glancing up from her screen and blowing on the halo of froth atop a cappuccino.

'Actually, I think it's a case of ARDI.'

'Oh, god, what's that? Not some hideous genital disease, is it?' Amber recoiled. 'There's a weapons-grade gonorrhoea during the rounds of the Pacific, apparently.'

'A-R-D-I – ABBA-related dance injury,' I explained. 'My over-exuberant Mum manoeuvres, circa 1982, have left me in need of a Zimmer frame.' I winced as I shuffled towards the armchair facing them. 'Christ, it hurts to bend my legs. I'll only be able to go up the stairs backwards, on my bum.'

'Well, you were burning up the dance floor like one of the Spice Girls.'

'Yes – Old Spice,' Amber said, 'judging by the ensuing chiropractor bills.'

'Ignore her. She's just jealous. Women have been treated like second-class citizens for centuries. Now it's our turn to have some fun. Just look at it as reverse sexism. So, I will take that second helping of beefcake, thank you very much. Toy boys are more effective than a Kegel8 miracle machine. My fanny muscles are now so strong I could suction my way up a wall, like a vaginal Spider-Woman.'

Amber and I took a moment to process this image. As we stared agog at our older sister, she changed the subject. 'So, tell us, how was the rest of your night?' Emerald probed, pruriently. She radiated excitement like a heater. I could have roasted chestnuts on her.

Don't blurt every graphic, gruesome detail; they'll only piss themselves laughing, I told myself ... before immediately blurting every graphic, gruesome detail – because that's what sisters do – and concluding by opening my bathrobe with a dramatic flourish. 'And then there's *this*!'

'Oh my god. Well, *that's* something a person hopes they won't live long enough to witness!' Amber said, shielding her eyes.

'What on earth . . .?' Medically minded Emerald knelt down for a closer inspection. 'It gives "read my lips" a whole new meaning,' she chortled.

'That lip reader is *shouting*!' Amber added, now bent double with laughter.

It wasn't exactly the sympathetic reaction I'd been hoping for. 'It's not funny! I think I must have had an allergic reaction to his aftershave. I could kill that dim-witted motherfucker!'

This set my sisters off on big, gulping guffaws. Usually Amber's idiosyncratically perfect vowels gave the impression that she'd learnt elocution from a sequestered British monarch, but not this morning.

'Motherfucker,' she repeated, snorting away.

'It's a motherfucking boat all right,' Emerald managed to add. 'Chock-full of mother-fucking motherfuckers.'

I stood, legs akimbo, listening to them laugh at my expense. My hot-pink, swollen labia had parted my pubes in the most comical way. It gave 'bad hair day' a whole new meaning.

'Look, it's great to see my sisters finally getting along, it really is, but what the hell am I going to do about the Mick Jagger impersonator between my legs?!'

'Getting along?' Emerald's eyebrows collided for a perplexed moment. 'Hey, I'd get on with Amber all the time if she wasn't always saying mean things behind my back,' she backhanded, all merriment evaporating.

'What?' Amber pointed an admonishing coffee spoon in Emerald's direction. 'I do not say mean things behind your back! Although *you* do. Mum says that you're always calling me vain, before adding how lucky I am to be "photogenic" – which basically means I look crap in the flesh,' she fired back.

'I never said that! Mum told me that *you're* always saying I'm fat, and that clearly there *was* a thin person inside me, but I ate her,' Emerald retorted.

Amber turned to scrutinise our older sister. 'I would never say that! Mum told *me* that you said I'm too thin. She said that you liked the skirt I wore to her birthday barbecue, but then commented how lovely it is that my spindly legs don't seem to bother me.'

'Too thin? Is there such a thing?! When we discussed taking the kids to Disneyland she said your response was, "Good idea! Americans are so obese; Emerald might even look slim there." She said you reckoned that my body wasn't so much a temple as a disused warehouse.'

'Oh my god. You went to Disneyland years ago! You've been nursing that wound all this time? Especially when it's not true. Why would I ever say that? Besides, it's *my* body Mum finds unacceptable. When my teenage bra cups did not runneth over, she said, "Unlike Emerald, you've got no tits, so you'd better make sure you keep your teeth nice."'

'What?' Emerald baulked. 'She told *me* to get a breast reduction to look more like *you*. Ugh. I loathe my big, pendulous Celtic breasts, inherited from *her* of course! I don't know how Mum actually breastfed the two of you as her boobs are in *my* body.' She looked down at her breasts, which were currently attempting to escape her nightdress in different directions.

'And then she puts *me* in the middle to sort it all out,' I sighed. 'I'm like a human ping-pong ball, bouncing between the two of you. It's bloody exhausting. And Mum's vile to me too, you know. Just before my birthday, I suggested we go out somewhere, just the two of us, and have a lovely time . . . And do you know what she said? "I don't want to have a lovely time, I just want to be with you."'

'Ouch.' Amber winced. 'But you're her favourite, Ruby. Being the youngest and all . . . Well, you were, until your infamous birthday speech.'

'Favourite? No, I'm just the most easily manipulated. I have no doubt I was a mistake – mostly because she's often told me so. I honestly think she only had children in case she ever needed an organ donor.'

Emerald snorted. 'It's true. The woman makes *Medea* look like good mother material. Forget Child Disability Assistance, we need *Mother* Disability Assistance.'

'Do you think it's too late to put ourselves up for adoption?' I suggested.

'Yes, it's not as though we don't have good grounds. Remember when I gave up smoking?' Amber inquired. 'I thought Mum would be so terribly proud of my achievement, but do you know what she said? "Just have one more and see if it sticks."'

'She did exactly the same thing to me when I tried to go on a diet,' griped Emerald. 'She put a plate of chocolates and a sponge cake on the table and said, "Dieters invariably put on weight, so it's best to just carry on as normal. Go on, you know you want to."'

'Mum's manipulated us all. It's a classic divide-and-conquer tactic. At least we know to buy her some worming tablets and flea powder for Christmas, as she's such a bitch. So now we've cleared that up, can we call a truce?' I suggested.

Amber's smooth cheek twitched. Emerald thumped a sofa cushion – *Bam! Bam! Bam!* – then said, 'Yes, okay. A truce.' She placed her nail polish bottle on the table and extended her unpainted hand to Amber.

'A truce,' Amber chorused, closing her laptop and taking her older sister's hand warmly in her own.

'Great. Then can you please pay some lip service to my problems? I'm on fire here!'

'Okay, calm down. Just take some deep breaths,' Emerald advised, trying to suppress her laughter.

'I need a doctor, not a Lamaze class – despite these childbearing lips.'

Emerald's laugh exploded, like a sneeze. As Emerald fanned my fanny with a magazine, Amber got on the cabin phone and, struggling to talk without tittering, made a medical appointment on my behalf.

'How was *your* night?' I asked Emerald, to take my mind off my discomfort.

She grinned up at me. 'I think my cub gave positive reports . . . if I understand "lol" and "grt" correctly.'

I snatched the magazine out of her hand and hit her over the head with it, then very gingerly dragged on the baggiest sweatpants I could find. Swathed in Emerald's voluminous trackie daks, I waddled off to see the ship's doctor, my siblings' laughter ringing in my ears all along the passageway. En route I chided myself for following Emerald over to the dark side. I wondered if the captain could make an announcement – '*We apologise for this temporary loss of service. Normal middle-aged mum activity will resume at the end of this routine midlife crisis.'*

Our boat was due to dock at New Caledonia the very next day. With a sprained groin and swollen labia, how the hell was I going to get around the island? On my personal vulva-powered hovercraft, obviously. Wincing and mincing my way into the elevator, I promised my nether regions that I'd learnt my lesson. I was officially off men as a genre. Husbands were bad enough, but lovers were insufferable. In fact, celibacy had never looked so attractive.

With each painful step along the corridor, I contemplated exactly what men had ever done for me. Now that women are economically independent and can impregnate ourselves, if vibrators could change car tyres and clean gutters, would we need blokes at all? I wondered. Harry always argued that men are better at some things – parallel parking, insect-wrangling, jar-opening, elk-stalking and map reading, for example – but if a bloke can determine the exact kilometre-per-litre ratio of a five-hour trip through the Tasmanian wilderness, where he then effortlessly locates a remote fishing haven that's not even on a map, then why can't he find a G spot?

I pussyfooted down the hall on E deck and into the doctor's waiting room, which resembled an upmarket day spa. A distinct lavender aroma hung in the air. Crossing to the reception desk, I ruminated that if more evidence was required of male inferiority we could just examine what excites the average male – food, footy and lingerie models. The trouble is, I'd clearly got all excited about nothing . . . and then married him.

The doctor's receptionist, one of those radiantly healthy,

flashing-white-teeth types, handed me a clipboard with a registration form to be filled in. I leant on the high counter and dutifully ticked the box for F not M, and then one for my religion. Oh, how I wished I could tick a box for a female god. For starters, a female deity wouldn't have done such a rushed job. Forget seven days. She'd have planned for seven months, so that more thought could be given to bull ants, flies, crocodiles, wasps, sharks, megalomaniacal world leaders with orange hair, cold-callers, earthquakes, tidal waves, bushfires, famines, pain during childbirth, appendicitis and religious extremism. Cancer and serial killers would also have been deleted at first draft stage. A born multitasker, a female god would also have done something about the annoying lost-sock mystery that tormented me on a weekly basis – although, maybe they'd just seen married couples in action and no longer wanted to be paired?

Besides the wisdom of Sock-rates, a female god would ensure women would never again be condescended to by car mechanics, exploited by tradesmen, paid less than male colleagues, overlooked for promotion, groped on crowded buses or trains, or told in a court of law that they were 'asking for it'. Eve would no longer be shouldered with the blame for the whole eviction from Eden, either. That duplicitous snake would be put on trial for entrapment.

When I reached the relationship status question on the form, I paused. What was I now – married or single? A female god would also ensure plagues of locusts and rats were visited upon all misogynists, from bearded types who don't allow women to show their faces, divorce their husbands, drive or play sport, to unfaithful husbands, oh, and himbos who lost their erections at the first sight of female pubic hair.

A female god would also reprogram women's brains to stop obsessing about unfaithful husbands and himbos who lost their erections at the first sight of pubic hair. The obsession with waxing would also wane.

The medical form had now progressed to questions about age and weight. *Hmm.* With a female god, cake would have no calories and cocktails would be a detoxing health drink. Botox, collagen and face lifts would also become totally passé, because a feminine deity would make sure that men found older women irresistibly attractive. Men would just learn to read between our lines. And there'd be news for Newton, too – a new law of gravity would ensure that women's bits only sagged upwards.

Tracksuit pants with elasticated waistbands would be the height of fashion. Female footwear would be flat all day and then turn into a fetching yet comfortable stiletto at night. Men would go to training schools to learn to put down the toilet seat and feign interest when women are shopping or gossiping. Cooking classes for blokes would also be compulsory – a true recipe for success. After all, the way to a woman's heart is through her stomach. That is *not* aiming too high.

Men would also be able to stop and ask directions without feeling they were being castrated. It dawned on me that it was more than likely that Superman is only constantly flying about in his pants because he's lost, but too embarrassed to ask anyone where the bloody hell he is.

A female god would also insist on not just sex education but also relationship education in schools so that toy boys like Wayve, raised on porn, understood that a woman is not just something to lie down on while having sex. Nor would they reject a sexual partner just because of a couple of incy, wincy baby stretch marks.

I then filled out the section listing the number of children I had and whether the births had been C-section or vaginal. Now, if god were female, either blokes would give birth or the womb would become an attractive handbag arrangement, like a kangaroo pouch but designed by Prada or Pucci – the Kangarucci.

The next category on my form was profession – which was another tricky question of late. 'Working mother', I wrote, thinking that another top priority for a female god would be to help underappreciated, exhausted working mums who are always running late. I thought back to when my kids were small. I was often so tired I'd put the kids under the sink and the lethal household substances within reach. To ease stress, a female god would install pink lanes next to bus lanes, reserved for mothers, to ensure they got to the school gate on time. Oh, and maternity leave would extend to a decade.

I handed back my patient questionnaire to the receptionist, then tentatively lowered my buttocks onto the edge of a plastic bucket chair. Out of habit, I checked my phone for any correspondence from my spouse. How long had I been waiting for a message from my husband to turn up? Harry was making Godot look punctual. There were lots of fun emojis from my kids and the daily chastising email from my mother (the woman could whinge for Australia), but when I discovered that all of my Harry-shaped inboxes were still empty, I concluded that, best of all, a female god would make sure that marriages don't break up for religious reasons – that is, because he thinks he's a god and she doesn't.

I tossed my phone back into my bag and sighed deeply. Yep. I was over men, altogether. Forever. Once the boat docked in Sydney I planned to retreat to a convent to knit my own yoghurt and do a little light whittling. Apart from my son – okay, and my nephews – oh, and the cute guy who serves coffee in the surf shack on the promenade – I pledged there and then that, from this day forward, I would never spend time in the company of the male of the species. Not ever again, never, ever.

13

I despaired as I heard a male voice call me in from the waiting room with a gruff 'Next'. Clearly my late-onset allergy to the male species had not been made clear to the onboard medical staff. If only there'd been a tickable box on my form. Allergies to penicillin – no. Allergies to male doctors – yes.

'So, what ails thee?' the medic asked without looking up from the paperwork in front of him. He was sitting behind a steel desk shaped like a kidney. His voice was brusque and he chewed his words. The crumpled trousers of his scrubs were mint green. His matching shirt wasn't wrinkled, but he wore it as if it were. Somehow simultaneously youthful and grizzled, he was in his late forties and showing every minute of it.

'I think I've pulled a muscle,' I said, to the top of his tousled head. 'In my groin.'

The doctor glanced at me sideways in a brooding, half-amused way.

'No. Not like *that*,' I hastened to add. 'I think it's an ABBA-related dance injury. It's so easy on a cruise to forget that you're no longer twenty-six, you know?'

I examined the doctor more closely as he scribbled on his notepad. His thick wave of dark hair, flecked with grey, was swept back from his broad forehead in a somewhat theatrical pompadour. Haggard and world-weary, he had a touch of the dissolute Irish poet about him despite his broad Aussie accent. The doctor definitely gave the impression of being a tall, dark and handsome type. He then stood up – and up, and up – and confirmed this.

'With no responsibilities, well, it's like being a kid again.' Disarmed and annoyed in equal measure by his silver foxiness, I found myself prattling. 'The hardest decision I've had to make since coming aboard is how many umbrellas to put in my cocktail. Anyway, my first time at the disco last night, a bit of impromptu choreography to "Waterloo" – and, well, here I am.'

'At our age, it's safest to do those manoeuvres horizontally,' the doctor growled, stretching his back. 'That's my advice. Though, why any woman with half a brain would waste time fraternising with these macho hottie-hottie-dumb-dumbs is completely beyond me. Hop up onto the couch.'

'I think "hop" may be too optimistic a word.' I flinched, adding indignantly, 'And I didn't come on board for those "macho hottie-hottie-dumb-dumbs", as you so eloquently call them. I just wanted to go on a cruise with my two sisters, and booked the first available one.'

The doctor peered at me over his reading glasses once more. 'You booked a cruise of your own free will? Well, there's no need for a urine sample, as you're clearly not taking any mind-expanding drugs.'

If my tentative climb up onto the gurney hadn't left me wincing from pain, I would have lobbed a zinger back in this objectionable doctor's direction. Once in the supine position, however, the barbed retort I was planning came out sounding a bit like a strangled moose, because the doctor had started probing my upper thighs through my borrowed tracksuit pants. Biting my lip, I just stared at his scuffed shoes – shoes that had gone out of fashion *wars* ago.

'Dear god, the conversations I've had to endure,' the doctor went on, acerbically. 'I had one young bloke in here who actually said, "Doc, my ears have been popping and I was wondering if it's due to our change in latitude?" Okay, bend your right knee . . . This Einstein also wanted to know if he advanced his clock ahead one hour, would breakfast still be at the same time in the morning? Okay, now push back against my hand . . . Another brainiac wanted to know if the water in the toilet was fresh or salt. I had to say, "I dunno, kid, I've never tasted it." Only this morning I heard another gormless gorilla asking a member of the crew, "Hey, mate, do these stairs go up *and* down?" . . . So, does it hurt more here or there?'

'Ouch! There. Definitely there!' Once I'd caught my breath, I added, conversationally. 'Yes, these "cubs" are not exactly Mensa material, are they?'

'Densa, more like it . . . Now lift your other leg.'

'I overheard one young guy ask the entertainment officer about arrangements for the last night on board. He wanted to know if he should put his bags outside the cabin before or after he went to sleep,' I conversed, hoping to distract myself from the strain pain.

'Genius!' said the jaded medic as he gently massaged my legs, pinpointing the source of my discomfort. 'Well, finding yourself accidentally on a cougar cruise must be the pits. I dunno what's worse, having to make small talk over dinner with boys who have the personality of a paving tile, or listening to a band who are busy demonstrating that knowing only three chords does not have to be a barrier to a career in music . . . Does it hurt if I press here?'

'*Yes!*'

While he adjusted my limbs, I appraised the surly man looming over me. There was something about the set of his shoulders – squared, braced, alert, like a caged animal ready for flight – that caught my interest. 'If you hate cruising so much, why did you take the job of ship physician?' I probed him back.

'Let's just say that the attention I give to my debt is unremitting. I foolishly signed a three-month contract. Can you bend your other knee for me now? This is my first cruise and I already can't wait to get the hell off. I'm just praying for Somali pirates . . .'

'Might be a long wait as we're, you know, in the *Pacific*. Where did you work before here, then?' I asked, in another effort to take my mind off his painful prodding.

'Doctors Without Borders. A job I loved, but lost.'

'Lost?'

'Yeah, it's probably with my car keys someplace.'

'Seriously.'

'There's not one shred of evidence to support the notion that life is serious, I'll have you know,' he verbally sidestepped. 'Push back against my hand.'

'So . . . you lost your job because you have a sense of humour?'

'Well, yes, actually. I annoyed my boss, this total wanker desk-jockey jerk, by making a joke at his expense on Twitter. Now bend your leg inwards for me . . . He'd mounted his high horse and was galloping off into the self-righteous sunset about something or other. I tweeted back a jokey comment. Sadly, he didn't find it funny.'

'What did you say?'

'That the clitoris has eight thousand nerve endings and still isn't as sensitive as a white male git on the internet.'

I snorted out a laugh, as unexpected as it was loud.

'So, I'm on gardening leave. Until I learn to be a bit more "PC" and "woke" and not hit "trigger points" for people on their "emotional journey". And then, when I've "evolved", I'll go find a cure for malaria, or perhaps even something more difficult to locate, like, I dunno, Vladimir Putin's moral compass, and life will go on. Okay, now press down as hard as you can.'

Despite my physical discomfort, I couldn't suppress a half grin. 'Yes, well, I'm having a career rethink too, actually. Although it might be time to finally face the fact that I'm never going to make it as one of Kylie Minogue's backing dancers.'

The crotchety doctor gave a twinge of a smile – a twinge that vanished the moment he noticed that I'd noticed it.

'Okay, hop – sorry, slide down off there and take a seat. You're right. It's a groin strain. Ice the inside of your thigh to reduce the swelling. Take anti-inflammatory pills every four hours for the pain and, when you feel able, do some stretching and strengthening exercises. I'll give you a sheet of suggestions. Is that it?'

'Well . . .' I slowly swung my legs over the side of the gurney and slithered to the floor like an otter down a riverbank. 'There is one other . . . It's a bit embarrassing . . .'

'Are you talking about the carpet burn on the end of your nose?' the doctor inquired. 'I've already clocked that. Dash of Savlon and perhaps some better judgement.'

'It's a sheet burn, if you must know. And no, I didn't get it *that* way. It was just a mistimed dive-bomb manoeuvre to ensure minimum naked exposure in front of a younger man, which I don't really want to go into . . . Or it could be a disco ball graze, I'm not sure.'

'Uh-huh,' the doctor said, warily.

'And, well, thing is . . .' I paused, too mortified to mention it. 'I have something similar . . . at the other end.'

'Do you want me to take a look?'

'Good god, no! I'm just a bit swollen and irritated. Probably an allergic reaction to aftershave.'

'Cheap aftershave can inflame the sensitive tissue of the clitoris. Fragrance sensitivity is an adverse reaction to chemicals in scented products, causing redness, swelling and vesicles, or skin rashes. Does that sound like what you're experiencing?' he asked, matter-of-factly, pen poised.

'Um, yes, probably. His aftershave did make my nose get itchy and irritable, too, you know, when we were kissing . . . But do you have to write that on my notes?'

'What? Itchy nose?' he teased. 'Oh, you mean "irritated clitoris". Well, I could use a euphemistic alternative from the slang of my Queensland youth. Love button, devil's doorbell, clitty litter, crotch nipple . . .' He counted expressions off on his fingers. 'Clisaurus, quimberry, cherry chapstick, love nub. We're so eloquent in the Deep North. But, if you like, I could just limit my clinical record to your groin strain. I'll write you a prescription for some soothing steroidal anti-itch cream for the . . .'

'Hooded prawn?' I suggested, lowering myself gently onto the edge of flesh-coloured chair facing him. 'We're pretty eloquent in my neck of the woods too.'

He only smiled with a corner of his mouth but there was a twinkle in his eye – the ophthalmic version of a broad grin. As the doctor rummaged through his desk drawer for his prescription pad, he added, 'A cool wet compress will also help, plus avoiding the, um, irritant. So, in other words, take it easy on the disco dancing, toy-boy consumption and bottomless vino. Wine stoppers were invented for a reason, you know.'

I bristled at his condescension – one of the very reasons I'd gone off men. 'Yes, sure. I have two weeks of my vacation left, so what better time to give up wine and sex? I mean,' I added, sarcastically, 'there's still masturbation and reading, right?'

The doctor looked up from his prescription pad. 'I only like *one* of those activities.'

'Oh?' I shot back, 'I didn't realise you're dyslexic. How sad.'

Pausing in his prescription writing, the doctor gave me a shrewd, searching look.

'I can still read *you* like a book. You've discovered that your husband's having an affair, so you're seeking revenge by bedding random boat meat and pretending you're enjoying it. That's what I actually diagnose – a chronic case of husband uncertainty syndrome.'

I was taken aback at the accuracy of his analysis. Who was this rude, impudent man, determined to annoy the tooth enamel off me? Gone were the days of me letting a man have the last word. Nope. From now on I was strapping on a bulletproof bra and shooting from the lip.

'And what *I* diagnose is arrogant, up-himself doctor syndrome. But there's no known cure for that, sadly . . .

except the sack. I could report you for about a gazillion breaches of professional ethics right now. I won't be doing that, however, because it will only get you dropped off at the next port with a healthy severance package, which is exactly what you want, am I right?'

The doctor gave a surprised laugh. 'Touché,' he said. 'You're the only patient who's seen through my little ploy. But I am genuinely intrigued as to why a seasoned, intelligent woman would be interested in the gauche, shallow attentions of these adolescent oiks.'

As I cautiously pushed up to standing, I felt my feminist ire rise along with me. 'Not that it's any of your business, Doc, but why is it okay for men to date younger women, but not vice versa?'

'Hey, I don't make the rules, I just enjoy them.' He shrugged. 'My last girlfriend was twenty-eight . . . But in truth, she bored the bejesus out of me. All those selfies and Instagrams of her food. *Why?*'

I limped towards the door. 'Okay, thanks for your time. Although, should I thank you or maybe just get you struck off? Decisions, decisions, decisions!'

'What you don't know,' the doctor post-scripted, the indifference in his eyes evaporating for a moment as he looked at me intently, 'is that those "cubs" you seem so attracted to target women in the nightclub to play the "Whaling Game".'

My hand was on the doorhandle, but I remained in the room, half turned towards him. 'What's that?' 'It's a vile, sexist game where young men compete to find, bed and "harpoon" the fattest female in the bar.'

I thought of my 'Kardashian-esque' sister, Emerald, and

cringed on her behalf. But then again, why should I believe anything Captain Curmudgeon had to say? 'You're so cynical,' I said, defensively. 'I just hope it's not contagious. Do you have the mental version of hand sanitiser in your office? Just to be on the safe side?'

The doctor sighed, despondently. 'Sadly, I kid you not. It's all about quantity, not quality. The hottie-hottie-dumbdumbs are keeping score. Apparently conquests are rated by looks, age and performance. Women are counted and cruelly catalogued, and then the info is shared on WhatsApp. I'm new here, so I'm still working out who's who in the zoo. But I do know that those "cubs" get together and tell each other every sordid detail. In their sleazy terms, a woman can be a "reheat" or a "freshie". The player with the lowest score has to buy everyone's drinks on the last night of the cruise.'

I blushed right down to the roots of my hair. Was that what last night had been about? Was I nothing more than a notch on a jock's jockstrap? Or, had this doctor just graduated from med school with a specialisation in sarcasm and contempt? Not all young men were like those he was describing. I thought once more of my own goofy, gorgeous son and my nephews, and their mates, who were all laconic charm and devil-may-care derring-do. There must be some boys on board of a similar, likeable ilk? But, then again, my son and nephews and their mates would never come on a cougar cruise.

'You know this for sure? Or is it just something you think? If you'll pardon the exaggeration.' I was really getting better at this ballsy, take-no-prisoners routine.

The dyspeptic doctor laced his hands, put them behind his head and rocked back nonchalantly in his chair. 'I don't worry about what other people think. After all, they don't do it very often,' he said, gesturing in the general direction of my track-suited nether regions. 'Obviously. And no, I'm not making it up. I've overheard the Whaling conversations with my own ears, unfortunately.'

My journalistic instinct kicked in. If I were interviewing this pessimistic smart-arse, what would I ask? 'On second thoughts, what I diagnose *you* with, Doctor . . .?'

'Quinn.'

'Doctor Quinn, is deep insecurity. Why else would a man of your age hide behind this pathetically barbed banter?'

'I could ask a woman of your age exactly the same thing.' He fiddled for a moment with the sheaf of papers on the desk before him and allowed the remoteness to creep back into his face. 'In my case, I hide behind barbed banter because saying to your face that you're a bloody idiot is considered rude in most social circles.'

'You know, thanks for the cure. If laughter really *is* the best medicine, I'll be better in no time, because you are a complete joke.'

'If you have a problem with me, please write it nicely on a piece of paper, put it in an envelope and shove it up the captain's arse.'

'Good try, Doc, but I'm still not going to help you get that severance pay,' I said, slamming the door on my way out.

My face was flushed and my temples were pulsing. Men were ruining my life on a daily basis. Clearly I had a huge bullseye on my back. Tomorrow we were due to disembark at Lifou Island. I couldn't wait to get out of this murky aquarium and flop onto the shore, alone with my dear sisters.

Men: can't live with them, can't . . . No, just can't live with them, I concluded, adding the misanthropic medic to my long list of blokes I never, ever wanted to see ever again.

14

'Oh, god, it's *you*,' were the doctor's not-so-warm words of greeting the following evening.

'Believe me, I'm not exactly shitting confetti with joy at being here either.'

'What is it this time?'

'Look, is there another doctor in the medical centre I could see? Preferably a woman?'

'Nope. Sadly, as I've taken the Hippocratic oath, not wanting you to die is kind of in the job description, so I guess I'll just have to save you. Take a seat.'

'That's just it. I can't . . . Sit down, I mean.'

'Don't tell me you re-triggered your fragrance sensitivity?'

'No. Good god, no. It's another problem entirely. My bum, actually.'

The doctor arched a curious, slightly suggestive brow. 'Let me guess. A hens' night that got out of hand?'

'No, nothing like that.' I felt my face turn hot enough to fry an egg. 'Like most sane women, I don't like to be beaten . . . not even at Scrabble. Thing is, I spent the day snorkelling with my sisters. The only downside to the tropics is that the turquoise water is so warm, and we stayed in for *hours*. My rashie protected my arms and I reapplied sunblock to the backs of my thighs, but I didn't notice my cossie riding up as I swam. I now have a hotter arse than Beyoncé.'

Doctor Quinn snorted. 'Excuse me while I laugh my own arse off.'

'It's not funny.'

'Really? Isn't laughter the best medicine? I seem to recall a rather annoying patient telling me that only yesterday.'

'Well, laughter is not going to help me sit down for dinner.'

'Still, surely laughter is the shortest distance between two people?' the doctor said with mock sincerity.

'The idea of anyone wanting to get close to *you* is laughable,' I responded, folding my arms.

'Well, I'd better take a look.'

I approached the desk, and the amused stare of its attendant. It was beyond mortifying to be back here, with my sunburnt tail between my legs. I gingerly lifted my skirt to reveal my blazing red, blistered buttocks. I thought back with longing to my perfect morning. Sometime during the night our ship had quietly moored off Lifou – one of the Loyalty Islands, in the New Caledonian archipelago. When we Ryan girls woke and drew back the curtains, the crystalline waters, pristine white beaches and steep coral cliffs were so breathtakingly beautiful it inclined us all to the adjectival. Having exhausted our supply of superlatives over breakfast, I'd suggested putting in an urgent request to Stephen Fry via Twitter to airlift in some even bigger adjectives.

High on excitement, we caught the tender into a jetty nestled in the crook of a turquoise cove. Disembarking, we were greeted by a line of palm trees with spiky Rod Stewart hairstyles, rising up like exclamation marks shouting 'WOW! WOW! WOW!' We soon found ourselves mimicking the palm trees by also speaking in exclamation marks. 'Amazing! This whole, empty, glistening beach is really all ours?!'

With sherbet-winged parrots taking flight, and fish darting through the coral in their colourful underwater choreography, the island was utterly perfect. Even the shrubs had that happy and contented, 'talked-to' look.

The hardest thing about snorkelling is not talking – especially when Amber and Emerald, post truce, had forgotten their differences and suddenly had so much to say to each other. Best of all, the buoyancy of the saltwater had taken all pressure off my groin strain.

Diving and floating around atolls, I lost myself in the riot of soft corals and swaying anemones, their bright maws greedily agape. I was so enthralled by this multicoloured world – so entranced by the silent aquatic symphony of silver, sparkling shoals of angel-, lion- and triggerfish darting in unison, as though following an invisible conductor's baton – that I hadn't noticed I was burning. Sun-savvy Amber had worn a full-length burkini, and Emerald's deeply unattractive but practical ensemble of long-sleeved rash shirt, knee-length board shorts and daggy surf hat had also kept the burning rays at bay. My exposed crescent moons of white butt cheek were now pulsating with red hot pain.

'Cold compresses to take the heat out of the skin, aloe vera gel to relieve the pain, ibuprofen to reduce swelling, a water-gel burn dressing to alleviate discomfort at night, and drink plenty of water,' the doctor recited. 'Well, this is definitely going to put a damper on your toy-boy bedding.' He chuckled. 'No bed rest for you, young lady. If you *can't* resist those hottie-hottie-dumbdumbs, then I advise you to only make love sideways. Then your cub can say that you really are his "bit on the side".' The doctor chortled, clearly thinking he deserved an award for his Wildean wit.

I shot the doc a scathing look. 'I'm a journalist, you know. A journalist on a *news desk*. Everything you have just said is totally inappropriate. Just be warned. Anything you say may be taken down and used against you.'

It was a blatant attempt to make myself sound like a dynamic, empowered, super-successful award-winning journo – instead of a laughable hack who penned such groundbreaking exposés as 'Local Scout Hall Cooker to be Cleaned More Often'. And, my most recent scoop, 'Midget Rapes Nun, Then Flees in UFO'. No wonder I'd called my cat Pulitzer – it was the only way I'd ever get to say that I had one.

'Hop up on the bed and I'll apply an urgent unguent.' He could not keep the amusement out of his voice.

I gazed up at the gurney with the same apprehension with which Ranulph Fiennes must have surveyed Everest from his base camp as he faced up to the fact that he was the oldest person ever to attempt the ascent. With my groin strain and singed behind, it was going to take me nearly as long to get up there as his mountain climb. Abashed and flustered, I just kept talking to ease the tension. 'You may look down on the cougar cruise,' I said, defensively, 'but for women who've been taken for granted or ignored, or betrayed by their husbands, well, some horizontal refreshment can be very healing.'

'How can bedding a male bimbo with the IQ of a crash-test dummy raise a woman's self-esteem?'

The gel he applied to my pulsating arse was incredibly soothing but did nothing to cool my temper, which was heating up by the second. 'Not that it's any of your business,' I seethed, 'but yes. I had a revenge bonk and it was great. What a night. The guy was half your age and he blew my mind,' I lied, craning my head to peer over my shoulder at the impertinent, party-pooping medic. 'I'm feeling liberated. Reborn. Resurrected. And why not? Why can't women play the same enjoyable field as you blokes?'

'You really wanna know?' He paused, then added, 'I know I go on about those cubs being as thick as the plank I'd like to make them walk, but I have to admit, they're not *all* stupid. Some of them are able to sum up a woman's net worth to the nearest FTSE share with one long, cool, calculated look. Okay, you can get up now.'

I pushed up onto all fours so I could dismount without smudging the gel or stretching my loins, a complicated manoeuvre requiring such dexterity it could have scored me perfect tens in Olympic gymnastics.

'A fool and her money are soon married,' the doctor warned, washing his hands at the sink. 'And on a cougar cruise, a bludging bloke can find a wife he can really bank on. Do warn those sisters of yours. If either one is a woman with money to burn, a toy boy will be her match.'

A punster. Hmm . . . I liked that. Shame it was the only vaguely likeable thing about the insolent, arrogant ratbag.

'*Do you take this woman to the cleaners, for fifty per cent of her income, from this day forth, for richer and richer? You bloody bet he does.*'

'Ha! You doctors can't talk!' I retorted. 'Now, open your wallet wide and say "Ahhh". Luckily, I took out travel insurance to foot your preposterous bill.' Although astounded by the quack's familiarity and rudeness, I was also wise to his ploy. 'But hey, Doc, be as rude and crude as you like. I'm still not going to report you for unprofessional behaviour, so you can kiss that severance pay goodbye, pal.' I rearranged my skirt and slid into my sandals, eager to depart.

The doctor shrugged. 'ABBA-related dance injuries, facial sheet grazes, labial contact dermatitis and a sunburnt arse – clearly, living is dangerous to your health, Ms Ryan. Just try not to be a hazard to yourself from now on, okay?' He opened the door and signalled to the receptionist to send in his next victim – sorry, I mean patient. 'Oh . . . and thanks for the laugh, Ryan. You really are the butt of your own joke today.' He squeezed out another chuckle.

Once more, I found myself executing a melodramatic flounce away from his office. No matter what happened – shark bite, Ebola, leprosy, not even alien abduction and anal probing – absolutely nothing would get me back here. I was not going to subject myself to his odious company again. Hell, I'd rather gnaw my way through my own ovaries.

15

Madame Ovary, I presume? That's what I thought when I found myself back in the medical centre waiting room the very next day, cursing my luck. I was looking forward to a third encounter with Doctor Dour as enthusiastically as I'd look forward to amateur appendix removal minus anaesthetic. The bloke had the bedside manner of Jack Kevorkian. I contemplated donning scuba goggles or using my swimming towel as a burqa, anything to hide my identity. I just wanted to retreat to my bed and hang a sign on the door reading *TODAY IS UNDER CONSTRUCTION – THANK YOU FOR YOUR UNDERSTANDING.*

'Rope burn,' I explained, entering his surgery, palms extended to obscure my face.

Doctor Quinn looked up from the book he was reading, uncrossed his legs, which were kicked up on the desk before him, rocked even further back in his swivel chair and grinned.

'Well, I knew you were highly strung, but not in a masochistic way. Although being the dominant one is actually very masochistic, in my view. I mean, all that time-consuming effort and financial outlay. Then there are all those knots that need

memorising, and . . .'

'Rope burn from abseiling,' I clarified, coolly.

I then explained how, over breakfast that morning, as our ship docked in Port Vila, Vanuatu, I thought my sisters had been chatting excitedly about canapés. I was under the impression they were planning on taking me to a local restaurant, but they meant *canopies*, not canapés, as in rainforest canopies with zip-lining and abseiling.

Now, I have a head for heights. Thanks to my journalistic job, I'm the Edmund Hillary of social climbing. Well, okay, maybe just the lower social slopes, inhabited by local surfing champs and footy heroes. But, dangling above the tree tops from a flimsy rope, I'd reached new heights – of terror. When I saw the harness I was to be strapped into, I'd clung to my sisters like Robinson Crusoe to his life raft.

'We're doing this for *fun*?' I queried, aghast. 'Other than, say, the bubonic plague or a tsunami, could there be anything less fun than hurtling through thin air held up by a bit of dental floss?'

Both my sisters remained unperturbed. Emerald was like a bouncy labrador, the type that causes chaos with its wagging tail. She was whooping her way across the leafy canopy at breakneck speed, not caring how many times she snagged or lurched or accidentally flipped upside down. Amber, on the other hand, was like a cat – standoffish, quiet, a touch superior, surveying the route with a calculating eye before eventually nailing the task with the finesse of a highwire trapeze artist.

After completing the course, my sisters stood together on the platform on the other side of the rainforest canopy and cheered me on in stereo.

Emerald cupped a hand to her mouth and shouted out, 'Don't be a wuss!'

'Any intelligent person, even a reasonably bright fungus, could see that leaping into the unknown like this is a stupid idea!' I'd shouted back to them.

'Carpe diem, remember?' Amber urged.

'Does the word "*splat*" mean anything to you*uuuuu!*' My sentence changed direction when the insouciant French ropes instructor suddenly shoved me forward. I screamed and squeezed my eyes shut as wind whistled through my hair. After what felt like an eternity, but was probably about thirty seconds, I felt a wrench. Certain that my right arm had been torn from its socket and was already hitchhiking back to the boat without me to order a cocktail, I was amazed to realise that I'd simply landed in my sisters' warm and welcoming arms. They hugged me simultaneously and congratulated me on conquering my fear.

My older sisters approached the abseiling part of the adventure with similar ease. Emerald, giving a goofy grin, just stepped backwards over the cliff edge, descending the vertical drop in jerking fits and spurts, guffawing merrily on route. Amber stood back to observe the other abseilers for a while, before nimbly rappelling earthwards with the smooth motions of a *Mission Impossible* agent.

I could hear them calling to me from the forest floor. Emboldened by my unexpected zip-lining success, I let the instructor belt me up, stood with my back to the drop, leant slowly back and gingerly inched a foot over the ridge. I might have made it unscathed, too – except that, in my apprehension, I dropped my goddamned gloves.

'Anyway,' I told the doctor now, 'abseiling turned out to be the most nerve-racking event of my life that didn't involve a gynaecologist.' *Or coming to your wretched surgery, for that matter*, I mentally added. 'Nobody warned me to pack adult Pampers. Hence the panic. Hence the fact that I dropped my gloves. Hence the rope burn.'

The doctor looked at me with grizzled amusement.

'Vanuatu's so fascinating, isn't it?' he finally said, getting up from his desk to examine my lacerated hands. 'Over a hundred distinct languages are spoken in a country with a population no greater than that of a large Aussie town. Virtually every group of villages has its own lingo. Colonialism exacerbated the islanders' difficulty in understanding one another, since Vanuatu was ruled jointly by the UK and France. That's why Bislama, a pidgin form of English, became their national language. And it's quite straightforward, really. A womb is a "basket blong pikinini". Flippers are "dakdak sus", or duck shoes. A tumour is "rabis mit", meaning rubbish meat,' he decoded. 'A bathroom is a "rum blong swim". A bra is a 'bag blong titi.' And 'bagarap' means buggered up, which you've clearly done.'

'And what's a rude, supercilious, self-important doctor in Bislama? A "pain blong backside", possibly?'

'I seem to recall from your last appointment that you've already got one of those. And now, rope burn.' As the doctor cleaned the wounds on my palms with disinfectant, he gave another annoying little chuckle. 'Abseiling without gloves. I can cure a lot of things, but there's no cure for idiocy, you know.'

'Yeah, well, you must think I'm an idiot if you thought I'd fall for what you said about the "cubs" keeping score. Seems to me you only diss the young studs in a pathetic effort to increase your own chances with women, which are limbo-low, by the way,' I pointed out in a frosty tone.

'Are you kidding?' The doctor grinned. 'These dumbarse "cubs" are having a fantastic effect on my self-esteem. Male airheads are the most efficient way of making a bloke in his late forties look fascinating and super-intelligent,' he said, eyes twinkling.

'In your wet dreams,' I scoffed. My irritation at this man was almost enough to make me forget the pain of my various ailments.

When the doctor had finished his ministrations, I stood up to leave. 'Thanks. I'm a huge fan of your work. Let's make sure we never do this again some time.'

Famous last words – the kind of last words that, hubris dictates, usually indicate it's time to pull the emergency brake on an out-of-control, runaway train.

16

'Okay, I now diagnose a case of chronic hypochondria.' The doctor smirked as I appeared the next day at his surgery door.

'I am *not* a hypochondriac,' I bristled.

'Then hypochondria must be the only disease you *don't* have.'

'Jellyfish sting. Can you believe it? Not even Billy Connolly could turn this journey into a witty anecdote.' I lifted my T-shirt and revealed the thick red welts on my abdomen.

'Yep, that looks nasty.'

'There are some stings in other more, um . . . sensitive areas.'

'Skinny dipping, eh?' The doctor stood and began to assemble equipment to bathe my wounds in soothing antihistamine lotion. 'Just a tip – knowing the location of all venomous creatures in the vicinity is really the minimum precaution one should take before exposing one's naked body to the elements.'

'Really? Thanks so much! I wish I'd thought of that!'

I'd actually spent a sublime day on Mystery Island – population zero – with my sisters. The palm-tree-fringed beaches and coral caverns so resembled a storybook fantasy that I'd expected to see singing mermaids riding foam seahorses. It's taboo to live on the southernmost island of the Vanuatuan archipelago, but grass-skirted locals had paddled over from nearby Aneityum Island to slice open coconuts with machetes for thirsty visitors, then entertain with traditional dance.

Strolling far from the crowds around the white, silica-sanded beach, we Ryan sisters had found a secluded, shaded spot and braved a skinny-dip. It had been Emerald's idea. 'Come on! As you said, Ruby, it's the first time we've been away together like this since we were kids – but this time there's no parental supervision. So, let's muck up!'

'We can do synchronised swimming,' Amber had laughed, peeling off her clothes. 'Just like we used to do in the pool at home. Except naked!'

'I just hope we don't get caught in a rip. Otherwise it will be the most embarrassing winch up to a rescue helicopter in human history,' I joked, stripping off and cantering after them into the lagoon. The water is, after all, my natural habitat. At school I'd won every swimming carnival, but Mum had put the kibosh on professional coaching because 'men don't like muscly girls'.

Giggling and squealing with juvenile joy, we formed a circle and touched toes, making starfish shapes then improvising other aquatic choreography. The water was so silky and warm, and our comedic camaraderie so cosy, it had been pure, purring perfection – until the pain.

The doctor, inspecting my oozing blisters, interrupted my reverie. 'Could be worse, though. These islands are said to still be home to some cannibal tribes. With your penchant for getting yourself into hot water, I'm surprised you're not simmering in a pot somewhere.'

'Cannibals don't eat witty women, because we taste funny,' I shot back. 'Clearly *you'd* be safe, too, because you're far too bitter for anybody's palate.'

The doctor was obviously relishing my chagrin at being back here in his clinic. 'I thought you might have realised by now that you are not entirely suited to the great outdoors, Ms Ryan. But off you go, day after day, despite the damage to your physical wellbeing. I think it's a case of persistence beyond the call of talent. Unless'—he raised a sardonically amused brow—'you're just making excuses to see me again.'

I reminded myself that it would take forty-two muscles to frown, and only four to stretch out my arm to slap the taciturn and irritating bastard. Instead I fired a furious look his way. If my eyes could shoot out fatal rays like the ones in sci-fi movies, he'd have been incinerated instantly.

'You know, GPs will soon be replaced by computers, so you won't have to subject yourself to the indignity of tending to actual patients.'

'Well, a computer did once beat me at chess. But it was no match for me at karate,' he said.

I was truly tempted to make a complaint about him now. But I also wanted to get back to my sisters. Emerald had booked us into the spa for a facial and pedicure. Yes; normally scruffy Emerald, who'd always acted as though her body were only there to carry her intellectual head around, had suddenly taken to beautifying. She'd started exercising, too, which was equally out of character. Each spring when Amber warned us that it was time to get 'beach body ready', Emerald would reply, 'If I'm by a beach, and I have a body, then I'm ready.' But not anymore. Push-ups, sit-ups, lunges – the woman was constantly on the move.

Much to my amazement, Amber had declined Emerald's invitation for some spa pampering. Although normally polished and perfect, she'd recently preferred slouching around in tracksuit pants – *elasticated* tracksuit pants – making it all the easier to graze on more and more food. Protein and veg only, of course – she'd still die rather than eat a carb – but nevertheless, her new motto seemed to be, 'My home is girth by sea.'

'Honestly, I'm like a boa constrictor. I just go to the buffet and unhinge my jaws. But instead of lying around digesting for, oh, say, six months or so, I simply go and consume another meal just like it three hours later. It's heaven!'

I'd promised to meet Amber at the sushi bar later and accompany her to watch the ballroom dancing, followed by a martini ice slide party, whatever the hell that was. 'It's the first time in forever that I'm doing things just for me!' she'd enthused. 'And, look at this.' She'd shown me her phone. 'I've only Skyped the kids twice!'

All of these interesting developments would be discussed in detail when we three met up for our daily cackle over a cocktail. So, I really had no time to waste on this irritating human haemorrhoid.

I wanted to strut out of his office but could only manage a half-limp, half-lope. A groin strain, a swollen labia, a red-hot arse, rope burn and a jellyfish sting – surely that had to be it; there was no way the fickle fairy of fate could deliver any more body blows with that bloody wand of hers. Because if I was forced to see this up-himself, pissant medic just one more time I'd be tempted to rearrange his smirking facial features with his own scalpel, while explaining to him, with caustic condescension, that apparently dying can also be seriously damaging to your health.

'By the way, thanks, Ryan,' he called out after me, with a chuckle. 'I can always count on you to brighten my day.'

17

By the time our ship had moored in Mare, New Caledonia, we girls were getting used to paradise.

'Right,' Emerald announced as the tender came to clamorous life and zoomed towards shore. 'Time to explore the beach in search of exotic creatures.'

Amber displayed all the eagerness of a limpet at her veterinary sister's suggestion. 'I think we've seen quite enough odd creatures aboard HMAS *Toy Boy*.'

'Yes, Em, you haven't exactly been exercising berth control,' I punned.

'Oh, ha-ha.' Emerald rolled her eyes good-naturedly. 'I'm talking about the Pacific leaping blenny. Or *Alticus arnoldorum*, if you want to be posh about it. It's a unique fish that lives on land and can leap huge distances. You simply must come with me to see it.'

'Ugh, no thanks. Ruby and I prefer our fish in the past tense – on a plate. We'll probably eat one of your leaping blenny's on our food tour of the local market, won't we, Rubes?'

'A food tour? You can't be serious. I can't believe you still have room to eat anything after all the food we've consumed on board. Ruby's definitely coming with me,' Emerald said. 'Aren't you, Rubes?'

The familial tug-of-war was settled, however, by my groin strain. The only place I felt no pain was in the weightless water. And so, having agreed to meet back on deck for a sunset cocktail, we went our separate ways.

Alone on the seashore, I breathed a sigh of relief so huge it was probably mistaken by nearby sunbathers for emphysema. Beyond the palm-tree-dotted beach lay the turquoise bay, distantly semi-circled by the frothy breakers of a coral reef.

Stashing my bag behind a boulder, I donned a sun-savvy rash shirt and, this time, long board shorts, and fixed my goggles and snorkel. Then, pretty certain that I was not in the running for the Ms Mare New Caledonia Style Awards, I plunged into the silky sea and swam effortlessly out into the cove. A warm sense of calm washed over me as I watched the majestic stingrays, with their theatrical Batman capes and stage-villain grins, the shy sea turtles, the giant gropers, with their pouty Mick Jagger lips, and the colourful choreography of iridescent fish darting through coral without a care in their weightless world.

Soaking up the silent grandeur of the majestic reef, I lost track of time. The turquoise water was so warm I practically grew gills. I felt completely at ease, apart from one moment when a blacktip reef shark took a long look at me, then gave an expression that said 'I already ate' and slunk off into the deep.

When my arms and legs were nearly numb from exertion, I finally bobbed my head up and trod water while clearing the mist from my mask. Gazing up at the blue skies, with their curlicues of clouds, I felt so happy that I should have had my own cloud to walk upon, marked number nine. I realised, with a jolt, that I hadn't thought of Harry today, not once. And even remembering that I hadn't remembered him didn't make me cry.

A warm breeze rippled across the water. The air itself seemed to waver, the tropical humidity suffusing it with an aqueous opalescence. Blissfully content, I was about to turn back towards the shore when I heard a cry – faint at first, but then a louder 'Hoy!' I trod water some more, turning in a semi-circle. Shielding my eyes against the sun's glare, I finally discerned the outline of a windsurfer on the horizon, and there it was again – an unmistakable cry for help.

Readjusting my goggles, I swam in strong strokes towards the castaway. After five minutes, I surfaced and lifted my fogged goggles to check my direction. The person lying across the stranded board suddenly came into focus as though a binocular lens had been turned.

'Oh, Jesus. Just when I thought this day couldn't possibly get any worse,' the doctor grouched.

'Gosh, it's just so hard to believe that you're single,' I replied, my hair floating about my face like red seaweed. I took in his broken mast. The waterlogged sail blew in and out faintly, like cheeks half-heartedly puffed with air. 'Not a natural windsurfer, I take it? A case of "*persistence beyond the call of talent*", perhaps?' I touchéd. 'How did you snap the mast, for god's sake?'

'I'm not too sure. I just leapt on, the wind went *whoosh* and next thing I know, I'm headed for Tahiti. I tried to turn the bloody thing around, but I had no idea how and must have yanked too hard because, well . . .' He gestured to the broken pole.

'You had no idea how? Wait, do you mean you went windsurfing with no instruction?'

'I only popped ashore to buy some indigenous nose flutes, or whatever it is you clichéd tourists do, then, on the spur of the moment, I decided to try windsurfing – a decision possibly influenced by the three daiquiris I downed in quick succession at the beach bar. You see, when I'm not on duty, my philosophy is to get as plastered as possible so that there's absolutely no chance of my having to save anyone from anything on my day off.'

'And it didn't cross your mind that, without being able to turn around, you might end up marooned on some volcanic island in the vicinity of Hawaii?'

'I just hope it's extinct, because you would no doubt take a volcanic eruption as a breach of copyright,' he retorted.

'Seriously, didn't you think it might be wise to, I dunno, maybe have a few lessons before you took off into the open ocean?' I quizzed. 'You're always saying the "cubs" on board are so stupid, but clearly *you're* the one who should join Densa.' Oh, I was enjoying this. 'And while we're talking about stupidity, why is it that all Aussie blokes are so keen to risk blood loss, broken limbs or waterlogged lungs in your leisure moments?'

'Well, I wasn't anxious about blood loss until now. As I'm drifting further out to sea, I am kinda getting a bit worried about the big fish with fangs below, because my legs are just, you know, dangling here in the water like shark biscuits. I'm a farm boy, don't forget. Lend me your goggles so I can see what's down there,' the doctor demanded.

I declined his invitation. 'If you see a shark in the water, you don't have to worry, mate, because it saw you a long time before you saw it. If it wanted to eat you, you'd be dead already.'

'Oh, that's *so* comforting.'

'Well, luckily I'm *not* a doctor, so saving you is not in my job description at all. I'll alert the dive centre to come and get you . . . eventually,' I said, relishing our role reversal. 'Okay? Bye.'

I was about to pull on my goggles and stroke back to shore when I noticed his leg. Or, rather, the absence thereof. His left leg was amputated from the knee down. Attached to his stump was an Oscar Pistorius–type blade.

When he noticed that I'd noticed, his dark eyes glittered but he said nothing. I didn't know what to say, so I dog-paddled in awkward silence for a moment.

There was no way I could leave now, despite how annoying I found the man.

I quickly calculated the distance to shore. It was only about one kilometre. 'Can you swim? I mean, with your . . .' I still hadn't quite worked out how to mention it, and the bastard doc chose not to make it easier. 'I suggest we just ditch the board and freestyle in together.'

'You seem to be forgetting my whole shark phobia,' he admitted, glancing apprehensively down into the depths.

'Most creatures are scared of humans. We hurt sharks far more often than they hurt us.' I'd been around Emerald for long enough to know that. I hauled the top half of my body up onto the board, on the same side as the doctor. 'Let's kick the board in to shore,' I said, and started a frantic cancan in the water.

The doctor tried his best, but his right leg was much better at displacing water than the blade, so the board began moving in a circular direction.

I checked our position against the headland. It was then

I realised we were in a rip – a current that was dragging us out of the inlet towards the open ocean.

'Look, why don't I swim to shore and raise the alarm? You just lie on the board and wait. Okay?'

I shoved on my goggles and slid back into the water. I was freestyling fast towards the shore, diagonally, to cut across the rip, when my eyes focused on the sandy-ribbed bottom of the sea. It looked like pale corduroy. But it also seemed to be moving oddly. At first I thought it was just reflective ripples made by the rogue tide. But with a sickening thud of my heart, I realised that the sand was alive with sea snakes.

I turned around and snorkelled at breakneck speed back to the broken windsurfer. My legs were kicking so frantically, I must have looked like the horizontal, aquatic version of Riverdance.

'Sea snakes,' I panted, scrambling aboard, my tangled hair now resembling a writhing mass of what I was avoiding in the water. I hugged my knees to my chest. 'I hate snakes. They're bad enough on land, slithering around, swallowing their prey whole. Some snakes can eat something ten times the size of their own heads, did you know that?'

'Sounds like certain cruise passengers,' the doctor interjected.

'But snakes in the water is just wrong. Plus, they're so venomous.'

'*But surely most creatures are scared of humans. We hurt them much more than they hurt us,*' the doctor contemptuously paraphrased. 'So, what now, Jacqueline Cousteau?'

I thought for a moment. 'The dive boats will be coming back soon from beyond the reef. We'll just have to wait to be rescued. Jesus. What a misadventure. It's like being in a bloody Hemingway novel – *The Old Man and the Sea*.'

'Oh, ha-ha. Middle-aged, at the most.' The doctor also dragged his whole body up onto the broken windsurfing board and positioned himself cross-legged, facing me. We sat there in uncomfortable silence – the time racing by as though it were only a year or two.

'So, how shall we pass the time? I suppose we could sing the harmony line to "Kum Ba Yah" ad nauseam?' he suggested.

'Well, as we're clearly doomed to spend the next god-knowshow-long marooned together, you might as well tell me what . . . I mean, I don't want to pry . . . Stop me if I'm being rude, but what . . .'

'Happened to my leg? I wondered when you'd ask. Most people just inquire if I have to take my leg off to have sex.'

'And what do you say?'

'"Oh, so *that's* what's meant by a leg-over." '

I smiled and nodded, hoping to encourage him to elaborate.

'Croc attack. The croc was called Hagrid. It was living in the lake out the back of our medical camp in Burkina Faso. I thought we had a rapport but turns out he just saw me as lunch.'

I looked at his dark, dancing eyes. It was impossible to tell if he was serious or not.

'To be honest, I didn't lose the leg doing anything heroic at all really. No croc wrestling or saving wounded from war zones . . . I was out jogging. Trod on a landmine. Decades on from the civil war in Angola and it's still one of the most mine-contaminated countries in the world. That's one day I should *not* have put my best foot forward.'

I drew a shuddering breath. 'I'm so sorry. That's horrific.'

'I'm sorry I've been a bit of a prick,' he admitted after a beat. 'And you were right. I really was hoping you'd report me. I cannot wait for my cruise contract to end.'

'Will you go back to Doctors Without Borders?'

I saw his shoulders slacken. 'I wish I could go back to my old job, but the truth is, I left under a bit of a cloud.'

'The tweet about the clitoris having eight thousand nerve endings and still not being as sensitive as a white man on the internet that, um, rubbed your boss up the wrong way?' I laughed.

'No. Truth is, I found out I was operating on a man who'd raped about ten women, and, well, I "accidentally" genitally mutilated him.'

My mouth opened and closed like a puppet whose ventriloquist had laryngitis, while I tried to think of something to say. 'Um, I think that's a little more than "leaving under a cloud". It's more like leaving under a cyclonic typhoon and possible asteroid onslaught. What were you thinking?'

'What I was *thinking* is that the food crisis that's gripping parts of southern Ethiopia is all because of ethnic violence – violence that has driven nearly a million people from their homes. Doctors Without Borders treated more than two hundred children in two weeks for severe malnutrition. The grim freight of human suffering I've seen – well, it's scarred my retinas, and maybe my psyche a little bit,' he confessed.

His eyes caught and held mine. My irises are the palest blue possible, but the doctor's molten chocolate orbs got even darker as his story deepened.

'And, of course, rape is a weapon of war . . . and this cocksure dipshit was bragging about his many "conquests". I was draining his acute perineal abscess, STD-related, and performing a circumcision due to multiple infections. It was only supposed to be a little dice and splice, but – well, I was so war-weary and shell-shocked, I couldn't even really remember which end of the syringe went into the patient. And oops, what a shame! My scalpel slipped . . . which meant I took off more than the tip, leaving a bit of a stump.'

I was appalled and intrigued in equal measure. 'Well, one thing's become clear. Now I know why you doctors wear those little green masks – so that nobody will recognise you when you're out of the operating room. So, what happened?'

'The official line was that it was an accident. But then I got ratted out to my supervisor by my girlfriend, who didn't quite appreciate the irony of genitally mutilating a rapist, apparently. And so, here I am.' He let out a sharp, contemptuous bark of a laugh. 'At least it taught me to never trust a woman again.'

'Well, maybe not a millennial who takes photos of her food to post online. And hey, big news – life lets you down. You're not the only one. It's like when I got my first period and didn't immediately want to waterski or play tennis in a white miniskirt. That's when I realised that existence was *not* going to live up to my expectations. The world is clearly a deranged place, and humans are lurching to the right while the planet implodes environmentally. We're all going to hell. All you can do is try to behave a little stylishly en route.'

'Stylishly? In that outfit?'

'Hey, at least I won't get sunburnt and have to go and see the ship's doctor, who's a complete bastard, by all accounts.'

The start of a grin began to tug at his mouth. 'So, what about marriage?'

'Well, that's an interesting offer, as I've only known you for about five minutes,' I replied, cheekily.

'Ha-ha. No, I mean, was I right? Are you unhappily married?'

Disarmed by the sun and our precarious situation, I let my guard down for a moment. 'Well, if you really want to know, my husband of twenty-eight years recently flunked the practical exam for his marriage licence. I told him to do something to himself that only an incredibly athletic person could ever do, then booked a cruise and buggered off.' I sighed.

'Ah . . . hence the sheet burn on the nose, I suppose.'

'Doctor–patient confidentiality?' After he nodded, I continued in a small voice, 'I wasn't very accurate on the old truth-ometer about that one-night stand I had. It was actually a total disaster. He lost all interest. I think it was the shock of seeing pubic hair,' I blurted.

'What? Really?' The doctor laughed. 'Well, speaking as an old bushranger, I can't help but feel sorry for a young man who can't cope with a stroll in the long grass. The poor buggers have been brought up on porn, where everyone's shorn. However, I must confess to being slightly jealous of him, whether or not he got lost in the jungle.'

I didn't look in the direction of the doctor but I felt his gaze brush warmly across my face and smiled, despite myself. 'What's your name? If one of us is going to have to eat the other to survive, we might as well be on a first-name basis, don't you think?'

'Brody. Brody Quinn.'

'Ruby Ryan. But you already know that. I'm no doubt filed at the medical centre under "most annoying patient". Or "status dramaticus".'

And then he really smiled. It was a slow, genial glow that started in his eyes and pulled at his lips until his face was wreathed in radiant delight. I almost gasped at the sudden and spontaneous warmth of it.

Marooned on our paddleboard, awaiting rescue, I ascertained certain things about the ship's doctor. Firstly, that he wasn't as awful as I'd first thought. And secondly, that he was incredibly sexy, even without a full complement of limbs.

Drifting in the sea, we had nothing to do but talk. In a nutshell, this is what I gleaned. Brody's daredevil father had taught him to ride horses and motorbikes, fly planes and to parachute. In his teens he'd ridden with a camel train across a desert. 'A big desert,' Brody said, reminding me that Queensland is nearly eight times the size of Great Britain. 'The correct answer to "Are we there yet?" was generally "No," ' he explained.

He'd eaten snakes, once used the corpse of a sheep as a sleeping bag, and rowed, naked, in a bathtub down the Brisbane river to raise money for his friend's kid who had cancer. He spoke Indonesian and Portuguese. He had a black belt in karate. He'd survived an attack from a cassowary, which he said looked like an unusually stupid emu wearing a party hat but was actually one of the world's most dangerous birds. Growing up in Queensland, he'd got good at dodging crocodiles, too . . . although he was more concerned about crocodiles in uniform, dictating to civilians in war-torn climes.

While we talked, he didn't do the usual self-obsessed male monologue. He also asked me questions – perspicacious, sensitive questions, about my life, my childhood, my passions. After an hour or so, with cramp setting in, the doctor readjusted his sitting position. As he balanced himself, his hand brushed my flank, giving me an instant jolt of pleasure. My nipples tingled without permission, and I coughed to cover my embarrassment. Brody patted my back gently, and this time not only did my nipples tingle insubordinately but there was also a bit of a cooee from my nether regions. An involuntary shiver shimmied up my thighs and said hello to those eight thousand nerve endings.

Stop it! I ordered my loins. *You know how this turned out last time – mortal humiliation and the inability to walk past the pingpong table in case Wayve has given his mates a detailed description of his trek through your Amazonian rainforest.*

But it felt as though we had enough electricity between us to power the broken windsurfer not just back to the beach but on a record-breaking, round-the-world trip. Brody gave me a look that only just fell short of igniting my hair, and I felt myself moving towards his mouth. 'Wait.' I stopped abruptly. 'What about the breach of doctor–patient ethics?' I gulped.

'As we're going to drown at sea, does it really matter?' he said, smiling roguishly.

He moved towards me this time, but the board tilted and rocked, and we both nearly slid into the sea. And so, balanced on our board, we just sat and gazed at each other, holding hands. We gazed for so long and with such absorption that neither of us noticed that the tide had turned. It was bird song that alerted us to the fact that we'd drifted free of the riptide and were now floating towards the shore. A breeze scented with cinnamon and nutmeg tickled my face. From the trees came the most exotic chorus – birds carolling, frogs baritoning and insects percussing in a hot hum of happy greeting.

We dragged the board up under the trees then walked along a dappled track. The jungly hills quickly gave way to a fringe of civilisation. The doctor moved at a saunter, carrying himself casually, even languidly, despite the leg blade. He hailed a battered rust bucket driving down the road and paid some locals to take us back to the jetty.

I retrieved my stashed beach bag from behind the granite boulder, peeled off my wet board shorts and rashie, and slipped a shift over my swimming costume. Brody, meanwhile, explained to the water sports staff where to find his broken windsurfer, palming them a tip.

'What are you doing tomorrow?' I asked him, fizzing coquettishly as we walked towards the tender. Coquettish fizzing? Really? At my age? Who was I? Pussy Galore?

'Working, sadly.'

'Oh, well, in that case, I think I'm going to be feeling quite sick in the morning.'

'Ah, yes, and what ailment do you think you'll be contracting between now and then?' he asked with a cheeky grin.

'I don't know . . . a stubbed toe? Diphtheria? A vampire bite, maybe?'

As we walked along the jetty, Brody Quinn put his warm hand on my shoulder and an electric current zapped straight down my body and mowed a lightning bolt clear through my lady garden.

'You know it's totally unprofessional for a doctor to flirt with a patient,' he flirted.

'Well, I'll just have to *stop* getting sick, then.'

He then ran his hand down my bare arm, so, so slowly and softly and for such a long, lingering time, that when he finally pulled away I had to check that I still had my bikini bottoms on. Even though we were now on land, I felt more at sea than ever.

Brody gave a slow, honeyed smirk. 'Make sure you stay well, though, otherwise things will just get weird for you, me and my potential parole officer.'

After I caught my breath, I replied, 'Sure. In fact, I seem to be feeling one hundred per cent better already.'

18

By the next morning I'd come to my senses. The last time lust had triumphed over prudence, I'd ended up with a space-hopper for a labia and a fear of overhearing comments from cubs about my pudenda being awarded national park status. Clearly the windsurfer encounter could be explained away as a severe case of mutual sunstroke – our brains had simply broiled in the tropical heat.

When Brody rang my cabin, I told him, 'I need to talk to you about yesterday.'

'Yeah, I wanna talk about that too,' he said. Great – it seemed the good doctor had also come to his senses. I agreed to meet him on the quoits deck at the back of the ship. Nobody ever went there. Amber had ordered breakfast in bed – possibly the first such meal in her life – and Emerald had nicked out to the boutique to try on more strapless, asymmetrical, off-theshoulder, bodycon and bandage dresses; of late, my once-frumpy sister was having more costume changes per day than Cher at an arena gig. With my sisters otherwise engaged, it was the perfect opportunity for a rendezvous with the doctor to apply an emotional tourniquet.

Judging from what the doc had told me on the broken sail-board, both our wheels of fortune had run over rusty nails of late and gone very, very flat. There was no need for us to create an even bigger accident. My tummy-compass told me that getting together with Brody Quinn wouldn't just be a car crash but a head-on collision between two flammable oil tankers.

But when I pushed open the big, heavy deck door, Brody waved wildly, as though summoning rescue. He was leaning up against the rail, gazing out to sea. As I approached, he ran a hand through his turbulent hair. The gesture was oddly enchanting.

'I think I just saw a dugong. Have you ever seen a manatee? Sailors of yore thought that they were beautiful mermaids, which shows how long those guys must have been at sea,' he joked, nervously. Nerves, from the misanthropic medic? What was going on?

'So, what did you want to tell me?' I asked.

'Something weird happened this morning. When I woke, I was in a good mood. You may have noticed that I, um, have a gravitational pull towards melancholy. And then something else bizarre happened – I heard myself singing along to a song on the radio. It gets worse – I did a weird little dance in my cabin. This is very concerning behaviour. I mean, I must be coming down with something. I was trying to diagnose myself but then I thought that you might have the antidote, or may even be the cure?' The look he gave me was amused, sexy and tender. This was not what I'd been expecting. 'Anyway, what did you want to tell me?' he added.

There's something about the sea; the way you can inhale it and feel its transformative properties slipping into your bloodstream. I was standing near to him now, breathing in the lovely ocean scent – tangy, astringent and seductive. His half-smile made me desperate to touch him, to caress his neck or, even better, run my fingers down his tanned arms and lace my fingers into his capable, dexterous hands.

Instead of delivering my prepared speech, I found myself leaning in to him. Brody bunched my bright curls in his hand and drew me closer. And then, ever so slowly, he put his mouth on mine. His breath was sweet as caramel. I kissed him back and was soon floating upwards, brushing the clouds, light-headed and happy.

Whereas Harry was muscled, with big thighs, powerful shoulders and calloused hands – a durable man – Brody was lean and lithe, but wiry. There wasn't a hint of the gym here. No vanity pec-flexing. Just effortless and easy masculinity. There was a caged energy about him that set my pulse pounding. His fingernails were gnawed and his shoes scuffed, but he had a worldly, hard-won edge that excited me. And what excited me the most was his apparent longing for me. There was a certain priapic affability concerning his trouser area that was both flattering and compelling.

'You know I don't trust easily. And I've been burnt recently, as I told you, betrayed by someone I confided in – which is how I ended up losing a job I love. I swore off women after that. But there's something about you. I feel as though I've known you for a long time. That sounds ridiculous, right?'

No, I thought. The really ridiculous thing was that I felt the same way. Clearly the abrasive Mr-Darcy-repulse-and-infuriate trope doesn't only work in Regency novels and clichéd rom-coms. I promptly realised Jane Austen had been right all along.

'Sorry, Ruby, I keep interrupting you. What did you want

to say to me? The thing is,' he went on, not drawing breath, 'yesterday I felt something I haven't felt for ages. Hope. It was like finding an air pocket in a ship that's going down . . . It must be how prisoners feel when they walk out of the gates. Shit. You've got me mixing my metaphors now. Sorry, I interrupted you again. I'll shut up. If doctors talk, you know, we have to charge,' he said, eyes twinkling. 'What did you want to say to me?'

I wanted to tell him everything I was feeling – my qualms, the fact that I was unstable, nuts, possibly in the middle of a nervous bloody breakdown, dodging friends, alienating my kids, pretending to have cancer, lying to my sisters – that, in fact, the Sphinx's riddle was less confusing than I was to myself right now – but I felt the words float away.

When I said nothing, he kissed me again – a kiss that left me misty with desire. He moved in front of me this time and leant me back against the railing, and kissed me for a long, luscious time. Kissing Brody was the most aerobic thing I'd ever done. His kisses required a lifeguard.

What was happening? Who was this man? In between kisses, never letting go, he kept opening up. He told me more stories about his time in Africa, when he'd escaped vigilantes by running through a forest fire, and, another time, by wading through rapids. And then there was the day out jogging when he didn't quite escape.

He also specialised in slightly crooked smiles and possessed a velvet touch that could make a woman's skin tremble. He was wild, reckless, anarchic, anti-authoritarian and, yes, he also had a gloomy, pessimistic, Eeyore streak, so at odds with the kindness and humanitarianism he displayed in his job. As a doctor, he'd devoted his life to those who were suffering in conflict zones – apart from the time he'd 'accidentally' castrated a warlord rapist, of course.

Nor was he gloomy all the time. When we sat in the deck-chairs and ordered tea, his medical anecdotes made me laugh so hard that at one point Earl Grey shot out of my nose. Not my best look, especially as the warm wind was already making a comedy of my coiffure, but it only made us both laugh harder. And then there was the fact that I felt I had so much to say to him.

Best of all was his penchant for puns. When it was time for Brody to report for duty in the medical centre, he called our parting from the quoits deck 'quoit-us interruptus'.

How, I wondered, was I to convey all this to my sceptical sisters?

'I don't know what this is,' Brody said, his hand on the heavy deck door. 'But whatever it is or isn't, you can't tell your sisters.'

'But I tell my sisters everything.' *Well*, I thought with a sharp pang of guilt, *not quite everything*. 'Maybe this is all a ruse on your part just to get your severance pay,' I joked.

But for once Brody did not smile back. 'Getting romantically involved with a passenger is a "chicken or beef" offence – as in, that's what the air steward offers you when you board the first flight home in disgrace, because your contract will be terminated.'

'No redundancy package?'

'Shit, no. In fact, I would probably have to pay them hush money. Or face getting struck off. I don't mind getting the sack – in fact, I hope I do – but I don't want to lose my medical licence. The board code of conduct prohibits relationships between doctors and patients, for obvious reasons. And, I hear that prison libraries are chronically short of Hemingway novels like *The Middle-aged Man and the Sea*,' he said, his eyes gleaming with playfulness once more.

'Is that right? Well, you could go on the run, but those police composite sketches can make a man look ten years older, which would be awfully cruel for a bloke your age,' I teased him.

'Ha-ha. You'll pay for that later,' he said – a fairly innocuous comment that, for some reason, set my nipples on fire again.

As he dashed off to work, I tried to get my head around what had just happened. Maybe I'd started my menopause and the doctor was my hot flush? Maybe he was a fantasist, and all his heroics were invented? Maybe he thought I was getting divorced and was after my settlement payout? He could be one of those guys he'd warned me about, who could suss out a woman's bank balance with one look. This gave me pause. Because, come on, what red-blooded man could fancy *me* – a middle-aged, middle-class, boring suburban mum? I mean, not even my shadow wanted to follow me. Clearly the bloke was self-medicating from his doctor's bag. And, anyway, wasn't my new motto 'All men are guilty until proven innocent?' I made a vow to break off these shenanigans. I would call him after his shift and make it clear.

And yet, catching my reflection in a nearby porthole, I noticed that I was beaming like I'd just had a vitamin B12 shot.

19

The Mexican monarch butterfly migration, the synchronous fireflies of North America, Chile's flowering desert, the migration of the Christmas Island red crab, the treacherous odyssey of the Serengeti wildebeest – there are many great wonders in this world, but nothing amazed me more than the day I saw my sister Amber eat a carbohydrate. Not just one bite but a whole plate of gnocchi's worth, followed by tiramisu, a Golden Opulence sundae, and two chocolate-truffle profiteroles. This was unbelievable behaviour from a woman whose dessert habits usually stretched no further than a lick of a sultana with a cup of skimmed air. The woman who'd spent her life lecturing the rest of us on the weighty subject of calorie intake, a monotonous mantra involving orders to take omegas and drink activated charcoal smoothies, was now mainlining cake and cocktails.

There were other weird and wonderful things happening, too. By the second week of our cruise, Amber had packed away all her make-up and chic summer capsule wardrobe in du jour shades and taken to slobbing about in Emerald's board shorts and Birkenstocks. By week three she'd stopped shaving her armpits and brushing her hair. Catching a glimpse of her one morning, I thought it might be time to schedule an audition for her in a reboot of *The Witches of Eastwick*.

'I've discovered my middle-age superpower: I'm invisible! The cloak of invisibility is upon me. And it's so fucking liberating,' she exclaimed.

She'd also started to swear with relish, and her shoulders now shook when she laughed. And when Amber laughed hysterically, it wasn't long before she started snorting in the most deliciously unladylike manner. Our mother would have been horrified.

Emerald, on the other hand, who was known for looking as though she'd dressed in the dark choosing items from a charity bin, had started sashaying around the ship in her designer clobber with the kind of walk that should always be accompanied by the brass section of a big band. She'd restyled her hair, too, dropped a few kilos and looked ready to run a marathon – or she would be if her feet were not clad in dainty, bejewelled sling-backs. Emerald had always berated Amber and me for torturing our poor tootsies in high-heels – she said it was akin to Chinese foot binding and other archaic cruelties – but now she clackityclacked in vertiginous stilettos everywhere she went.

'Well, I have been getting a lot of exercise,' Emerald explained, flicking the loose elastic of her shorts as we took up our sunbathing spots on the pool deck. 'Not from bloody gym sessions or dieting, ugh,' she said, grimacing, 'but from toy-boy dodging. Hiding from a cub you've shagged involves a lot of ducking and diving, which is incredibly aerobic.'

I knew what she meant. That very morning, on the way to meet Brody, I'd glimpsed Wayve on the lido deck and immediately dropped to the ground and crawled out of sight, keeping my head down as if I were dodging enemy fire.

'Oh, god, don't look up. Here comes one now,' Emerald gasped.

I paused in my application of sunscreen to scan the row of board-shorted cavaliers barrelling our way. 'Which one?'

'The bloke I kicked out the other night, remember? I could put up with the tattoo on his bicep that read *Death Before Dishouner* – spelt D-I-S-H-O-U-N-E-R, I kid you not – but not the tat on his chest, which read *Never Don't Give Up*.' She lifted her open book to an inch below her eyes, watching his approach like a detective on a stakeout.

'Oh, yes.' I cringed, laughing. 'That's definitely a grammatical faux pas too far.'

'Couldn't he have just inked *I'm an idiot* on his forehead in a magic marker?' Amber suggested.

'Exactly. Anyway, he keeps coming back for more. I've rejected him three times now, quite vociferously. I'm "ghosting" him, I believe is the parlance, and he's hoping I'll "zombie" him, which means continuing where you left off with someone you've ghosted, apparently.'

Emerald pulled her sunhat down and buried her face in her zoology book, which, in terms of camouflage, proved as effective as a bikie hiding out in a nunnery. A toned hunk peeled away from his pals, strode up with the gait of a horse wrangler and placed one thonged foot on the end of Emerald's sun lounger. This vantage point offered Amber and me a direct line of sight up the leg of his board shorts, which is how we discovered that he was going commando.

'You're ghostin' me, aren't ya, ya stuck-up cow?'

'Well, as a vet, I have saved many a calf with this very hand.' Emerald fluttered her freshly lacquered fingers in his direction. 'So, that's not really an insult to me, darl, more of a job description.'

'Bitch!' the big flummoxed bloke replied, demonstrating that the sun protection factor of his sunscreen was higher than his IQ. 'You just used me an' that.'

'It's a cougar cruise, kiddo. That is kinda the point. Just doing what it says on the box.'

'Literally,' I said, sotto voce, prompting a stifled giggle from Amber, who was supine on her sun lounger. That was another thing that had changed: Amber, who usually avoided the sun like a vampire, had taken to tanning.

'And I won't be haunting you, either . . ."Haunting",' Emerald clarified for her perplexed sisters, 'means getting back in touch after a long period of silence in a noncommittal way, by following the guy on Twitter or watching their Snapchat stories.'

This exchange made me feel so much better about Brody's 'whaling games', 'reheats' and 'freshies' revelations. After the young stud had harrumphed away, I said, 'Why don't you give these guys marks out of ten and score them. You know, ratings on looks, performance, et cetera. I'm sure they're keeping score on us . . .'

Emerald chuckled. 'You seem to have forgotten that I'm a vet, Rubes. Someone will call the RSPCA and report me for cruelty to dumb animals.'

While I laughed with relief, Amber looked up over the spine of her latest unreadable, Booker Prize–winning hardback – one of those interchangeably turgid tomes with *Death, Famine* or *Road* in the title, and said, 'Emmy . . .'

At first I thought my middle sister was about to open up a discussion on the American awards for excellence in television, but then I realised, amazed, that she was addressing our big sis by an affectionate abbreviation she hadn't utilised since childhood. 'If you're so obsessed with grammar and spelling, why don't you join us for the quiz this afternoon? With our combined expertise, the Ryan girls will win hands-down.'

'Thanks, possum, but I'm not really a quiz person.'

'Trying new things is the best way to stay young. You never know what's inside you.'

'Oh, but I do, darl – Brendon, Cillian, Guy, Joaquin, Shane, Zane, River and Hanif.' Emerald laughed. 'And I know what's inside you, Amber – almond croissants, spaghetti carbonara, crème brûlée and cake. It's so great to see you getting an appetite for life.'

'Literally,' I interjected once more. 'When we came aboard you were so thin, your pyjamas had, like, one stripe.'

'It's the chocolate soufflés. They're like eating clouds,' Amber said, dreamily. 'I don't know what's come over me, but I feel as though for years I've subsisted on a diet of anxiety and insecurity, my hunger only occasionally assuaged by the smallest gulp of attention from my husband and kids. But not anymore! Now I'm stuffing my face so regularly at mealtimes I need to get a cab from the dining room back to the cabin.'

'All *I'm* craving is a hunky spunk on a bed of lettuce; or, rather, matelot en croute.' Emerald licked her lips.

'Ah, the joy of being cooked for,' Amber sighed, blissfully. 'And cleaned for.'

'So true. Any woman who says she gets high on housework has inhaled way too much cleaning product,' I agreed.

'The closest I've come to housework is giving my cabin a sweeping glance.' Amber beamed serenely.

'And the only bucket we've seen is the one with the champagne bottle in it,' Emerald added.

'I have raised the laziest kids,' Amber said, slamming her book shut. 'I don't know how I've done it. But do you know what I just realised? I haven't FaceTimed them in days. Not even a WhatsApp message or a text.'

'Fan-bloody-tastic! Now, promise me you'll give up your tutor too,' Emerald lectured. 'As if being a parent isn't stressful enough! What, with balancing meals, supervising digital detoxes, and discouraging tattoos, side-boob, piercings and the perception that the *Love Island* contestants are role models.'

'You know what? You're right. I really don't have to add tutoring on omniscient narrators and quadratic sequences into my already over-booked schedule,' Amber concurred.

'Mind you,' I joked, 'I do have one burning question for your tutor – when did parenting get so hard? The exam is multiple choice. Are you an over-anxious parent? a) Yes. b) Yes.'

'What parents desperately need is a lesson in how to chill out about parenting,' Emerald said. 'Let me tutor you in how to forget about being perfect. First, pour yourself a big cocktail. Second, put on your headphones so you can't hear your whiny kids' demands . . .'

'Then pop your feet up and dive into some "continuous prose", otherwise known as a novel,' I finished the thought.

'Speaking of which, I'm so sick of this pretentious crap,' Amber said, and with that, flung the huge hardback across the deck.

I'd never seen her do something so reckless. 'Well done, sis.' I applauded, amazed. 'Go to the top of the class.'

'Oh, quick! Look at that albatross,' Emerald said, pointing out the magnificent bird, with its massive wing span, gliding effortlessly above the boat's bow. 'The babies leave the nest and fly to sea and don't land for two years. Unlike our kids, who never really leave the frickin' nest. My kids might be away at uni, but they still bring home all their dirty laundry and expect me to iron it.'

'This break has been such bliss it's made me think about flying the nest to escape my own kids,' Amber admitted.

'Well, I didn't think a cruise would float my boat,' Emerald confessed, 'but I haven't thought about work once. If only we didn't have to go back. Why don't we just take a gap year, girls? Gap years are so wasted on the young.'

'Um, Em, having trysts with twenty-two-year-olds *is* your gap year,' I reminded her.

Both my sisters spluttered with laughter, their earthy chortles sounding like cars on gravel. When they'd calmed down, Emerald said, 'Okay, so *I'm* rediscovering my mojo, getting fit, not thinking about work and reinventing myself as a smoking hot sex goddess. I had a facial, for god's sake! And wore gold hotpants to the Big Band Bash in the Molecular Bar. Me! And Amber's eating and tanning and letting her hair down – her chin hair – and having "me time", while wishing she'd sent her kids off to boarding school the minute the umbilical cords were cut, and, I can't believe it, wearing leggings and flip-flops . . . But what about you, Ruby? What's new with you?'

Amber's eyes narrowed, her gaze quizzical and calculating. 'Yes, you look different somehow. Are you feeling okay?' she asked, anxiously.

'Me? Oh, yes. Fine. I'm just worrying about the flak we're going to cop from Mum when we get back,' I said quickly. 'She's sent me a couple of extremely curt emails. We'll have to buy matching Mum-proof flak jackets.'

'What's that on your chin?' It was Emerald's turn to scrutinise me now. 'Is that beard rash? You've been snogging some love god, haven't you, you, cheeky minx!'

My lips felt as though they'd been novocained. 'W-w-what?' I stammered. 'No, I haven't.' Oh, god, I was lying to my sisters again. I'd become so adept at lying, I really only had two options: join Her Majesty's Secret Service or become a conservative party politician. But I'd promised Brody – and I was clearly in enough trouble with the karma police as it was. I broke out into a sweat that had nothing to do with the tropical sun. I felt like an adolescent, all angst-riddled and blush-ridden. 'Must be a snorkelling mask rash,' I ad-libbed, rolling onto my stomach so I could bury my face in my towel.

'I didn't know you needed a snorkel to "go down"!' Emerald jested.

'I dunno what you're talking about . . .' *Liar, liar, pants on fire!* How many pairs of pants had I immolated on this cruise, I vaguely wondered.

'Now that you've rolled over, I can read something imprinted onto your back. Hmm, what does it say? *Life boat cover – remove only in emergencies.*'

'Really?' I momentarily fell for Amber's ruse and rolled onto my back again.

'I was only joking, Ruby, but you're blushing bright red. So, you *have* been making out with someone?'

'No! It's not stubble rash. It's just . . . it's just . . . an overexuberant facial scrub.' I was a bad sister. I should be made to wear a large badge identifying me as a 'sister trainee', I scolded myself.

A ruckus by the pool saved me from further interrogation by my nosy siblings. Not that I didn't want to talk about Brody with them, despite his warnings; I just didn't know what I wanted to say. Anyway, there was nothing *to* say, because I was ending it, before I fell flat on my face – well, fell flat on both of my visages, because I'd become so two-faced of late I was positively bi-facial.

'*Right, laaadeeez!*' boomed a familiar American-accented voice over the tannoy. I recognised the counterfeit buoyancy of Brent, the entertainment officer, and spied him at the edge of the pool. It seemed to me that nobody could speak that enthusiastically without Class A narcotics being involved. '*It's time for the SPLASH Competition. So, tell me, ladeez, do you like to get wet?*' he said lasciviously.

A few of the tipsier female passengers whooped accordingly.

'*Well, I'm about to make you very, very wet indeed. I'd like our heftiest males to report poolside, pronto. Points will be given for water displacement. If your belly flop wets the ladies on the upper balcony, double points. A little pathetic squirt that gets none of the ladies wet won't get you any points. This is a competition where size does count, don't you agree, laaadeeez?*'

The cocktail-clutching women clustered around the pool squawked their inebriated agreement.

'*And, laaadeeez, I'll be needing you to hold up fingers for points, ranging from one to five. It ain't gonna be pretty. Rough seas poolside, people! To kick-start proceedings, I've drafted in a few of our more substantial crew members. Give it up for BORIS and FLABBA!'*

On cue, two of the crew shambled forward, wearing bathrobes and clownfish caps à la *Finding Nemo*.

'Okay, you big bruisers, show us what you've got.'

With painful reluctance, both draftees sheepishly shed their robes. Barrel-chested and bulging of stomach, their massive groins were incongruously clad in teeny, weeny, bright red and white budgie-smugglers. Shuffling self-consciously towards the diving boards, both crew members looked as though they'd rather endure a freak wave, an iceberg, hull flooding, a full-on pirate invasion or Robinson Crusoe–type marooning than face this public humiliation.

'Boris! Step forward, bro.' The tallest, biggest bloke trundled to the pool edge. *'Boris is one of our sous chefs. So, how have you been training for your belly flop, dude?'*

'Well, I've been eating a lot,' he replied, half-heartedly.

'Not your own cooking, I bet!' Brent scoffed.

The big chef looked genuinely baffled and hurt. But the entertainment officer had turned his attention to clownfish number two.

'So, Flabba, as one of our valuable deckhands, can you tell us what your secret is for keeping in such fine physical condition?' Brent condescended.

'Rum and cokes,' Flabba joked, trying to be convivial.

'Great. So, you already have brain damage, that's good – no need to alert health and safety! Right, are there no other takers for the splash competition?' Brent gave a cursory glance around the crowd. *'Okay then, let's get started.'* Brent climbed to his observational perch on the lower diving board. A blast of Carole King's 'I Feel the Earth Move'

sounded from the speakers. '*Now, if there's a tie, we'll have a "sudden death mode", where I choose the prettiest ladies on board to push you in simultaneously, then see which woman gets the wettest.*'

'God,' Emerald said, leaning up on her elbows for a better look at the entertainment officer's peacockish display. 'This wet analogy is making me dry.'

'Yes,' I muttered. 'I'm pretty sure that bloke's only ever had one long-term lover – his right hand.'

A crestfallen Boris climbed onto the high diving board and flopped in first, sending up a tidal wave of water to drench the front row of women, who squealed playfully. Boris emerged moments later, his pale belly pink from the impact.

'*I didn't realise it was whale-spotting season!*' The entertainment officer wisecracked, showcasing flawless white veneers. '*Only, Boris didn't get that way eating krill, did you, duuuuude? Ladies, your verdict please.*'

The audience of tipsy females hollered and hooted their piña-colada-fuelled encouragement, holding varying numbers of digits aloft.

'*Right, Flabba. Your turn. I want* pain. *We're looking for bruised nipples. I want you bright red from your Adam's apple to your ankle, and all the dangly bits between, bro.*'

Flabba reluctantly ascended the ladder to the top diving board then propelled himself forward. Midair, he suddenly jerked into a half-dive in an effort to soften his entry into the water.

'*Oh, shame, Flabba, shame. There's a technical term for what you did. "The butt-pucker". You chickened out, dude! Now, do it again, and this time I want a double tsunami with a twist.*'

The reluctant, sodden contestant number two was about to climb back onto the diving board when an angry voice reverberated across the deck. Passengers swivelled in the direction of the commotion. My heart did a little tap dance when I realised it was Brody in his Listerine-green medical uniform.

'Hey, bud, release these crew members immediately.' Brody snatched up some towels lying on the end of a sun lounger and chucked them at the shanghaied, dripping men.

'*What? Why?*' the furious entertainment officer demanded, all charm evaporating from his voice.

'It's a breach of health and safety rules. If there's an emergency, the crew's on call. Imagine if some poor guest requires mouth-to-mouth resuscitation and wakes up to find herself in a lip-lock with a half-naked clownfish,' Brody improvised, climbing up onto the lower dive board to address his adversary face to face. 'She'll be psychologically scarred for life. Besides, both these men have abdominal issues. I need them excused on medical grounds.'

The two half-drowned, dragooned crew members seized their moment. Boris and Flabba swiftly disappeared below decks.

'*Oh, for Pete's sake.*' The entertainment officer gnashed his cosmetic orthodontia, increasing his resemblance to a piranha. '*You are such an a-hole, Quinn, you know that? Getting the crew involved is naval tradition.*'

'So is administering one hundred lashes with the cat-o'-ninetails, but we don't do that anymore,' the doctor retorted. 'Mind you, you'd probably misinterpret that as foreplay.'

And then the medic gave a little bounce on the diving board. It wasn't a big movement, but it was enough to propel the entertainment officer off his perch on the end of the board, arse-first into the pool. Brent's ungainly, scrambling, sprawling fall, landing right next to the wall, created a wave of water big enough to knock two women right off the edge of the pool.

'Oops!' the doctor said.

Emerald and Amber cheered with delight and held up their hands, giving the doctor a perfect five.

I surreptitiously held up both hands – because Doctor Brody Quinn was a perfect ten.

20

I am going to sleep with him, I told myself as I feigned fatigue, claimed a headache and waved my sisters ashore for a full day's fun in Noumea. (My loving but competitive sisters fought over which one of them would stay to take care of me, which only amplified my guilt, but I finally fobbed them off. I know, I know, straight to jail, do not pass Go.)

I am going to sleep with him, I told myself as I shaved my armpits and legs and moisturised every inch of my flesh.

I am going to sleep with him, I told myself as I *pfffted* with one spray and *pfffted* with another.

I am going to sleep with him, I told myself as I put on my laciest, sexiest, most temptingly sheer peekaboo underwear, purchased from the onboard boutique.

I am going to sleep with him, I told myself as I drew the curtains in the cabin and swept the ornamental pillows off the bed.

I am going to sleep with him, I told myself as I checked my phone one last time to make sure there was still no communication from the absentee infidel, otherwise known as my soon-to-beex-husband. *I am going to sleep with him*, I said, flicking on the 'Do not disturb' sign.

I am going to sleep with him, I told myself as I opened the door at his knock to find the ship's doctor standing there, all tousle-haired and gimlet-eyed.

'I can't do it,' were the first words out of my mouth after he'd crossed my bedroom threshold. 'I'm too nervous.'

'Oh, good. Me too.' The doctor sighed with relief.

'Don't you like sex?'

'Of course I like sex. It's a pastime I rank just above breathing. It's just that I don't want to break up a marriage. Are you sure it's over with your husband?'

'Yes . . . No . . . I don't know. I don't know what I'm doing. This is ridiculous. I'm acting like a teenager, except with wrinkles instead of pimples.'

We stood in silence for an agonising minute.

'Your sunburn looks a bit less hideous today,' he finally said.

Insofar as I'm aware, no one had ever used a second-degree burn as a flirtatious manoeuvre before. If this were a rom-com, Brody would have placed his hands around my waist and drawn me so close I'd be able to inhale the musky spice of his skin, taste his warm breath on my face and feel the pulse of lust stir in him as he gnawed his way through my lingerie with his teeth. But we weren't in a film. We were two strangers, one of whom was still married and sneaking around behind her sisters' backs, and the other, well, a misanthropic, possibly psychopathic doctor who'd butchered a man in surgery and had lost his leg to a landmine or a crocodile or a crazed girlfriend.

But then he looked at me with those piercing eyes and that crooked smile, and there it was – the pang of lust. Pang is putting it mildly. Calling it a pang is like saying that a meteor hurtling towards earth is only a little life-threatening.

'The trouble is, I've been married to the same man for twenty-eight years. Harry was my boyfriend at school, for god's sake. I've only been to bed with one other bloke since I got married, and that was a total disaster. It's made me worry about how I look naked. I mean, I have had two children . . .'

'Hey, I only have half a leg, so I think I trump you there. A stump trump.'

'Okay, true. But the light's so bad in here, I can't see if I have any chin hairs, even with the illuminated make-up mirror.'

'You have lights around your mirror?' the doctor asked, amazed.

'Yes, it's on the dressing table.'

'You have a dressing table?'

'Yes, over there by the coffee machine.'

'You have a coffee machine? I'm dying for a cup. Where's the milk?'

'In the fridge.'

'You have a fridge?'

'It's by the walk-in wardrobe.'

'You have a walk-in wardrobe?'

'It's next to the bathroom.'

'You have a *bath*?' Brody poked his head into my marbled ensuite, adding, 'With bubble bath and expensive conditioner and a shower cap? Well, not anymore you don't.' As he stretched up to retrieve the little bottles of luxurious lotions from my shower shelf, a band of stomach showed between his jeans and his T-shirt – a taut, muscled band – and I was suddenly lighting up all over like a Christmas tree.

As Brody pocketed the toiletries, I joked, lamely, 'I think you're more aroused by my cabin than my curves.'

'Sorry. My shower's so small, I just soap the walls and spin around. The cabin's so tiny I have to draw up a roster with myself to determine which days I can breathe. It ain't so glamorous below decks, I can assure you. And I'm one of the luckier ones. As a doctor I get my own berth.'

We stood facing each other awkwardly once more.

'Look, forget the coffee. Do you want to go on deck and get a cocktail?' I asked. 'Or . . .?'

Brody ran his fingertips gently down my arm. 'I think "*or*" would kinda hit the spot.'

'The G spot, I hope. After all, you are a doctor, right?'

The doctor cleared his throat and would have said something witty, I'm sure, except my tongue was down there already. Then Brody's hands were on my hips. Not the way Harry grabbed me, like a drunken octopus, but with purpose and passion. And then it was as if someone had pulled the pin from a hand grenade. We tore at each other's clothes and scrambled onto the bed. I hadn't felt this kind of urgency since I'd been at the front of the queue for the Boxing Day sales. I yanked off his T-shirt and jeans while he ripped off my knickers. I tugged at his boxers and then he took off his prosthetic leg – okay, not your average bit of foreplay, but at this stage I couldn't have cared if he revealed a pair of cloven hooves.

I could no longer speak, but what I lacked in lucidity I made up for in enthusiastic moaning and gasping. I felt like an astronaut who'd crash-landed on an unexplored planet. It was a sensation I vaguely remembered: bubbly, aerated, light, sparkly – sequined, even. What was it? *Desire*. Ah, yes, that's what it was. Hot, red, raw, half-crazed lust. There was no time to worry about stray chin hairs or belly stretch marks, because he'd pulled me on top of him and I was shimmering. I felt my spine arch and heard a long, low, slow moan, which, I realised with a shock, was emanating from my own lips.

As the reverberations shuddered through me, I couldn't remember the last time I'd experienced anything like this. It felt like rediscovering a long-lost talent from my youth; like executing a perfect pool backflip, shinnying up a tree or cartwheeling endlessly across a green field.

The range of sound effects available to me as a human seemed inadequate, and I wished I were a bell so I could ring and chime and peal out my pleasure.

I awoke, mid-afternoon, to find myself entwined with the doctor, our bodies warm and luxuriant beneath the sheets. I poked my head out of the blanket.

Brody, a blur of messed hair and briny bed smells, smiled and reached over to smooth my hair back from my face. Then his hands moved down onto my breasts, ever so gently.

I'd always thought that my sex life with Harry was good. He was quite sensitive in bed, meaning that he hugged me afterwards – well, until his arm went numb and he rolled me off – which was practically a Byron love poem in the Insular Peninsular.

But this – this was something totally different. Parts of my body that I didn't even know I had were speaking to me. I was like a pinball machine of pleasure, with lights and whistles and bells and flippers going off frantically all over.

I sighed with longing, but suddenly broke free from his kiss.

'Wait! I've got to tell you the truth.'

Brody looked at me with wary intensity. 'Oh, Christ. You're not really estranged from your husband?'

'No. Not that.'

'Phew, okay . . . You caught herpes on that one-night stand – the gift that keeps on giving? Or crotch critters? This is a floating STD zoo, you know.'

'No. And, yuck, is it?'

'Um . . . you're really a bloke?' His eyes glimmered mischievously.

'No! The truth is, I don't write for a major national newspaper. I write for a local rag. I pen groundbreaking pieces about a kitten that choked on a mouse, a man who got stuck in a toilet or a patient who was given a pillowcase instead of a hospital gown.'

'Okay. Time for me to tell you the truth,' Brody said, with equal fervency. 'I didn't lose my leg jogging. I was staggering home, pissed, from a staff party, and wandered off the path into an area that hadn't been de-mined. So, it was my own stupid fault. Mind you, if they instigated random drug and alcohol testing of medics in conflict zones, there would be no Doctors Without Borders left.' He reached for me again. 'Moving on . . .'

'Wait,' I said once more. 'Orgasms this great deserve a good soundtrack and a swipe of lipstick. Here, choose a song.' I handed him my iPhone while I leapt out of bed to reapply lip gloss.

'Hmm . . . The Doors, "Light My Fire"? What about "Sexual Healing"? No, it's gotta be "Whole Lotta Love", Led Zeppelin.'

'I was thinking something classical . . . Zeppelin are a bit, well, pedestrian.'

'Pedestrian? Sure – and the pyramids are just a pile of rock.' Brody was going to expound on this theory, but just then I slipped back into his arms. 'I would pick apart that pathetic prejudice of yours, but I've never won an argument with a naked woman . . . So, you choose.'

As I fiddled with my phone to find the soft, wafting Ravel I craved, Brody did a little light tuning of his own. Forget Spotify – my nipples were soon so erect I could have picked up Classic FM. His mouth then moved slowly down my body, and stayed there for a long time. Clearly, if Brody ever gave up the medical profession, he could definitely win a medal for breaking the world underwater endurance record. And, I was pleased to note, there was nothing cheap about the doctor's aftershave.

The next time I woke, the sunset had turned on its dimmer switch and the day was dying slowly, turning from gold to russet to an aubergine bruise. The sea shushed on the side of the boat – *shh, shh, shh*, as though conspiring in our secret.

I felt so contented and happy that even the palm fronds on the hills outside the window seemed to be waving in a friendly way. Hell, even the bend in the bananas in the bowl on the coffee table made it look as though they were smiling.

'Wow,' was all I could say. 'Is it like this for you every time? I mean, is this . . . normal? It's not normal for me. But maybe you make every woman feel like this?' I blathered, intrigued and overwhelmed.

Brody raised his head and met my eyes. His eyes were wide and seemed to shine with delight. 'No. It's not normal at all.'

Then this is something, I thought. *This is really something.*

I smiled too, a big, radiant beam, like a cartoon of a besotted teenybopper.

What was happening? This was supposed to be a transient, fleeting, you-make-me-feel-alive-again fling thing, not a proper romance. He kissed me once more, and I slipped into the moment like a warm bath.

Oh, fudge, I thought as I went under. *Oh, fuckity, fuckity, fudge fuck.*

21

'*Attention: woman overboard!*' That was the announcement I kept waiting to hear over the ship's public address system, because I'd dived in the deep end, with no life jacket. It was as though my vag had its own private sat-nav system – a twat-nav, which kept leading me back to Brody against all my better judgement.

The following week was a nonstop sexual gymkhana. We had sex everywhere and anywhere – standing up, backwards, on the shuffleboard deck, on his surgery gurney, in my cabin, in his cabin, once in a lifeboat and twice in the morgue. 'It's too public. I couldn't possibly . . . I couldn't . . . I can't . . . Okay, I can . . . Oh, right, I clearly *am*!' became my catch cry.

Time ceased to exist between us. All I could think about was the spicy, delicious smell of Brody's skin. And all he could think about, he said, was unwrapping me with all the breathless anticipation and excitement of a kid on his birthday.

I felt haloed in happiness. When Brody kissed my neck, I floated so far above cloud nine I could have waved to the International Space Station.

Who had I become? I didn't know myself. I was making love like a wild hippie girl, with my hair flinging around. I was also sneaking around behind my sisters' backs. If they thought I was behaving oddly, they put it down to my 'condition' – which I still hadn't got around to debunking. I know. Bad, bad sister! I wanted to confess but had left it so late now that it was doubly embarrassing – 'Sorry dearest sisters. But you know me! I was going to procrastinate but didn't quite get around to it.'

Justifying my behaviour to myself required contortionist levels of cognitive flexibility – let alone being able to explain it to anyone else. Mind you, my sisters didn't seem perturbed. That's because they were blissfully busy with their own pursuits – Emerald swinging from the chandelier with a toy boy between her teeth and Amber obsessing over both the quiz and the cuisine.

After breakfasting with Emerald and Amber I would pretend to have spa appointments, then would meet Brody between his patients. After dinner with my sisters, I would feign a yawn and stretch luxuriously, all the sooner to get back to him. Boris and Flabba (whose real name, I had discovered, was Joshua), the loyal crew members Brody had saved from public humiliation at the hands of the creepy entertainment officer, happily acted as lookouts and decoys when needed.

After having sex all night, I would creep out of Brody's cabin at dawn, vowing not to have sex with him again until I'd sorted my life out – I was, after all, still a married woman – then, ten minutes later, I'd be back, knickers at half-mast, legs wrapped around his waist, my whole body a quivering wreck. *Self-discipline, that's what I'm famous for*, I'd chide myself while nibbling his neck. But somehow all that mattered was that Brody keep on doing what he was doing. And then do it again.

When we weren't together, we texted like infatuated teenagers.

Brody: *How do I love thee? Let me count the ways: 1. From behind. 2. From the side. 3. . . .'*

Me: *That was mind-blowingly good. I'm coming straight back to give you a standing ovation.*

Brody: *Meeting you is the best thing that's ever happened to me. I feel as if I've been shot in the backside by a rainbow. Jesus, Ruby. I think I'm falling for you.*

Me: *Thank god. I was beginning to worry that all of this hot sex was for nothing.*

My reply to this message was flippant, but when I read that he was 'falling for me' my heart did such a massive leap I thought either there was a kangaroo hiding out in my bra, or that I was having palpitations and needed an air ambulance. Or that I was falling for him too.

Of course you're not in love, I lectured myself. Not in the least. I'm not discombobulated in any way, shape or form. After all, I always floss my ears, run a comb through my teeth, spritz my pits with hairspray and bouffe up my hair with a spray-on deodorant offering twelve-hour protection.

But, if what Brody and I were doing was so, so wrong, then why did it feel so, so good? Falling in love is like going to the doctor and being told that you need to put *on* weight. And who wouldn't love that?

In the tender light of Brody's gruff adoration, I felt luminous. The doctor seemed to treasure me, despite my pathetic journalistic career writing stories more likely to litter the ground than break it. He seemed to cherish me despite my citing the 'five ingredients' cookbook as my culinary bible. He liked me even though I was a paid-up member of Underachievers Anonymous. He even liked waking up next to me in the morning, when my hair was sticking up in all directions, with yesterday's mascara smeared under my eyes. The deranged idiot seemed to adore me in spite of everything.

'I feel like a rescued mountaineer clinging to a Saint Bernard dog, with its brandy barrel,' he said, one day, post coitus.

'A dog. Thanks. That's an analogy I'll treasure,' I taunted. 'I'm also very handy for sniffing luggage at airports.'

'No, what I mean is, you've rescued me from cynicism. I'd stopped believing in people. I've been betrayed too often, and by people close to me. I've seen too much. Man's inhumanity to man and all that. The fickleness of fate on the front line is grim – cuddling dying babies, or stitching up mutilated bodies only for them to be put back into the battlefield to get blown up all over again. It takes its toll. I kept a kind of mask on at all times. But somehow you got under my defences, Ruby Ryan. I don't think you realise what a huge thing it is for me to trust you.'

Something cracked open in him then, and I saw straight through to his heart.

'I dunno,' he continued. 'I feel as though life is making something up to me; that the universe is apologising, sort of. It sounds self-absorbed, I know, but it's as if god's kinda quickly glanced up from all that warmongering in Syria and Afghanistan to throw me a bone.'

Fondness spilt and rippled across his face. With his tender fingertips, he then played me like a keyboard.

'I am awake, right?' I whimpered, surrendering to the pleasure.

But was I? It was just all so magical – sailing through the opalescent ocean, phosphorescence flashing in the bow waves, the Milky Way sprawling above us, moonlight shimmering on the waves . . . It was a midsummer's night dream. Perhaps I was drugged, like Titania? He did have access to the pharmacy, after all. Was the doc spiking my drinks? Was that the explanation for how I'd been hijacked by my libido?

But our attraction wasn't just physical. We talked about everything, delighting in shared favourite music, authors, films, poets and box sets, as well as alike politics and world views. Both 'recovering Catholics', we swapped memories from our church-dodging, free-range childhoods, me running wild by the sea, Brody running wild in the bush. Our conversation thrummed and trilled around us – it was a symphony of chat. I just had so much I wanted to say to him, and vice versa.

He made me laugh, too, with his medical anecdotes, like one about some kids who had broken into a house and snorted a white powder they found, then fell ill because what they had thought was cocaine turned out to be the cremated remains of the house owner's father and his two Great Danes.

And then there was the couple rescued from floods outside Brisbane after surfing down a swollen river on an inflatable sex doll. They thought it'd be fun, until the doll snagged on a tree and they were marooned there overnight, clinging to its deflating plastic appendage. Brody treated them for cuts and bruises and hypothermia, while also explaining why blow-up dolls are not an approved flotation device.

Even better, his death-by-cunnilingus tale. Brody had

saved a woman who had tried to kill her husband by putting poison in her vagina and then asking him to perform oral sex on her. The intended victim said he became suspicious when he noticed an unfamiliar odour emanating from his wife's coochie. The woman, clearly a criminal mastermind, didn't know that vaginas are porous. Realising that his wife was probably absorbing a majority of the poison intended for him, the husband very kindly brought her to the hospital.

'And they say chivalry is dead!' I laughed.

I reciprocated with tales of my less-than-illustrious journalistic career, with its many comedic mishaps, concluding candidly – 'Trouble is, I thought that by now I'd be getting helicoptered in to book festivals, dashing on stage to give the keynote address while still maintaining salon-perfect hair. I thought I'd have an access-all-areas pass, a bodyguard, a restraining order against a stalker fan, a scandalous libel lawsuit and everything!' I joshed. 'But what have I actually achieved? Zilch. An unfinished novel in a bottom drawer.'

'Yeah, well, during high school I believed my true calling would be representing Australia in tennis at the Olympics, and, if that didn't pan out, I could always fall back on winning the Nobel Prize for curing cancer. Now look at me. Sitting on my arse, pensively considering my future. I've had to abandon many of my former career ideas – lead guitarist, astronaut, trapeze artist – though I still have high hopes for one-legged pole-vaulting and sit-down comedy.'

I laughed, but added more sombrely, 'I can't believe that I'm fifty. Fifty! The years have stolen by so surreptitiously, it's as if my life's been dressed in combat fatigues.'

'I know exactly what you mean . . . But maybe this trip

has been the catalyst you needed? This could be the turning point in your life. Your epiphany. Or, at least, a catharsis.'

'I assume they're medical terms for orgasmic bliss?' I teased, running my fingertips lightly up his thigh.

Brody, aroused but also annoyingly ticklish, snorted with laughter; a snort that made me cackle so loudly it set Brody off again until we were both bent double, like kids. Our laughter was a tap we couldn't turn off. In his small cabin, hidden under the waterline like a submerged cave, we seemed to move outside of reality, in a timeless universe of our own discovery.

As the ship got closer to Sydney, we embraced so that neither might see the other's face, and made love with a new and intense passion of impending loss. Two days out of Sydney, the dreamy underwater mood of the cabin seemed more fragile than ever as we spun our cocoon of breath around each other.

I continued to meet my sisters for meals and cocktails each day. They took my new blissful state as evidence that the cruise was doing me good. It was clearly doing *them* good. Amber had taken to slobbing around the cabin in her PJs, watching rom-coms, only emerging occasionally to eat her way through the dessert menu. 'I always believed that the only way to live a long life was to drink what you didn't like, do what you didn't want to and eat what you had to. Now I've realised that you don't really live longer, it just *feels* that way,' she said when I bumped into her in the gelato bar.

'Oh yes, the heart specialist's diet – if it tastes good, spit it out. I too refuse to live like that,' I concurred, spooning salted caramel gelato into my mouth, ravenous after hours of sex with Brody.

'And anyway, who wants to live longer when all your carbeating, alcoholic, carnivore friends and beloved sisters are dead?' Amber added, shovelling a chocolate fondant down her throat. 'I've had no desire to check up on my family, either,' she marvelled. 'Three weeks ago, if my kids had asked me to pogo to the South Pole on a knitting needle, I wouldn't have batted an eyelid. But if they asked me now . . .' She shrugged.

'You'd look for a loophole in their birth certificates? Well done,' I said, rewarding her with a big, happy kiss on her forehead.

I occasionally glimpsed Emerald around the ship, swinging an inflatable penis over her head at a pool party as she danced with some muscled stud whose budgie-smuggler bulge was severely testing the limits of lycra, happily chasing a terrified member of the Sonic Groove Duo around his turntable, or licking whipped cream off a cub's nipple piercing at the R-rated comedy game show.

'The worst thing about being the oldest sister is having to be a good example. It's much more fun being a terrible warning,' Emerald laughed as we sipped sunset cocktails. 'And I don't see it as "sleeping around", either.'

'Of course not!' I agreed. 'You're just having a brief dabble in amorous philanthropy.'

'Exactly. I'm not only in it for the kinky thrills. Although they're not bad either! But I really wanted to get my confidence back. My sex life with Sandro has been like trying to thread a needle with overcooked spaghetti,' she confided. 'On the Love Boat, though, I've bedded the type of studs who wouldn't have looked twice at a nerd like me back in high school.'

This time it was Emerald I rewarded with a big, happy kiss mid-forehead before the old twat-nav steered me back to Brody's cabin.

On our last day at sea, as I dressed, I noticed Brody's face was fogged with gloom. 'What's the matter?'

'I'm ill, because once we make port, my favourite patient is going to stop coming to see me with fake illnesses.'

'They were not fake!' I pinched his arm. 'I really hated you at first.'

'Ditto, darl. I wouldn't have fucked you if you were the last woman on earth,' he said, unbuttoning the blouse I'd just buttoned up.

'I hope you at least have the intelligence and self-awareness to know that the feeling was extremely mutual,' I said, as we ripped each other's clothes off once more. It seemed that the only reason Brody liked me to get dressed was for the pleasure of disrobing me all over again.

Afterwards, I rested my head on his broad chest and gazed at the low ceiling that had been the sky of our world for the past week, and said, impetuously, 'If I just seized the day and left my husband, if I threw caution to the wind, would you come with me?'

'Yes', he said, simply.

I lent up on one elbow, surprised, delighted and terrified in equal measure. 'What? Are you sure? I haven't given you much time to think about it. This is the emotional equivalent of a knee-trembler in an alley after the pub's shut, I've just skipped all the foreplay.'

'One thing treading on that damn mine taught me is to live in the moment. Nobody's guaranteed a second act.'

My eyes searched his face. Did this really mean as much

to him as it did to me? 'I feel that – oh, god, it sounds so corny. Cliché alert! But I feel nobody ever really knew me before I met you.'

Brody put his hands around my waist, pulling me so close I could feel the pulse of blood in him and the warmth of his breath. 'I feel that way too. But what about your husband?'

I shrugged. 'Harry was the only nice guy in my school. He gave me a Nick Cave album, *Kicking Against the Pricks*, and on school disco night he fingered me behind the smoke machine. Needless to say, a few years later we got married and had two children. And I thought we were happy. But clearly I was lying to myself. I should have listened to the little voice inside me saying "Is this all there is?" Obviously, I've been a bit depressed since my babies were born.'

'Really? Crikey. How old are they?'

'Eighteen and twenty-one.'

Brody laughed, but then added, seriously, 'Good point, though. What about your kids?'

'Zoe's just finished school and is taking a gap year. She's fruit-picking near Byron Bay now and going travelling in Asia in the new year. And Jake's trying to find a place to move out with mates from his apprenticeship course.'

'If captains can perform weddings at sea, I don't see any reason they can't perform divorces as well,' Brody suggested.

'That's a bit drastic,' I said, laughing. 'I've only known you for three weeks. I'm not sure I'm ready for the full husbandectomy.'

'Fair enough. But I do think we need to find out what this is, between us,' Brody said solemnly. 'Don't you?'

'But what about your contract with the cruise company?'

'I'll just break it and jump ship. I'll say I got a

twenty-fourhour virus – a twenty-four-hour virus that will last for at least the rest of the summer.'

'No severance pay?'

'Nope. But it's worth it, Ruby. Much to my amazement, for the first time in a long time, I'm looking forward to Christmas. Because look what Santa gave me for a present,' he said, laying me back on the bed and kissing his way down my body. 'I love the salty taste of your beautiful quim,' he said.

Finally, a doctor who didn't believe in giving up salt! This was my kind of medic. Once more, the sounds I was capable of making seemed insufficient to express what I was feeling. I wished I were a rooster so I could crow. No one had invented the noun (or is it a verb?) that I needed right now. All I could do was beam, ecstatically, and perhaps execute a handstand on the end of the bed.

The truth is, Brody and I just couldn't resist each other. We had about as much control as a white-water raft in a category five hurricane.

Brody lifted my calves onto his bare back, his mouth never leaving my body. And then later we nodded off, my heartbeat chiming in time with his breathing. Deeper and deeper we both sank, together.

22

'A toast!' Emerald declared, raising her champagne glass. 'Let's
drink to our livers!'

'And the transplants!' I added.

We were lounging in the jacuzzi on the top deck,
marvelling at the southern sky in all its glittering glory, as
the warm, tropical night purred around us.

'And thank you, Ruby, for making us come along.' Amber
tapped her plastic glass against mine. 'I can't begin to tell
you how much this trip has meant to me. Put it this way:
I've had so much fun laughing, teasing and chatting with my
beloved sisters that I've gone from Skyping home every five
minutes to thinking, "Do I even *have* children?"'

'Me too!' Emerald said. 'My kids insist on having their
"safe spaces", but then *I* get yelled at if I get their non-binary
pals mixed up with the sexually fluid flexitarians.'

'Where is *our* safe space? That's what I want to know.' I
laughed along with them.

'On this bloody boat, actually,' Emerald said. 'Oh, I just
don't ever want to get off.'

'Me either,' Amber added. 'We've both paid you back, by
the way. The money's transferred into your account. I would
have paid double for this time together.'

'Triple,' Emerald agreed.

My eyes widened. My sisters agreeing, again! Would miracles never cease? 'Thank you, girls, but there was no need. It's been worth every penny. I too am now a cruise addict. I will need to go to meetings.'

'It's changed me, this trip. I'm not taking that crap from the kids when I get home,' Amber vowed. 'Not from Scott either, the lazy, hypocritical dipshit.'

'Good for you!' Emerald enthused. 'Surely, the simple rule should be that if a woman is earning the bacon, her husband should cook it.'

'And, if a wife is wearing the proverbial pants, he should launder them for her on a regular basis, too,' I suggested.

'What every busy working mum wants is an iron man. Not a bloke in lycra on a racing bike, but a man holding the starch bottle and a basket of laundry.'

'Well said, Ruby! And if Scott and the kids don't do more to help around the house, well, I'll be doing what Ruby said, and looking for a loophole in my marriage certificate.'

'What a fantastic idea! I'm shaking things up as well,' Emerald pledged. 'This trip has given me back my self-esteem. And not just physically. Although, sexually, I've been like a squirrel, storing up nuts – I've had enough orgasms to get me through the winter.'

'So we've heard,' Amber said, flaring her eyes but smiling at her sister with affection.

'I want my sex life back with Alessandro. It's not an unreasonable demand. But he has to work at it too. And, I mean, what's not to love? Look at these two babies.' She pointed at her breasts, released from their bikini top and bobbing in the jacuzzi bubbles like two pale puddings fizzing in froth. 'Otherwise, I'll also be looking for a loophole in *my* marriage certificate.'

On cue, one of the toy boys Emerald was avoiding strolled past, flanked by two muscled mates. Emerald's conquest was an inhabitant of the man-bun brigade – one of those guys who smokes a great deal of dope and believes that crystals are more medically sound than vaccinations.

'Sit on my face, babe,' Man Bun said, bragging for the benefit of his brawnier pals, whom he now fist-bumped in turn.

'Why? Is your nose bigger than your cock?' my older sister shot back. 'Can't you see we're on a girls' night?'

I caught Amber's eye. Our laughter exploded and crackled like popcorn. I didn't know why I'd ever worried about Emerald and the 'whaling game'. She knew exactly how to handle beasts of all kinds.

'So, what was wrong with Man Bun?' I asked, when he'd stomped off after his unimpressed mates.

'He kept asking if I was an Aries or a Taurus. In the end I told him that *my* sign was "Do not disturb".'

That set us off again. When our laughter had abated, Amber said, 'And what about you, Rubes?' She topped up our champagne from the bottle, which had been leaning at a rakish angle in a bucket by the hot tub. 'What's been the best thing about the trip for you?'

'That's easy. My sisters getting along with each other. And being out of range of our evil mother.'

'Oh, by the way, bad news,' Amber sighed.

'Boris Johnson and *Playgirl* have agreed to centrefold terms?' I suggested.

'Worse. Mum's learnt to use WhatsApp. I have about ten messages on my phone berating me for abandoning her.'

'Really? She's attacking me on Messenger. I've been getting daily bulletins from Planet Grim since we left Sydney,' Emerald said.

'Well, let's just ignore her until we get back. United we stand, divided we're screwed,' I said.

'I dunno why we even bother being nice to her.' Amber sighed, then swigged down another big gulp of champagne. 'She's probably just going to leave her whole estate in trust to a cat retirement home or her hairdresser or something.'

'We're already out of the will, didn't I tell you?' Emerald reported. 'God, I meant to, but in all the rush and fuss . . .'

'What?' Amber's head spun to look at her.

'Well, you know about Mum's volcanic temper . . .'

'What did Dad call her?' I asked. 'Oh, I remember: Lady McDeath.'

'Yes. Well, in short, Lady McDeath told me that if we abandoned her to come on this cruise, she'd leave all her money to the Catholic Church.'

'Fuck!' Amber swore – something she did now.

'Hey, it was always on the cards. She never forgave you for marrying a Protestant, Amber. Nor me an atheist, which is even worse. That's another reason why she's always liked you the best, Ruby. Because you married a good Catholic boy.'

'Not so good, it turns out,' I said, sourly.

Amber patted my hand consolingly.

'Although, it's true,' I acknowledged. 'Mum thinks Protestants make the baby-sacrificing Aztecs and missionary-nibbling cannibals of Africa look civilised.'

'But the real reason she's leaving her money to the church is so that prayers will be said to get her out of purgatory,' Emerald clarified.

'Gosh, it's ridiculous, isn't it?' Amber bemoaned. 'A rich sinner can get a fast-track VIP pass through purgatory by donating to the Pope's Prada shoe fund. But paupers, not so much.'

'I doubt that any number of prayers could get our mother out of purgatory, anyway,' Emerald jibed. 'The truth is, Mum's an evil, hypercritical, she-bitch from hell . . . But, of course, I wish her only the best.'

'Well, *I'm* not saying prayers for her. Not after being cut of the will, after all I've done for her,' Amber grumbled.

'All *you've* done? Surely you mean all *I've* done. Mum's always complaining to me that you do nothing for her, Amber.'

'What? I do *everything*. She's always saying *you* don't do anything for her, Emerald, and that she can't believe how selfish you are.'

One minute of conversation about our mother and our sib-ship was drifting into troubled and treacherous waters. My emotional shipping report was issuing a red light warning – icebergs ahead. I immediately went into policewoman mode, stopping the verbal traffic with my hand. 'We *all* do far too much for her. *Mommie Dearest* is the closest thing we have to a home video.'

'Hopefully she'll be senile soon and won't be able to play us all off against each other anymore. "*If only you had your* sister's *figure . . .*" ' Amber mimicked. ' "*Oh, your* sister *doesn't do it like that.*" '

' "*You mowed the grass too short. Your* sister *knows better . . .*" blah blah blah,' I added.

'Senile? Jesus.' Emerald interjected, in an alarmed voice. 'What *are* we going to do with her when she eventually goes gaga?'

'You have the most practical house, Emerald – mostly on one level. Surely you should take her in?'

'Oh, yes. That would be second on my list of fun things to do – right after a clitoridectomy,' Emerald snapped. 'Bugger that. *You* should take her in, Amber. You have the biggest house.'

'That would be second on *my* list of fun things to do, too – right after having a bubble bath with Hitler,' Amber said, scowling.

'Well, I'm not looking after her either – not without combat pay,' I added. 'Let's face it, within a week we'd all be in an institution, sobbing and braiding our hair.'

'There's clearly only one solution,' Emerald stated baldly. 'We're just going to have to smother mother.'

This comment was so unexpected that Amber and I guffawed hysterically at Emerald's audacity.

'I'm serious. Pets are better off than people, d'you know that? They can be humanely put down when the time comes.'

'Maybe we *could* take her to a vet – she is such a cow at times,' I joked, thrumming my fingertips thoughtfully on my chin. 'Ah, if only we knew a vet . . .'

'Ruby's right. Surely you've got enough sedative to put a rhino to sleep,' Amber asked Emerald. 'Those opiates are thousands of times more potent than morphine, right?'

'Well, yeah, we could drug her with a ram sedative,' Emerald riffed. 'But we'd have to put a plastic bag over her head and probably gas her with helium to make it seem as though she'd killed herself. But why should *I* bloody well do the dirty deed? Amber, you know all about poisonous plants, don't you?'

'Sure. Oleander tea. Or there's the flowering *aconitum* plant. Farmers use it to kill foxes. It's known by lots of other names – monkshood, wolf's bane, devil's helmet, blue rocket. Have you heard of it? Even contact with unbroken skin can kill.'

'Let's do that, then. And if we get caught, I'm sure we can get the jail sentence commuted to a few psychiatric sessions after we tell the story of our lifetime of psychological abuse,' a slightly inebriated Emerald reasoned.

'Yes, we'd be out of prison in three or four years and then there'd be a bidding war among the TV networks for our exclusive interview,' I conjectured, lightheartedly.

'Ruby, you could give it to her. I mean, if *you* get caught, it's not as though they can give you a life sentence, right?' Emerald concluded, matter-of-factly.

'Emerald!' Amber sobered suddenly. 'You know that we don't talk about . . .' She chose her words carefully, eyebrows emphatically raised, '*Kev.*'

I jolted awake. *Kev?* I thought, startled. *Who's Kev?* I had a vague recollection that it was someone I should be worried about. Then it hit me like a falling grand piano. I'd completely forgotten about my fake cancer. Now would be the time to confess all and set my siblings straight. *This very second. Now. NOW!*

'I . . . I . . . I . . .' If ever I'm a contestant on *Mastermind*, prevarication will be my specialist subject. It wasn't that I was still waiting for a spine donor. No, it was really just that I had something more important to admit and didn't want to get sidetracked. *One bombshell at a time*, I rationalised through a fog of champagne.

'Oh, Ruby, I know you don't want to talk about that thing we're not talking about,' Amber said, softly, 'but I just want you to know how much I love you. And that you're our priority. Isn't she, Emerald?'

'Bloody oath. When we get home, whatever you need, Ruby, your sisters will be there for you.'

'Um, that is so, so lovely, girls. I can't tell you how touched I am. Only . . .' I took a deep breath and then stepped out into the emotional minefield. 'I'm not going home.'

I might as well have thrown a firecracker onto the home stretch of the Melbourne Cup. Both my sisters spun their heads in unison to look at me.

'What?' asked Emerald.

'What?' echoed Amber.

'I've fallen in love.'

'What?' Emerald said again.

'What?' echoed Amber.

My sisters now cocked their heads to the side. It brought back memories of the backyard synchronised swim team we'd pretended to be part of as kids, and in the lagoon the other day – only I was clearly out of sync. Shock had rendered the loquacious Ryan girls momentarily monosyllabic. For a few seconds, we broiled away in our bubbly, chlorinated cauldron in complete silence, till Emerald blurted, 'Who with?'

'With whom?' amended Amber, on autopilot.

'The ship's doctor,' I confessed, my face vivid with excitement. 'Which is why I couldn't tell you until now, as it's somewhat illegal because I have been his patient on the cruise. I'm sorry about that. But all the advice you both gave me at the start of the cruise about the menopause – try this herb, pop this pill – I discovered what I *really* needed is some simple HRT – that is, husband replacement therapy.'

23

'The doctor? The one who pushed the entertainment officer into the pool?'

'Yes. Isn't he all silver-foxy and fabulous?'

There was no answer except for the bubble and whirr of the jacuzzi.

'I'm so sorry I didn't tell you until now, but it's a breach of the doctor–patient whatnot, so he made me promise I wouldn't say anything. But I just had to let you know that I won't be going home with you tomorrow.'

'The ship's doctor? Yes, that's definitely a prima facie case of professional misconduct,' Emerald said, sounding serious.

'Sit on my prima facie,' I giggled. Since when did I get so giggly? 'Oh, girls, when he touches me, I feel as though a cyclone has spun me up into the stratosphere and landed me softly on cloud ten,' I added, in a rush. 'I've fallen in love. Just like in the movies. God, he's so good in bed our headboard needs an airbag! I'm not kidding. I've kissed him so much I can't believe my lips aren't in a splint. It's thrilling, frantic, romantic, dirty, dangerous, all-consuming, mind-blowing, tender, surprising, emotional, freaky – and then, sometimes, just fun. He says my red hair is as bright as daylight. Oh, and he's so funny. Seriously. Thank god he's a doctor, as I may haemorrhage from humour.'

My sisters, however, didn't seem to be finding my revelation remotely amusing.

'When? When exactly did this happen? You've been with us most of the time,' Amber asked, bewildered.

'Well, remember when I got that sheet burn on the nose and pulled my groin and my fanny was on fire and you booked me an appointment with the doctor? Well, I thought he was the most arrogant ratbag I'd ever met. But then I sunburnt my bum and had to go back. It was hate at second sight, too. Then there was the abseiling accident, and jellyfish sting, and it was hate at third and fourth sight – or slight, actually, because we couldn't stop bickering. But, well, turns out it was actually your whole basic Beatrice and Benedick *Much Ado About Nothing* scenario, because in Mare I got stranded with him on a broken windsurfer and, as he thought we might drown at sea, he let down his defences. And it turns out we laugh at the same jokes, we watch the same box sets, we love the same books . . . I never thought anything would happen between us. But it did. It has. And I've never felt more in love or more alive!'

I beamed at my older sisters, who were still just staring at me, mouths agape. Sensing they were not as pleased by this romantic turn of events as I'd hoped, I went in for a harder sell.

'Brody's capable, kind and brave – he worked for Doctors Without Borders, you know, risking life and limb, literally . . .' I paused, but quickly decided that the whole leg issue was probably a detail too far at this juncture. 'He's single, never married, can cook, is emotionally articulate, plays the guitar, laughs at my silly jokes and loves cunnilingus. What's not to love? I've landed on my feet – and my back – at the same time!' I was now gushing more than a Texan oil well but it was such a relief to let it all pour out.

But still they stared.

'I've never met anyone like him,' I persisted. 'He's the sort of guy who can punch a crocodile to death, rip out its liver for dinner and then bivouac the night away under its flayed hide while trekking in the wilds of the Congo.'

'The Congo? Who takes a holiday in the Congo?' Emerald narrowed her eyes suspiciously. 'Are you sure he's not a fantasist?' 'Where's he from, this Doctor Love?' Amber delved, distrust ringing in her voice. 'Is he a Sydney boy?'

'No, he's from . . . out of town.'

'Where? The Fifth Dimension?' Emerald scoffed.

'Maybe we should ask his care-in-the-community worker,' Amber suggested, sarcastically.

'A little town near Bundaberg,' I said, not liking the way my big sisters were ganging up on me. Yes, I loved it when they agreed, but not when they agreed that I was wrong.

'Oh, *great*!' Emerald's voice dripped sarcasm. '"What do you think of Ruby's boyfriend?" "He's a . . . well, if you pardon the expression, a *Queenslander*!" Part of the bloody redneck brigade who lost us the last election and got us the climate-changedenying dinosaurs who are driving us towards extinction.'

'A banana bender? Oh, Ruby. That's too, too much. I need another drink. Urgently.' Amber hauled herself out of the hot tub to seek alcoholic reinforcement.

'Ruby, you don't need a doctor, you need a *psychiatrist*,' Emerald admonished.

'What's the matter, Emerald?' I asked her, pointedly. 'Did you get up on the wrong side of somebody's bed this morning?'

'Okay, fair enough. We've all had some fun in the sun. But it's just a holiday romance. The high life on the high seas has had its way with you. Once you're ashore these feelings will evapo rate, like sea mist. *Pffft!*' She snapped her fingers.

'You don't understand! I crave his touch. His voice. His eyes.'

'Oh, puh-*lease*, you sound like a cheesy lyric from a mawkish eighties love ballad.'

'I know,' I giggled. Again! 'Isn't it *great*? And at my age. All this endless advice women are given about how to deal with menopause: eat more kale, which is really just cabbage with good PR. Drink eight glasses of water a minute. Take up Pilates. Give up yoga. Take progesterone biocompounds. Give up coffee. Whack *in* vaginal salves. Whack *on* oestrogen cream. But love is the drug that works. I've never felt better! Which is why I'm not going home. My kids have fledged. And clearly Harry's marriage vows should have said "Till death do us part – or till someone hotter comes along." When we get to Sydney, Brody's jumping ship and we're heading up the coast together to see what happens. I'm going to relaunch myself.'

'You're not a ship, Ruby. You can't just break a bottle over your own bloody head,' Emerald said, sternly. 'Mind you, the way you're talking, I think you already have and that this is the concussion speaking.'

'I'm so happy, Emmy. I feel like a wilted plant that's been watered and cared for and brought back to life.'

'Okay, what have I missed?' Amber asked, lowering herself back into the jacuzzi, clutching a fresh bottle of champagne.

'Your sister thinks she's a pot plant, apparently.'

'Chemistry, passion – call it what you will. But it's there and it's real. And it's allowed me to get over Harry's betrayal.'

'Infidelity is about so much more than sex, Ruby,' Amber counselled, topping up our glasses. 'People have affairs because they don't feel appreciated. They feel neglected, or ignored, and crave intimacy. They enjoy the feeling of being wanted, needed, desired. Harry may have been looking for an emotional connection, someone to open up to. Now you know that, it could be the very thing that fixes your marriage.'

'Amber's right, Rubes. Listen to your older, wiser sisters. This doctor thing, running away and all, is a very bad idea.'

'It's all Kev's fault.' Amber wiped tears from her eyes. 'You're spiralling down a rabbit hole like Alice in Wonderland. None of this is real.'

'Neither of you are in love, so you can't understand,' I sulked.

'Okay,' Emerald said, 'I admit that it's better to be in love than, say, in a fatal car crash or an iron lung. But it's just as painful. Nothing good can come of this, Ruby. Better to end it now.'

'Emerald's right. It's nothing more than a mirage.'

Amber constantly agreeing with Emerald seemed more surreal than anything I was saying. '*Marriage* is the mirage,' I retaliated. 'I thought I had a happy marriage. I thought we had a good sex life. I know now it was dull and perfunctory. Yes, we talked during sex, but only to ask when he was going to hang the shower curtain or pop to the shops to buy a new pool sweep. I thought my husband loved me as much as I loved him. But we've been away for nearly three weeks now and *not one bloody word*. We're just joined together in holy acrimony.'

'Look, keep calm when I say this, Ruby, darling, but maybe Harry's still coming to terms with the shock of . . . *Kev*,' Amber whispered, sombrely.

The only way I could keep calm about 'Kev' was to undergo a lobotomy – but, come to think of it, I'd already had that, the moment I lied to my sisters. Perhaps I'd been sleep-walking and doing sit-ups underneath stationary vehicles that day, I thought darkly, but said, instead –

'Look, just say you contracted cancer tomorrow. What would you regret? Not the things you've done, but the things you *haven't* done. Right? It sounds trite, I know. But I don't want to die before I've learnt how to live.'

'That *is* trite. Who *are* you?' Emerald asked, perplexed.

'Trite, but true. Why not live every day as though it's your last? That's what I'm trying to do. Which is why I'm not going back to my old life. Clearly my husband has moved on.'

'Forgive Harry, Rubes. The Anglo-Saxon attitude to infidelity is so unforgiving. We need to think like Europeans and not drive couples to divorce, causing kids to suffer. What about Zoe and Jake?'

Amber had successfully prodded my maternal guilt gland. I thought of the frosting of freckles across Jake's soft cheeks, and the way Zoe liked to wear her wild hair up, in a wiry strawberry-blonde halo. I loved them so much, but . . .

'My kids no longer need me. Anyway, all my life I've censored my behaviour – either worried what Mum would think or what my husband would think, or what my kids would think, or what society would think . . . Well, what *I* think now is that my kids are leading their own lives, so why can't I live a little? Zoe's on her gap year. And Jake's moving in with his apprenticeship pals. As it is, I only ever see them when they want to borrow my car,' I joked. 'My ship's come in – literally. Can't you be just happy for me?'

Once more, the only sound was the jacuzzi, fizzing and frothing. Even the hot tub seemed to be hissing its disapproval.

'Haven't you ever wanted to shake off the labels that have been slapped on you your whole life – loving daughter, doting wife, devoted mother, reliable co-worker – to do what you want and not what is wanted of you? Is that so bad?'

Hiss, hiss, went the hot tub.

'Can't one of you say something?'

'What I can say is,' Emerald began, 'the only thing you're divorced from is reality. Running away with a man you've known for only a few weeks is the most reckless, insane, stupid bloody idea you've ever had. And, as your older sister, I completely forbid it.'

'Seconded,' said Amber, firmly.

I shook my head. First, in amazement that my older sisters were agreeing on every goddamned thing; and secondly because, for once, I was not going to do what they told me to. All my life my sisters had known they could get me to do anything, mostly because I so wanted them to like me. I was six years old when they got me to steal money out of Mum's purse, and seven when they made me hide a visiting priest's towel so he'd have to streak from the bathroom to his guest bedroom. It had only taken me fifty years to work up the courage to defy them. I'd finally reached the twelfth step of my low-self-esteem program. '*Hello, my name is Ruby Ryan and I am no longer a low-self-esteem addict.*'

And it wasn't just my sisters who had a tendency to ride roughshod over me. I thought for a moment of all the career opportunities I'd turned down to look after the kids or support Harry's business or appease my mother. But now I was the headline in my own news scoop – 'Betrayed Wife and Jaded Mum of Two Discovers Late-Life Romance – oh, and Multiple Orgasms'. Brody knew how to make a girl wake up smiling. High-kicking and horseback riding might be difficult after the previous night, but smiling – a cinch. And, for once, I wasn't going to give up what felt right.

'It's time you both let me make my own mistakes. Only, it's not a mistake. It's the best thing that's ever happened to me.'

Emerald put her arm around my shoulders. 'It's clearly just your fanny talking. And I should know. Mine's been chatting away for weeks!'

'I think so too, Ruby,' Amber said. 'You're just having a severe libido attack. Time to get real.'

'But, Emerald, you're the one who said how splendid it is when the sex is so intoxicating that it takes over your whole imagination. You said you'd jump off tall buildings or stop speeding trains just to feel that life force. Didn't you?'

'Yes, but I wouldn't throw over my whole life . . . what life you have left, I mean.' Emerald searched for the right words, other than '*You are batshit crazy*', which I could tell from her face she felt most succinctly summed up the scenario. 'Have you told Doctor Love about Kev?'

My deceit kept catching me unawares. Now was the time to come clean about the misdiagnosis. I girded my loins, drew in a deep breath – then shrank back in fear. I was just too bloody cowardly. I decided to write them an email outlining the whole sorry saga. I'd send it on the first day back on dry land, when I was out of range of their fury – especially now that Emerald sported stilettos sharp enough to perform a labial augmentation with one quick kick. Amber had developed a foul-mouthed tongue sharp enough to cut glass. That would give them time to cool off and hopefully forgive me.

'Well?' Amber prodded.

'No . . . But it wouldn't matter. Brody's in love with me.'

My sisters sat there, their faces as animated as Easter Island statues.

'And if the kids look at me as if an alien has taken over my body and say "What have you done with our real mother?" I'm just going to smile and say, "Maybe this *is* your real mother!"'

'What do you mean?' Emerald's Easter Island statue moved its judgmental jaw.

'Well, for years you two have been comparing hot flushes and fanning each other, but you never told me the good things about the menopause. I feel, well, liberated! It's given me licence to behave badly. After decades of mollifying overwrought teens about their pimple breakouts and broken hearts, or pacifying Harry over car dents or shopping bills or whatever, my family will just have to tiptoe around *me* for a change. The expression "The change will do me good" has never seemed so apt. Yes, I feel guilty that I'm not behaving as a selfless mother should, but maybe I'm feeling guilty because deep-down I'm not feeling that guilty at all!'

I hadn't meant to say so much, but I was on my fourth glass of champagne and feelings were bubbling out of me. I was more bubbly than the jacuzzi in which we were poaching.

'Our smashed-avocado-on-toast-munching brunching-snowflake kids are right about one thing, though. We need to live our best lives. Which is why I want to lie in the arms of the man I love and banter in bon mots and down daiquiris, post-coitus, all through Christmas.'

My sisters gave me a pitying stare that said loud and clear that they now suspected our mother must have drunk during her pregnancy with me.

'Come on!' I crashed my plastic flute up against their glasses. 'Be happy for me. It's our last night at sea and it's smile o'clock!'

I beamed, basking in the moonlight, before downing my champagne in one jubilant gulp.

'Oh, and by the way, he's missing half of one leg.'

24

Planning is a vital part of any trip. Just ask Scott of the Antarctic.

Maybe I was waiting in the wrong place? I had gone out on deck before dawn to watch the ship gliding through the heads of Sydney Harbour, snaking towards the city lights then sliding majestically into port, to dock in the shadow of the Coathanger.

I'd jumped the queue to disembark early, collected my suitcase then taken up my post at the designated spot. Excitement effervesced in me. I didn't recognise myself – before this cruise the most spontaneous thing I'd ever done was to buy a vacuum cleaner on the spur of the moment, because it was on special, then pay for a taxi to lug it home.

My eyes raked the crowd streaming off the ship. I was searching for his mop of tousled hair, inquiring chocolate eyes and those cheekbones a girl could shave her legs on.

Leaning up against the terminus wall, looking out over the sparkling harbour, I thought back on the past three weeks, which had so seismically changed the lives of the Ryan sisters. Not only were we now friends, but Emerald had gone from dejected, cynical kicked cat to top-order predatory feline, and Amber had stopped being the perfect parent, started laughing at life and learnt to let her heart stop eating itself – as well as other dietary tips involving carbohydrates. And I had found love – oh, and also my G spot. Much to my own astonishment, I was now planning a romantic adventure with a man I'd only just met. I had things in my fridge that had been around longer than Doctor Brody Quinn. And yet, here I was – flying by the seat of my pants. Hell, I had frequent flier pant miles.

I knew my sisters didn't approve, but for the first time in my life I was not going to let them dictate my destiny. As my older sisters, Emerald and Amber had always done everything before me and done it better. Compared to my confident, competent siblings, I always felt that I was a runner-up in the human race. Hell, I'd practically worn their hand-me-down clothes while they were still wearing them.

But now a *Fuck it, I'm Fifty!* feeling had kicked in. It was time I did something for myself. I mean, if not now, when?

I checked my watch again, scanning the dock as passengers filed ashore and wandered through the jumble of suitcases, searching for their name tags. But it was my sisters I soon saw striding purposefully towards me. I'd been hoping to escape with Brody before they had time to track me down; I'd already composed an email to them, ready in my outbox, explaining about the misdiagnosis and begging them not to worry and to please forgive me.

'Don't try to talk me out of this.' I shook my head emphatically. 'For once in my life, I'm following my instincts. So what if my behaviour raises a few brows?'

'Ruby.' Emerald addressed me in the calm voice she used to soothe feral dogs and grieving pet owners.

I felt as if some terrible fate was gathering, like a storm far out at sea. 'What is it?'

'Brody's not coming.'

'Yes, he is. It's all planned.'

'Last night, after you told us about him, well, we tracked him down and revealed your . . . situation.'

My heart was like a heavy-metal drummer in my chest. 'What situation?'

'Your Kev situation. It wasn't fair to let him give up his job and make plans with you when your future is so uncertain,' Emerald said bluntly.

I felt a spasm of nausea in the pit of my stomach.

'Darling Rubes, you're clearly not in your right mind, which is why you're making such rash decisions,' Amber added.

Panic sluiced through me. 'What did you tell him?'

'That you need to be with your family right now. Which is why I also rang Harry late last night,' Emerald said. 'He's been sulking, big time, at being falsely accused in front of all his friends and family of something he swears he didn't do. And he was also sucker-punched by news of Kev's appearance. He needed time to process it all. But he's forgiven you—'

My face flushed, as though I'd spent too long in a hot bath. 'Forgiven *me*?! That's a bit rich.'

'He swore to me that he's never been unfaithful. And, while you've been away, he's realised how much he loves you. He's arriving any minute now to tell you so himself,' Emerald went on.

I felt numbness spread across my lips. 'What? But Brody will be here any minute.'

'Ruby!' Emerald barked in a glottal bass. 'Brody's not coming.'

Tears of anger brimmed at my eyelids. 'But I've had a Kevectomy. I don't have cancer. It was all a mistake!' I blurted.

'You're in remission?' Amber asked, her face alight with joy.

'Ruby! That's amazing! Oh my god . . . But how do you know?' Emerald interrogated.

'No, no, you don't understand. I never had cancer in the first place.'

Emerald's face froze in disbelief. 'What?!'

As Amber grappled with her feelings of relief, shock and confusion, her mind was slow to grasp the reality of what I'd just confessed. When she finally spoke, her voice was petulant with disdain. 'Wait. You never had cancer? The cancer was a *lie*? But I carried your suitcase! I let you win at Scrabble. And Monopoly. And cards, come to think of it . . .'

'It was a misdiagnosis. And you didn't "let" me win, Amber. You two are always underestimating me,' I lashed out.

Both of my sisters were doing a pretty good imitation of the tropical fish we'd been snorkelling with these past few weeks. I watched their mouths opening and closing, silently.

Finally Emerald's lips set like granite. 'When did you find out about the misdiagnosis?' she asked, her voice cold and metallic, like an antipodean Dalek.

'The day after my birthday party. I was going to tell you, but I *so* wanted you both to come on the cruise to patch up your differences and become friends again – which we have! And then, once we were on board, well, we were having such a lovely time and all getting on so well, and you were both so happy. I knew you'd be furious that I got you on board under false pretences . . . So, I just kept putting it off. Then we were having so much fun that I forgot all about it. And then, of course, I had bigger things to tell you. Like the fact that I've fallen in love and am running away!'

My sisters' eyes were bare and round as full moons.

'I really, really did want to tell you that I didn't have cancer. But somehow it was so good to be dying that I kinda started to wish that I really was!' I said, tap dancing in quicksand.

'Don't you worry about that, Ruby, because I am going to kill you,' Emerald seethed.

'I'm sorry, okay? Don't be angry with me.' My lips trembled. 'I just didn't want to ruin our holiday, which is why I decided that the best time to tell you was just as soon we got back to port. Which I'm doing now, right?' I added, desperately.

'Only because we forced you to confess! I cannot *believe* you lied to us! And lied, and lied, and lied . . .' Amber said shrilly.

'I've written you an explanatory email, begging your forgiveness. Here!' I opened the email on my phone. 'I've just sent it to you both.'

But it was too little, too late. Both sisters glowered at me, with hands on their hips.

'This whole trip was a bloody lie, just like your stupid infatuation is,' Emerald declared. 'We don't need a doctor to make a goddamned diagnosis, Ruby. It's increasingly clear that your midlife crisis has started without you.'

'I mean, the scheming, the manipulation, the emotional blackmail . . . Do you know who you remind me of? Our mother,' Amber stated, coldly.

'I'm sorry. Truly. I just didn't want our holiday headline to be "Enjoy Your Trip to Paradise – or Possibly Hades".'

'I can't believe you would put us through all this worry and anxiety and pain,' Emerald smouldered, 'and then joke about it!'

'It didn't look as though you were in that much pain as you shagged your way through every toy boy on board,' I retaliated. 'The ship's fire officer was about to close down your cabin due to overcrowding. And as for you, Amber. Don't judge me about my marriage. You're supposed to be so blissfully wed, but in truth you'd rather have a plane jettison its chemical toilet on your head than get down and dirty with your husband.'

'Marriage is not a happy experience for any wife,' Amber prickled. 'But we all just get on with it.'

'Yes,' Emerald echoed. 'Just go to Bunnings, buy yourself some wood and some nails and then build a bridge and get over it.'

'Well, I don't want to "just get on with it" or "get over it". I refuse to go to my grave in instalments. Remember when you said, Emmy, that the thing you missed most in life was great sex, mostly because you can remember having it? Well, I'm having it. Lots of it. And I'd do anything to keep having it. It's my last hormonal hurrah, like you said. I'm *glad* I got the misdiagnosis. Otherwise the alarm would not have gone off on my mortality. Getting cancer was the best thing that never happened to me,' I concluded, illogically.

My sisters just kept staring at me, gobsmacked. It was as if I were sending postcards from a parallel universe.

'Look, you're just at a tricky time in your marriage,' Amber placated. 'If your marriage was a week, you're kind of up to Wednesday afternoon – too far from the last fun weekend and too far from the next. But you'll get there.'

'Well, I still intend to carpe the hell out of the diem no matter *what* day it is. And, anyway,' I said, peeved, 'shouldn't you two be just a little bit pleased that I'm not actually dying?'

'Of course we're pleased,' Emerald said, through clenched teeth.

'Then be happy for me. You've totally underestimated Brody, too. He wouldn't abandon me because of a cancer diagnosis. It would only make him love me more. Ask him yourselves, as soon as he gets here.'

Emerald and Amber exchanged a glance. I stabbed at Brody's name on my mobile. The call went straight to voicemail. I tried again. And again.

'The thing is, Ruby,' Emerald finally said. 'We told Brody that you *wanted* him to leave you alone. And that he had to allow you to be with your husband and family in your final months. We told him that you wanted us to tell him that it was all over, not to contact you and to leave you in peace.'

'And that, as a doctor, he should respect your final wishes. As a doctor who has broken the law and could be struck off,' Amber added, with earnest insinuation.

It was then that the real tidal wave of panic rolled in and pulled me under. 'You *blackmailed* him? Why? Why have you sabotaged my one chance at love and happiness? Mum was right – you're both jealous, selfish, horrible siblings.'

I observed then that it's a good idea to love one's enemies, just in case your friends and family turn out to be two-faced, rotten rats. I'd just turned to run to the gangway and fight my way back on board when I saw my husband striding across the dock towards me, flanked by my brothers-in-law.

If I'd been on a plane, an oxygen mask would have dropped from the overhead panel at this moment. *Mayday! Mayday!* All I could do was adopt the brace position.

25

Harry propelled himself towards me with such force that I steadied myself for a punch. But he hugged me instead. I thought about smiling in greeting, but decided it was just a waste of facial muscles.

'I still love you,' my husband said rapidly. 'So much.' He raked his blonde hair, the colour of ripe wheat, out of his anxious face. 'I know I should've been in touch, but I was so pissed off, to be honest. I couldn't process it all – the way you put me down in front of all our mates. I thought we were happy and then, *kapow*!'

I raised a combative brow. 'Our happiness warranty expired when I found out you'd been cheating on me.'

'But I didn't! That's bullshit. Those stupid texts were just harmless bloody in-jokes with an old client I was trying to keep sweet, which you totally misinterpreted. I swear on . . . on Don Bradman's grave. Whatever happened to innocent till proven friggin' guilty?' His face crumpled.

I saw Emerald and Amber greeting their own husbands. Scott was wearing the standard uniform of the intellectual male – rumpled linen shirt with a trail of food stains, like a menu, down the front, faded chinos covered in ink stains, and a pair of white Crocs, which looked as though he had two huge paracetamols strapped to his feet. As he hugged

her, I thought it took all of Amber's considerable strength
of character not to show that she found the whole look
extremely irritating.

Emerald, on the other hand, launched herself at
Alessandro with a feline moan of pleasure. With his dark,
curly hair, forearms like glazed cudgels and bodyguard
build, if he didn't have that ruthless look so common to
hardened Mafiosos, the man could have been a male model.
'Hi, babe,' he said, his voice as composed and calm as a
hotel receptionist, then vaulted out of Emerald's grasp on
the pretext of picking up her suitcase.

Harry steered me out of earshot of the others and said,
'I was a complete dickhead not to get in touch, I know. But
one thing's for sure, Ruby – I missed you.' He clutched me
to his chest in a bear hug. 'All the little things that annoyed
the bejesus out of me – your inability to kill a spider or get
a lid off a jar . . . The way you can't read the paper without
bloody well demolishing it, or fold maps back up along the
creases – Well, I find all those little habits so endearing now.
I really do. It sounds nuts, but I wanna be with you every
moment of every day – especially when you can't get a lid off
a jar. I really, really missed you – I missed you all the time,
like when I couldn't find the salad spinner – where is that
bloody thing kept, by the way? – or when I was trying to
fold the washing without creasing it – how do you do that? –
and in the mornings, when I couldn't find clean overalls and
was late for work. I mean,' he blundered on, 'you're the only
the person who can look in the bathroom cabinet and find the
toenail clippers, which aren't there.'

'So,' I recapped, incredulous. 'You love me because
of my toenail-clipper-locating abilities, washing-folding

prowess, clean-overall-finding powers and salad-spinner storage?'

'No! Yes . . . Look, what I'm trying to say is, it's the little things in a marriage that add up to make the big picture. And that picture is . . .' Harry squirmed with discomfort. The word was on his tongue, but he just couldn't spit it out. 'Love,' he finally regurgitated.

Harry's comment was so treacly-sweet it wouldn't have been out of place on a British boarding-school pudding. When I was too astounded to respond, Harry ploughed on nervously.

'What happened to those two kids who used to surf and sail together, and swim in the nuddy down at Bundeena Beach, and make love in the moonlight, and laugh till our lips fell off?'

'They got busy cheering on toddlers for pooing in the potty,' I explained, flatly.

'You're right, Rubes. And when we weren't applauding bowel movements we were doing the bloody school run and attending parent–teacher nights and taking it in turns to drive across town at one in the morning to pick up kids from festivals, and arguing about pocket money, and parties, and which one of us was the most exhausted.'

'Dear god, I was so bored helping with math homework I could see my plants engaging in photosynthesis,' I concurred with a sigh.

'Exactly, hon. We lost each other in there, somewhere. But all the reasons we fell in love, Ruby, way back when we were kids – well, they're still there. And in the time we have left, I wanna rekindle it all . . .'

My face registered a look of mild surprise and then

deepening horror as it hit me that, of course, Harry didn't know about the misdiagnosis. Nor could I guess how he'd react to the news that I'd hijacked my sisters to come on a cruise on false pretences. I experienced a colonic flutter as my sphincter battened down its hatches. Why, oh, why hadn't I come clean way back in the beginning? Of the many, many misdemeanours of my life, this was by far the stupidest thing I'd ever done. I took a deep breath and tried to steady my nerves. There was no need to panic, I told myself – a handy little phrase which often means 'Take those cyanide pills *now*.'

But before I could blurt out the whole surreal tale, Emerald, who'd been eavesdropping, suddenly barrelled back into the conversation. 'Do you have my sunscreen?' she asked, winking at me. 'Has Ruby told you the great news? It was a misdiagnosis. She got the doctor's apologetic email this morning,' she gushed. 'It's miraculous. She has told you, hasn't she?'

Harry's double take was so cartoon-comical it could quite possibly have caused whiplash. 'Is it true?' he asked, warily.

I nodded. Hey, I'd been lying for weeks, why start being honest now? Nauseated at the level of my deceit, I just tried to maintain an enthusiastic facial expression. I smiled until my face cramped. The gauzy, leaden atmosphere around Harry suddenly lifted. His eyes started to burn and his chin to tremble.

'Seriously? Is this for real?' he asked, falteringly.

I felt like the demented heroine in a Tennessee Williams play who'd forgotten her lines and had no prompt. All I could do was nod away like a bobbleheaded toy dog in the back window of a car.

Harry's face, which had been ravaged with despair, lit up. He let out a baritone boom of a laugh.

'Bloody hell! I was about to organise a marathon with the footy boys and the surf lifesavers: "Run for Ruby". And I deadset hate running! But I was sure as hell going to run one for you.' He laughed again and hugged me to his chest once more, wiping tears from his eyes. 'Come on. Let's get home and tell the kids the amazing news. Zoe's still up at Byron, but we can Skype. And Jake's asleep on the couch, chucking a sickie.'

'Um, the kids already know that it was a false alarm and that I'm okay.'

'What? You told them before me?'

I glanced at Emerald, pop-eyed, signalling SOS.

'Ruby wanted to tell you the good news in person,' Emerald ad-libbed.

'Oh, love.' Harry melted. I relaxed for a moment into the familiar comfort of his big, solid arms, my face mashed up against his scruffy shirt. He smelt like home, like pool chlorine and a hint of Christmas. I felt it all, then, our long history, in vivid, colourful flashbacks – the pregnancies, the births, the cute things our kids did and said, like the time Zoe came home from her grandmother's to report that for tea she'd had 'elephants and chips', which apparently decoded as 'an elegant sufficiency'. And the time Jake, aged nine, had written us a note to say that he'd discovered his superior intellect and was clearly a 'genus'.

I thought of the weight of our shared mortgage, which we'd only just paid off together after years of scrimping. Maybe it *was* just a Wednesday in the week of our marriage. Maybe Thursday and Friday would be so much better . . .

not to forget the hedonistic weekend. Perhaps the passion I shared with Brody truly was just a mirage, the cruise ship nothing more than a floating Brigadoon.

Harry had sworn on Bradman's grave that those texts were just meaningless, stupid banter with an old customer, which made *me* the adulterer now, come to think of it . . . Although there was nothing adult about it. No, it had been wild, rash and reckless. Maybe my menopause had started and Brody was my hot flush? A hot flush made flesh?

Harry checked his watch. 'Come on. We'd better get our skates on!' He called to the others. 'We're smack-bang in the morning rush hour, of course, which is a bit of a bummer. Traffic jams are so bloody bad in Sydney these days you can have an oil and grease change and a full friggin' service without losing your place in the lane,' he chuckled, relief rolling off him in waves.

Harry was always ready to laugh at the world. It was one of the things about him I'd fallen for – that sanguine, devil-maycare, she'll-be-right-mate Aussie insouciance, so at odds with the stressful atmosphere I'd known in the Ryan family home.

Alessandro and Scott hugged me, expressing joy at the excellent medical news and generously putting my birthday outburst down to shock and grief and alcohol. Amber and Emerald waved goodbye as they followed their husbands to Alessandro's SUV. Harry tilted my bag onto its back wheels, put his arm around my shoulders and guided me out of the terminal and towards his Hire a Hubby van, which was parked precariously, half up on the kerb.

'You look like a sunbeam in that dress.' He smiled.

I felt the chill of the sea breeze cut through the flimsy silk and shuddered.

While Harry put my suitcase in the back of the van, I surreptitiously checked my phone one more time. Nothing. I stabbed at Brody's number and again it went straight to voicemail. I strapped on my seatbelt. Crosscurrents of feeling were pulling me to and fro. This is what it must feel like to be drowning, I realised. As Harry manoeuvred the van onto the road, I discreetly pressed redial five or six more times. Still nothing.

As the van nosed its way into the traffic, Harry chatted on amicably about the kids, the traffic, the weather, the cars – he'd lent mine to Jake, hence the van.

'So, I've stacked the fridge with mangoes, prawns, camembert and lamingtons – the four essential food groups. I'm just so glad you're home, hon! Jake held a "gathering" just after you went away, because I am the best dad *ever*, as well as being a pushover. I'm afraid the carpet's suffered, along with some of the more delicate pot plants, which some of the boys puked their pizza into. Then I had to drop off Zoe to her farewell party before she left for Byron Bay, which turned out to be a bit of a rave and set off a brief and kinda challenging flashback! I had to hurry home to a nice cup of tea and *Antiques Roadshow*,' he joked.

As Harry turned the car south, the city unscrolled on my right. After the calm of the high seas, the honking horns and dashing pedestrians jarred on my nerves. Sydney at peak hour seemed to be braying at me like a drunken man laughing too loudly in a restaurant.

'We had a mini cyclone while you were away, too, which the Bureau of Meteorology didn't bloody well notice until next morning, when they woke to discover that the Opera House had washed away to friggin' Parramatta.'

His voice sounded distant, as if it were coming from the bottom of the ocean. I tried to tune in to his chatter but an unpleasant buzzing had started in my ears.

'"Chance of showers", the weather bloke had said. "Chance", note. So I painted the fence with Jake, and then we went for a surf till – *WHOOSH!* Down it came! Buckets of the stuff. Six inches of rain in about five minutes, then press repeat all night long.'

I watched the brutish flow of cars racing towards the city on the opposite side of the highway.

All I could think about was Brody's velvet-brown eyes, his crooked smile, his touch, his warm mouth on me.

'Next morning, the same weather dickhead says, "It rained quite heavily last night," which kinda understated the ferries sinking to the bottom of the harbour and the soiled undies of the pilots who had to swoop around in holding patterns for hours on end. I mean, this was bloody biblical. The national park nearly joined Atlantis; the streets were covered in yachts . . .' Harry glanced over to see if I was finding his musings amusing. '. . . and chockers with blokes saying "Dude, where's my car?" Mate, I think you'll find it's in Tasmania by now.'

I clenched the handle of the car door, realising I craved conversation with my husband about as much as I longed for an audition in Harvey Weinstein's semen-caked hotel suite.

I nodded and said 'Hmm' but did not look Harry's way. I just stared at the oncoming suburbs as if it were my own doom that approached with slow, winding inevitability.

'Work's been good, but. This guy called me to fix

something that nobody had been able to work out how to mend. Condescending prick he was, too . . . Anyway, I gave the machine a quick thwack with my sledgehammer and it shuddered into life. I then billed the bastard three hundred dollars. He got all pissy and said, "That's a bit steep, isn't it, mate? I want an itemised bill." So, I wrote – "For giving the engine a good thwack, a buck. For knowing where to thwack it, two hundred and ninety-nine dollars.'"

I'd heard him tell a similar tale so many times. Harry was set on repeat – just like my life. My head started to throb with the measured insistence of a metronome.

Walking into my house an hour later felt dreamlike. Gazing through the kitchen window, the shimmering turquoise of our kidney-shaped swimming pool against the bright green grass was so Hockney-esque I felt as though I'd fallen into a frame. Was any of this real?

Jake leapt up from his position on the couch and embraced me. After expressing his delight that I was home and well, he went straight back to watching re-runs of *Love Island*. Why would my son want to spend his spare time watching people with nothing to do not doing anything, when he could just watch his parents' marriage? Although our son was still technically living at home, he was always out partying and then sleeping it off. I felt sure I'd catch up with him again sometime this millennium.

Zoe Skyped in from Byron and blew me kisses. 'Wow, Mum, you look great. The cruise really did you good.' After a quick stopover at home for Christmas she was heading off to Asia and would also probably pop in some time in the next twelve months via India, Sri Lanka, Ibiza or somewhere over the rainbow.

I walked around my home feeling like a terrapin exploring the familiar edges of its aquarium. Even though Harry had made an effort to tidy up and the warm, late spring sunshine was streaming through the balcony doors, it felt like a holiday home in winter – cold, stale, paling into significance.

Molasses-slow minutes dripped by as I unpacked my suitcase, opened the mail and put on the washing, stuffing the machine full of clothes he'd touched, unbuttoned, peeled to the side or ripped off in the throes of passion.

I hated cooking. The last time I'd baked was when I'd accidentally burnt my buttocks while snorkelling. On automatic pilot, I started making a dressing to go with the prawns. The whisk beat against glass bowl: *tap, tap, tap.*

I took a shower before lunch, thinking, *This is a metaphor for my life – Shampoo, rinse, repeat . . . shampoo, rinse, repeat.*

An hour later I walked heavily into the bright, crisp heat of the sunlit backyard to hang up the washing. Eucalyptus blossoms trembled like soft clouds, translucent and tenuous before my gaze. Although the garden was abuzz with butterflies and bees, and fragrant with frangipani flowers, it felt like a prison wherever I turned.

Soon would come the long, hot, dry summer, in which tempers frayed as the grass turned brown and the sweet scent of dying jacaranda flowers drenched the heavy air. An emptiness was beginning somewhere within me; I felt a withering, a falling away. Pegging up my clothes, which were now washed clean of Brody's scent, birds started to chatter in the trees that crowded the garden. I listened to the sound of the crow, its long, forlorn cry. I knew just how it felt.

I spent the afternoon in the garden, digging energetically

at weeds. As the day cooled, I paused to draw breath. With remote fascination I watched a blue tongue lizard pounce on a smaller one, which dropped its tail and escaped, darting away, reborn. The next thing I knew, I was grabbing my handbag and dashing for the door – scrambling, skidding, scuttling across the concrete apron in the middle of the road, running for the train. Running for my life.

26

Was it possible to wear off a fingerprint from over-texting? That's what I wondered all the long, long way back to Circular Quay on the infuriatingly slow, all-stops train.

At first, I tried wry humour: *Brody, I think you'll find that your mobile phone will generally be more useful when you a) remember the 'mobile' aspect and b) not have it on silent – unless you're in a Trappist monastery, and forgot to mention it, you know, because of the whole non-talking policy, ha-ha.*

Then I tried pleading: *Please, please, please answer so I can explain everything. I'm begging you.*

Then anger: *Who are you? A hottie-hottie-dumb-dumb? Or maybe you're president of Trump's pussy-grabbing academy? Have these past two weeks meant nothing to you?*

It surprised me how desperate I was to see him. It was a hard, physical longing, like a craving for water in the desert. When the train finally shuddered to a stop at Circular Quay station, I pushed through the barrier, hurling other poor passengers out of my way. After a sprint that would have given Usain Bolt a run for his money, I arrived, panting, at the cruise terminal – just in time to see the ship I'd disembarked that morning pulling out into the harbour, newly stocked with passengers.

Standing at the back of the cluster of friends and family who'd come to farewell their loved ones, my face crumpled like a chip packet. I was blindsided by a queasy swell of emotion. Feeling faint, I grabbed the sleeve of a uniformed man to steady myself. I read his identification badge, discovering that he was, in fact, a water taxi driver. 'Do you know where that ship's going?' I demanded.

'Out there somewhere.' The bearded boatie gestured to the ocean beyond Sydney Harbour.

'Oh, you mean the largest, deepest water mass on the planet, which covers more than sixty million square miles and is thirteen thousand feet deep, otherwise known as the Pacific?' I could not keep the edge of hysteria out of my voice.

He hitched a nonchalant brow. 'Ah, yep.'

'Could you be just a tad more specific about the Pacific?' People were starting to look at me strangely.

'I dunno. Ask *them*.' The water taxi driver pointed to a couple emerging from a black hire car. A pair of manicured feet encased in diamante-studded high heels led to two impossibly long legs, which disappeared into a leopard-print miniskirt, above which protruded two massive breasts, draped in a sea of shimmering blonde hair extensions, all of which was topped off by a botoxed visage in designer shades. The woman had enough gold jewellery around her neck to induce curvature of the spine, and that was without factoring in the overweight bloke weighing down her arm. With his mashed-up nose, dyed black hair so perfectly smooth it looked plastic and a T-shirt that read 'I dig Western Australia', you didn't have to be Hercule Poirot to deduce he was some kind of mining magnate.

The taxi skipper explained that these were the uber-rich residents of the ship's penthouse apartment. The bloke was an iron ore exporter, apparently. Their flight from Perth had been delayed and they'd missed the departure deadline, so had booked his water taxi to whisk them out to the ship. When the harbour pilot was disembarking Brody's ship near the heads, these tardy passengers would be allowed to board. It was highly irregular, but the captain was making an exception due to the size of their walk-in wallet.

After clearing customs at record speed, the Glamazonian clattered her way along the gangplank to the waiting speedboat. I leapt the rope barrier, ignoring a raucous 'Oi! You!' from a customs officer, and trotted along beside her. 'The man I love is on that ship,' I said mournfully. 'Please, will you let me hitch a ride?' I let out a choking sob. It was all too much. Since I had turned fifty a month ago, my life had gone from calm, ordered mundanity to reckless, perilous insanity, and I wasn't quite sure how.

The trophy wife peered over her saucer-sized sunglasses. 'Well,' she adjudicated, 'you've got that jaundiced, ill look, which means you've either just eaten a bad oyster, you're comin' down with the flu or that you're truly, madly, deeply in love.'

'It's love, unfortunately, which is the worst affliction on that woeful list.'

'Ain't that the bloody truth!' She laughed and gave her shrugging consent. 'Hey, it's no skin off my nose job.'

Which is how, moments later, I was bouncing and jouncing across the harbour at speed, in hot pursuit of a disappearing ocean liner. Our plucky little boat skimmed past the Opera House in a hiss of spray and then zipped at a loose clip past

Shark Island, towards Manly. The cruise ship now loomed before us like a huge white whale.

The trophy wife, it transpired, had met her future husband while working at a 'skimpy' bar in Kalgoorlie – so called because waitresses work in their smalls. Having ascertained the details of my doomed love affair, she asked the water taxi skipper to call ahead to request the presence of the ship's doctor in the docking area.

'Sorry, no can do,' he growled.

The trophy wife gave him a laser death stare. 'Don't play dumb with me, mate. I'm much better at it.'

'But . . .'

'I'm also wearing a G-string two sizes too small and feeling mean as fuck, so if you like your scrotum attached, just *do it*!'

The water taxi skipper promptly radioed the bridge. As he relayed the message, I wondered what kind of cruise was currently heading out. Brody had told me of the many different themed, niche cruises on offer on the high seas. 'Bare Necessities' swingers cruises, with dress code 'clothing optional', or the 'Walking Dead' cruise, with zombie-related activities, or the 'Star Trek' cruise with Klingon pub crawls for die-hard Trekkies. Looking at the gold-plated, diamond-studded couple before me, I couldn't quite see them opting for the knitting and crochet cruise, or the 'Meow Meow' experience for dedicated cat lovers.

The mining magnate's main squeeze had had so much work done she gave new meaning to 'manmade'. But she'd acquired Mother Theresa–like status in my mind because, at her request, Doctor Quinn had been summoned to the boarding area and would be waiting for me. Hell, I was so grateful I'd have given her a kidney if I could. 'Good luck,' she said, crunching my fingers in a chiropractic handshake.

The water taxi steered in next to the chugging behemoth, matching its speed and minimising the gap between the vessels. I watched as the ship's crew lowered an aluminium stairway. To passing vessels our little skiff must have looked like a remora attached to a larger marine animal. This was a run-of-the-mill manoeuvre for an experienced taxi skipper, but seemed to be somewhat alarming for the magnate, who was quivering like a jelly at the thought of edging his way to the speedboat's foredeck, which was the closest point to the cruise ship, and climbing aboard rung by rung. He grimaced, flashing a gold-tipped incisor, and firmly shook his head.

Leaving the trophy wife to coax her anxious hubby aboard the ship, I mountain-goated up the ladder in a few leaps. Two burly crew members immediately clambered down into the idling taxi to retrieve the suitcases of the unpunctual passengers.

When Brody realised who had ordered his urgent appearance on deck, he gave me the sort of look usually reserved for a strangely vacant person you see sauntering into a fast-food restaurant wearing a 'Life Sucks' T-shirt and holding a chainsaw.

'You should be with your family,' he said brusquely, putting down his medical bag. His dark eyes had gone dull, as if filmed over with layers of disappointment. And his hair, which usually curled in an unruly shock, now lay flat and lifeless.

'But I don't have cancer!' I exclaimed. 'It was all a mistake.'

Brody's expression softened to one of baffled delight, then disbelief. 'But why would your sisters lie to me?'

'Because I lied to them.'

'What? Why?' His brow pulled into a frown.

'I know it sounds nuts. The truth is, I did receive a cancer diagnosis. Terminal. On my fiftieth birthday. I went into meltdown. I got drunk and told everyone what I really thought of them. All I wanted to do with the time I had left was patch things up with my two warring sisters. That's why I booked the first cruise I could. Only, then I found out it was a misdiagnosis. But if I'd told my sisters, they wouldn't have come on the trip. So, I postponed telling them. And then we were all having so much fun that I put it off again. And again. I know it was wrong.' I grabbed hold of his hands. 'But the medical scare made me see life differently. It made me want to live in the moment – as though every day is my last. And then I met you and fell in love and forgot all about the cancer, until my sisters told you that I didn't want to see you anymore.' I grabbed hold of his hands. 'But I do! I do! Life is in two acts – the trick is surviving the interval. The cancer misdiagnosis was my interval, and you're my chance at a second act. It'll be like adolescence in reverse. A lovely rebirth!'

I beamed up at my beloved. When Brody's face didn't move, I just held my smile in place as if waiting for an unseen photographer to complete his work.

The trophy wife was finally aboard and was looking at me with a mix of incredulity and pity. The crewmen now scrambled back down the ladder to fetch the seasick mining magnate.

Brody extricated himself from my grip. 'Who lies about having cancer?' Hot anger crackled in his voice.

'Okay, I deceived my sisters and got them to take a three week holiday under false pretences, I lied to them about cancer, then lied to you by not telling you that I'd lied to them. I put my own pleasure and happiness first, and forgot all about my friends and family . . . But name one *really important* shortcoming?' I joked, desperately.

But my normally loquacious, witty, quippy love god was struck dumb. When Brody finally did reply, he said, 'If Oliver Sacks was still alive, he could have written you up in one of his books, as you clearly have an incredibly rare personality disorder.'

'You're the incredibly rare one. Which is why I adore you, Brody Quinn.' I was speaking in a tone of voice I'd never heard come out of my mouth before. It was as though I'd unlocked a secret level of my vocal cords that was velvety and alluring. 'Can't we just stick to our plan, head up the coast?' I persevered. 'We'll work it out. Jump ship. Come back with me now in the water taxi . . .'

'Where to? A psychiatric facility?'

'Well, I *am* crazy – crazy in love with you. Flabba and Boris can forward your stuff.'

'You *must* have a brain malfunction if you think I'd want anything to do with a woman who lies about having cancer. I'm a doctor, for fuck's sake. And if you can lie about that, what else can you lie about?' he added, keeping me fixed in his unflinching gaze.

'I'm not lying when I say I've fallen for you. I'm your Saint Bernard, remember? With the whisky barrel?'

'Yeah, and then you bloody well bit me. I told you what a *big* thing it was for me to trust you. And now I find out you're a liar.' His rebuke reverberated across the deck. 'The chances of my trusting you now are about as probable as Tonya Harding making a return to professional figure skating.'

The magnate was finally aboard, all flushed and flustered, and the harbour pilot was making ready to leave the ship. It was now or never.

'Please forgive me.' I seized Brody's arm. 'It was all a mistake that started with the misdiagnosis.'

Brody's face hardened – he was closing in on himself, like the sea swallowing a skimmed stone. 'Why should I believe that? You're clearly a fantasist. I mean, who *are* you? For all I know, you do this to all the men you pick up. Just leave me alone.'

'But . . . I love you,' I said, falteringly, feeling the bump as our relationship hit an iceberg and began to go the way of the *Titanic*.

Brody gave me a look that made it clear his love for me had joined a witness protection program and that I was on the list of Australia's least wanted. 'I never want to see you again. Men, escort this stowaway off the ship,' he ordered the crewmen.

The two seamen frogmarched me back to the ladder and stood watch while I descended to the waiting water taxi.

After landing aboard with a thump, I looked back up at the ship's deck, but Brody was gone.

As the little speedboat peeled away from the mothership, I achieved a personal best for self-loathing. No wonder he didn't want anything to do with me; *I* didn't want anything to do with me either, I thought, bleakly.

'Anythin' I can get ya, kid?' the skipper asked, a bit alarmed at my ashen visage.

'Um . . . a sprinkling of Valium and a heroin chaser?' I replied, weakly.

'Right. I was thinking more along the lines of a sick bag or a bottle of water.'

'Does it come with any strychnine?'

I craned over my shoulder to watch the huge cruise ship veer right at Watsons Bay on its journey out of Sydney Harbour. My ship had sailed. Panic constricted my trachea for longer than I feared healthy in a human being. The low, thick sky bulged with grey dampness. Seawater hit the bow, hissing like a snake. By the time the next wave had reared up and collapsed in a spatter of spray, I could feel tears starting to well. The sea had turned snot-green and choppy. The wind was carving huge escarpments out of the water before my eyes. A massive wave, like a malicious grin, loomed up before us, its white fangs biting into our flimsy-seeming boat.

There'd been storm warnings on the radio, but no mention of the emotional gale that had blown me off course. No mood meteorologist had urgently interrupted the scheduled programming to forecast the psychological cyclone that was approaching.

I was suddenly crying so passionately that it took me a while to realise that the sky was weeping with me. The torrential summer rain came in icy sheets across the harbour, stinging my skin.

I took shelter in the tiny cabin, where I curled into a ball and sank down, deep in thought, which, I had to admit, had been totally unfamiliar territory of late.

Why *should* Brody believe a woman who could lie about having cancer? Why *had* I lied and deceived the people I loved? *Maybe I am like my manipulative and scheming mother*, I thought with dread. If only I could talk to someone who understood me . . . But the only people who did were my sisters, and they were rightly furious with me.

As the boat laboured its way back to shore in the storm, I breathed in shallow gasps. I wondered if this was how a fish felt, lying on the bottom of a bucket, mouth opening and closing, drowning in air.

27

December 1st

Dear friends and family,

I'm sorry this is a group email, but I just wanted to let you all know that the cancer scare was a misdiagnosis. This is a mixed blessing, considering that most of you now want to kill me. I can only apologise for my insane behaviour at my birthday bash. Clearly I was a) deranged with worry and shock, and b) drunk.

If you can find it in your hearts to forgive me, that would be huge. If you want to send me a one-way ticket to a colony for social lepers, that's also to be expected. But I'm just so sorry I maligned my husband, who is totally faithful. I want to make it clear that my kids are the light of my life. I'm also sorry I was bitchy about my friends – I'm actually just off to the vet to get my claws done. And I was completely out of order about my mother, who single-handedly and heroically raised three teenage daughters after our dad died. Mum, I owe you the biggest apology of all. I'm sorry.

And to my dear sisters I say, life's not worth living without you, so please be friends with me again.

Okay, that's enough grovelling for one day, or I'll have

no skin left on my kneecaps. Anyway, here's hoping some of you can forgive me, because, at the moment, I don't know whose name to write in the 'In case of emergency, please notify' sections of official forms, which is truly tragic. Meanwhile, I'll be here staring at the sky, hoping for an incoming asteroid with my name on it.

Remorsefully, Ruby.

I wasn't sure exactly how this email had been received but I was aware that the looks I got from people in the supermarket or at the gym or on the boardwalk at the beach had shifted from wariness to pity. Old friends and colleagues who'd been snubbing me altogether now greeted me with a cool formality. They looked at me curiously, as if I had spinach in my teeth or had tucked my skirt into my undies.

My mother was the first vulture to feast on my carcass. When I answered the rat-a-tat of her many-ringed hand on the front door, she greeted me, her youngest daughter, with all the enthusiasm with which she might welcome a gangrenous pustule.

'What have you done to yourself?' she said, the implication being, 'you look like shit'. She made lip-farts when she disagreed with anything her daughters said or did. As I now apologised in person, my mother had a chronic attack of lip flatulence.

The morning light struck my mother's face starkly, accentuating the lines beneath her foundation and deepening the shadows under her eyes. Her handsome face had sagged of late, and although the flesh was still like tanned leather, it no longer stretched so tautly over her cheekbones. Her grey eyes, though still sharp and clear, were sunk more deeply in her face; the shrewd watchfulness there now half hidden. Her hair, usually bleached blonde, shimmered with touches of grey at her roots and temples. Our indomitable mother was ageing. A small, not unpleasant sadness caught briefly in my throat. But just as I was feeling compassion for the family matriarch, Ruth's viper tongue lashed out.

'You're damn lucky Harry took you back, after your monstrous outburst, as well as having squandered all his money on a luxurious cruise with your sisters . . .' She twisted the diamond rings on her arthritic fingers.

'The girls have paid me back, actually, because they had such a good time. They—'

'. . . not sparing a thought for your poor, abandoned mother.'

She pushed past me into the kitchen, where she took up position at the head of the table, then began, in a monotone, to go down the long, baleful list of my faults. I sat under her level, ice-grey gaze and ruminated on my mother's character. My conclusion? That Mrs Ruth Ryan does have some good points – if you like flesh-eating bacteria.

'Considering your many foibles, it's no wonder Harry strayed. Now you know what it felt like for me.' She dug her painted nails into my soft warm forearm, as if trying to draw blood. 'Do you think I wanted to stay with your *father*?' She said the word as though it were toxic. 'After all his humiliating betrayals? I stayed because it was my duty.'

I felt florid – as if my face were too near a heating coil on a stove. 'Harry didn't stray. It was all a misunder—'

'Once a woman walks down the aisle, her fate is sealed.'

'Women are not envelopes, Mum. We—'

'Although, of course, I had many admirers. I could have taken my pick of men. Unlike you.' My mother bared her crocodile smile. 'A plain jane like you – well, what other man would want you?'

I bit my tongue – the crocodile was obviously on a fishing expedition. My mother's eyes were always watchful, like a Kakadu salty: feigning sleep, but in reality poised to strike at the first sign of vulnerability.

'As for the hateful lies you told about *me* – I've decided to forgive you. Because it's the Christian thing to do.'

When I didn't rise to the bait, my mother held her mouth pinched up like a rectum. 'But you're still out of the will. I'm having it altered when my solicitor's back from holidays, after the ordeal of Christmas is over. Where is your lippy? You look like death warmed up without it.'

Clearly my mother was running late for her joy and euphoria seminar. The woman made the Supreme Leader of the Islamic Revolution look perky. Her once-beautiful face bore the deep marks of habitual dissatisfaction. You could smell disapproval on her, like BO oozing out of the armpits of a synthetic blouse on a scorching hot day. After criticising my housekeeping, cooking and child-raising skills, she departed in her new Mercedes, a recent purchase funded by selling off even more of Dad's shares, without a backwards glance.

Normally I'd have immediately found Harry to vent my fury about my mother's vindictiveness, but after my abrupt departure back to the boat for no plausible reason, leaving the prawns to go off on the kitchen counter, we'd turned into the kind of husband and wife who behaved towards each other with a distant courtesy. Expectation weighed like a thick blanket over our every move. Harry was doing everything he could to make himself agreeable. All the jobs he'd put off for eons – clearing the leaves out of the gutters, digging a fishpond, installing a compost bin, painting the laundry – were being ticked off his to-do list with dutiful good humour.

Hearing Ruth drive away, Harry appeared in the kitchen doorway. 'Ding dong, the witch has gone! I still can't believe she can appear in daylight, being, you know, a vampire. Do you like the fishpond so far? And what about the rockery I've started? Are they making you happy?' he asked with trepidation.

'Yes, I'm really happy,' I replied, doubtfully.

Harry walked slowly out of the room, disquieted and puzzled, feeling my cool, pale gaze on his back.

I wasn't trying to be disagreeable; but I just couldn't settle. I didn't even buy a whole litre of milk in case I decided to scarper once more. I constantly found myself shuffling aimlessly around the house like Marlene Dietrich in her later years.

One of the little niggling things that had always irritated me about my husband was his habit of splashing pool chlorine onto his T-shirt and bleaching it in pointillist spots. Every T-shirt he owned ended up Jackson Pollock-ed. I'd frequently offered to take over the job of mixing the pool chlorine but he always made out how difficult it was to get just the right balance – a cup of chlorine, stabiliser, acid, more pH. He took such care over this cocktail of chemicals and yet clearly could not adjust the chemical imbalance in our marriage. Since my birthday party we were out of whack as a couple and growing algae.

Was this to be my life? I reflected as I did the housework. Spending our weekends with Harry rotating his tyres, and me swishing a wettex around the toilet bowl rim and taking lint off clothes that were washed with a loose tissue in the pocket, while pretending to the women in my book club that life was *sooooo* busy, when in truth my most current reading material was the steam iron warranty?

I pep-talked myself into finding happiness in the little things that life offered, but things that used to make me happy – the joy of discovering a forgotten twenty bucks in a jeans pocket; having my parking ticket validated by the cinema; the free foundation sample in a magazine – meant nothing now. If I'd been back at work, even seeing an article by a colleague I disliked be spiked by the editor, usually an office highlight, would have left me flat. And speaking of the office, I was so desperate to get back on the job that I would have spiked myself on a daily basis, impaled there on the editor's desk, just for a whiff of newsprint. Not only is writing better and cheaper than therapy, but it would take my mind off my many misdemeanours and painful longings. My boss, Angela, knew about my misdiagnosis, but refused to answer my calls about coming back to work.

In bed one night, as Harry laboured above me, my nose tucked into his shoulder, I ticked off all the experiences in life that were overrated – oysters, yodelling, experimental opera, expressive dance, sorbet, cricket – eventually concluding that there was nothing as insipid as sex with a husband when your heart is not in it. It was like dancing with no music.

After Harry fell asleep, I slipped outside. Beyond the jagged outline of the suburban houses, the lights of Sydney glowed invitingly in the distance. In the other direction, across the bay, lay the jet-black expanse of the national park.

The southerly buster had brought a chill to the evening air. I breathed deeply and felt my body tingle in the coolness. It made me think of Brody's touch. By day I walked through a world full of carefree, happy people who had not just lost the love of their lives, and at night I silently cried myself to sleep.

Our house was all Italian tiles and big windows. During the day, its rooms were seared with light. I used to so enjoy opening the blinds every morning. But now I opened the blinds then quickly closed them again, convinced that the best way to start the day was to go back to bed. Curled around my pillow, I'd watch the ABC weather report, but was so fogged with sadness I'd somehow not tune in properly until the presenter had passed Sydney and was now making predictions for Melbourne, Adelaide, Perth. If only there were a reliable forecast of my moods. When could I look forward to a bold, sunny front approaching?

My eyes in the mirror were pink and watery, like a laboratory rabbit's. I'd also lost my appetite, felt constantly tired and often nauseous. Plus, my head ached, all the time. I didn't seek a medical opinion. No, I could self-diagnose this one – chronic love sickness, with no known cure. It was remiss of the Department of Health not to issue a warning that falling in love with a doctor can be seriously hazardous to a woman's health.

When symptoms persisted and then became worse, I put it down to the peri-menopause. It had finally arrived and was clearly kicking in with a vengeance. I needed a panacea. What I really needed was someone with a good bedside manner. But Brody was off exploring somewhere exotic and aquatic, exact coordinates unknown. An alternative cure would be a big dose of my sisters – but Emerald and Amber were still both ignoring me.

Ten days before Christmas, I poured myself a giant gin and emailed them.

Dear Only Two People in Australia Who Ruby Ryan Actually Likes,

Since my exile into Social Siberia I've been so frantically busy, what with the Aldi sale and the dishwasher filter needing changing.

As you know, my bitchy boss at the newspaper put me on sick leave. She knows I'm one hundred per cent fine, but has obviously finally realised that I'm wholly unnecessary and was basically only in the job for the free parking, and that my work could easily be done by a wombat with a dictaphone. This means that I suddenly have quite a lot of spare time, and quite a lot of leftover birthday chocolate to eat and vodka to drink, if either of you are hungry or thirsty?

Now unemployed, I spend a lot of time learning Spanish by watching El Chapo *on Netflix. I can now say 'Where are the drugs?', 'Kill him slowly', 'Torture a confession out of him' and 'Give it to me, big boy'. The neighbours must think I'm running a brothel or a meth lab. I also watch re-runs of* I'm a Celebrity . . . Get Me Out of Here! *all night, just to remind myself that there are people out there far more desperate than I am.*

Actually, I'm working on a pitch for my own reality TV show, in which middle-aged mums abandon all logic and fall in love with unobtainable men, and make total fools of themselves, alienating their beloved sisters in the pathetic process.

Anyway, if you have it in your hearts to forgive such a person and meet up for a drink, I'll be in the Sandy Bay beach bar this Friday, where I'll be buying the drinks and eating my words (yum!). Oh, and, by the way, you'll actually be buying, as both my cards have been cancelled after being overdrawn when I paid for a very expensive cruise for three. Thanks for reimbursing me, which you didn't need to do. But it's just as well you did, as my reality cheque has bounced. If I don't find employment soon, I may have to sell the children.

Bring nothing but love (and credit cards), and prepare to slag off the boss who hasn't taken me back yet. We will drink to my excellent new future, in whichever fast food joint offers me a job first.

Love, Ruby

P.S. I am actually thinking of starting up a toy boy boutique for women of a certain age, with a man buffet, shopper loyalty cards and time-share husbands. They'd have to be trained in an appreciation of Jane Austen, be emotionally intelligent and good at massage. What do you think – my next start-up? To discuss.

Amber was the first to send a reply via our sisters Messenger group. *Someone has clearly stolen your Prozac. Whoever they are, I hope they're happy.*

Emerald's sarcastic message said simply *Who is this?*

I tried again. *Emerald, I know you're super busy. If it's easier I could come around to your place?*

Emerald: *No. My dog hates you. He'll probably bite your legs, and you can't afford to lose any more length there.*

Me: *Are you two going to meet me for a drink?*

Amber: *Thanks, but I'm completely knackered from all the Christmas party catering. I dress like Iris Murdoch these days so don't want to be seen in public. I'm turning down all invitations too, except to book club. Do you remember Leyla Khoury from school? I've just joined her club, as well.*

Emerald: *You seem to be booked up for a book club every bloody night. It's a wonder you have any time to read.*

Amber: *At least I don't only read wine labels like someone I could mention.*

Me: *Instead of discussing the book, you could just discuss why you didn't have time to read it. Or maybe start an abridged book club or a pamphlet club for busy working mothers.*

Amber: *What I want to discuss is if you're okay, Ruby.*

Me: *I can't tell you because I'm too busy slamming my head against a wall. Though, I do feel slightly better than I did yesterday – as evidenced by the fact that I'm vertical – but it's still, well, how can I put this . . . an absolute fuck-up. Have you both forgiven me for deceiving you?*

Emerald: *Sure. Just ignore this voodoo effigy of you and vial of ricin I'm carrying in my pocket.*

Me: *So, it's a yes to meet up for a drink then?*

Emerald: *No. I'm either at work inoculating pets for the kind of Christmas holidays in Europe that I can't afford, or at the gym running on the spot like a hamster on a wheel to keep the weight off. I'm only communicating to send you the Christmas Day job list. Amber, I've got you down for your Thai salad, plus your fab pav and meat for the barbecue. I'm doing the ham and turkey. Mum's making her Christmas pudding, complete with sixpences and cyanide. Ruby, due to your culinary prowess, oysters, prawns, nibbles, etc. Maybe a potato bake if you promise not to burn down your kitchen.*

Me: *I'll put that request into the swill I've been calling my 'thought process'. But, be warned, my take-charge-planning gene is horribly frozen.*

Emerald: *Christmas Day is forecast to be 33 degrees, so I suggest doing everything possible before 10 am. I'll then just fan myself until late afternoon. Harry and Sandro will barbecue, as usual, and Scott's in charge of the bar.*

Me: *I will require a lot of numbing alcohol.*

Amber: *Heartache is painful. But it'll pass.*

Me: *Brody's not a gallstone, Amber. You're talking about the potential love of my life.*

Emerald: *Stop being ridiculous, Ruby. This is the time in life when we should be knitting doilies and eating lamingtons. Yes, I ran around like a teenager on the cruise. But it's time to get back to real life. Okay?*

Amber: *Emerald's right. Try to stay calm and be positive. This time of the year is stressful enough.*

Me: *The most stressful things in life are death and moving house, apparently. And then there's divorce, which is death and moving house combined.*

But I was typing into a void, as both my sisters had signed off. I sighed sadly. Life really was going to be the death of me.

★

One week before Christmas, in a show of seasonal goodwill, and after eating enough humble pie to stock an entire patisserie, I was finally invited back to work. My first assignment? A front page scoop on dog poop – a dream come true! At first the staff were so surly towards me they made Vlad the Impaler seem helpful. But by day three things were back to normal. I tried to be interested in conversations about gazebo extensions and the merits of kidney-shaped pools over rectangular, the pros and cons of buying a boat and cricket scores, while all the time bleeding inside. Bleeding? It was more of an emotional haemorrhage. I couldn't believe that people I knew were talking about house prices and cricket scores and whether Harry and Wills would patch things up after Megxit, completely oblivious to the fact that my world had imploded. The only thing that even vaguely amused me was the office party, where at least my colleagues could *admit* they were drunk and not getting any work done.

I was looking forward to Christmas with the same enthusiasm as a turkey might, but with five days to go and my fairy lights still not strung up, the tree lying at half mast, I suddenly went into a frantic Yuletide frenzy of holly-bedecking and eggnogwhisking, contracting chronic hand cramp from the penning of two hundred Christmas cards. *It gives new meaning to 'cardiac arrest'*, I messaged my sisters. Emerald joked back that Christmas had been cancelled. *Apparently you told Santa you'd been good and he died laughing.*

The very thought of gift-wrapping made me want to

garrotte myself with a string of tinsel. *'Comedy rapper'*
does not refer to Ali G but to a description of my present
wrapping technique, I messaged them once more. Amber
sent an emoji of a terror-stricken face, but had no time for
actual words.

Still, I was more adept than Harry. When wrapping my
present, he laid out the wrapping paper on the table, then
accidentally cut straight through an antique tablecloth given
to us by his mother. Which made me wonder via our sisters
Messenger group how Christmas had ever really caught on. *I*
mean, three wise men? Yeah, right. But they were both too busy
to banter – or possibly still pissed off with me. I wasn't sure.

Two days before Christmas, I couldn't put off the present
purchasing any longer and dragged myself to the shopping
centre, the large glass towers of which rose up above the
surrounding suburban houses like tombstones. It took so
long to find a parking spot I thought I'd probably missed
Christmas altogether. I then panted through department
stores in a desperate hunt for last-minute gifts for my
picky brothers-in-law, followed by a frantic dash through
the supermarket for the necessary ingredients for my
potato bake. Carrying my own body weight in chips, dips,
drinks, napkins, nuts, potatoes, mince pies and marzipan –
enough stuff, in fact, to establish a comfortable wilderness
homestead – I then tried to find my way back to the car.
Where the hell was it again? I'd been so distracted and
irritated, I hadn't paid enough attention to where I'd parked.
After two futile attempts in two different parking areas, I
realised I'd have to hire a car to find my car.

The taxi rank was at the other end of the huge shopping
complex. On and on I trudged along endless fluorescent

corridors, passing elves in budgie smugglers and carol singers in bikinis, and endless glossy promotional photographs of festively festooned couples smiling at each other as they happily hung curtains and drilled nails in DIY cupboards, cruelly mocking the fraught misery of the average suburban scene of attempted IKEA assemblage, which had embittered couples turning their power tools on each other, shouting, 'Die, evil scum!' within minutes.

I was slogging past the food hall towards the escalators when a wave of nausea almost knocked me off my feet. I lurched left and steadied myself on the shoulder of an exhausted Santa who was chowing down on a spring roll during his lunch break. He was wearing the full red suit, requisite fluffy white beard, eyebrows that resembled toothbrush bristles and the suitably wrung-out expression of a man who'd been sitting all day letting kids pee on his lap while they whispered the brand names of skate and surf boards into his ear.

I felt myself swoon and then collapsed onto his lap, where I promptly vomited into my handbag – the handbag that contained the car keys I'd have to fetch out when I finally found my car. But I felt too sick to care. Bent double, barfing, two things dawned on me. First, that I was going to be a headline in my own newspaper: 'Fifty-Year-Old Woman Arrested for Refusing to Get Off Santa's Lap'. And, second, that I really was sick. There was no doubt in my mind that it was cancer. I felt it in my gut. It would be poetic justice, wouldn't it? The medical karma I so richly deserved. And, of course, the worst part was, nobody would bloody well believe me.

28

'**R**uby Ryan?'

My head emerged from the hood of my cotton top like a meerkat peeking out of its burrow. I trudged from reception into the doctor's office like a condemned woman to the electric chair. The decor, I noticed, was flesh coloured. I sat down on a hard chair facing the doctor's desk, which squatted on a faded rug. The name on the desk plate read *Zahra Hanbury*, but our family doctor was on sabbatical. The locum greeted me with brisk professionalism.

'And what brings you here today?' she asked with perfunctory politeness.

'Unexplained weight loss, constant fatigue, loss of appetite, nausea, headaches . . . It's cancer, clearly,' I stated.

The doctor, who was around half my age, showed about as much interest in this self-diagnosis as she would if I'd read her the specifications from the back of a manual for a fridge freezer.

'Been consulting that well-known quack Doctor Google, have we?' the locum diagnosed. 'Let's just take some actual medical tests, shall we?'

I extended my arm for a blood-pressure check then looked away from the needle at the cheap walnut panelling on the walls and the commercial grade rust-coloured carpet on the floor. Tests were pointless. I knew I was doomed. At least I'd get to pen my own obituary for my paper. 'Fate struck while the irony was hot,' I would write. Through the window, grey clouds sloshed across the sky like jumbled washing. A sense of foreboding as heavy as a winter coat pressed down on me. As I left the medical centre, the cloudy laundry overhead had thickened. It was only when I got to my car that I realised it was smoke – bushfire smoke billowing up the coast. It seemed ominous and apocalyptic.

On Christmas Eve I dragged myself from the office back to the surgery for the results of the tests. I couldn't think of a less appealing rendezvous. A barbecue with Hannibal Lecter held more allure. Sitting opposite the doctor, I could feel my blood coagulating with fear. I actually flung my hand over my eyes like a damsel in distress about to be tied to a railway track. 'Give it to me, straight,' I said. 'Is it pancreatic?'

'Congratulations,' the doctor said.

'What? It's not pancreatic cancer?'

'On your pregnancy.'

I fell back against the plastic bucket seat in a fugue of shock, my eyes bare and round as light bulbs.

'There must be some mistake. I mean, I'm fifty!' I looked at the locum the way a monkey must look at a medical researcher – knowing such experiments need to be conducted for the sake of knowledge but still pleading for release.

'A lot of women your age presume they're peri-menopausal, so they forgo contraception,' she explained. 'When they get the symptoms of pregnancy, they put it down to the change of life.'

My life was about to change, all right, but not in the way I'd foreseen. I started squeaking like a lost kitten. My smile became unhinged. To make matters worse, the estimated date of conception that the doctor gave was vague enough that it could either be Harry's or Brody's.

Driving home on autopilot, my whole body felt numb. The realisation that life hasn't quite turned out the way we thought it would hits us all at some point. It's prompted by many things – a lover leaving, kids flying the nest, neighbours' designer pool cabanas, and . . . *falling accidentally fucking pregnant aged fucking fifty and not knowing who the fucking father is*. I slammed the steering wheel with both hands. *WTF?* What the fuckity, fuckity, fuck? To keep it or not to keep it? That was the (insert *pregnant* pause) question.

I had no idea how to break the news to Harry. Maybe I could lessen the blow by telling him something much worse first, like, I dunno, 'My mother's moving in.' But that would only give him a heart attack and mean a drive back to the medical centre. I decided not to tell him until I'd figured out what I was going to do. But when Harry opened a bottle of wine after he got home from work, the smell made me retch. Plus, I had a sudden craving for mashed potato. I gnawed away at bowls of the stuff like a barnyard animal – all under Harry's watchful and wondering gaze. Next would be spaghetti sandwiches, Tim Tams and mustard, and ice cream on toast. We'd had two children – Harry would surely recognise the signs. It was pointless trying to keep it from him. And so, I reluctantly asked him to join me at the kitchen table so I could reveal the results of my test.

'I've got something to tell you.'

'I hope it's that you've won twenty grand on a scratchie,' he joked, nervously.

KATHY LETTE

I wriggled in my chair and contemplated using my serviette as a balaclava. All I wanted to do was go and lie down in a cordoned-off chalk outline to see if it would fit.

But after I brusquely broke the news of my impending abortion, Harry took a beat, then emitted a joyful shout loud enough to be heard in an Antarctic base camp.

'That's friggin' awesome!' he exclaimed. I realised that, in his mind, pregnancy explained away my strange behaviour and mood swings. The relief he felt that my withdrawal was biological and not psychological was seismic in its immensity.

'But I'm not going to keep it, Harry,' I added, gravely. 'Of course I'm not. It's more likely that my mother would release a death metal album than it is that I would keep this baby.'

He gazed at me blankly for a moment. 'Why not? The kids are about to bugger off. The nest will be empty. What could be better? This is just what we need to bring us closer together!'

'We're too old to be parents again.'

'But a baby will keep us young. A baby. Can you imagine? Wow!'

I made a noise like a tyre going flat. Realising that I wasn't showing the right level of enthusiasm, I curled my mouth into what I hoped was a smile but was more like a rictus. My toes curled up as though I were wearing a pair of Turkish slippers.

'Be serious, Harry. What sane people our age would want to spend one more second of their lives making rocket ships out of loo rolls?'

'I have a say in this too, Ruby. And, hey. At least, as an

older mum, you're programmed to the baby's schedule – up all night drinking.' He winked.

And if I didn't drink before *having a baby at fifty, I definitely would after*, I thought grimly.

'And I'll take such good care of you, love. I'm gonna treat you like a princess. Because I do love you so, so much, Rubes.' His voice sounded so sickly sweet I was worried he might slip into a hyperglycaemic coma.

'Are you, ya know, craving anything else? You always get the munchies when you're up the duff. What do you feel like? Malaysian? Vietnamese? Waffles? New carpet and a car upgrade? They're the pregnancy cravings you got last time. Whatever it is,

I'll race out and pick it up. Well, what do ya know!' he laughed. 'There's lead in the old pencil yet.'

Of course, what I didn't tell him is that I wasn't at all sure which pencil had written my fate.

My forced smile now felt as though some multi-legged tropical insect was climbing across my chin. As soon as Harry had scooted off to get me some salted caramel chocolate and some Tabasco, I lay on the hammock by our turquoise pool, feeling the evening cool. It was that time of day when the sun normally looks like a knob of butter in a red hot skillet, sizzling and caramelising into a golden brown, but today due to the bushfire haze the sky was end-of-the-world-eerie and sinister.

What was I going to do? Harry wasn't a bad person. He had a big heart. He was a good dad. He was kind to animals and kids. He volunteered for Nippers and school barbecues and firefighting. And then there was all our history . . . Perhaps I could make a go of it with my husband? And this could be our new beginning? Maybe Brody was nothing more than a foolish fling. But if so, why did I so crave the miraculous comfort of his smile?

Many of my middle-aged friends were desperately groping for a ripcord to parachute out of their marriages. But jumping off into the unknown has its hazards, too. There was no guarantee of a safe landing. When lust evaporates you could just be lost. Maybe it was better to just stay strapped into my marital safety belt, ride out the buffeting winds and hope for bluer skies? But it was only fair to tell him about my affair – after which he might not want me anymore, anyway. I felt driven to reveal the truth – but feared I was being driven by Ted Kennedy at Chappaquiddick. Anyway, I couldn't tell him now, on Christmas Eve, with Zoe due home any moment and Jake putting his electrician skills to work by happily stringing up extravagant lights around my haphazardly decorated tree.

I know what you're thinking – *Don't tell another lie, Ruby Ryan!* You just want to fling yourself forward and shake me until my fillings fall out, don't you? And I'm with you! I really am. While I wouldn't call myself an intellectual – I mean, I'm clearly not the kind of girl who sits around splitting atoms in her spare time – I had never before realised the true depths of my stupidity. If it's any consolation, at this point, nobody could have liked me less than I did. There's a cream to cure people like me, you know; haemorrhoid cream, because I'm such a pain in the arse.

Above me, seagulls squawked like teething babies. The sound repulsed me. Any slight angst I had was soothed by simply burying my face in a beach towel for half an hour and screaming and screaming and screaming.

29

On Christmas Day, it's a good idea to tell each family member what to bring to lunch – that way two people don't show up with the same sexist or racist opinions and get thrown in the pool. This was the Ryan motto.

Our family always celebrated Christmas lunch beside Ruth's backyard swimming pool. The sisters divvied up the courses and the boys manned the bar and the barbecue while the six cousins played Marco Polo in the deep end, forgetting to be 'cool' and harking back to the fun they'd enjoyed as little kids.

My mother still lived in our family home – a palatial manor on the furthermost point of the Insular Peninsular, on a big, broad block that looked out across the mouth of the river to the swaying eucalypts of the national park. The area is an architectural minestrone, with residents playing out their fantasies in bricks and mortar. A Swiss chalet with a gabled roof and ornate carvings rubs up against a Japanese-themed minka with sliding doors, opposite a Mexican ranch house. Ruth's plantation-style French colonial mansion is the most imposing on the street, and nicknamed by we Ryan girls 'The Swank-ienda'.

Ruth's current neighbours were rich footballers, property developers and daytime TV hostesses, who all unapologetically put the 'nouveau' into 'nouveaux riches'. Christmas oneupmanship was high on the agenda, epitomised by the residents' annual competition to determine who had the most sensational decorations. Despite global warming angst, the bushfire season starting earlier and lasting longer, and summer temperatures so intense that local chooks had taken to laying hardboiled eggs, no electrical wattage was spared in the flashing, disco-dancing reindeers, gyrating polar bears, strobing 'Ho Ho Ho's, and frenzied elves and Santas sleighing back and forth across suburban roofs in a phantasmagoria of fluorescent choreography. On and on they flickered across the sky, even in full, blazing sunlight.

Stunned pedestrians staggered from throbbing cul-de-sac to cul-de-sac. My mother's street attracted the most sightseers. My favourite of her neighbours, an old surfie dude in a fibro shack, who'd refused to sell out to the developers, had just one homemade neon sign on his front porch. It was a simple, luminous arrow pointing back towards his neighbours' houses, above one flashing word – 'WANKERS'.

Even on Christmas Day, gawping crowds meant that the roads leading out to the point were blocked with suburban SUVs. We trundled along behind these standard parental-issue behemoths at a geriatric pace. Zoe and Jake reverted to ironic, kiddie-type whining, with exaggerated 'Are we there yet?'s. Although they were joking, it made me have serious second thoughts about my secret baby on board. When we finally arrived at the family home, my mother swung the front door open wide and made a sweeping gesture, like a French courtier, to indicate that we should enter. The look she gave me was so searching and shrewd that when she said, flatly, 'You're late,' for a sickening instant, I thought she was talking about my period.

My mother's harsh face suddenly appeared to have the fragility of ancient, drying paper. Ruth hesitated and for one fleeting moment I actually imagined she was going to say something nice. 'Potato bake?' she said, peering down at the huge baking dish I was clutching. 'So glad you took me at my word and didn't go to too much trouble.'

I sighed. *Here we go*, I thought, resignedly. My mother was good at being mean the way a shark is good at being predatory. Today, even the big windows in her sunny, deep waterfront home seemed cold and unfriendly. Despite the brightness outside, it felt cold in here, as though sunlight never entered.

With forced geniality, my mother offered a cheek to her grandchildren to be kissed, then turned to Harry. 'Harrison.' Her eyelashes whisked up and down his frame. 'I didn't get the memo that it was fancy dress.'

Harry glanced down at his shirt front to look at the colourful stingray chasing a board-shorted Santa across his broad chest. 'It's my new Mambo shirt. I thought it was kinda festive?' he said, the wind taken out of his sartorial sails.

In silence my family trailed our matriarch through the house and out onto the big, rolling, billiard-table-green lawn, which stretched all the way down to the bright-blue bay. Harry caught my eye and rolled his orbs behind his mother-in-law's back, but once we'd joined the clan under the patio awning it became obvious that Ruth's antagonism wasn't aimed solely at us. It seemed the whole family had entered a hard-hat area.

When Amber presented her famous pavlova, a huge and impressive pagoda of strawberries and passionfruit, the meringue whipped into curlicues and covered in creamy foam, Mum adopted the sort of pained expression that made me think she was trying to suck her face out of the back of her skull.

'Pavlova? *Again?* It's become quite your signature dish, hasn't it? I was rather hoping for something more *special* for one of the lord's holiest days.'

Amber wilted like a perm in a sauna and put her magnificent pav back into the esky.

Scott was Ruth's next victim. 'Oh, look who's just arrived. That feisty champion of the common man! So, how's the pro-bono work going? Of course, you couldn't indulge your do-gooding side if your wife didn't work so hard. A wealthy wife is quite a labour-saving device. It's obvious you hit it off because you have *so* much in common: Amber owned a waterfront home, and you wanted one.' Our mother laughed, to make out she was only joking, which she clearly wasn't. 'I now pronounce you Man and Mansion. That's what Father Gallagher ought to have said at the altar. Prawns, anyone?'

Ruth was obviously 'coming the raw prawn', as our Dad, a lover of colourful Aussie vernacular, was wont to say. Even decades on, our sadness at losing our darling dad in a car crash was a constant hum, like tinnitus. It was just always *there*. The loss was felt even more intensely on Christmas Day, because he'd been the cheerful buffer between mother and daughters.

The food started curling in the heat as soon as it hit the table – ham, turkey, salads – and tempers were running nearly as high as the temperature. As Ruth handed around platters of oysters and seafood, her fuchsia-painted lips slapped together in a wet percussion of rebukes to all and sundry. Emerald and Alessandro were her next victims.

'A caftan, Emerald? What a sensible idea for someone as big-boned as you.'

'I've actually lost six kilos, Mum, thanks to Ruby taking us on that cru—'

'Although, isn't it interesting that, in a gulag, there's never anybody "big boned" or suffering from "water retention", is there? Isn't that "food for thought"? I imagine you're on a starvation diet for *that* kind of nourishment, Emerald, being married to a mechanic. Intellectual sustenance is the one thing you really *should* be hungry for. When did you leave school again, Alex?'

Alessandro, who hated being called Alex, bristled, but replied politely, 'Sixteen. Once I'd wised up to how many graduates were bumming around on the dole and saw the moolah I could make in trade, I reckoned getting an apprenticeship was a no-brainer—'

Ruth cut him off. 'Yes, no wonder it's lucrative. A mechanic is just someone who picks your pocket from underneath your car. Still, at least you know that Emerald married you for love. How else would she stand all these years of talking about differential shafts and lubricant.' Ruth's fake smile was so intense it could irradiate soft fruit.

'Lube,' Alessandro corrected his mother-in-law, through clenched lips. 'Lube greases the steering system and suspension to keep moving parts that touch from wearing each other down. Maybe I should have brought some today.'

'So . . . shall we get the barbecue fired up?' Harry suggested with urgency.

The three brothers-in-law fell on each other with relief. They grinned and slapped each other's shoulders, then, taking a bucket of prawns and a plate of oysters, retreated to the barbecue at the bottom of the garden for their annual corroboree.

Emerald popped the champagne with alacrity and filled her sisters' glasses to the brim. Today's Christmas spirit was clearly going to come from a bottle.

'Oh, look, the tide's gone out already,' she said, refilling her glass with a fizzing *whoosh*.

The kids fell on the prawns like squawking seagulls then leapt into the pool. Ruth Ryan quite liked her grandchildren – they were still malleable. Talk turned to the kids' plans for the future, the safest conversational option. It was only during her third champagne top-up that Emerald realised I wasn't drinking.

'Why aren't you drinking?' she asked, amazed. 'After the hottest, driest year in history, we're saving water by drinking alcohol.'

'I just . . . I just don't feel like it,' I prevaricated.

'Are you sick?' my mother asked. 'Actually, you don't look at all well. Even worse than usual,' she added, true to her style.

'Thank you, Mother. I can always count on you to brighten my mood.'

Ruth rummaged in her handbag for a lipstick. 'And you can brighten mine by putting on a bit of lippy.'

'Actually, Mum's right. You do look a bit peaky, Ruby. Are you okay? A friend of mine, Leyla, works as a receptionist at the medical centre, and she told me at book club that she'd seen you there twice this week,' Amber probed.

'Oh, god. You haven't gone and actually got cancer, have you?' a tipsy Emerald joked.

'Well, now, that really would be funny,' my mother said, a smile acid-etched onto her face. All she needed was a black chariot drawn by howling, multi-headed hellhounds to complete her 'Dark Mistress of Torment' image.

A fierce desire to shock my merciless mother down to her very hair follicles came over me in a rush. 'I'm just feeling a little bit nauseous, you know, because of the baby.'

All three heads jerked in my direction like a small school of hooked herring.

'What baby?' Emerald, who'd been up since dawn trying to arm-wrestle a naked turkey into the gynaecological position in order to stuff chestnuts up its orifice, had developed the demeanour, aching legs and mood swings of a member of a long-haul cabin crew. There was no point messing with her.

'The baby I'm carrying. I wasn't going to say anything till the three month mark, or until after the termination,' I added, to shock my staunchly Catholic mother even more, 'but—'

'*What?*' Amber said, similarly flabbergasted. 'How can that be? At your age?'

'No, it can happen,' Emerald espoused. 'The famous changeof-life baby.' Fuelled by champagne, my oldest sister ploughed on without thinking. 'Especially, biologically speaking, if the vagina hasn't had time to become hostile. Vaginas love new sperm. With a new lover the vag hasn't had time to build up immunity. It's a very, very warm and welcoming place indeed.'

'New lover? What the hell does that mean?'

We three sisters were sitting facing the swimming

pool – our backs to the path that ran down the garden to the barbecue below. Only Ruth, with the pool behind her, had noticed Harry's reappearance, but had chosen to say nothing. She just sat there, gimlet-eyed, in full Madame Defarge mode, with her imaginary guillotine and invisible knitting. We swivelled in unison to face him.

Emerald's words hung, irretrievable, in the air. For a moment, all that could be heard was the splash and splosh of the cousins frolicking down the deep end, and the cackle of the kookaburras, who were clearly in on the joke.

'What do you mean, "new sperm"?' Harry asked again, aiming his barbecue tongs at Emerald like a weapon.

As elephants in rooms go, this one was more like a woolly mammoth. Emerald and Amber's eyes jumped to mine. I just kept smiling until my face cramped and my teeth felt like they would fall out. Remorse racked my whole body. I figured now would be a good time to fake a terminal illness – say, necrotising fasciitis – or possibly to emigrate to New Zealand.

'Tell me!' Harry demanded. 'What the bloody hell's going on?'

I wanted to throw myself in front of my husband like a fire blanket to protect him from what was about to be revealed. I tried to speak but seemed to have a live eel halfway down my throat – that's what it felt like, anyway. 'I . . . I . . .' I was suddenly sweating more than a Russian athlete about to take a drug test. 'I met a man,' I began, finally grabbing the elephant by the trunk. 'On the ship. I was going to tell you—'

'Oh, and, what, you decided not to tell me until *now* so that I could have a heart attack at leisure in front of your entire fucking family?'

'Somehow I don't think this is quite what's meant by Secret S . . . S . . . Santa,' Emerald slurred, in a drunken attempt to alleviate the tension.

I glanced towards my mother, expecting sanctimonious fury. But she was wearing the smug expression of a preacher, or a saleswoman; someone who knows they're about to command the room. In fact, it turned out that my mother had been waiting for this moment for a quite a while. The baby bit was news to her. But it didn't compare to the information she'd been nursing like a precious piece of porcelain, a treasure, to be revealed when the time was right. She'd obviously fondled the evidence regularly, weighing up its worth, evaluating its price and its power.

'Harrison,' she said, in a measured voice, her eyes glittering with spite. 'I never thanked you for your old iPhone, which you kindly passed on to me. It's been an invaluable source of information.'

'What? Oh . . . good,' Harry said, distractedly, his eyes welded to my stricken face.

'Yes. Especially about you. I know you told me you'd erased all your . . . "data", I believe is the right word? The grandkids might say I suffer from a technology deficit disorder, but when my daughters abandoned me to go on their luxury cruise I was forced to teach myself to use the contraption. One day I was pressing things randomly and a message popped up on the screen from something called "WhatsApp". I followed what you might call a text chain . . . A chain that led me to a very startling conclusion.'

Harry's eyes now darted towards Ruth. A layer of sweat glistened on his tanned face, wet moons rapidly appeared in the armpits of his shirt, and his thick, sun-bleached blonde hair suddenly seemed to stick in lank strands to his forehead.

'You see – the thing about men, girls, is that they're lazy. They'll just make do with whatever's lying around the home . . . even when it comes to gratifying their carnal appetites.' Ruth's bejewelled hands twitched like spiders on the tabletop, and a malicious smile shrieked across her face.

It had seemed for one astounding moment that my mother was coming to my defence. But I should have known better. 'What do you mean?' I asked, bilious with what I hoped was only morning sickness.

'Why don't you ask your cherished sisters? The ones you so kindly took on a cruise, completely forsaking your poor, lonely mother, who loves a cruise but has no one to go with. Six months, I'd say, the affair lasted. Judging by the messages. Being both self-employed, I'm amazed either of you found the time.'

Amber's laugh vibrated on a high, metallic note. Harry looked at my sister, sheepishly. And that's when I knew. My heart scrambled and foundered as the truth hit me, hard as a punch. The pain came, rapid and intense, like opening the blinds on a summer's day when you have a hangover. The knowledge that my sister had slept with my husband settled on my heart, compressing my chest in a vice grip that would never let go.

A shark can smell one tiny droplet of blood in one hundred litres of water. It then traces its prey by following the electricity that is discharged by a terrified animal. My mother gave a gloating grin, her bleached teeth bared. It was the grin of a Great White going in for the kill.

The rest of us were frozen, speechless, as our offspring

splashed on in the pool, oblivious. The shimmering bay sparkled at the edge of my vison. I fought the urge to run down the garden and throw myself into it.

What my mother had revealed was so surreal that I lost the power of speech. I sat, welded to my wrought-iron chair. My mind rejected what I'd so clearly heard. My entire body felt hollowed out by the bright white light of a nuclear blast. I was a shell of my former self. My tongue felt suddenly swollen and unyielding. When some words finally came out, they sounded foreign in my mouth. 'You had . . . an affair? With Amber?' I ventriloquised.

Amber's normally alabaster cheeks blazed red, becoming two expressionist splatters of colour.

'I can't believe it,' Emerald gasped. 'Miss Goody-Two-Shoes. It seems, Amber, that you have entirely failed to grasp the concept of loyal sisterhood – the very first rule of which is not sleeping with your bloody brother-in-law.'

I turned on Amber, eyes ablaze. 'But you said you hated being touched?'

'Just not by *your* husband, obviously,' our mother qualified, helpfully. 'You laid the table today, didn't you, Amber? Forks on the left, and knives in your sister's back?'

All the comments Amber had made on the ship, encouraging me to forgive Harry, came back to me in a rush: 'Therapists believe an affair can rescue a marriage'; 'It's not about assigning blame, but finding the roots of the infidelity'; 'All marriages can suffer from a little fidelity fatigue'; 'We should be more European, and forgive adultery . . .'

No wonder Harry hadn't contacted me the whole time I was away. He was no doubt desperately worried that Amber would confess. He was just waiting to see the lay of the land.

Literally. And why hadn't she confessed, instead of letting me continue to suffer?

I looked at my middle sister, dumbfounded, battling a desire to knock her to the ground; to pull her hair and pinch her, hard, and Chinese-burn her arms, the way we did when we were girls. I could feel myself reverting. It was primal. It was instinctive. It was survival. It was biblical – siblings smiting each other.

'Oh my god, Amber! The grief you gave me for lying, when all the time it was *you* who was telling the biggest lie of all! Why? Why did you do this to me?'

Amber seemed to have become a finalist in a fixed smile event.

'Tell me, Amber – with brain trepanning, is there pain afterwards?' Emerald quizzed, sarcastically. She'd got herself drunk to avoid Ruth's verbal bullets, but was now behaving just like her, shooting from the lip. 'What were you thinking? Or rather, not thinking . . . Well, say something, for god's sake!'

'I . . . I . . . I'm so sorry,' Amber finally stage-whispered.

'That's it? That's *all*?' Emerald threw up her hands in disgust. 'You'll have to come up with something better than that, sis.'

'It's just, well – Scott tried to put together this flat-pack furniture cupboard and built himself in – I had to call Harry to rescue him. I made Harry a crepe suzette to say thank you. And he was so grateful. And then, you know, Harry started to pop round with that tool belt of his and just fixed everything Scott was too busy saving the world to mend. Pretty soon nothing in my house smoked when I plugged it in, leaked oil, or made a funny clunking noise

286

anymore. And then I'd feed him to say thank you and . . . he liked my cooking so much and, for once in my life, I felt so *appreciated* . . .'

I reacted to these words as though they were gunfire and dropped my glass in surprise, which smashed into smithereens on the flagstones. Once more, the reassurances Amber had uttered on board the cruise boomeranged back at me: 'Infidelity is about so much more than sex'; 'People have affairs because they don't feel appreciated'; 'They want to feel wanted, needed, desired'; 'They are looking for an emotional connection . . .'

'Jesus, Harry! You made me feel so guilty that I'd accused you of being unfaithful. You even swore on Donald Bradman's grave!'

'Yeah, well, if you knew me at all, you'd know I don't even like bloody cricket,' Harry said, petulantly.

A darker thought clouded my mind. All over the Insular Peninsular, photos of Harry's ruggedly handsome smiling face were tacked to noticeboards or beamed out from under fridge magnets, offering his 'Hire a Hubby' services. How many other lonely, unappreciated women had taken up his offer? And in how many ways? 'Jesus, Harry. Exactly how many ladies love the tradies?'

'What? None! Gimme a break.'

'Why should I believe you?' I seethed.

'Look, I can't explain it either! I know it's an inexcusable act of first-grade scumbaggery. But Amber so reminded me of you, but a more confident, successful, domesticated version, I guess. And she kept feeding me. Oh, the food. The tarts, the trifles, the banana cakes, the lamingtons – how can a lammie taste that good?'

'*What?*' I repeated, duly horrified. 'You betrayed me for some banana cake and a lamington?'

'My dick just went into overdrive and the rest of me was forced to follow. I don't know what got into me. A midlife crisis, maybe.'

'Oh, puh-lease! How can you have a midlife crisis when you've never left puberty?' I fumed.

'And Amber was so chuffed by everything I did. She heaped praise on me all the time. Unlike you. You never even mention all the DIY I do for you. She really appreciated me.'

His words echoed in my head like an explosion. 'Appreciation? What about how unappreciated I feel? Doesn't that count? Appreciation for what you do? You're not a surgeon wielding a scalpel, Harry. Hammering a shelf over a woman's sink to hold unpaid bills is not exactly rocket science.'

'Hey!' The voice was Scott's. He was striding up the garden path, waving his barbecue fork. 'The steaks are nearly done,' he said. 'We're waiting on that platter, Harry. What's the ho, ho, hold up?'

Amber's eyes were fixed straight ahead. Her face was blank and her lips moved as if she were reading from an invisible book.

'What?' Scott asked. 'What are you saying? Speak up. I can't hear you.'

'I'm sorry,' she whispered.

'Mate.' Harry's flat, ironical voice had developed a tremor.

'What?' Scott asked again. 'What have I missed?'

Nobody spoke for a full minute. Nerves jangled more than the reindeer bells on the plastic Santas sleighing across Ruth's roof.

'Apparently your wife has been having an affair with her brother-in-law,' Ruth said. 'Forget the turkey, Harry. Your goose is well and truly cooked,' she concluded with sour glee.

From Scott's limitless legal lexicon only one feeble word sprang to his erudite mind. '*What?*'

Alessandro appeared behind him then, sausages piled high on a plate, just in time to hear a stunned Scott say to Amber, 'But I always have to initiate every encounter. You're just not that into it. Sex, I mean.'

'Only with you, apparently,' a tipsy Emerald took aim once more.

Amber turned on her. 'Shut up, Emerald, you're pissed! And, anyway, you can't talk. Exactly how many toy boys did you shag on the cruise? I lost count.'

I put my head in my hands. Catastrophes were piling up on each other like an acrobatic group.

Now it was Alessandro's turn to utilise the word du jour. '*What?*'

'Well, I'm not getting anything at home with Mr Limp-dick h . . . h . . . here,' Emerald slurred. She had clearly drunk enough to achieve that level of volubility where no secret goes unshared. 'What did you think was gonna happen, Sandro, if you put me on a sex diet? I have appetites, you know,' she added, taking a ravenous bite of a steaming sausage.

The humiliating visual metaphor was not lost on Alessandro, but once more, 'What?' was the only word that sprang from his lips as he tried to fathom the Grand Guignol scene playing out before him.

'Al can't get it up?' Harry asked, amazed, without thinking. 'I thought he was the Italian stallion?'

Everybody was staring at Alessandro now. He dumped the plate of sausages down on the table, grabbed a beer from the esky, twisted the top off the bottle and took a husky slug. 'Yeah, well, why bother?' he shot back, in a snarky and facetious tone. 'I'm second in importance in my house to the bloody dogs. I get the newspaper after the puppies. The only thing my wife truly loves are those goddamned animals, whereas *I* reckon animals are at their best on a barbecue. I especially hate dogs. Dogs have far too many teeth for a supposedly friendly creature. If I *had* to have a pet it would be a crocodile, so it could just eat all the fucking others.'

'You hate animals?!' Emerald flared. 'How can you say that when you know it's my passion?'

'Maybe if you stopped absent-mindedly scratching me behind the ear and saying "Good boy", I might feel a bit differently. As it is, you might as well start throwing me a tennis ball to chew on.'

'You know I love you, Sandro. But you push me away constantly.'

I'd always presumed my tough oldest sister would only ever cry if, say, the local artisan cake shop got wiped out in a tsunami. But our time away together on the cruise had clearly changed her. Tears sprang to her eyes. She mopped at her face with a napkin.

'Bullshit, Emerald. You only keep me around because your clinic's losing money – all those rescue animal ops you do for free. You'd bloody well sink without my financial input.'

'Why didn't you come to *me* for money if you're in trouble?' Amber asked Emerald, consolingly.

I couldn't suppress an indignant gasp. 'Oh! *Now* you're

feeling sisterly? The only animal behaviour going on right now is from my own sister. I can't believe it, Amber. I'm in shock. I don't even know what to say to you.'

'Ruby, I'm desperately sorry. We all make mistakes, okay?' Amber's pretty face flushed red again and the lines on either side of her mouth deepened in dismay. Attack being the best form of defence, she raised a combative eyebrow and then took aim with the only ammunition she had. 'Just like you, with the ship's doctor.'

'The ship's doctor?' Harry asked me sombrely. 'Fuck. Is he . . . the fresh sperm? Is he the father?'

Now it was time for Scott and Alessandro to '*What?*' simultaneously.

'We're having another baby,' Harry said, flatly. 'I thought it was mine.'

'I thought it was the menopause,' I elaborated.

'You can't possibly keep it, Ruby. Everyone knows that, over fifty, there are two things a woman should never do – be seen in natural light and have a s . . s . . . sprog,' Emerald stammered.

'*Jeezus Christ.* It's just one big sexual lazy Susan with you, isn't it? Spinning from one sister to the next. Can't you keep your dick in your fucking pants?' Scott bellowed, grabbing Harry by the scruff of his Mambo shirt. In the ensuing scuffle, buttons popped and material tore, dissecting a reindeer and decapitating a snowman.

I could not believe what was happening. All our lives were being pulled apart like Christmas crackers.

'I can't fucking believe it. I thought we were mates!' The noise Scott emitted as he punched Harry in the face sounded similar to the cry of a rhinoceros being fed into a food processor. Harry flailed one beefy arm in front of his face in defence, but Scott managed to land a punch on the bridge of his nose, drawing a dark comma of blood. While Harry reeled, Scott drove his clenched left fist hard into Harry's abdomen.

Amber's face became a little, balled-up fist. She jumped on Scott's back and thumped him. 'Stop it, Scott. It's not his fault! It's all *your* fault. If only you'd ever encouraged or praised me! Harry didn't take me for granted. He loved my food. Unlike you. He thanked me profusely after every bite!' Amber seemed to have mistaken her husband for a piñata. She was banging and whacking and thwacking his back as though he were full of treats. Her gleeful animation seemed to be bordering on the thin edge of hysteria. 'You always told me how gentle Harry was in bed – I wanted that. For a man who spends every waking moment so engrossed in human rights cases, my husband has a hard time being human. Whereas Harry actually talked to me – not monologued, but really talked. He would sit at the kitchen table and chat for hours.'

'I think you did a bit more than *chat*, Amber.' I was trying to make my teeth grind more slowly so as to muffle the sound of disintegrating enamel.

'You have no idea how lonely it is being married to him. I sometimes think about getting myself taken hostage, just so Scott will take notice of me outside the bedroom. And what about my human rights?' She pummelled her husband's back again. 'You can catch despots who launder millions of dollars but don't know how to wash your own underwear. Really?' Then Amber, who hated hugging, slid off her husband's back and splayed her arms to me. 'But what I did was wrong.

Deeply, profoundly wrong. Please, please forgive me. I was not in my right mind.'

I winced away from her, feeling a queasy mixture of horror and also some grim satisfaction that at least my accusations about Harry's infidelity had been proven, despite his gaslighting. But with my own sister? It was like being dropped straight into a Greek myth.

'Do you think she's on something?' Emerald asked me.

'Yes. My husband's face, unfortunately,' I replied, gutted.

'The *emotional* libido, that's what's important to women,' Amber addressed her husband's vinegary expression. 'Not just sex, sex, every bloody day, over and over and over. Wham, bam, no thank you, ma'am.'

'Sex every day, over and over and over . . . Jesus, have you any idea how lucky you are?' Emerald said wistfully, glaring with resentment at her well-built but impotent spouse.

'Why didn't you two just swap husbands? That would have solved everything!' I tried to shout, but my voice was juddering and broken. 'Have some husband replacement therapy.'

'You always say that I hate to be touched,' Amber said to me. 'That's not true. Emotional tenderness and connection, that's what I've needed so desperately. But the whole Harry thing just made me feel more miserable and lost and self-loathing. I was still stressed, and barely eating. It wasn't the answer. But it did force me to look harder for the deep affection I so craved. I tried to tell you both on the cruise but the time was never right. I've finally found what I was looking for. With . . . with . . .' She began gesturing like a heroine from a Jacobean tragedy. '. . . with Leyla.'

I rubbed my ears. Surely I'd misheard? I was beginning to think that it would be safer to fly an American jet into Iranian airspace than attend a Ryan family gathering.

'What?' said Scott, in the same voice he'd use in court to shout 'Objection!'

'Who?' asked Harry.

'Leyla Khoury. We were at school with her. Almond-eyed, Lebanese, good at maths . . .'

It took a beat for this momentous revelation to sink in for the frazzled family.

'Khoury . . . You mean the doctor's receptionist?' Emerald asked. 'The one you're in a book club with?'

'Yes.'

'A book club for two, where you slip between each other's covers?' Emerald sought clarification. 'No wonder you've been at "book club" every bloody night!'

'You're into *women*?' a dazed and amazed Scott asked.

'I don't know! I'm into Leyla, that's for sure. She's so soft, so kind, so gentle . . . so slow. I've never known slow before. Slow sex in a fast world. Women don't want a Tinder app, they want a Tender app. Well, I do anyway.'

Christmas, I thought, *the gift that just keeps on giving*. The whole family continued to stare at Amber, gobsmacked into rare silence.

And then there came a slow hand clap. The family focus shifted back to Ruth, who was lounging comfortably in her chair, feasting her eyes on the fallout.

'Oh, yeah, by the way, thanks for dropping me in the shit, Ruth. And on Christmas Day. Thanks a lot,' Harry addressed his mother-in-law, bitterly. 'Why don't you just finish things off by sodomising me with your fucking Hoover?'

'Yes, Mum. How long were you holding on to that grenade, waiting to lob it into my life?' I demanded to know. 'You wanted to maximise the casualties, obviously. Why else would you wait until Christmas Day?'

'Well, now you all know what it feels like to be cheated on. Not so nice when it happens to you, is it?' Our mother's tissue paper Christmas hat had tipped across her forehead like a witch's fringe. 'We've had every sort of failure in our family. Alcoholics, adulterers, homosexuals, gamblers. But, in truth, you're all the most bitter disappointments.' She rose up like a cobra ready to strike, hissing through clenched teeth. 'When I finally die – of shame, no doubt, after today – I'm bequeathing a little legacy to each of the grandchildren, but the rest I'm leaving to the church, the only part of my life that has never let me down,' she said, with all the melodrama of a Dickensian denouement.

I took a deep, shaky breath and marshalled all of my energy for a final desperate surge, like a drowning surfer paddling for the wave that will rescue them from the rip and get them safely to shore. 'I've never wanted to admit it to myself, Mum,' I said, with surprising tranquillity, 'but you really do hate us, don't you? Why?'

Our mother's cheeks sucked in to make valleys in her face, and her eyes glinted like metal. 'Your father was the most feckless, irresponsible, selfish man on god's earth. And you girls worshipped him. Even when I'd discover another of his sordid little affairs, you'd always take his side. You even covered up for him! I just hope he's writhing in his gruesome grave,' she said venomously.

The Ryan girls looked at our mother with pained astonishment.

'Wow, Mum,' I finally said. 'You'd be discharged from a Saudi hit squad for being too brutal, do you know that?'

Ruth's false nails, which were sharp enough to disembowel an echidna, raked a scratch down my arm. As an imaginative child, I'd taken more beatings from mum's feather duster than my sisters for telling tall tales. 'I've told you a million times, do not exaggerate!' Ruth would yell while whacking away at my legs. The pain of the scratch was the catalyst I needed.

'I don't know why Dad married you, but I'd be very surprised if it didn't involve some kind of satanic ritual at some point.'

Ruth fluttered her bejewelled fingers in the air, shooing away the conversation as if it were a mosquito. 'What better way to hurt him, than to hurt all of *you*!' Her voice was firm and punitive – the kind of voice that God would have used to part the Red Sea. 'At least your father confirmed my Catholic faith. Yes. He taught me that there really *is* an afterlife; I finally had a life after he died.'

A shocked silence descended once more onto the Christmas gathering. Punch-drunk, reeling, raddled, stupefied and combat-fatigued, we all just stared at our matriarch. Some ants crawled across Ruth's hand. I hoped they were the South American flesh-eating type. Finally, I spoke up on behalf of my sisters. 'Well, Mum, you've definitely brought religion into our lives, because now all of us really do know what it's like to be in hell.'

Then, extracting Amber's famous pavlova from the esky by my feet, the youngest, most polite, most pliable, most intimidated Ryan daughter smashed it into our mother's face.

*

The younger members of the Ryan clan had clambered up out of the pool some time ago and had been watching the melodrama unfolding beneath the gazebo. They were so startled not one of them had checked their iPhone or taken a selfie or Instagrammed anything for at least, oh, twenty minutes.

Bella: 'If only we'd brought them up better.'

Jake: 'It's pathetic, really. I mean, *this* is our gene pool?'

Zoe: 'Is it too late to put ourselves up for adoption?'

Alice: 'Oh, shit. The worst thing is . . .'

Justin: 'There's something worse than this drunken display?'

Alice: '. . . now there'll be no Secret Santa.'

30

The Insular Peninsular has everything in common with the Wild West, except for, well, dress sense, lingo, gun laws – oh, and access to abortion. But Christmas Day had left the Ryan family feeling like they'd been in a shootout in the O.K. Corral.

It was, without doubt, the worst Christmas any of us had ever experienced. Lunch had been abandoned, uneaten. Presents were left unopened, beneath the tree, Santa's secrets never to be revealed. There was only the prospect of a month of ham sandwiches to indicate that Christmas had even happened at all.

Lying in the darkness that night, Harry and I were as far apart from one another as it was possible to be in a double bed. I'd expected him to go sleep on the couch, and he'd expected me to abandon the marital bed. It was your classic stand-off, except, well, lying down. We hadn't spoken to one another since lunchtime. I actually had no plans to speak to him for the rest of my life. My last words to him were, 'You're a total arsehole, only not as useful. Why don't you make like Santa and only visit us once a year?'

I tossed and turned as images I'd buried kept flashing into my head – my husband's concupiscent glance down Amber's cleavage at a family gathering; his eagerness to help Amber out any day and, more worryingly, any night, at a moment's notice; the number of plumbing emergencies Amber phoned up about, which, curiously, always seemed to coincide with Scott's trips interstate; my naive appreciation of Harry's concern for my sibling, imagining it only proved what a great guy I'd married. Why had I turned a blind eye to all those red flags? Helen Keller could have seen it coming.

By two am, the only thought on my mind was whether I should cap off an otherwise unproductive day by flogging my handyman husband to death with his tool belt.

'Hmm,' I addressed my pillow. 'A husband who had an affair with my sister, a psychotic mother, an unwanted pregnancy at fifty, a broken heart and a dead-end job . . . Who says you can't have it all?'

After a fitful pre-dawn doze, I awoke consumed with rage at my mother's vicious timing. Her selfish performance had given me a strong desire to anchor her with weights into a pool of piranhas. Couldn't she at least have waited till Boxing Day to box our ears with such brutal news? I determined then and there to book in for an abortion. I mean, how could I bring another human into this dysfunctional family? Especially if the poor kid was carrying any of Ruth Ryan's sour and acidic gene stock.

A feeling of defeat had settled over the house, acrid and thick, like the sulphurous bushfire smoke that clung to everything it touched. Mother Nature was in meltdown and so was I. Watching the sun rise over the sea, the bitter taste of remorse flooded my mouth. My whole life I'd allowed myself to be intimidated by my overbearing mother. I realised that I wasn't suffering from multiple personality disorder – I didn't even have *one* personality. But no more.

Fifteen minutes later, after rolling over a couple of kerbs and taking out a letterbox en route, I wheeled to a tyre-screeching halt outside my old family home and catapulted across the nature strip to my mother's door. I rat-a-tatted my knuckles on the glass panel in the same way my irritable and impatient mother announced her arrival anywhere. No answer. I stabbed my finger on the doorbell, repeatedly. My mother was clearly resting after the exertions of machine-gunning her entire family with psychological shrapnel – a day that forevermore would be known as 'The Christmas Day Massacre'. Determined to finally speak my mind, I scrabbled around in the rockery for the hidden spare key, speared it into the lock and let myself in.

'Mum?!' Met by silence, I wondered briefly if she'd gone back to the bottle – memories flooding back of Ruth's many drunken stupors, when she would sometimes be found lying in a pool of piss on the bathroom floor when we girls got home from school.

My march into the kitchen became less confident as girlhood terrors returned. Was my mother lying in wait with the feather duster for a quick, painful thwack around the legs?

The big glass doors opening out onto the terrace were still wide open. I walked outside, trying to keep my nerve. My mother was lying, asleep, in the banana chair. Her paper Christmas hat sat at a rakish angle. Yesterday's lunch lay uneaten and swarming with flies on the table.

'Mum?'

The eyes of dingoes are yellowish grey, and alert yet neutral. That's what Ruth Ryan looked like now, staring straight ahead, unperturbed. A shiver of ghostly shock ran through me. I shook my mother gently by the shoulder. Her body crumpled, as if my gaze had shrivelled her.

A jolt of pain and panic spread instantaneously through me from top to toe. I felt as though I were on a sinking ship and hadn't paid attention during the muster drill, so had no idea how to find my lifeboat station. When I noticed the traces of pavlova still on my mother's face and hair, a pathetic, wretched sob wrenched its way out of my throat.

I killed her! was all I could think. Quickly followed by *I'm an orphan.* But how could I be an orphan? It sounded so *Jane Eyre.* An orphan is a poor heroine in a dusty old novel who ends up in a workhouse.

I felt as though I'd been dropped through a wormhole into a crack in time. My unaware sisters were living above it. On their timeline, our mother was not dead. After sobbing bitterly for a five full minutes, I turned on my phone and texted my sisters through my tears.

SOS. Come to Mum's immediately. Emergency. This is not a drill. Repeat: This is not a drill.

31

'What are *you* doing here?' were Emerald's first words to Amber when they met on the porch as I opened the door. '*You* should be languishing in the outer ring of the seventh circle of hell.'

'You can't make me feel any worse than I already do.' Amber closed her eyes and smacked the heel of her hand against her forehead. 'Clearly it's the most vile, thoughtless, stupid thing I've ever done in my whole life.'

'Stop calling yourself stupid. You're going to ruin it for everyone else.'

A hungover Emerald had come straight from bed and was still wearing her brand-new silk pyjamas, bought in the ship boutique to replace her regular moth-eaten cotton nightie. Amber was still wearing the clothes she'd worn on Christmas Day, an uncharacteristically simple cotton shift and flat sandals.

'Why haven't you changed since yesterday?' Emerald asked.

'I've been driving around all night with a boot full of prawns, trying to work out what to do with the rest of my life.'

Emerald rolled her eyes so far back in her head she could probably see her synapses zinging. 'Not lying face-down on either of your brothers-in-law would be a start. So, Ruby, what the hell is so urgent that you dragged us both over here at sparrow's fart?'

I was standing numbly in the doorway. Neither sister had taken into account my ghostly complexion.

Emerald pushed past me and stomped down the hall towards the kitchen, with Amber trailing after her. Emerald then grabbed the nearest utensil from the countertop and swivelled to face us. 'Don't mess with me. I'm all out of oestrogen and I have a fondue fork,' she said, only half-joking. 'So?' she asked me. 'What's up?'

Blood beat in my ears. 'Mum's dead,' I said tonelessly.

Everything suddenly seemed slow, as though we were all moving through deep water in dive suits. My sisters looked at me for a silent eternity, though the clock on the wall behind them recorded it as eighteen seconds.

'No!' Amber choked.

'Are you sure?' Emerald demanded. 'Where is she?'

I led my sisters to the grim scene on the backyard banana lounge. We made a semi-circle around our mother, all of us stupefied by the power of death.

Amber and I instinctively looked to our elder sister for guidance. Emerald was the practical and level-headed sibling; she would know exactly what to do. Emerald's superior maturity became immediately apparent when she gasped, hysterically, 'What the fuck do we do now?!'

'I don't know!' Amber's voice seemed pitched an octave higher than usual. 'You're the medical one. Shouldn't you do CPR or something?'

This galvanised Emerald into professional mode. She immediately felt our mother's bejewelled wrist.

'So, is she . . . you know?' Amber asked, in an annihilated voice.

'Dead?' Emerald said. 'As a dodo. Deader than a weekend in Dapto,' Emerald said, lapsing, in her woe, into inappropriate black humour.

Shock has a terrible texture to it. The world around you, normally solid and implacable, suddenly looks thin and translucent.

'Oh, god,' Amber exclaimed. She was pointing at an orange vial of pills poking out of the pocket of our mother's dress. She picked them up and read the label. 'Fentanyl.'

'Opioids,' Emerald said. 'And look.' She indicated a vodka bottle amid the debris and detritus of yesterday's uneaten lunch that I didn't remember being there.

'She's Catholic. Mum would rather die than kill herself,' I said.

'Unless she was helped,' Emerald stated.

The idea that it may not be a natural death hit all three of us at the same time with cyclonic impact. Despite the fact that the soporific heat of a scorcher was already declaring itself, the morning air thick with abundant insects and birds, the menthol coldness of winter suddenly descended onto our garden. Mistrust banked up around us like a slow drift of snow, making everything icy and treacherous.

'So, what *were* you doing here so early in the morning?' Emerald asked me.

'I came to give Mum a piece of my mind.'

'Is that all you gave her? Remember what you said on the boat – that if you killed Mum you'd be out of the mental hospital in two to three years and then there'd be a fat book contract waiting?' Emerald's sharp accusation went into me like a blade. My skin became overly sensitised to every molecule of air, and my bare arms were definitely registering a threat.

'I was being facetious!' I pinned my older sister with a reproachful glare. 'Besides, *you're* the one who said you wanted to smother mother.'

Emerald snorted in disdain. 'Oh, come on. You know I was joking. Besides, why are you letting Amber off the hook?' she added. 'The person you go to bed with says a lot about you; sleeping with your sister's husband says that you are clearly a two-faced psycho.'

We were suddenly circling each other like Cold War spies. Newly orphaned, we three strong, capable, working mothers quickly reverted to little girls, bickering like spoilt brats.

'Yes, I've done something vile and unforgivable, but I am *not* a psychopath. I'm sorry, but if anyone's a psychopath, it's *Ruby*,' Amber shot back. 'Or have you forgotten introducing us to "Kev"? Although, Emerald, you did say you have enough morphine to put a rhino to sleep. Ram sedative, that's what you recommended. With a plastic bag full of gas and helium, to make it seem as though she'd killed herself.'

'What?! *You're* the one who knows how to induce multiple organ failure from poisonous flowers, Amber. Devil's helmet, you called it. No antidote,' Emerald counter-claimed.

'Oh, and what's my motive? *I'm* not the one with money troubles,' Amber parried. 'Alessandro told us how much debt your practice is in, Emerald. And what about Ruby's baby? A new baby costs a fortune. Being cut out of Mum's will is clearly the last thing *you* wanted, either,' she said, turning to face me.

'The will,' I said, snapping us back to reality. 'Mum's

solicitor is still on holidays. She told me she was going to deal with it after Christmas. Do you think she got around to signing the new version?'

It didn't take us long to find it. The sealed envelope addressed to the solicitor was sitting on her writing desk, beneath the watchful eye of a framed image of the Virgin Mary. It was stamped, ready for posting.

'Look away, Mary,' Emerald said, as she tore open the letter.

We fumbled around in our respective bags for our reading glasses, then pored over the pages, heads banging. Our mother had made handwritten amendments to the document, scratching out our names and citing the Catholic Church as her sole beneficiary. She had carefully initialled each of the amendments. The document was signed, dated, and witnessed by two of her hairdressers. Emerald took the will into the kitchen, rummaged through the drawers and found a box of matches. She stood over the sink, match poised to strike.

'We mustn't. It's illegal,' Amber stated, but I could hear the touch of a plea behind the assurance in her voice.

'No, we mustn't,' I agreed, gnawing my nails all the way up to my wrists.

'Although . . . nobody will ever know,' Amber added. 'Except for the three of us.'

I had now chewed my nails nearly all the way up to my elbows. We caught each other's eyes over our reading glasses. And then as one, we signalled a covert middle finger by pretending to adjust the frames on our noses. It had been our secret code since we were kids, giving a subversive middle finger without being caught by our parents.

'A pact.' Emerald laid her hand out flat in front of her. Amber placed her hand on top – then I added my own quivering palm to the fleshy tower. 'In sisterly solidarity.'

'In sisterly solidarity,' Amber and I chorused.

We nodded our agreement and Emerald lit the match. We watched in silence as our mother's new will and testament flamed into black curls and disappeared in a fug of smoke.

Emerald scooped up the ashes and deposited them in the compost bin, then called the police to report Mum's death. As we waited for an officer, she poured herself a large whisky and sat nursing the bottle with her legs dangling into the pool, pristine silk pyjama pants rolled up. I resorted to comfort eating, grazing straight from the fridge with a spoon. Amber started frantically cleaning, binning spoilt food, putting on the dishwasher and polishing surfaces, using a flannel to manically wipe down anything that didn't talk back.

The police officer, a middle-aged, no-nonsense woman with salt-and-pepper hair, arrived half an hour later. She offered perfunctory condolences then moved straight outside into the backyard. Watching through the window as the officer examined our mother's body, I felt as though we were in a play. This impression was only heightened, half an hour later, by the arrival of a grizzled badge-flasher who introduced himself as Detective Tyson.

Sisters have an emotional patois only we can understand – we can speak fluently to each other only using eyes. What our eyes were saying right now was *A detective? Why?*

The detective summoned us into the backyard a few moments later. 'I'm sorry for your loss,' he growled in a ten-pack-a-day voice. He peered at the world from beneath veined, saggy eyelids and his hair appeared to have been groomed with salad tongs. 'When there's an unexpected fatality, we usually rely in the first instance on good old-fashioned door-knocking and talking to friends and family. When suspicions are aroused, we tend to work backwards from the scene where the death occurred,' he monotoned, utilising the brute vocabulary of his profession. 'An officer has spoken to your mother's neighbours. Apparently, some of them overheard a quarrel here yesterday.'

Our secret sisterly ocular semaphore resumed its bewildered broadcast.

'Do any of you have any plans for the next few days?'

WTF? our eyes said to each other, more loudly this time.

'I'll probably just be sitting around tweezing my stray facial hairs,' Emerald replied, before adding, curtly, 'We have a funeral to organise, so obviously we'll be here. Why do you ask?'

'We'd just prefer it if you didn't leave the area while we conduct our inquiries.'

Inquiries? The whole house was suddenly smudged with unspoken thoughts.

'We'll need to investigate and send our reports to the coroner, who will make a decision about whether to hold an inquest.'

'An inquest?' Emerald remarked, brusquely. 'Why?'

'Sleeping pills and alcohol have been located in the vicinity of the dead body. Toxicology reports take a while, so, in the meantime, it's routine to determine the approximate time of death as well as any possible motives, alibis . . .'

'Alibis?' Amber repeated, wide-eyed with disbelief.

'Yeah, well, usually the victim's will is a dead giveaway.

As in, who's gonna benefit?' The detective smiled without warmth. He now stood like a conquistador, with his scuffed black shoe on the pebblecrete lip of the pool.

Emerald put her lips through a series of gymnastic contortions. I thought she was going to cry, then realised she was merely trying to hold back from a giggling collapse.

'How can you find this funny?' Amber asked, agog.

'How can you not?' Emerald rebutted, emitting a raw, guttural bark. 'Mum's still making our lives a misery – even from beyond the bloody grave.'

I laughed then too, a bravura burst, bordering on mania. 'You see, Detective, our mother was to parenthood what myxomatosis is to rabbits,' I tried to explain between bouts of mirth.

This simile set Emerald off once more. Her explosion into a barrage of throaty howls caused Amber to also succumb, windmilling her arms to keep her balance as she rocked back and forth.

If any neighbour had glanced over the garden wall at this moment, they would have seen three sisters weeping with laughter over their mother's corpse. It would warm the cockles, it really would. Although, perhaps not those of Detective Tyson, whose cockles remained decidedly, icily, cold.

'So,' he addressed Emerald, 'just out of interest, where were you between the hours of four pm yesterday and one am this morning?'

'I was on the beach for some of it,' Emerald tittered. She sat down, suddenly winded from laughing. Amber collapsed onto one of the wrought-iron seats beside her.

'Can any witnesses vouch for your whereabouts?'

Emerald let out another huge guffaw at the absurdity of it all. 'Her husband.' She hooked a thumb in Amber's convulsing direction.

This comment caused Amber to instantly sober up. 'Oh, really? Why?'

'Scott came around. You hadn't come home, apparently. And you weren't answering your phone. He needed comforting. Alessandro was totally bladdered by then. So, Scott and I went for a walk on the beach.'

'And just how much comfort did you provide?' Amber asked, her perfect white teeth clenched. 'Your usual full body pillow, I presume?'

Emerald shrugged, which prompted Amber to jump to her feet. 'What happened? Answer me!'

'Look, we snogged. That's all. Don't blame me. Ruby put the idea in my head.'

'What? No, I didn't!' I protested.

'You're the one who said that Amber and I should swap husbands.'

'Oh my god!' screeched Amber. 'You shame me for having a fling with Harry and then make out with my husband? Unfucking-believable.'

'It's a very different scenario, Amber. You're now into tits and clits, remember? With Leyla,' Emerald replied. 'Besides, nothing more happened. We were both off our trolleys by then.'

The detective was looking from one Ryan girl to another, as though at an unruly tennis match between McEnroe-type racquet-brats. With twitching fingers he cracked open the cellophane of a packet of cigarettes, which he was clearly trying to give up, then disappeared in a bloom of smoke. 'Do you want to talk me through the details of this particular shit-show?' he said.

I realised that I'd become strangely detached from my feelings of grief and shock – I felt no tears, no ache in my throat, no rage, just an odd calm. As the only trained reporter in the vicinity, I felt it incumbent upon me to summarise the situation for the confounded copper.

'I'm sorry, Detective Tyson, but, you see, it's been a rather stressful Christmas. Our mother entirely failed to grasp the concept of maternal love during her lifetime, which is why she chose Christmas Day to reveal that my husband Harry had a fling with my sister Amber, because he likes her cooking, apparently. Amber's husband is the sexual equivalent of a binge-eater, while Emerald's husband is a lapsed vagetarian – he now totally avoids vag,' I elaborated. 'Basically, we're three menopausal women whose dreams have collapsed, just like our pelvic floors, which we seem to be trying to cure with some HRT – husband replacement therapy.'

The detective collapsed in a wheezing phlegm-fest. 'Don't worry. One of these days I'll be out of therapy,' he said, lighting up another cigarette from the butt of the last. 'So, let's unpack this more slowly, shall we, girls?'

But we were saved further humiliating interrogation by the shrill of the doorbell. Relieved at the reprieve, Emerald bounced off to open it. A few moments later, she called down the hall. 'Ruby? Your HRT just arrived.'

I crossed to the kitchen doorway and looked towards the front door. A figure ambled out of the blinding sunshine into the darkness of the hall. I blinked against the brightness as my eyes adjusted. And there, backlit by the dazzling morning sun, stood Doctor Brody Quinn.

32

'Ruby.'

As soon as I heard his voice a pang of longing corkscrewed through my body, which responded instantly, like Pavlov's salivating dog. A lobotomised grin was the best I could manage.

'Brody.' I stumbled to a halt before him. Wide-eyed and wild haired, clothes dishevelled, I imagined I looked like a hair-care-magazine reject, or the 'Before' photo in a makeover feature.

'Look,' Brody began, with no preamble, raking his hands through his springy hair. 'I'm sorry about the radio silence. Our ship got as far as Vanuatu, but then the winds picked up. There was rather a lot of offshore, which was presently onshore, and vice versa, and soon there were more trees resting on the upper decks than is desirable. The ship got blown into a reef, then laid low in port for a bit, before limping back to Sydney for propeller repairs. I got severance pay and joined some of my medical mates from Sydney who were off on a professional retreat at a wilderness lodge in Tassie. I was just drowning my sorrows in drink and wallowing in the general bollocks of being cross and hairy and living in squalor when one of the doctors started talking about a case she'd had recently, of a mother and daughter who shared the same initials . . . And how her practice had sent a letter revealing stage-four, terminal pancreatic cancer to the daughter instead of the mother. Well, needless to say, my ears pricked up. And I just want to say that I'm sorry I didn't believe you . . . The lodge insists on digital detox, otherwise I would have contacted you straight away. Anyway, as soon as I got back to the mainland yesterday I tried to call you, but your phone's been off. So, I got your address from a mate who works for the cruise company. But I didn't want to go to your house, you know, to avoid the testicular trauma and compound fractures that might greet me upon my arrival. I mean, have you told your husband about us? Are you even still married?'

I was too stupefied to speak. I just kept looking up into his tanned, open face and remembering his lovely lips on mine while trying to fathom what the hell he was attempting to say to me.

'Anyway, obviously now I knew your mum's initials and, like a lot of people her age, it turns out her address is in the phone book. So, I headed for the Insular Peninsular. You know I like to experience exotic, distant places with unfamiliar customs,' he joked. 'I thought I could find out the lay of the land, and also see if your mother could use my help.' Brody paused in his explanation for a moment to look at me more closely. 'Do you need to sit down? You're white as a ghost.'

'Yeah, well, a mother dying will do that to a girl.'

Brody didn't look remotely surprised. 'Ah. I'm too late, then. Pancreatic cancer is a bugger. One in four people die within a month of diagnosis, making it the deadliest of the common cancers. It's what killed Alan Rickman, Aretha

Franklin, Luciano Pavarotti, Patrick Swayze, Steve Jobs . . .
If a scan shows cancerous cells in the pancreas, it's not
unusual to be sent straight to palliative care without further
investigation.'

'I'm sorry, Brody – I haven't had much sleep. What are
you saying, exactly?'

'Well, the cancer diagnosis, as I'm sure you know by now,
was actually meant for your mother. Ruth Ryan and Ruby
Ryan. Same initials. Easy mix-up.'

'*What?*'

'Your family doctor is Zahra Hanbury, right?'

My breath seemed too loud, as though I were scuba
diving and running out of oxygen. 'My mother had terminal
pancreatic cancer?'

'Yes. Oh, shit. You still didn't know? I did a little light
sleuthing over a bottle of red one night. Your mother made
Zahra promise not to tell the rest of her family. Patient
confidentiality and all that. Zahra only confirmed it to me
when we were six cab savs to the wind. I'm so sorry for your
loss, Ruby,' he said, kindly. 'When did she die?'

'Last night. I found her body this morning.'

Sympathy pooled in his beautiful eyes. 'Oh, god. Clearly
you've had a pretty quiet Christmas, then.'

'Ah, yes . . . you could say that.' Little black dots danced in
front of my face, and I felt sweat prickling on my upper lip. I
was on the verge of flying apart like an exploding supernova.

Brody put his arm out to steady me. 'Are you okay?'

'No, not really. Our mother didn't do big, warm-hearted,
positive, life-enhancing emotional displays. She did sarcasm,
sulking and revenge. Which is why she chose Christmas Day
to reveal that my husband, Harry, who loves to eat, had a

fling with my chef sister, Amber, because I'm a terrible cook. Which is undeniably true. Everything I make ends up tasting like linoleum, with the texture of paving stones. Only now Amber's come out as lesbian, which means I'm supposed to forgive her, as apparently the affair was just a stepping stone on her sensual journey of self-discovery. Meanwhile, my other sister, Emerald, who is sexually malnourished because her husband Alessandro's as limp as William Shatner's toupee, made out with Amber's cuckolded husband, Scott. So, in short, all our marriages and friendships fell apart simultaneously, and then our mother died. Apart from that, everything's just fine. Fab! Tickety-boo. Except, oh yes, now Detective Tyson suspects foul play.'

'Foul play? Jesus, Ruby. I'm pretty sure you have the killer instinct of a Chihuahua.'

An overwrought sob was working its way up through my body. I tried to suppress it, but it escaped through my nose, uninvited. After a raucous bout of my crying in his arms, Brody said, 'I've always thought distant relatives are the best kind. And the further away the better. Come on. Let's sort this out.'

His warm hand was on my shoulder as he steered me gently back down the hallway. His competence overwhelmed me. I began to envy his patients. Hell, I began to wish for a serious ailment. When he lowered his hand to the small of my back, I felt a rush of blood to a part of my anatomy that was totally inappropriate on the day that my mother had drawn her last breath.

When I walked back into the kitchen with Brody in tow, Amber's face registered a level of surprise last seen on the faces of the congregation at Oscar Wilde's wedding.

'Detective Tyson?' Brody said.

'All day, every day,' the world-weary detective drawled.

Brody shook hands with the detective then produced his own ID that identified him as a doctor. In a steady, calm voice, he explained about Mrs Ryan's terminal pancreatic cancer, an affliction she'd kept secret from her family. He gave a name and number for Doctor Zahra Hanbury, who'd be able to confirm the diagnosis.

Amber and Emerald looked at me, startled. I delivered ocular confirmation that, yes, our mother had been terminally ill. At least it explained her lack of sympathy at my own 'diagnosis'.

'Like all docs, you're clearly hell-bent on flapping your gums until you've worked up to a Force Ten Gale,' the deadpan detective droned, putting away his notebook. 'But the mother's diagnosis does shed new light on the investigation. We're still going to have to get a toxicology report and possibly a full post-mortem, so nobody is to leave the general area, is that understood?'

Brody rang the nearest forensic medicine department, identified himself and made a joke about operating a 'skeleton staff' over Christmas, which helped him to sweet-talk the pathologists into hurrying along the report in order to eliminate any uncertainty and get the death certificate signed so that we Ryan sisters could bury our poor mother.

When Ruth's body had been loaded in the back of the coroner's van, Emerald and Amber started the grim ritual of calling relatives and friends, planning funeral readings and flowers, and writing death notices. It was the worst time of year to try to organise a funeral, as the whole country was on holiday.

'Are you two okay to work on this together?' I asked my warring sisters. 'Because I, um, have a private consultation booked with a heart specialist.'

Amber raised her eyebrows. 'After the despicable thing I did to you, Ruby, and after all we've been through in the past twenty-four hours, I don't judge anyone anymore, as long as they're not carrying a bomb or a blood-splattered relative.'

'Religion is a sham and god cannot logically exist. But, despite that, we will organise a lovely Catholic service,' Emerald stated, and ratified the temporary truce by hooking them both up to a bottle of gin in order to fortify themselves for the grim tasks ahead. I gestured for Brody to follow me down past the deep end of the pool, where we could sit on a frangipani-canopied swing seat facing the cobalt cove.

'Thank you,' I said, squeezing his arm gratefully.

'I bet you say that to all the men who get you off a murder rap.' Brody gave his devilish smile. 'I owed you a favour, anyway.'

'Really? Why?'

'For curing my chronic sceptic-aemia. There's no prescription for that. And, if you still feel the same way . . . well, I think I need a daily dose. Doctor's orders.' A mischievous grin split his face.

I was reeling. No wonder it's called Boxing Day: I was doing ten rounds with fate and I was on the ropes, fate clearly winning.

When I didn't respond, he added, 'Okay, I drink too much, I lie on my tax returns, I get the sack too often for speaking my mind, and I have a few minor felonies on the books, but name one *really important* shortcoming?' he said, cheekily.

Dumbstruck by his reappearance, I could only gaze

at his tanned forearm, then up at the square set of his broad shoulders, then at his face and the smile lines that parenthesised his full mouth, which made me think of those kisses that so electrified my palate . . .

When I still didn't speak, Brody persevered.

'You said you hate your job. You said that your kids don't need you. You said that your marriage is over. You said you wanted adventure before dementia. Well, so do I. I'm planning to ply my trade for a while in New Guinea. Local non-profits and NGOs are begging for doctors to come work there. Then I thought maybe I'd move on to Fiji, the Solomons, Samoa . . . Doctors are needed everywhere. It's always been my dream to follow in the footsteps of James Cook and Robert Louis Stevenson, and explore that big, beautiful Pacific. It's one of the things that convinced me to sign up with the cruise company. For the first time in my life, there's nothing holding me back. No debts. No contracts. No commitments. I've changed my phone number so nobody can find me. I'm free as a bird – an exotic tropical bird, exactly the kind I'd like to study in the wild. With you by my side. You know, now that I'm a recovering cynic.'

Brody was wreathed in hope, his face alight with expectation. No commitments. No contracts. No debt. Nothing holding him back. His words rang in my ears. How could I rain on his happiness parade?

I couldn't believe the mess I was in. At my age I should be quilting, golfing, scrapbooking and possibly mastering calligraphy while contemplating my vegie patch, not angsting over the paternity of an unplanned pregnancy. Usually when my life fell apart, I took to cooking with wine – only forgetting to add any food. But what the hell was I going to do *this* time? Mind you, foetal alcohol syndrome was about the only drama missing from this whole surreal scenario. I didn't want to tell him about my positive pregnancy test, the one test you can't cheat on, until I'd made up my own mind. Last night I had been determined to terminate it, but today I found myself vacillating.

Could I really keep it? Was I too old? Fifty-year-old men have babies all the time, so why not women, too? And, as the potential father, wouldn't Brody also want to have a say? But how could I tell the man I'd known intimately for only three weeks that I wasn't peri-menopausal after all, but possibly carrying his child? The man who was just rejoicing at having no commitments. And what if it came out of the womb carrying a spanner instead of a stethoscope? How could I say all this succinctly? There just didn't seem to be a Hallmark card to cover it.

'You are allowed to be happy,' Brody said, in his gentlest, most hypnotically soothing voice.

Finally I found my voice. 'A few months ago I was leading a soft, gentle, safe little life. Now look at me! I've been misdiagnosed with cancer, alienated all my friends and family, fallen in love, found out my husband is sleeping with my sister, and discovered my mother's dead body,' I said, in a voice just one decibel shy of histrionics.

'A woman of your magnificence is never broken, Ruby, only bent. Run away with me and I'll straighten you out,' he said lasciviously, eyes twinkling.

I squeezed his hand. 'The world needs more good men like you.'

'No.' He squeezed my hand back. 'It needs more bad women like you.'

Realising that I wasn't showing the right level of enthusiasm at his sexy suggestions, I made my mouth twitch into what I hoped was a smile, but felt more like a grimace. What on earth was I going to say to him? I took a few mental runs at this conundrum, but felt like a pole-vaulter who kept smacking her forehead on the crossbar. And so, in desperation, I settled on something ambiguous. I focused my eyes on the midriff buttons of Brody's linen shirt, kept them there and said, lamely, 'There are complications.'

'Like what? Not money worries. We have my severance pay, if that's what's troubling you.'

I was creeping across the conversational terrain like a ninja. Light as air. 'But New Guinea? Jeez. There's a lot of jungle up there, right?' I said, stalling for time.

'I believe so,' he laughed. 'The whole unwaxed pudenda.'

'The trouble is, life in New Guinea is not like *The Jungle Book*, Brody,' I busked. 'Real animals don't want to befriend you, they want to *eat* you, instantly. Especially mosquitoes. The mosquitoes are probably already texting each other saying, *She's coming! The Aussie with succulent flesh.*'

'Well, they can bugger off, because that's all mine,' Brody said, placing his warm hand on my inner thigh. He smiled his familiar, crooked smile and my fanny did a fast fandango. Memories of our liaison could unravel either one of us in a heartbeat.

'With these pissant, Pentecostal, coal-fondling conservatives in power, it's a good time to get out of the country, just like our indifferent prime minister jetting off on a Hawaiian holiday. Crossing the bridge into the peninsula today,' Brody went on, 'I noticed that the welcome sign's been vandalised. Instead of reading *Welcome, please drive slowly*, it says, *Welcome, please die slowly*. It reminded me of how you said you wanted to live a little.'

'But not in New Guinea. There are so many insects. I'd need to drive around in a big Aerogard can.' With immense concentration and willpower I managed to arrange my features into a semblance of cavalier composure. 'I holidayed in the North Queensland rainforest once and a huntsman got into my room. You may think that a thwack with a towel is the best defence. I, on the other hand, screamed for a SWAT response team.'

He laughed. 'Huntsman spiders can't hurt you.'

'Really? It's called a *"hunts" "man"*. There must be a reason for that. The clue is in the name! Nothing like roaming your own bedroom with a net and tranquilliser dart to relax you before sleep. And what about the cockroaches in the tropics? Jesus. Tropical cockroaches could use me as a chew toy. They're the kinds of creatures that can drag you into the Underworld.'

Brody withdrew his hand from my thigh. 'Is it the leg?' he asked, stonily.

'No! Of course not.' I studied my feet with forensic detail.

'Maybe you just felt sorry for me? Well, you shouldn't. Disabled people are just as capable of being complete dickheads as anyone else.'

'Yeah, I think I've worked that out already,' I teased, halfheartedly.

'Then what? What's changed?'

I felt his gaze like a breath on the nape of my neck. The rational side of my brain wanted to tell him but the emotional side would rather perform a self-administered appendectomy. With a cocktail fork. Blindfolded. While hanging upside down from a trapeze wire.

'Come on. Say something. I've been describing you to my friends as a woman with a Dorothy Parker mind in a Mills and Boon suburban world. It's time to break free. Time to write that book. A funny, quirky, mad, original book, just like you. Come on. Speak to me. Words are what you do, Ruby Ryan.'

And yet, no words formed on my tongue. If I'd been in the mood to joke I would have called it a pregnant pause.

'What happened to that free-spirited, fun and fabulous girl who rode me as if I was a bull at a rodeo? You told me that there was so much life to enjoy in your second act.' He ran a hand through his unruly hair. 'You said it was like adolescence in reverse; a lovely rebirth.'

Rebirth. Did he have to choose that particular word? It wasn't fair to dump this dilemma onto him. I was a big girl. It was up to me to handle it. And there was something else – I didn't want him influencing my decision one way or the other. He'd never had children, so maybe he would want to keep the baby. And then, what if I didn't? Did he have legal rights? Cataloguing all of the obstacles we faced, I fell into a trance of indecision. When my lips remained in neutral, Brody got to his feet.

'I'm sorry, Ruby.' I loved the way he said my name, in that warm, velvety tone. 'I just presumed . . . or hoped . . . I mean, nothing like this has ever happened to me before. But the timing – your mother's just died. Our timing's always wrong. We have the timing of a bad talk show host. Or, rather, the . . . timing . . . of . . . a . . . bad . . . talk . . . show . . . . host,' he joshed, trying for last stab at levity to lighten my mood.

I had to tell him. I would tell him. It was now or never. We would work it out together. But just as I made up my mind to confess all, he took me by the shoulders.

'Unless,' he said, tentatively, 'you're happy again, you know, with your husband. Or maybe you just feel too guilty about your kids? Try as I might, I can't really imagine what that feels like. I never wanted kids, which is why I had a vasectomy.'

It was now me, not Brody, treading lightly around landmines.

'You had a vasectomy?'

'Yeah, in my twenties. I just knew that I never wanted to be tied down, with my non-existent bandwidth for routine and predictability. So, you can be straight with me. What the hell's holding you back? Is it guilt about your family? Or . . . maybe'— a shadow passed across his handsome face—'you just don't love me as much as I love you?'

My mouth flopped open like I was a beached fish. There was *definitely* no Hallmark card for this. *Yes, I love you madly, but, oh, by the way, I've still been screwing my husband and now I'm preggers with his sprog.* A tremor of helplessness went through me. My lips stiffened in an effort to say just so much and no more. Finally I replied, robotically, 'Well, family is important at a time like this.'

I peered behind me to catch a glimpse of the ventriloquist who was uttering these words in my voice. This is *not* what I wanted to say. What I wanted to say was 'Take me, I'm yours, you crazy, half-legged, horndog!'

But I just kept on staring at the pool, listening to the mechanical octopus making its methodical rounds, sweeping the tiles back and forth, back and forth . . .

When I finally looked up, Brody had gone. I exhaled. I hadn't even realised I'd been holding my breath.

A moment later I was racing out the front door. My eyes raked the street in both directions. Wiping away tears, I could feel my heart gazing up at me quizzically, asking in between beats, '*Are you sure you want me to keep doing this?*' I glimpsed him then, moving off at speed through the spotted gums. If there'd been a mist, it would have enveloped him, accompanied by violin strings and a fade to black. But instead he was swallowed up by a gang of kids with new Christmas surfboards, mooching down to the beach in search of a wave.

'Come back!' I called out. 'I've gotta tell you something. *I'm up the duff!*' But a wind had come up and it blew the words back in my face. I fumbled for my phone and stabbed at his number, forgetting that he'd changed it. I looked up again and he'd disappeared.

Defeated, I dragged myself back to my mother's home, catching my reflection in the hallway mirror as I passed. I appeared even more dishevelled, wide-eyed and wild-haired than before. My earlier look, of a hair-care-magazine reject, seemed positively poised and groomed by comparison to what I now resembled: a deranged kind of outback woman who hatches abandoned emu eggs in her bra. It was enough to send a shiver up one's spine. But, of course, I had no spine, because it had turned to jelly.

33

The week between Christmas and New Year's day was hot – the kind of hot that makes a woman think that the only reason bras were invented was for the unparalleled joy that comes from taking one off.

The days that followed Mum's death were a time of intense activity – but it was like jogging through treacle. The only other period in my life when I could remember feeling time so suspended, when I'd lived so intensely in the present, was after birthing my babies. Hours seemed to rush by and minutes dragged, with everything telescoped into the here and now.

Thanks to Brody's intervention, the death certificate had been issued swiftly. It stated that Ruth had died of natural causes, exacerbated by her weakened condition from pancreatic cancer and a lifetime of heavy drinking. My sisters and I met with the priest, designed the order of service, and tried not to kill each other. The way we were going, it could be a four-for-one funeral.

We couldn't even pick out clothes for our mother to wear for her cremation without falling out. Amber had selected the kind of age-appropriate frock that had been fashionable around the time of the Boer War.

'Mum'd hate that to be the last thing she ever wore!'

Emerald snapped, tossing it back into the wardrobe. 'We should bury her in her leopard-print tankini.'

'What about pearls *and* a sequined sarong?' I suggested, attempting to placate. 'And what about underwear? Do we need to choose underpants? Surely we can't let Mum go commando?'

'I suppose you'll be taking Emerald's side in all matters from now on, won't you, Ruby?' Amber sulked. She flounced off to answer the doorbell, hips swishing, then reappeared in our mother's bedroom carrying another huge bunch of flowers. 'From Mum's lawn bowls club. Aren't they magnificent!'

'Why do people send flowers? Who wants dying things at a time like this,' Emerald griped. 'There's an organisation who build dunnies for villages in the developing world. If mourners want to make a gesture, they should just give money to this toilet twinning scheme. I've twinned with a latrine in'—she took out her phone to read the details—'Htawadum, Kachin State, Myanmar.'

'Well, that settles it. There's no way I'm letting *you* handle Mum's estate.' Amber huffed. 'If we let you do the finances our whole inheritance will be funnelled into flushing away poverty. Literally.'

'And what's wrong with that?' Emerald flared. 'Can't you ever stop thinking of yourself for one nanosecond? You're the one who's been running around putting little stickers on the back of the paintings and furniture you want to keep, and drawing up a spreadsheet of the valued possessions you want first dibs on.'

'Flowers and latrines are *both* fine,' I mollified. Attempting to cut through my siblings' mutual resentment was like trying to saw raggedly through a frozen loaf of bread with a butter knife. We were right back to where we'd been before the cruise.

Before we left for the funeral home, Amber threw together an Ottolenghi salad and summoned us to the kitchen table.

'Pass me the hummus, will you?' Emerald asked, falling into a chair and pointing to the tub on the counter in front of Amber.

Amber ignored her. The kettle clicked off and she slowly warmed the teapot.

'For god's sake, it's not as though I'm asking for your stash of Colombian cocaine, Amber. Just pass me the bloody tub.'

I leapt up out of my chair as if electrocuted, to fetch the tub in order to short-circuit the clash.

'Can I get *you* anything, Ruby?' Amber then asked with the most courteous of smiles.

'Yeah, you could take that knife out of her back,' Emerald said through a half-chomped mouthful of salad.

'I could say the same to you. Liberated feminist, or amoral slut? Defend your answer,' Amber retaliated.

We drove our mother's new Merc to the funeral parlour. While my sisters fought over which one of them should take the wheel, I diplomatically slipped into the driver's seat. The bickering and niggling continued in the car – especially over who should give the eulogy at the funeral.

'As the eldest, it should be you, Emerald,' Amber decreed.

'Jesus Christ, no! I'm far too atheist. I find it hard to square the idea of a loving god with the existence of ichneumon wasps, which lay eggs in caterpillars that then hatch and consume the poor thing from within. Not to forget famine, war and childhood cancer, oh, and sisters who screw their brothers-in-law.'

'Oh, god, have you ever thought of *not* giving your opinion, Emerald? I really think it's an option we should explore,' Amber said, scathingly.

'Let's explore you speaking at the funeral, then. You never seem to want to shut up at other times.'

'Don't be ridiculous. Look at me. I haven't done my roots, my nails are chipped, and I'm living out of my car boot, where my only change of clothes is a beige tent dress and Birkenstocks.'

'Well, that's true,' the perfectly groomed Emerald said, giving her sister a full body scan. 'I've seen better dressed salads.'

By the time I'd reverse-parked into a tiny spot right outside the funeral home, I was so fraught and overwrought from my sisters' arguing that I dropped the coathanger holding the clothes Ruth was to be cremated in. I scrambled to snatch up the bra, shoes and sequined Carla Zampatti frock from the dirty pavement. 'I'm so sorry, Mum . . . Oh, god, girls. I'm talking to a bra,' I said, then hugged the dress dangling on its hanger as if Mum were inside it. It was the first time I'd hugged my mother for as long as I could remember.

'Oh, Mum,' I said, between sobs, 'I'm sorry you were so unhappy. I'm sorry I threw the pavlova into your face. And I'm sorry you got sick. How did it happen? God has clearly been on sabbatical for the past few years and left a hopelessly unqualified intern in charge.'

'Is that what you're going to say? At the funeral?' Amber asked.

'What? No. Why should I have to speak? I'm the youngest.'

'Because you're our wordsmith, Ruby,' Emerald stated. Amber nodded her agreement.

It was the first time they'd ever called me that. It made me feel as though I'd won the Booker Prize.

A few days later, in church, people who barely knew Ruth Ryan were sobbing and blowing their noses. The church swelled like a throat with the sound of hymns and organ. Our mother's church book group, about ten imperious women, sat in the first few pews on the right. When some of their ex-husbands appeared with new, shiny young brides on their arms, the bookish dames glowered and closed ranks, whispering behind liver-spotted hands how *dare* they turn up again after all these years.

I sat in the front left pew, flanked by my warring siblings, contemplating the notes I'd written about what to say at this coming out party for a ghost. *Our mother had enough chips on her shoulder to open a casino. She left a substantial amount of money in her will to the Catholic Church so that prayers would be said for her, but no amount of prayers could get our mother out of purgatory. It's more likely she's already terrorising the inmates of hell. Oh, and we burnt the will because where there's a will, there's a way!* was what I wanted to say. But when I rose to my feet, I said, instead –

'We all know that none of us gets out of this place alive, but losing a parent is always so difficult to take. I know that some of you have a rather peculiar conviction that it's only a temporary parting – don't tell Richard Dawkins! But I'm not religious, so have nothing comforting to say about where our mother has gone. Our father was a great traveller and often said that he thought death must be a rather fine adventure, as he could think of no one who'd ever returned from the trip. So, bon voyage, Mum. My sisters and I have agreed that we will make a handsome donation to this church our mother so loved – just as soon as women are allowed to be ordained as priests.'

I glanced at my sisters, who gave me the thumbs up.

'My mother was an intelligent, contradictory and complex woman, but she did give me the greatest gift possible – two warm, witty, wise and wonderful sisters. I'm going to call them up now. Emerald, Amber?'

My surprised siblings glowered up at me in surprise. Emerald shook her head and Amber tch-tched but, reluctantly, they joined me at the front of the church and faced the congregation. I extracted three lipsticks from my pocket and shared them around.

'In honour of you, Mum, the woman who taught us that everything is made better by a bit of lippy.' I painted a red slash of colour across my lips and my sisters followed suit, laughing through their tears. 'And because nobody wore lippy as well as you did, Ruth.'

And then I peered over my reading glasses, caught my sisters' eyes and pretended to adjust my specs up the bridge of my nose, with a covert middle finger.

The next day we took delivery of the cremation urn. We placed Ruth on the kitchen counter and contemplated our next move.

'So, where shall we sprinkle her ashes?' Amber spoke first.

'What about the designer shopping outlet? It was her favourite haunt,' Emerald suggested.

'The club and the pub were her favourite haunts,' Amber corrected.

'What about Kurnell beach?' I said. '"Birthplace of a nation" . . . or, the site of Invasion Day, although it made her furious to hear us call it that. But she did love it there.'

'It's a good idea, but it's illegal to scatter human remains in public places without council permission,' Emerald countered.

'That's okay. We'll just fill our pockets with Mum's ashes, cut holes in the seams, then walk along, dropping her in instalments like the tunnel diggers at Colditz.' I demonstrated, sauntering around the kitchen, surreptitiously shaking my pockets.

'I think we should sprinkle her under the casuarinas. Wind blowing through casuarinas sounds like moaning, and you how she loved to moan,' Emerald said, and we all snickered. 'And then we'll know where to go when we miss her.'

'Oh, god, I laughed so hard I just had a little LBL – light bladder leakage,' Amber uncharacteristically confided.

We laughed even more when we arrived at the beach and realised we'd forgotten our mother. She was sitting back at home on the kitchen counter. We drove back for her urn at top speed and this time strapped her into the front seat, just like old times, apart from the lack of commentary on our appalling driving/bad parenting/poor grooming/lack of lippy.

We parked among the flowering gums, then walked towards the water in the bright heat of the summer afternoon, serenaded by cicadas.

What upset me far more than the act of scattering the ashes was how they were packed. Shredded newspaper padded out the urn. I kept catching glimpses of headlines from my own local paper – the usual trite stories often penned by my own hand: 'Seagull Steals Dentures'; 'Drunk Falls on Face'; 'Man's Penis-Enlarging Vacuum Pump Stolen – Wedding Dreams Shattered'.

The pointlessness of my life and the inevitable approach of death was laid bare, right there, in black and white. No wonder I suddenly felt as though I'd been buried alive.

Moments later, standing at the water's edge, watching our matriarch bobbing on the tide, we girls clung to each other like barnacles on the hull of HMAS *Family*, storm-tossed in big, unchartered seas. Through grief we had coalesced into one familial organism, made mute by memories.

'All I can think about is Dad's death,' I said, finally. 'I can remember the sound of our hearts splitting open. Can't you? We loved him so much. And he loved our mother, even if he wasn't all that great at showing it. So, there must have been some good in her. Mum can't just be a Disney villain. Something made her become the wicked witch.'

'Perhaps it was giving up work?' Amber conjectured. 'Dad made her do that. Maybe that's what gave her a touch of the Hedda Gablers? She was bright enough to have been running a company, but had no outlet for all that clever, ruthless scheming.'

'Plus, they were just so spectacularly matrimonially mismatched,' Emerald added. 'Yes, Dad was irresistibly charming, but he was also a womaniser.'

'God, yes! He offered matrimony to so many women,

both before and after he was married, that Mum called him Lord of the Rings, do you remember?' I said, and we found ourselves laughing again. 'Who knows what Mum was like before he hurt her. We always thought he had affairs because she was so awful, but maybe she was so awful because he had affairs. I mean, look at us, all bitter and twisted over a bout of infidelity. Mum was right about one thing – now we *do* know how she felt. Her bitterness morphed into sarcasm then carcinoma. We mustn't go that same way. We can start by forgiving her,' I said, firmly. 'And each other.'

'Are you sure you're the little sister?' Emerald asked, rubbing the top of my head affectionately.

'I'm so, so sorry about Harry,' Amber gushed. 'I was confused. A mess. A menopausal hot mess of hormones and despair and denial about my sexuality. I felt starved of intimacy to the point of insanity. Does that make sense?'

'I'm sorry about snogging Scott, too,' Emerald said to Amber. 'I wish I didn't need sex so much. But I do! Since the cruise, I've been so famished for bodily contact I've been tempted to give myself a strip search. If it weren't for a bra fitting last week at DJs, I wouldn't have had any sex life at all since we got back. If only I was an aphid, a wasp or a termite. They've dispensed with copulation altogether. Did you know that? They produce eggs that develop without any contact with sperm. You, on the other hand, Amber, are like a slug. They're bisexual, you know. Some species start off as one sex and turn into the other as they develop. It's just their nature. And one must follow one's nature.'

'What? Nasty and slimy?' Amber asked quietly.

'No,' Emerald corrected, 'adaptable and unique.'

I detected the ghost of a smile on Emerald's lips, which, much to my delight, Amber mirrored.

'I know I joked about it, but why *don't* you simply swap husbands?' I said. 'Emerald can live with Scott, whose sex drive's stuck in top gear. And you, Amber, can live in asexual bliss with Alessandro, the vagina decliner. That's perfect husband replacement therapy. We'll still be one big happy family. Our kids are so wrapped up in themselves, they won't even notice the change.'

'Yes, it's just recycling, really,' Emerald said sensibly. 'One woman's trash is another woman's treasure.'

'I don't know what I want, exactly, but I'm pretty sure it's not a man,' Amber said, softly.

'That's good, because I'm not ready to throw my husband in the garbage just yet. That's why I've started secretly slapping testosterone gel onto Sandro's skin when he's asleep. Men need hormone replacement therapy too, you know, but are too proud to admit it. I'm hoping it's going to be the fuel he needs to reboot his man missile before bats fly out of my forsaken fanny.'

Amber laughed, before asking gently, 'What about you, Ruby? What's your husband replacement therapy?'

'I'm upgrading, as it turns out. Yep, I'm getting a new and improved, renovated version of my old hubby. With a baby on the way, Harry wants to renew our wedding vows.'

'Really?' both sisters asked, in tandem.

'People live for so long now that the time from honeymoon to tomb can be seventy, eighty years,' I elaborated. 'Harry says that marriage should be a temporary arrangement, similar to a mobile phone contract. You should renegotiate, say, every five years. And that's what he's doing – renegotiating.'

'Just make sure you get a lot of perks in the package, starting with daily breakfast in bed,' Emerald suggested.

'And a foot rub each night,' Amber added.

My sisters wiggled their eyebrows mutely at each other for a moment before Emerald asked, with astonishment, 'So, you really are going to keep the baby?'

I shrugged. 'Harry wants it too badly.'

'But what about you?' Amber said, softly.

'Well, I put myself first once before, and look where that got me. Anyway, Harry says my affair with Brody was a real wake-up call. He admits he's been a selfish bastard and is begging forgiveness. He said that he was total prick to lie to me, and that he knows that if he hadn't cheated then I wouldn't have either.'

'I can never say sorry enough.' Amber chewed her lip, regret devouring her.

'But Harry did point out that he's not the only one whose pants have been on fire. And not just in our family, either. Fake news and conspiracy theorists, anti-vaxxers, Cambridge Analytica, climate change deniers, anti-abortion activists on social media, Putin, Brexiteers, they all just lie, lie, lie . . . He said that Trump has told about fifteen thousand lies while in office.'

'It's true. How many of our friends' hashtag "livingmybestlife" Instagram posts are putting a positive, filtered spin on misery and loneliness? All of mine, in the past, for sure,' Amber acknowledged.

'But he also promised that when we renew our vows, he would swear never to lie to me again.'

'Ah, but was he lying at the time?' Emerald asked, holding up crossed fingers.

Amber thumped our big sister in the arm, but it was good-natured. 'Well, we'll back you, Ruby, whatever you decide. Won't we, Emerald?'

'Yes. But I am not wearing any hideous, big, blancmange bridesmaid outfits ever again, is that clear? '

I shuddered. 'No bridezilla, I promise!'

The wind picked up. The waves were now a creamy froth, whipped in places into peaks more than two metres tall. The sun was slightly less direct now, already starting to slip behind a faraway scribble of trees.

'Bon voyage, Mum,' I said, and then we turned back towards the car.

'Are you limping?' Amber asked Emerald in the casuarina grove.

'God, it's such a bore,' Emerald admitted. 'I've got arthritis behind my knee apparently. Arthritis! Jesus. That's what old people get. I'll probably have to have an op.'

'Cheer up. The upside of having knee surgery is that you'll never have to give a blow job again.' I smiled. '"I'm sorry, but I'm not allowed on my knees. Doctor's orders."'

'Except to a man standing on a ladder,' Emerald quipped.

'Speaking of dicks,' Amber added, 'it's just as well you didn't go any further with Scott. He calls his appendage the Conquistador. Did I ever tell you that? Plus, all lawyers are workaholics. He'd soon have had you plea-bargaining for foreplay and outlining all your sexual requirements on a yellow legal pad.'

'. . . which he'd then take under advisement,' I riffed. 'And no affection after sex, right? Post-coitus it's more like, case closed.'

It was suddenly like old times, us tittering like schoolgirls at silly entendres and wonky wordplay. After we'd stopped giggling, Emerald said, abruptly, 'Do you think Mr Hire a Hubby can be monogamous?'

I considered this as I walked along between my sisters. 'He swears he only ever cheated once, with Amber. In twenty-eight years. So, he's already monogam-*ish*.'

'Oh, Ruby, I truly am sorry. Can you ever forgive me?' Amber said, earnestly, her face aghast. 'It was nothing more than a desperate cry for help.' Never was there a woman more genuinely suited to be the poster girl for guilt.

For the first time in my life, I no longer felt like the youngest Ryan girl, always trying to catch up to and please and impress my older siblings.

'Well, you can tell a lot about a sister by her hands. If she's holding a machine gun, machete or carving knife aimed at your chest, then she's probably still peeved,' I replied. 'But if not, then I'd say we've moved on,' I concluded.

I took hold of Amber and Emerald's hands and squeezed them tight, and they squeezed right back. Then we clung together in a slumped embrace, like exhausted boxers at the end of a long and bloody bout.

34

Emerald's arthritic knee stayed on my mind on the drive home, which was an unusual place for the synovial hinge of the femur, tibia and patella to be. 'Fancy meeting you at a joint like this?' I mused. I was only five years younger than my biggest sister. I didn't often think of ageing, but when I saw my face in the rearview mirror I recognised, with mild shock, the changes that had come over me. I noted the tiny lines radiating out from around my eyes and mouth, and how the skin was loosening over my cheekbones.

While I no longer expected to be swept up into a passionate embrace by a passing poetry-quoting brainiac with smouldering eyes, a bionic cock and a sizzling wit, mothering a child at fifty was far from being one of my life goals. But Harry's lack of paternity angst was gallant and stylish, and reminded me of what I'd loved about him in the first place. Besides this charming, laid-back attitude, he was also still trying so hard to please me. The man was redecorating and painting and gardening constantly. And cooking. When I got home that evening, wrung out and more fatigued than I'd ever felt in my life, dinner was waiting on the table – fish and coriander curry followed by pineapple upside-down cake, a craving I'd mentioned in passing that morning.

'Wow, Harry. What a skill set! All you have to do now is win *Dancing with the Stars* and your Man of the Year award will surely be in the mail.'

'Wait till you see what else I did for you today. You now have a new loo, with a directional massage jet, automatic lid, power deodoriser, heated seat, and rimless bowl with triple-jet tornado flush. It's a paperless bidet–toilet hybrid, apparently.'

'Is that a little, ah, toilet humour, or are you actually serious?'

'It's the latest Japanese model. I thought you'd get a kick out of it. When we renew our vows, that's gonna be one of them – to spend the rest of my life doing things to make you happy.'

I kissed him lightly on the top of his head, which smelt of sea and salt and summer, ate a delicious dinner, threw it up again into the new Japanese toilet while cursing the fact that morning sickness could also strike at night, then crawled into bed.

I was bone-tired but slept fitfully, and eventually woke in a cold sweat. I checked the time. It was only half an hour since I'd last woken. Sleep is one of my favourite things in the world. I often joked that it was the reason I got up in the morning. And yet, since Mum's death, it had totally evaded me. Finally abandoning all thoughts of slumber, I crept out of bed without waking Harry. I took a pee in the normal toilet in the hall, wondering if my husband really knew me at all. I mean, if I wanted to conclude my seated ablutions with a blast of hot air, I'd move to the hurricane belt in the American Midwest, or alternatively Canberra, where right-wing politicians were still arguing about the reality of climate change while our country went up in flames. I then slipped out into the front garden. The warm summer air felt silken on my skin. At the corner, a streetlight pushed feebly against the darkness that closed in around it. I walked slowly towards the beach, breathing the night's frangipani fragrance and tasting upon my tongue the sharp tang of the sea.

Mum's death had opened an old wound in me. The headlights zipping past on the distant highway brought back my father's car accident in a sickening rush. Even though he'd died decades earlier, I still hadn't entirely got used to it. Still, it was comforting that he stayed in my thoughts, silently guiding my actions and giving me parking karma when I needed it – 'Come on, Dad. It's raining. I need a spot, right outside the cinema.'

I may be a grown woman with weekly by-lines in a local newspaper and years of child-wrangling under my belt, but at my core, I will always be my father's little girl, I ruminated. I thought how much my father loved life and how he would want me to be happy and cheerful, and how I'd better do my duty to him and bloody well be so.

The big empty beach beckoned at the end of the road. The sand was cool under my bare feet. There'd been a bushfire in the tea-trees by the water's edge. A black calligraphy of branches was now scratched onto the landscape. I looked at the gnarled arms of the scorched trees, which curled and twisted against the moonlit sky as if in pain. Except then I realised I was the one in pain. I bent double suddenly to cushion myself against the short, sharp stabbing cramps. It felt like a long, long time before I could draw a proper breath. Every inhalation was a shallow, panicked little effort that brought no relief. I lay on the sand, curled up like a frightened echidna.

An hour later, I knew I'd lost the baby. Having been unsure if I wanted it or not, I now felt nothing but grief: deep grief and profound loss. I cried and cried as if my heart would break. I once more felt estranged from myself. I was like a book with the ending ripped out. What was to be my denouement? And then, lying there, a sticky mess in the sand, the world suddenly clicked into place. I felt as though I'd finally figured out that I'd been holding the map upside down all this time. After the pain and the sobs subsided, I walked gingerly back towards the house. Under the searchlight beam of the big full moon, at last I saw clearly what I had to do.

35

'Ladies and gentlemen, friends, family, workmates.

'Once upon a time there was a woman who discovered she'd turned into the wrong person. I've gathered you all here on New Year's Day, at ridiculously short notice, to toast my dear departed mother, and also to apologise for the last time we were all together, on my fiftieth birthday a few months ago. Proving that star signs mean nothing at all, on the day when my very own newspaper's astrologer had predicted that I would find "happiness and joy, because the moon was in Neptune", I got misdiagnosed with cancer, discovered my husband had been unfaithful, insulted all of my family, friends and work pals, got iced out of my job and alienated everyone in the Insular Peninsular, my kids included.

'When I sobered up, I seriously considered an emergency operation to have my voice box removed. But I've learnt a lot in the meantime – mostly that it's pathetic to find fault with others while overlooking your own foibles. Of which, clearly, I have many. Anyway, I've written down what I want to say this time, so as not to make any big boo-boos. And because, well, I am a writer, after all.'

I liked saying that out loud and not being embarrassed about it. I took out some typed sheets of paper from my dress pocket, the same sparkly dress I'd worn at my ill-fated party, placed them on the lectern and started reading.

'First of all, I wanted to use this mini wake for Mum as a chance to say sorry. And, being New Year's, to beg you all to let me start over. The main thing I'm sorry for is that I didn't really forgive my mother while she was alive. Our father broke her heart, and hurt metastasises into blame and rage, which means, sadly, we girls never knew what Ruth was like before she started drinking and hating.

'But you only find heaven by backing away from hell, right? Which is what my sisters and I are doing, backing up as fast as we can. We're not allowing Mum's bitterness to poison us. So, I just wanted to say thank you, with the deepest love and gratitude, to my sensational sisters, who are my fortune and my blessing, and whose unbridled love, loyalty, inexhaustible wit, warmth and joy light up my life on a daily basis.'

I looked down from the stage of the Sea View function room at Emerald and Amber, who were standing arm in arm and smiling up at me. I winked, and they winked back in unison.

'And now, to my darling kids . . .' I searched the small crowd for their sunny faces and beamed over at them. 'Zoe, Jake, I would take a bullet for you, you both know that. And not just a light graze either, but a full-on *Peaky Blinders*–type machine-gun body strafe,' I ad-libbed. 'You constantly lift me up two octaves on the happiness scale without even realising you're doing it. And I want you to know that whenever you feel lost or like you can't find your place in life, I will always be your bookmark. The truth is, though, I have complete faith that you won't ever lose your way.

'My darling Jake, who will soon be a qualified electrician, has just joined the volunteer firefighters, like his dad, and I couldn't be more proud.' I blew a kiss towards my son, then deadpanned, 'But, wait. Is that actually you? Because most kids consider a Facebook post right up there with the Dead Sea Scrolls, I've only seen the top of my son's head for, oh, about a decade.'

A ripple of warm laughter from other parents ran around the room. I gave an involuntary shudder, remembering how different it had felt the last time I'd stood on this stage, gazing out at the stunned faces of the people I loved.

'My darling Zoe, I'm so proud of you too. She got great results in her HSC, an ATAR in the mid-eighties, and is now about to leave for Cambodia, where she's going to do volunteer work in a school run by a non-profit organisation.' I rested the pages on the lectern and spoke off the cuff again. 'Mind you, I'm only assuming this because the inquiry "Has anyone seen my passport?" has been echoing around the house for the past two days. This usually tends to happen during the first call for boarding at the airport, so that's a slight improvement. I probably won't see her again until she's married and needs me to babysit. Which is how it should be. Only in American sitcoms do mothers and daughters discuss the minutiae of their lives with each other in funny, frank exchanges that always lead to hugging. Love you, hon.' I blew a kiss at my darling daughter, who blew a kiss in return.

'But once you fly the nest, kids, no moving back in, okay? Human beings are the only creatures on god's green earth who take their young back when they're fully grown. It's not natural. And, rest assured, if you have your revenge by locking me up in a maximum-security nursing home in thirty or forty years' time, I will personally come back and haunt you after, okay?'

This prompted another warm wave of laughter from the parents in the room. I went back to my script.

'And now, to my friends. Thanks for letting me slink back into book club, girls. Especially as we are doing Jeanette Winter-son . . .' I looked up once more and added, '. . . which is not a sentence she'd be entirely displeased with, I'm sure. We're also doing a book by "Anonymous", who will invariably turn out to be a married author writing about sexual infidelity. And, next, a biography of someone or other – although, surely, biographies are a fate worse than death. Speaking of which . . .

'To the school mums I say, we survived and lived to tell the tale! Goodbye to fetes and P & C meetings, and hello to spas in Bali, right? Yes, we've had our occasional clashes, but we've been there for each other through thick and thin . . . and thin and thin, lately,' I said, harkening back to my drunken birthday rant.

'To my colleagues, especially my boss, Angela, I know I whinge about the mundaneness of working on a local paper, but there are worse jobs, right? I mean, we could be off manually masturbating caged animals for artificial insemination. Although . . .' I gazed thoughtfully at the ceiling, as though reconsidering the merits of this option.

My workmates let out an irreverent whoop of support.

'And now, the biggest thank you of all, to my husband Harry. Harry has put up with my annoying ways at close range. And, miraculously, he still loves me, despite my dreadful cooking. I keep waiting for the hallucinatory drugs to wear off, but no. Even after the night I grabbed the very first package in the freezer for dinner, which turned out to be pet mince. Mind you, there've been some positive results from this "minor" culinary disaster. My husband now sits when commanded and fetches my slippers. Just don't judge him when he cocks his leg on a tree, okay?'

'It's puppy love!' Harry heckled, affectionately, from the audience.

'But, seriously, Harry, thank you for putting up with me for all these years. Can you come a little closer?' I beckoned him.

Harry pushed through the small crowd to the foot of the stage. He wasn't venturing any further, not after last time. So, I knelt down and pressed my face into his messy hair, tenderly kissing the top of his head.

'Harry says that all we need is a marital tune-up, like an emotional oil and grease change. Harry, darling, thanks for standing by me and for helping me raise our two wonderful children, and for offering to renew our marriage vows . . . Thank you, my love. Thanks, but . . .' I took a deep breath, reminding myself that I was no longer a cowardly custard pissant procrastinator. 'But, no thanks.'

A surprised gasp echoed through the crowd, followed by a sinking feeling of deja vu. For a moment, all I could hear was the murmur of the sea on the rocks outside as the day died through the big glass windows.

'It's stating the obvious, but when your last parent dies, there's no buffer left between you and lights out. I mean, can you hear that beating sound? Times's winged chariot, folks. You suddenly realise that tempus is fugit-ing like there's no tomorrow. When Harry asked me to retie the marital knot, I was so deeply touched . . . until I realised that the knot would be around my neck.'

I looked down at my bewildered husband and smiled compassionately.

'I love you, Harry. And I always will. But it's our kids holding us together, isn't it? They're the glue. But now they're leaving, well, there's an honest bit inside us both that knows we're busy covering up the cracks. In years to come, we'll just regret lying to ourselves. But I'm not lying to you now. It seems to me that women never got the memo that our lives belong to us; that we don't need a permission slip from the principal's office to ask really important questions, like, what do *I* want in life?

'I know what *you* want – to nest. But I've nested, goddamn it! I want to spread my wings. Okay, my bingo wings,' I joked, wobbling the flabby skin of my triceps. 'At fifty, it's time for me to face the fact that I will never be able to make a soufflé rise or head up a FTSE 100 company. Nor will I ever write a global best-seller that will wow Oprah and be optioned by Steven Spielberg. But what I *do* know is that my least favourite word in the world, besides "bathroom scales", is "*should*". As in, Ruby, you *should* suck up more to your boss. Ruby, you *should* keep a tidier house. Ruby, you *should* push your cuticles back. Ruby, you *should* do two hundred sit-ups a day. Ruby, you *should* have a pelvic floor your husband can trampoline off . . . My other most hated word in the English language is "could". You *could* have worked on a national newspaper. You *could* have written a novel. Well, I no longer want to be a person of cast-iron whims. Which is why, once Mum's probate is settled, I'm taking a little SKI trip – Spend Kids' Inheritance. Well, some of it.'

This statement was met with a shell-shocked silence. After a moment, though, Emerald called out, 'Good for you, sis!'

'Touché, Rubes!' echoed Amber.

'I'm drawing up my bucket list, or my *fuck it* list, as I prefer to call it. And then I'm indulging in some HRT – husband replacement therapy. Only that doesn't mean finding a replacement hubby, just a replacement life.

'I've already explained everything to Zoe and Jake, and they don't feel aggrieved. I pointed out that I've straightened their teeth, taught them to reverse park, finished their homework assignments, let them sweat in my clothes they weren't supposed to borrow. But they're cooked. They understand that it's my turn now. I don't want to keep putting things off until I "have time". Because that time never comes, does it?

'I know some of you are thinking that I'm not myself. But maybe this *is* my real self? Somewhere along the way, I feel as though I lost my identity. I may need to go to a police line-up and see if anyone can make an ID. But I know I don't want to be this person anymore – all decorative, demure and self-sacrificing. I don't want to sit at home tending my herbaceous borders. I want to *cross* borders, into exotic places. I want to get a pet quokka, and wear nothing but sequins. I want to be told off by my progeny because they saw me coming out of a nightclub at two am, and then reply, "Well, you're mistaken, kids. I wasn't coming *out*. I was going *in*!" I want to write a novel, not posthumously, or anonymously, but honestly. About dying.'

A traumatised gasp rose up from the audience. Not *again*, I could hear them thinking.

'What the fuck?' I heard my husband moan as he put his head in his hands. Clearly this performance of mine was rating high on the old Jerry Springer–ometer. Not wishing to be carted off in a straitjacket before I'd said my piece, I put down my notes and picked up my glass of champagne from the podium.

'About *cheating* death, I mean, before it's too late. So, please join me in raising a glass to my mother – to Ruth.' I saluted our departed matriarch.

'As I said at the beginning of this mea culpa, which is going on longer than *War and Peace*, so I'll shut up in a minute . . . Once upon a time there was a woman who discovered she'd turned into the wrong person. But no longer. My sisters and I have a new motto, don't we, girls? Growing old may be compulsory but growing up is optional. Adventure before dementia!' I shouted into the mic, before laying it down and polishing off my glass of champers in one long gulp.

I walked towards the front of the stage to enthusiastic whoops and cheers from my two loyal sisters. The rest of the function room stood spellbound in overawed silence. But then Leyla joined in the clapping, moving next to Amber and linking arms. 'I've Got Scott', who post-divorce would be demoted to 'I've *Not* Got Scott', glowered nearby, arms folded, clearly contemplating ringing Amnesty International to say that his pampered husband rights were being abused. I then saw Alessandro close the space between himself and Emerald and slide his arm around her. I noted how she leant into him affectionately. The surreptitiously applied testosterone gel was clearly working its hormonal magic. Sandro didn't cheer me on, but didn't look at me as though I had coronavirus, either, which was something, all things considered.

Legs trembling, I went down the steps, trying not to fall arse over tit, then made my way through the startled crowd. Sally from book club started to clap as I passed. Celeste and

Debbie, my two former 'besties', joined in, as well as some of the other school mums. It was just a few tentative claps at first, but soon crescendoed to cheering and stomping from most of my female friends, who I was sure must also nurse secret fantasies of running away. I fleetingly imagined myself standing in the alps of New Zealand, France, India, Peru or Switzerland, unable to throw a stick without hitting a retired headmistress, seamstress, stewardess or postwoman on a mountain bike.

I approached the big glass doors looking out over the cerulean sea. I'd nearly made my escape when Harry took hold of my arm. 'I'm a builder. I'm good at papering over cracks.'

I turned and held him close. 'Oh, Harry. It's thrilling to see our kids making their way in the world. And we should be so proud that our parenting's been competent enough to result in fabulous, fully formed, functioning adults. But, honestly, now that it's just the two of us for the first time in twenty-one years, do we still have anything in common?'

'Whaddya mean? Of course we do . . .' He trailed off.

'Be honest. How often have you thought, *It's irritating that she's such a bad cook, but she's a good mum.* I know I've said to my sisters a gazillion times, "Harry gets on my nerves occasionally, but he's such a great dad." But now parenting's no longer a daily requirement, what if all we're left with is irritation? Isn't it better to get out before that happens and salvage a friendship?'

'Jeez, Ruby. I didn't realise the dress code for today was "hearts on sleeves",' my crestfallen husband said. 'Did you have to do this so publicly?'

'I'm sorry, Harry. Ripping off the psychological bandaid in one quick wrench seemed the best way.'

'For you, maybe. I can't believe you spoke to the kids before you told me. That's some top-notch parenting right there, Rubes.'

'I wanted to get their blessing before I made my move. We both want different things, Harry, and we have to be brave enough to say it. That's why you had an affair. And why I followed suit. Besides, I didn't say *everything* in front of our family and friends. I didn't mention the fact that I found your work phone with loads of other sexts under coded, professional-sounding contacts like "Big Boys' Steel Erection", "Cox's Outlet" and "Knobs and Knockers".'

He dropped my arm. 'Oh.'

Women were moving in Harry's direction, hovering nearby with commiserative, comforting looks on their faces. A single, heterosexual man in Sydney attracts women like flies to a dropped chop. I had no doubt that Hire A Hubby's services would be in great demand.

'But it's all chardonnay under the bridge now. I love you. And I love our kids. We done good, matey,' I said, and brushed my lips across his forehead.

With my heart drilling hard in my chest, I walked outside onto the balcony. When the glass doors whooshed closed behind me, I took in a great gulp of raw sea air. My heart was still beating out a staccato rhythm against my bra but, for the first time in months, I felt the weight of despair lift, all my anxieties and neuroses suddenly in the rear-view mirror.

Bubbles of children's laughter floated up on the breeze from the beach below, as they paddled in the cool of the evening. The sky was a fluorescent tangerine and turquoise spectacle. Colour was seeping back into my sepia world.

I presumed the huge, flannel-grey clouds looming over the sky was bushfire smoke, but cool sprinkles suddenly peppered my face. It had been such a hot, dry, bushfire-ravaged start to the summer. The welcome sound of the rain grew louder and then exploded around me. I kicked off my shoes, flitted down the stone steps and felt the warm, wet sand between my toes. Then I was running and splashing up along the beach, towards the end of the Insular Peninsular, with the rain pelting down and the waves hissing and sighing onto the sand.

My plan was to quit work and head off on a big adventure – a case of 'have globe, will trot'. On my own. It would be the first time I'd been on my own in my whole adult life. I wanted to hoover up the sunshine and let the cares of life roll from my shoulders. Although, there was nothing to stop me detouring to some exotic Pacific locations along the way.

I reached into the pocket of my sequined dress, which shimmered in the sunset like a mermaid's scales. Extracting my phone, I punched in the number I'd got from Zahra Hanbury.

'Who is it?'

'You know how they always say, "If symptoms persist, you should consult your doctor?"'

'. . . Ruby?'

'Well, I seem to have a case chronic of doctor-itis.'

'Ah,' he said, and I could hear a smile surfacing in his lovely, warm voice. 'I believe that's only curable with a lot of bed rest in the arms of your favourite medic.'

'Funny, that's what I diagnosed too. I mean, who better to

administer husband replacement therapy than a doctor with a good bedside manner?'

Brody chuckled. And I did too – a joyous burst effervescing up in us both like champagne. For so long I'd been telling myself that the trouble with the future is that it wasn't what it used to be, only to suddenly realise that the present had turned out to be beautifully gift-wrapped.

Acknowledgements

WITH THANKS to my darling sisters, Jenny, Cara and Liz, for their perspicacious editorial notes. For adding various bits of verisimilitude, thanks to Detective Niall O'Caroll, Doctor Clio Kennedy, Adam Hills, Steve York, Michelle Black, Angela Bowne, Fran Delano, Kate Shea and Patrick Cook. With love to my cherished mum, the crossword queen, for our daily dose of mental aerobics. Thanks also to Georgie and Jules, and Brian, for your unconditional love and days of laughter.

On the publishing side, thanks to Meredith Curnow and Kathryn Knight for nursing the novel through conception to the delivery ward. But next time, may I have a creative epidural, please?

And to PR queen Karen Reid, also known as Chopper, and my agents, Tara Wynne and Jonathan Lloyd.

To Zahra Hanbury and Jaynie Morris, good on you for supporting osteoporosis research and the Country Fire Authority of Victoria by bidding for roles in *HRT*. I hope you're both grateful I kept your pants on.

Finally, to all my female friends, enjoy your second act. Hope to swing from a chandelier with you soonish.

About the Author

KATHY LETTE first achieved succès de scandale as a teenager with the novel *Puberty Blues*, which was made into a major film and a TV mini-series. She has written 20 books which have been translated into 19 languages. Kathy has two children and divides her time between Sydney and London. Kathy is an autodidact (a word she taught herself) but has three honorary doctorates. She is a TV presenter, newspaper and magazine columnist and also an ambassador for Their World, the National Autistic Society and Ambitious About Autism. Kathy recently completed a tour of her one-woman show, "Girls Night Out", and is pleased to report that she didn't fall out with the cast.

Visit her website at www.kathylette.com and find her on X @KathyLette, Facebook/KathyLetteAuthor and Instagram @kathy.lette